ALSO BY ALLAN BLOOM

The Closing of the American Mind
Plato's Republic (translator and editor)
*Politics and the Arts: Rousseau's Letter to
  d'Alembert* (translator and editor)
Rousseau's Emile (translator and editor)
Shakespeare's Politics (with Harry V. Jaffa)

GIANTS
AND
DWARFS

Essays 1960-1990
ALLAN BLOOM

SIMON AND SCHUSTER
New York • London • Toronto • Sydney
Tokyo • Singapore

SIMON AND SCHUSTER
Simon & Schuster Building
Rockefeller Center
1230 Avenue of the Americas
New York, New York 10020

10 9 8 7 6 5 4 3 2 1

Library of Congress Cataloging in Publication Data

Bloom, Allan David
   Giants and dwarfs : essays, 1960–1990 /
Allan Bloom.
      p.   cm.
   Includes bibliographical references and index.
   1. Books and reading.   2. United States—
Intellectual life—20th century.   I. Title.
Z1003.B66   1990
028.9—dc20   90-42050
                                              CIP

ISBN 0-671-70777-9

Acknowledgments for permission to reprint previously published material appear on pages 388–89.

To my friends

Saul Bellow and Werner Dannhauser

Parce que c'était eux,
parce que c'était moi.

CONTENTS

PREFACE

MY TITLE is, of course, a reference to Jonathan Swift, who converted size of soul into size of body and thus made the spiritual and its various ranks palpable to us. He enacted our unending quest for a standpoint from which to judge ourselves and our times, and showed us how books are the borrowed ladders to that standpoint. He also reminded us of the fact that where there are giants there are also dwarfs, a fact not so dreary as it might appear, inasmuch as the awareness of the existence of giants gives us both an object of admiration *and* emulation. Lemuel Gulliver, in fact a dwarf, was able to live in the company of giants. This association was what put him at war with his contemporaries or, as he characterized them, the Yahoos. Swift teaches, above all, that the essence of education is the experience of greatness.

My title emphatically does not refer to the old saw "We are dwarfs, but we stand on the shoulders of giants." This expresses, in the guise of humility, too much self-satisfaction. Do giants let themselves be climbed so easily? Is it their function to carry dwarfs on their shoulders? Perhaps they were once so gracious but now have set us down on the earth and quietly stolen away, leaving us with an illusion of broader perspectives. The groundless assumption of intimacy with greatness soon gives way for a new generation which denies that there ever were giants and asserts that the whole story is a lie made up by their teachers to empower themselves. The giants are, I presume, looking down on this little comedy and laughing.

My point is encapsulated in my favorite statement on reading books. Xenophon tells how Socrates responded to Antiphon, the Sophist, who was trying to attract his companions or students away from him by claiming Socrates' life was not a happy one, particularly because of his great poverty.

Antiphon, as another man gets pleasure from a good horse,
or a dog, or a bird, I get even more pleasure from good
friends. And if I have something good, I teach it to them,
and I introduce them to others who will be useful to them
with respect to virtue. And together with my friends I go
through the treasures of the wise men of old which they left
behind written in books, and we peruse them. If we see
something good, we pick it out and hold it to be a great
profit, if we are able to prove useful to one another.

Xenophon comments, "When I heard this, I held Socrates to be really
happy. . . ." (*Memorabilia*, I, 6).

How naïve! It is a naïveté we would do well to recover. But, oh,
the difficulty of it! Rousseau understood this very well:

Our bombastic lapidary style is good only for inflating dwarfs.
The ancients showed men as they are naturally, and one
saw that they were men. Xenophon, honoring the memory
of some warriors who were treacherously killed during the
retreat of the ten thousand, says, "They died irreproachable
in war and in friendship." That is all. But consider what
must have filled the author's heart in writing this short and
simple eulogy. Woe unto him who does not find that en-
trancing!*

Rousseau's observation is even more appropriate to this passage, the
only one in the writings of Xenophon, who had experienced so much
and seen so many illustrious men in action, where he calls a man
happy.

To penetrate the meaning of that would be to understand the
peculiar genius of Socrates' way of life. A number of powerful words
naturally cluster around him—good, pleasure, friend, profit, and
books. Friendship, Socrates tells us, is the core of his life. And we all
treasure the idea of friendship, but it is really not a modern theme.
It is difficult to find a profound recent discussion of it. But here we
have at least hints of what real friends are, apart from the tainted
friendships based on pleasure or utility which are not enduring and
tend to make up the bulk of what is ordinarily called friendship. The
friend is the man with whom Socrates can talk about their shared
interests in the good. Good horses and dogs are not companions on
this hunt; only human beings are. Shared taste and interest are a real
common ground for them. And here we come to the core of what is

---

Emile, ed. Allan Bloom (New York: Basic Books, 1979), p. 343.

of concern to us: awareness of shared interest and nourishment for it come from books of the wise men of old. Lovers of the good become friends because they think about it with the help of wise old books. Suddenly and simply the possibility and the content of friendship come clear to us. Friends spend their lives together reading and talking about the life they would like to lead while they are leading it.

Such friendship, connected with books, it turns out, has been my deepest satisfaction and has furnished me amply with beautiful and pleasant experiences of an enduring and relatively self-sufficient kind. I say this to refute the contention that I am a grouch, a victim of *Kulturpessimismus*. That opinion is founded on the historicist premise that one is utterly a creature of one's own time and that any criticism of it means that one must be unhappy. If that premise were true, Swift could not have enjoyed the contempt he felt, and so comically expressed, for the education of his time. He had climbed from the shifting sands of his culture to a firm footing in timeless greatness. There lay his satisfactions. It is very difficult when one has lived with Plato, Machiavelli, and Shakespeare to take seriously what is being said about them by the humanities establishment in our universities today. But laughter, not anger, is what it provokes. The pleasure of theory, of looking at men and things, is independent. The art of living is knowing how to seek the always rare individuals who can share that pleasure.

Because the educational scene in the United States is now bleak does not mean that this will always and everywhere be so. As I write, there is in Eastern Europe a springtime of the soul. Serious men and women who know what freedom means, particularly freedom of the mind, are using their minds to recover the outlines of nature and seeking a language adequate to their aspirations for justice. They know the use of books and need them to think about their future. In Poland, Hungary, and Czechoslovakia, an admirably educated class of "velvet" revolutionaries is breaking the chains of a barbarous jargon which stood between them and the world and which constituted at least half of the tyranny which oppressed them, just at the moment when American intellectuals are subjecting themselves to other such jargons. If you need inspiration, look to Eastern Europe. There you can talk sense and talk freely.

These essays are a partial record of a life which began with Freud and ended with Plato in a search for self-understanding. The decisive moment of that life was the encounter with Leo Strauss. I was nineteen years old, and at first everything he taught was the absolute Other for me, an Other which, if it was true, seemed to deny my special individuality. But I finally learned from that great man that self-actualization depended on seeing what the human possibilities are and that they live in flesh and blood in old books. Since then the path to self-knowledge has been for me the interpretation of the books which teach about the philosophic way of life and which tend to be discrete mixtures of philosophy and poetry. The supreme example of this art is Plato's dialogues, which are nothing but the story of Socrates' life. Now I finally begin to divine what Nietzsche meant when he said that a man who chooses to be timely—that is, to live the deepest modern life—must be untimely, and to be untimely means to know the Greeks. I never made a plan for my life, although I often thought I should. But I now discover that there is a unity. This moth always circles around the same essential flames. They light the way to the fulfillment of youth's inchoate longings.

The essays are reprinted pretty much as they originally appeared. Giving way to the temptation to improve them would have led to infinite revision, bringing them into line with my latest reflections. And I am not at all sure that I am better now than I was then. I have taken the unusual step of including translations of the two little Platonic dialogues. They will give the reader the opportunity to read the texts in fairly reliable versions along with the interpretations. None of my interpretations are meant to stand alone; they are accompaniments of the texts they address and presuppose acquaintance with them. I try to be only the matchmaker, setting up the meeting of reader and book, to be forgotten after the marriage.

The first section of this volume is intended to introduce readers to my way of approaching texts and to some of the perennial questions presented in them. The second section gives an account of three of the teachers who introduced me to books and to the life of the mind. The recognition of their virtues is one of the primary benefits of the education I received. The third section indicates the reaction to contemporary intellectual life of one who has learned such books from such teachers.

Nathan Tarcov, as usual, told me what to do. Steven Kautz helped me do it. Judy Chernick and Terese Denov patiently put it all together for me.

Chicago, March 1990

WESTERN CIV

Fellow elitists:

If I were E. D. Hirsch—people do tend to mix us up—I might ask, "What is the literary influence on my salutation?" The answer is Franklin D. Roosevelt's salutation to another select audience, the Daughters of the American Revolution. He began his address, "Fellow Immigrants."

Roosevelt was gently ridiculing those ladies for believing that in America old stock constitutes any title whatsoever to privilege. That notion is a relic of the aristocratic past which this democracy supplanted in favor of equality or of privilege based on merit. Roosevelt was urbane and witty, this century's greatest virtuoso of democratic leadership. We, the immigrants or the children of immigrants, loved his act; he was on our side. Our enjoyment of his joke was enhanced by the acid of vengeance against those who thought they were better than us. F.D.R. knew how to manipulate such sentiments, and his slap at the D.A.R. was not entirely disinterested insofar as there were a lot more of us than there were of them. Moreover Roosevelt's enjoyment was quite different from ours. He was really one of them. His family's claims to antiquity, wealth, and distinction were as good as practically anyone's. It was certainly more pleasant to poke fun at his equals or inferiors than to show resentment toward his superiors. His was an aristocratic condescension. He condescended to rule in a democracy, to be, as was often said about him at the time, "a traitor to his class"—a neat mixture of man's perpetual striving to be first and the demands of a society where all are held to be equal. The psychology of democracy is complex and fascinating.

Address delivered at Harvard University on December 7, 1988.

That psychology determined the very unusual intensity of the response to *The Closing of the American Mind,* focusing on my alleged elitism. I was suspect as an enemy of our democratic regime. And the first and loudest voices in this chorus came from the Ivy League, particularly from those with some connection to Harvard—to the point where I thought of the old joke about the farmer who hears a thief in the chicken coop. Substituting the Harvard Coop, I imagined myself yelling, "Who's in there?" and getting the answer, "There's nobody in here but us antielitists." Everybody knows that Harvard is in every respect—its students, its faculty, its library, and its endowment—the best university in the world. Long ago when I, a Middle-Westerner, taught for a year at Yale, I was amazed at the little Harvard worm that was eating away at the souls of practically all the professors and students there, except for the ones who had turned down the opportunity to be at Harvard. *Elite* is not a word I care for very much—imprecise and smacking of sociological abstraction—but if any American institution of any kind merits that name, it is Harvard, and it lends that tincture to everyone associated with it.

Why, then, this passion to accuse others of the crime of elitism? One is tempted to attribute it to simple self-protectiveness. "If we say he is one, they won't notice us." But I suspect some, or many, acted from a more tortuous, more ambiguous motive: guilt. The leading principle of our regime is the equal worth of all persons, and facts or sentiments that appear to contradict that principle are experienced by a democrat as immoral. Bad conscience accompanies the democrat who finds himself part of an elite. He tries to suppress or deny to himself whatever covert feelings he might experience—I am sure that none of you has had them—of delight or superiority in the fact that he has been distinguished by Harvard, of how much better off he or she is than the poor jerks at Kalamazoo College, even that he or she deserves it, that superior gifts merit superior education, position, and esteem. A few might consciously believe such things, but since they would be at odds with the egalitarian opinions of democracy, they tend to become spiritual outlaws, hypocrites, and cynically indifferent to the only American principle of justice. The rest, to soothe their consciences, have to engage in casuistry, not to say sophistry. The simple democratic answer would be open admissions, just as there would be if Harvard were located in Europe, where such elitism is less tolerated. But nobody here really considers that. Harvard, I gather, intends to remain adamantly exclusive, implying thereby that there are significant natural differences among human beings. President Bok's way of squaring such elitism with democratic right-thinking is, apparently, to teach that the Harvard person is a doer of good works for society as a whole. This is in the spirit of Harvard's John Rawls, who permits people to possess and cultivate superior talents if they can be proved to benefit the most disadvantaged part of society. Whether this solution is reason or rationalization is open to discussion.

All this suggests the intricate psychology of the democrat, which we must be aware of in order to know ourselves and which we are not likely to be aware of without the help of significant thinkers like Tocqueville, Burke, and Plato, who see us from the outside and judge us in terms of serious alternatives to democracy. The charge of elitism reflects the moral temper of our regime, as the charge of atheism would have done in an earlier age. You couldn't get much of a response in a university today by saying that Allan Bloom doesn't believe in God. But you can get a lot of people worked up by saying that I don't believe in equality. And this tells us a lot about our times, and explains how tempting a career is offered to egalitarian Tartufferie. "Elitist" is not a very precise charge; but compared with the Ivy League, I would have at worst to be called a moderate elitist, and by persons other than those who are now making the charge.

The real disagreement concerns the content of today's and to-morrow's elite education. We are now witnessing the introduction of a new "nonelitist," "nonexclusionary" curriculum in the humanities and in parts of the social sciences, and with it a program for reforming the human understanding. This is an extremely radical project whose supporters pass it off as mainstream by marching under the colors of all the movements toward a more equal society which almost all Americans endorse. Not recognized for what it is, this radicalism can thus marshal powerful and sometimes angry passions alongside its own fanatic ones. *The Closing of the American Mind* was brought before this inquisition and condemned to banishment from the land of the learned. The American Council of Learned Societies even issued a report written by a panel of the new men and women which declared that there is now a scholarly consensus, nay, a proof, that all classic texts must be studied using a single approved method. Such texts are, we are ordered to believe, expressions of the unconscious class, gender, or race prejudices of their authors. The calling of the humanities in our day is to liberate us from the sway of those authors and their prejudices; Shakespeare and Milton, among others, are mentioned in the report. This puts humanists at the cutting edge of the battle against Eurocentrism. The battle is not primarily, or even at all, scholarly but moral and political, and members of the reactionary rear guard are the objects of special fury, the enemies of historic destiny. What kind of a man could stand in the way of deconstructionism, which according to Hillis Miller, one of its proponents, will bring the millennium of peace and justice to all mankind? Consequently the report deplored the "disturbing" success of *The Closing of the American Mind* and attributed it to that old bogey, "American anti-intellectualism" (of the Know-Nothing or McCarthyite variety, you see). The characters who wrote this report were sent by central casting for the movie version of *The Closing of the American Mind.*

Such responses were inevitable, since I am very much a critic of the radical reform being imposed on us, although I have always been a supporter and a beneficiary of the movements toward practical equality.

For my sins I have reaped an unabating whirlwind of abuse, paralleled in my experience only by Sartre's diatribes against his enemies and critics in *Les Temps Modernes* in the forties and fifties. (As I argued in my book, that Sartrean world was the conveyer belt for many of the views affecting us now.) I suspect that Sartre is the model for *engagé* critics who charged that my opinions stain my hands with the blood of innocents in Nicaragua, *les mains sales,* and called me, in a striking reminder of our McCarthyite heritage, "un-American."

People's angers teach much about what concerns them. Anger almost always disguises itself as moral indignation and, as Aristotle teaches, is the only one of the passions that requires speech and reason—to provide arguments which justify it and without which it is frustrated and withers. Anger proves man's rationality while it obscures and endangers reason. The arguments it adduces always lead back to a general principle of morality and then issue in blame—they would also lead to book-burning if the angry were not strongly constrained by our liberal society. Here is an example as reported by Richard Bernstein in *The New York Times* (September 25, 1988):

> A "MINUTE OF HATRED" IN CHAPEL HILL:
> ACADEMIA'S LIBERALS DEFEND THEIR CARNIVAL OF CANONS
> AGAINST BLOOM'S "KILLER B's"
>
> In some respects, the scenes in North Carolina last weekend recalled the daily "minute of hatred" in George Orwell's *1984,* when citizens are required to rise and hurl invective at pictures of a man known only as Goldstein, the Great Enemy of the state.
> At a conference on the future of liberal education sponsored by Duke University and the University of North Carolina at Chapel Hill, speaker after speaker denounced what they called "the cultural conservatives" who, in the words

of a Duke English professor, Stanley Fish, have mounted
"dyspeptic attacks on the humanities."
   There were no pictures of these "cultural conservatives"
on the wall, but they were derided, scorned, laughed at. . . .

I appreciate the *Times*' making explicit the resemblance to Sta-
linist thought control. Such sentiments represent the current establishment in the humanities, literature, and history. These professors
are from hot institutions like Stanford and Duke which have most
openly dedicated themselves to the new educational dawn called *openness*, a dawn whose rosy fingers are currently wrapped tightly around
the throat of the curriculum in most universities.

   The attack on *The Closing of the American Mind* brings this movement into focus, though it has misrepresented both the book and me.
There is a desire to make me into something other than what I am
so that I can be more easily categorized and demolished. In the first
place I am not a conservative—neo- or paleo-. I say this not to curry
favor in a setting where conservatism is out of favor. Conservatism is
a respectable outlook, and its adherents usually have to have some
firmness of character to stick by what is so unpopular in universities.
I just do not happen to be that animal. Any superficial reading of my
book will show that I differ from both theoretical and practical conservative positions. My teachers—Socrates, Machiavelli, Rousseau,
and Nietzsche—could hardly be called conservatives. All foundings
are radical, and conservatism always has to be judged by the radical
thought or events it intends to conserve. At first I was not, to use
Marxist language, even considered an objective ally of the Right—as
the very favorable opinions of the book expressed by Left liberals such
as Christopher Lehmann-Haupt, Richard Reeves, Robert Skidelsky,
and Conor Cruise O'Brien prove. But that was before the elite intellectuals weighed in. Their misunderstanding has something to do with
the fact that I am also not in any current sense a liberal, although
the preservation of liberal society is of central concern to me. The
permanent human tendency is to doubt that the theoretical stance is
authentic and suspect that it is only a covert attachment to a party.
And this tendency is much strengthened in our time when philosophy
is itself understood to be *engagé*, the most extreme partisanship. The
necessity of parties in politics has been extrapolated to the point where
it now seems that the mind itself must be dominated by the spirit of
party. From this perspective, theory looks pallid, weak, dishonest, and
sinister.

   Arthur Schlesinger, Jr., criticized me in a way which shows how naïve the views of contemporary intellectuals have become. He said, with a somewhat unsure grasp of what I wrote, that I am an absolutist whereas the authentic American tradition is relativist. To support this latter contention he cited—hold on to your seats—the Declaration of Independence's "We hold these truths to be self-evident, that all men are created equal and are endowed by their Creator with certain inalienable rights. . . ." He takes this statement of fundamental principle, *mirabile dictu,* to be evidence of the American Founders' relativism. Schlesinger made this astounding argument in a commencement address at Brown University, where he apparently thinks the students will believe anything.

It is a waste of time to defend myself when the charges allege that I said things I did not say, but it is perhaps useful to instruct Professor Schlesinger about the real question. I never stated, nor do I believe, that man is, or can be, in possession of absolutes. My language is not that of absolutes, a language not present in my writings. I tried to teach, evidently not very successfully in his case, that there are two threats to reason, the opinion that one knows the truth about the most important things and the opinion that there is no truth about them. Both of these opinions are fatal to philosophy; the first asserts that the quest for the truth is unnecessary, while the second asserts that it is impossible. The Socratic knowledge of ignorance, which I take to be the beginning point of all philosophy, defines the sensible middle ground between two extremes, the proofs of which demand much more than we know. Pascal's formula about our knowing too little to be dogmatists and too much to be skeptics perfectly describes our human condition as we really experience it, although men have powerful temptations to obscure it and often find it intolerable.

Socrates' way of life is the consequence of his recognition that we can know what it is that we do not know about the most important things and that we are by nature obliged to seek that knowledge. We must remain faithful to the bit of light which pierces through our circumambient darkness.

It is the theoretical life I admire, not some moralism or other, and I seek to defend it against the assaults peculiar to our time. Philosophy, the enemy of illusions and false hopes, is never really popular and is always suspect in the eyes of the supporters of whichever of the extremes happens to dominate. Mr. Schlesinger is an average representative of the relativism which is today's consensus on the Left. However, so eminent and perceptive an observer as Walker Percy, looking from the Right, says that he suspects that I am a nihilist, and he is supported in that view by much less responsible persons from the same quarter. I would respond to him with exactly the same arguments I made to Arthur Schlesinger. This equilibrium of criticism reassures me that I am in the right way, and it confirms my apprehensions about philosophy. It is neither understood nor desired. To the ones it is absolutism, to the others it is relativism; there is no middle; each camp shoves it over into the other. I am now even more persuaded of the urgent need to study why Socrates was accused. The dislike of philosophy is perennial, and the seeds of the condemnation of Socrates are present at all times, not in the bosoms of pleasure seekers, who don't give a damn, but in those of high-minded and idealistic persons who do not want to submit their aspirations to examination. Certainly Socrates is the source of a profound liberalism in relation to which Professor Schlesinger's version of it looks like a parody.

I conclude this digression by remarking that Professor Schlesinger's relativism is not real relativism but a curious mixture of absolutism and relativism typical of our time. Professor Schlesinger is absolutely and unquestioningly committed to democracy and wants to avoid people quibbling about it. He coyly says he does not believe in anything and that good and evil are just preferences, and then he entrusts democracy's fate to a hidden or, rather, a divine hand. I, for my part, doubt that there is any substitute for rational argument for all of its risks and uncertainties. Professor Schlesinger, no stranger to the fabrication of myths or ideologies, appears to be providing one for the tyranny of the majority.

Further, I am also not the leader or member of an educational reform movement, or any movement whatsoever. I respect persons like Sidney Hook who give the best of their energies to fighting threats to academic integrity. But that is not me. I have always been content to hang around the fringes of the intellectual establishment and look in, and am continually surprised that I can support myself that way. To attempt to change things would take me away from my natural activity, would delay gratification now for the sake of unsure futures. I suppose I think the most important thing is to think things through. My book is a statement—as serious as I could make it—about the contemporary situation seen from the perspective of our quest for self-knowledge. Not in my wildest imagination did I think it would appeal to anyone but a few friends and potential friends, a few students and potential students. When it became a hit, the genial American can-do traits surfaced. The prospect I described is publicly unendurable, and I was both criticized for not providing a cure and praised for having prescribed one. Perhaps a public debate about education is a good thing. But I am not a very active participant in it. I suspect that any confrontation with currently stronger forces only precipitates greater defeats for liberal education. Above all, I wish to avoid the self-absorption and corrosion I have seen in others who were principals in *causes célèbres*.

I have gotten a great kick out of becoming the academic equiv-alent of a rock star. This is partly because the eternal American child in me found it agreeable to experience peculiarly American success from the inside—to find out whether I had been missing anything. But mostly it was because I was afforded a close-up look at the closing of the American mind. I have had to learn, however, to watch out as it slams shut on me.

To the extent I am passionately affected by the spectacle I describe in the book, I feel sorrow or pity for young people whose horizon has become so dark and narrow that, in this enlightened country, it has begun to resemble a cave. Self-consciousness, self-awareness, the Delphic "know thyself" seems to me to be the serious business of education. It is, I know, very difficult even to know what that means, let alone achieve it. But one thing is certain. If one's head is crammed with ideas that were once serious but have become clichés, if one does not even know that these clichés are not as natural as the sun and moon, and if one has no notion that there are alternatives to them, one is doomed to be the puppet of other people's ideas. Only the search back to the origins of one's ideas in order to see the real arguments for them, before people became so certain of them that they ceased thinking about them at all, can liberate us. Our study of history has taught us to laugh at the follies of the whole past, the monarchies, oligarchies, theocracies, and aristocracies with their fa-naticism for empire or salvation, once taken so seriously. But we have very few tools for seeing ourselves in the same way, as others will see us. Each age always conspires to make its own way of thinking appear to be the only possible or just way, and our age has the least resistance to the triumph of its own way. There is less real presence of respectable alternatives and less knowledge of the titanic intellectual figures who founded our way. Moreover we are also affected by historicism, which tells us one cannot resist one's way, and relativism, which asks, "What's the use, anyway?" All this has the effect of crippling the natural longing to get out.

In *The Closing of the American Mind* I criticized doctrinaire his-toricism and relativism as threats to the self-awareness of those who honestly seek it. I pointed to the great sources of those serious ideas which have become dogmas and urged that we turn to serious study of them in order to purge ourselves of our dogmatism. For this I have been violently attacked as nostalgic, ideological, doctrinaire. The meaning is really "Don't touch our belief structure; it hurts." We ought to know, on the basis of historical observation, that what epochs consider their greatest virtue is most often really their greatest temptation, vice, or danger—Roman manliness, Spanish piety, British class, German authenticity. We have to learn to put the scalpel to our virtues. Plato suggests that if you're born in a democracy you are likely to be a relativist. It goes with the territory. Relativism may be true, but, since you are by birthright inclined to it, you especially had better think it over—not for the sake of good morals or good social order, at least in any usual sense of those terms, but for the sake of your freedom and your self-awareness.

Since I first addressed the issue of relativism, I have learned with what moral fervor it is protected and its opposite, ethnocentrism, attacked. This fervor does not propose an investigation but a crusade. The very idea that we ought to look for standards by which to judge ourselves is scandalous. You simply have to believe in the current understanding of openness if you are to believe in democracy and be a decent person.

This openness dogma was epitomized by one intellectual who, unencumbered by acquaintance with my book, ridiculed me for not simply accepting that all cultures are equal. He said that his opinion must be standard equipment for all those who expect to cope with "the century of the Pacific" which is upon us. His formulation set my imagination in motion. I decided it might be interesting to experience a Gulliver's travel to Japan to see whether we really want to set our bark on the great Pacific with a relativist compass and without an "ethnocentric" life jacket. We can weigh anchor at the new, new Stanford, whose slogan is now "Join Stanford and see the world." When we arrive in Japan we shall see a thriving nation. Its success clearly has something to do with its society, which asks much of itself and gets it. It is a real community; its members have roots. Japanese society is often compared to a family. These characteristics are in tune with much of current liberal thought in America. (Remember Governor Cuomo's keynote speech to the Democratic Convention in 1984.)

But the family is exclusive. For in it there is an iron wall separating insiders from outsiders, and its members feel contrary sentiments toward the two. So it is in Japanese society, which is intransigently homogeneous, barring the diversity which is the great pride of the United States today. To put it brutally, the Japanese seem to be racists.

They consider themselves superior; they firmly resist immigration; they exclude even Koreans who have lived for generations among them. They have difficulty restraining cabinet officers from explaining that America's failing economy is due to blacks.

Should we open ourselves up to this new culture? Sympathize with its tastes? Should we aim for restrictiveness rather than diversity? Should we experiment with a more effective racism? All these things could be understood as part of our interest in keeping up with the Japanese economic miracle. Or they could, in a tonier vein, help us in our search for community and roots. We recoil in horror at even having such thoughts. But how can we legitimate our horror? It is only the result of our acculturation, excess baggage brought with us on such voyages of discovery. If there are no transcultural values, our reaction is ethnocentric. And the one thing we know absolutely is that ethnocentrism is bad. So we have painted ourselves into a corner. And it is important to understand this. Those who shrug off such difficulties fail to recognize how important it is to have justice in addition to feeling on our side. Without justice we shall soon succumb to some dangerous temptations and have perhaps already begun to do so.

Many such lessons are to be learned on future voyages to the non-Western world. Discovery requires courage and resoluteness, as Heidegger will teach you. I wonder whether all the *engagé* critics who use his language are aware of what he means when he says that one has to face storms in the ocean of becoming. When little children speak of how bad ethnocentrism is, I know that they have been propagandized. It is too complicated a thing for them to understand. Condemning ethnocentrism is frequently a sign of intellectual, although not necessarily moral, progress. But it is only a first step. To recognize that some of the things our culture believes are not true imposes on us the duty of finding out which are true and which are not, a business altogether more difficult than the wholesale jettisoning of all that one thought one knew. Such jettisoning always ends up with the selective and thoughtless return to old ethnocentric ideas on the basis of what one needs right now, of what pleases one, of pure feeling.[1] But to travel one must spend a little time thinking about one's compass as well as the land one wishes to reach.

This problem has been nicely illustrated these last months by the

---

[1] Following this lecture, Henry Rosovsky, the legendary dean of Harvard College, exasperated by me, announced that he is a relativist. In the next instant he was complaining that I only look for the bad things in Japan and not the good ones.

case of Salman Rushdie, author of *The Satanic Verses*, which insulted the Muslim faith and occasioned the Ayatollah Khomeini's command to have Rushdie killed in England, or wherever he is to be found. There was general shock throughout the Western world at this, and writers, whose ox was being gored, rushed before the TV cameras to denounce this blatant attack on the inviolable principle of freedom of speech. All well and good. But the kicker is that most of these very same writers have for many years been teaching that we must respect the integrity of other cultures and that it is arrogant ethnocentrism to judge other cultures according to our standards, which are themselves merely products of our culture. In this case, however, all such reasonings were forgotten, and freedom of speech was treated as though its claims to transcultural status, its claims to be valid everywhere and always, are true. A few days earlier such claims were treated as instruments of American imperialism; miraculously they were transformed into absolutes. Leaving aside the intellectual incoherence here, this floating means to say we do not know from moment to moment what we will do when there are conflicts, which there inevitably will be, between human rights and the imperatives of the culturally sacred. You may have noticed that there has recently been silence about the case; this is partially because it is an embarrassment, and our convictions are weak. The serious arguments that established the right of freedom of speech were made by philosophers—most notably Locke, Milton, and Mill—and our contemporaries do not return to them to refresh their memories and to see whether the arguments are really good. And this is due not only to laziness but also to the current attack on the very idea of such study.

The educational project of reforming the mind in the name of openness has gained strength in the last couple of years and is succeeding in changing curricula all over the country. These changes are as great as any of the sixties but not nearly so noticeable because so easily accepted and now apparently so obviously right. From the slogans and the arguments echoed so frequently in the universities and the press one can judge the intentions of the reform and what is at stake. The key word is *canon*. What we are witnessing is the Quarrel of the Canons, the twentieth century's farcical version of the seventeenth century's Quarrel between the Ancients and the Moderns—the greatest document of which is Swift's *Battle of the Books*. Would that he were here to describe ours as he described theirs! The issue is what food best nourishes the hungers of young souls. "The canon" is the newly valued, demagogically intended, expression for the books taught and read by students at the core of their formal education. But as soon as one adopts the term, as both sides have—foolishly so for those who defend Dante, Shakespeare, and Kant—the nature of the debate has thereby been determined. For canon means what is established by authority, by the powers, hence not by criteria that are rationally defensible. The debate shifts from the content of books to how they become powerful, the motives for which they are used. Canons are, by definition, instruments of domination. They are there to be overthrown, *deconstructed,* in the name of liberation. Those who seek *empowerment* must overcome the prevailing canon, the main source of their enslavement. Curiously books are invested with a very great significance in all this. They are the causes, not mere epiphenomena, as Marxism would have it. Change the books, not the ownership of the means of production, and you change the world: "Readers of the world, you have nothing to lose but your canon." The language is the language of power. "Philosophy is the most spiritualized will to power." That is from Nietzsche, as is, more or less, all the current talk about the canon. "It's all about power," as they say, and in a more metaphysical sense than most know. Philosophy in the past was about knowing; now it is about power. This is the source of the deep drama being played out so frivolously about us. Intellectual life is the struggle of wills to power. Edward Said said at Stanford that the new university reforms were the triumph of postmodernism, meaning, among other things, that the curriculum which taught that the theoretical life is highest has been overcome. Underlying the discussion about non-Western content is a discussion among Westerners using entirely Western categories about the decline or end of the West. The suicide of the West is, by definition, accomplished by Western hands.

The *Times* report of the North Carolina conference gives the flavor of the public discussion: ". . . the conference's participants denounced what they said was a narrow, outdated interpretation of the humanities and of culture itself, one based, they frequently pointed out, on works written by 'dead white European males.' " That is *the* slogan. Above all, the campaign is against Eurocentrism:

> The message of the North Carolina conference was that American society has changed too much for this view to prevail any longer. Blacks, women, Latinos and homosexuals are demanding recognition for their own canons. "Projects like those of Bennett, Hirsch and Bloom all look back to the recovery of the earlier vision of American culture, as opposed to the conception of a kind of ethnic carnival or festival of cultures or ways of life or customs," Professor Fish said.

Replace the old, cold Greek temple with an oriental bazaar. This might be called the Chicago politics model. Overthrow the Waspocracy by means of a Rainbow Coalition. This has more or less plausibility as a political "strategy." Whether it should be the polar star in the formation of young minds is another question. It promises continuing wondrous curricular variations as different specialties and groups vie for power. I would need the pen of Flaubert to characterize it fully. I am grateful to Professor Fish for having described it so candidly.[2]

This is the popular surface of the movement, the publicly acceptable principle of everyone's getting a piece of the action in a nation that has bought into group politics. But there is a deeper, stronger, and more revealing side: "The conference buzzed with code words. When the speakers talked about 'the hegemonic culture,' they meant undemocratic domination by white men. The scholars particularly scorned the idea that certain great works of literature have absolute value or represent some eternal truth. Just about everything, they argued, is an expression of race, class or gender." This is academic jargon, one-third Marxist, two-thirds Nietzschean; but it points toward the metaphysics of the cosmic power struggle in terms of which we interpret everything nowadays. All books have to be reinterpreted to find the conscious or unconscious power motive of their authors. As Nietzsche puts it, "Every philosophy is the author's secret confession."

The other side in this struggle can be found in the words of W. E. B. Du Bois at the turn of the century:

> I sit with Shakespeare and he winces not. Across the color line I move arm in arm with Balzac and Dumas, where smiling men and welcoming women glide in gilded halls. From out the caves of evening that swing between the strong-limbed earth and the tracery of the stars, I summon Aristotle and Aurelius and what soul I will, and they come all gra-

---

[2]During the question period I discovered that this project has been a roaring success with at least some students. A Chinese, a black, an Armenian, and a person speaking for homosexuals wondered whether they were being "excluded," inasmuch as books by members of their "communities" are not represented in curricula in proportion to their numbers in the population. They seemed to think that Greeks and Italians have been in control of universities and that now their day is coming. One can imagine a census which would redistribute the representation of books. The premise of these students' concerns is that "where you come from," your culture, is more important than where you are going. They are rather like Plato's noble guardian dogs in the *Republic* who love what is familiar, no matter how bad it is, and hate all that is strange or foreign. This kind of demand is entirely new: you do not go to college to discover for yourself what is good but to be confirmed in your origins.

ciously with no scorn or condescension. So, wed with Truth,
I dwell above the Veil.[3]

I confess that this view is most congenial to me. Du Bois found our
common transcultural humanity not in a canon, but in certain works
from which he learned about himself and gained strength for his lonely
journey, beyond the Veil. He found community rather than war. He
used the books to think about his situation, moving beyond the corrosive of prejudice to the independent and sublime dignity of the fully
developed soul. He recapitulates the ever-renewed experience of books
by intelligent poor and oppressed people seeking for a way out.

But during the recent Stanford curriculum debate, a leader of the
black student group declared that the implicit message of the Western
civilization curriculum is "nigger go home." Du Bois from this perspective was suffering from false consciousness, a deceptive faith in
theoretical liberation offered by the inventors of practical slavery. *No
Exit.*

These opposing quotes truly reflect the meaning of the debate
over what is called the canon. The word has religious overtones. *The
Canon* is the list of books of the Bible accepted by the Catholic
Christian church as genuine and inspired. These books are supposed
to compel our faith without reason or evidence. Using a word like
canon arouses our passion for liberation from authority. This kind of
pseudoreligious characterization of practically everything is epidemic
in the post-Nietzschean period. God is dead, and he is the only founder. All kinds of abstract words, like *charisma,* determine our perspective on phenomena before we look at them, and harden the
opinion that power is the only thing, in the intellectual arena as well
as in the political arena. A canon is regarded as the means of indoctrination used by a ruling elite, and study is the process of entitlement
for entry into the elite, for distinguishing the dominators from the
dominated. In other words, the priests who teach the canon are empowered by the canon, and they protect their privileged position by
their teaching. They establish the canon and are established by it. So
you see why a professor like me defends the canon so ferociously.

One can go on weaving these webs of fantasy endlessly, and there
is an element of truth in them. Obviously books are used by nations
and religions to support their way and to train the young to it. But
that is not the whole story. Many books, perhaps the most important
ones, have an independent status and bring us light from outside our

[3]W. E. Burghardt Du Bois, *The Souls of Black Folk* (New York: The New American
Library, Inc., 1969), p. 139.

cave, without which we would be blind. They are frequently the acid which reveals the outlines of abusive power. This is especially true in a liberal society like our own, where it is hard to find a "canonical" book which truly supports our way unqualifiedly. It is at least as plausible that the books which have a continuing good reputation and used to be read in colleges have made it on their intrinsic merits. To be sure, traditions tend to ossify and also to aggregate superfluous matters, to be taught authoritatively by tiresome persons who don't know why they are important and who hold their jobs because they are virtuosos of trivia. But this only means that the traditions have to be renewed from time to time and the professors made to give an account of themselves.

One of the most obvious cases of a writer used as an authority to bolster what might be called a structure of power is Aristotle during the Christian Middle Ages. Scholasticism was a stifling force which had to be rebelled against in order to free the mind. But to take that Will Durant–like interpretation as exhaustive would be naïve. In the first place, Aristotle is something on his own. He survived the wreckage of Scholasticism quite nicely and needed no power structure prior to that time or afterward to insure the continuing interest enlightened men and women take in his works. Moreover, Aristotle's accession to power was a result of a revolution in Christianity which rationalized it and made it move a long way from revelation toward reason. It was the explosion of Greek philosophy into Christian Europe. That philosophy had been preserved and renewed among the Muslims. The challenge of reason presented by the Muslim philosophers precipitated a crisis in Christianity that was appeased but not entirely resolved by Thomas Aquinas. Aristotle sat among the Christian sages, but he inspired many to turn against them. Here we have a truly interesting case of the relation between the allegedly Western and the allegedly non-Western. Such cases speak against the canonical thesis rather than for it and are covered over by it.

It is a grave error to accept that the books of the dead white Western male canon are essentially Western—or any of those other things. The fact that I am doubtful about the non-Western craze suggests automatically, even to sympathetic critics, that I am promoting Western Civ or the like. Yet the very language used shows how enslaved we have become to the historicist assertion that all thought is decisively culture-bound. When Averroës and Thomas Aquinas read Aristotle they did not think of him as Greek and put him into his historical context. They had no interest in Greek Civ but treated him as a wise man, hence a contemporary at all times.

We smile at this naïveté, but they understood Aristotle better than do our scholars, as one can see simply by perusing the commentaries. Plato and Kant claim that they speak to all men everywhere and forever, and I see no reason to reject those claims *a priori*. But that is precisely what is done when they are taken to be parts of Western Civ. To the extent they are merely that, the appeals against them are justified, for Western Civ is clearly partial, demanding the supplement of all the other Civs. The strength of these appeals is in their demand for wholeness or completeness of understanding. Therefore, to begin with, historicism, the alleged primacy of culture, has to be called into question, though it is one of those opinions that has so completely captured modern minds that it appears indubitable. The quarrel is *not* about Western and non-Western but about the possibility of philosophy. The real issue is being obscured due to a political dispute. If we give in we shall allow very modern philosophy to swallow up all philosophers from Socrates up to and including Marx. Postmodernism is an attempt to annihilate the inspiration of Greek philosophy that is more effective than that of the barbarians with their Dark Ages after the fall of Rome, more effective because it is being accomplished by the force and the guile of philosophy itself. I am not asserting the truth of philosophy's old claim to break through the limits of culture and history, but I am asserting that it is the only question. It is neither a Western nor a non-Western question.

Nobody, or practically nobody, argues that natural science is essentially Western. Some efforts have been made in that direction, just as some feminists have tried to show that science is essentially male, but these efforts, aside from their admirable sense of the need for theoretical consistency, have not proved persuasive. There is that big rock of transcultural knowledge or truth, natural science, standing amidst us while we chatter on about the cultural basis of all knowledge. A serious non-Western putsch would require that students learn fifty percent non-Western math, fifty percent non-Western physics, fifty percent non-Western biology, and so forth for medicine and engineering. The reformers stop there because they know they would smack up against a brick wall and discredit their whole movement. Philosophy, they say, is not like that. Perhaps, but I have yet to see a serious discussion about wherein it differs. Differ it does today. But qualitatively? That question ought to keep us busy for a long time. Science is surely somehow transcultural. Religion seems pretty much limited to cultures, even to define them. Is philosophy like science, or is it like religion? What we are witnessing is an attempt to drag it away definitively to the camp of religion.

The universities have dealt with this problem by ceding the despised historicized humanities to the political activists and extremists, leaving undisturbed their nonhistoricized disciplines, which is where the meat and the money are. It is a windfall for administrators to be able to turn all the affirmative-action complaints over to the humanities, which act as a lightning rod while their ship continues its stately progress over undisturbed waters. Stanford shows its concerned, humane, radical face to its inner community, and its serious technical face to the outside community, particularly to its donors. The humanities radicals will settle for this on the calculation that if they can control the minds of the young, they will ultimately gain political control over the power of science.

The essential liberating texts have survived because they are useful. When I spoke of democracy and relativism in *The Closing of the American Mind*, I said only what I learned from Plato and a few others. I appreciate and need further information. So do we all. The serious scholars in non-Western thought should bring us the powerful *texts* they know of to help us. The true canon aggregates around the most urgent questions we face. That is the only ground for the study of books. Idle cultural reports, Eastern or Western, cannot truly concern us, except as a hobby. Edgar Z. Friedenberg once said that social scientists are always giving themselves hernias trying to see something about America Tocqueville did not see. That is why we need Tocqueville, and our neglecting to read him can be interpreted as an effort at hernia prevention. Nietzsche did not seek out Socrates because he was part of the classical canon German boys learned in school. He did so in spite of that fact. Socrates was necessary to him as the profoundest statement of what philosophy is and as the worthiest of rivals. Machiavelli was impelled by real need, not by conformism, when he sought out Xenophon. Male, female, black, white, Greek, barbarian: that was all indifferent, as it should be. Nietzsche reflected on Buddha when he wanted to test the principle of contradiction. That is a model of the way things should be. The last thing we need is a sort of philosophic U.N. run by bureaucrats for the sake of representation for all peoples.

Each must ultimately judge for himself about the important books, but a good beginning would be to see what other thinkers the thinkers who attract him turn to. That will quickly lead to the top. There are very few who remain there, and they recognize one another. There is no conspiracy, only the desire to know. If we allow ourselves to be seduced by the plausible theses of our day, and turn our backs on the great dialogue, our loss will be irreparable.

In my book I connected this radical historicism with fascism and

asserted that the thinking of the European Right had wandered over
to the Left in America. This earned me severe and unthinking criticism
(with the honorable exception of Richard Rorty). It seems to such
critics that I am one of those persons who trivialize unique and terrible
phenomena by calling anyone whom I don't like a fascist or a Nazi.
But I did not call persons active in the sixties those names. I said that
the language of the New Left was no longer truly Marxist and had
become imbued with the language of fascism. And anyone with an
ear for the speech of intellectuals in Weimar Germany will hear echoes
all around us of the dangerous ideas to which they became accustomed.
Since the publication of *The Closing of the American Mind*, fortuitously
there has been fresh attention paid to the Nazism of Martin Heidegger,
more and more widely recognized as the most intelligent figure contributing to the postmodernist movement. At the same time Paul de
Man, who introduced deconstructionism into the United States, was
revealed to have written, as a young man, pro-Nazi articles for a
collaborationist Belgian newspaper. In reading these articles I was
struck by the fact that if one suppresses the references to Hitler and
Hitlerism, much of it sounds like what one reads in advanced literary
reviews today. The lively debate around these questions has not been
very helpful, for it focuses more on questions of personal guilt than
on the possible relation of their thought to the foulest political extremism. The fact that de Man had become a Leftist doesn't prove a thing.
He never seems to have passed through a stage where he was attracted
by reason or liberal democracy. Those who chose culture over civilization, the real opposition, which we have forgotten, were forced to
a position beyond good and evil, for good and evil are products of
cultures. The really great thinkers who thought through what the turn
to culture means, starting from power, said that immoderation, violence, blood, and soil are its means. These are the consequence of
the will to power. I am inclined to take the views of men of such
stature seriously. Very few of America's end-of-the-West people are
attracted by these aspects of the problem of culture, although there
are some, I suspect, who do experience a terrible frisson of joy when
they hear them. However that may be, one always ends up by paying
a price for the consequences of what one thinks.

This is how the American intellectual scene looks. Much greater
events occurring outside the United States, however, demonstrate the
urgency of our task. Those events are epitomized by the Statue of
Liberty erected by the Chinese students in Tiananmen Square. Apparently, after some discussion about whether it should be altered to
have Chinese rather than *Eurocentric* features, there was a consensus
that it did not make any difference.

The terror in China continues, and we cannot yet know what will become of those courageous young persons. But we do know the justice of their cause; and although there is no assurance that it will ultimately triumph, their oppressors have won the universal execration of mankind. With Marxist ideology a wretched shambles everywhere, nobody believes any longer in communist legitimacy. Everywhere in the communist world what is wanted is rational liberal democracy that recognizes men's natural freedom and equality and the rights dependent on them. The people of that world need and want education in democracy and the institutions that actualize it. That education is one of the greatest services the democracies can offer to the people who live under communist tyrannies and long for liberty. The example of the United States is what has impressed them most, and their rulers have been unable to stem the infection. Our example, though, requires explanations, the kind the Founders gave to the world. And this is where we are failing: the dominant schools in American universities can tell the Chinese students only that they should avoid Eurocentrism, that rationalism has failed, that they should study non-Western cultures, and that *bourgeois* liberalism is the most despicable of regimes. Stanford has replaced John Locke, *the* philosopher of liberalism, with Frantz Fanon, an ephemeral writer once promoted by Sartre because of his murderous hatred of Europeans and his espousal of terrorism. However, this is not what the Chinese need. They have Deng Xiaoping to deconstruct their Statue of Liberty. We owe them something much better.

It is in this atmosphere, the awareness that we tread near the edge of the abyss, that I think and write. The American intellectual scene is bleak and ominous but certainly provides great theoretical exhilaration, if one can bear to observe it closely.

Books

Giants and Dwarfs:
An Outline
of *Gulliver's Travels*

GULLIVER'S TRAVELS is an amazing rhetorical achievement. It is the classic children's story and it is a rather obscene tale. Swift was able to charm innocence and amuse corruption, and this is a measure of his talent. I can think of no parallel: Hans Christian Andersen for children, Boccaccio for adults. But, most of all, it is a philosophic book presented in images of overwhelming power. Swift had not only the judgment with which to arrive at a reasoned view of the world, but the fancy by means of which he could recreate that world in a form which teaches where argument fails and which satisfies all while misleading none.

Gulliver's travel memoirs make abundantly clear that he is a Yahoo in the decisive sense. He says "the thing which is not," or, to put it into Yahoo language, he is a liar. This does not mean that I do not believe he underwent the adventures he relates; but he does have something to hide. A small bit of evidence can be gleaned from his own defense of his conduct with a great Lilliputian lady, who had conceived a passion for his person. Gulliver grounds his apology on the alleged fact that no one ever came to see him secretly. But immediately afterward he tells of the secret visit of a minister. We can only suppose the worst in the affair between the lady and Gulliver. And we may further suppose that Gulliver has certain hidden thoughts and intentions which are only to be revealed by closely cross-examining him.[1] He indicates this himself at the close of his travels when he swears to his veracity. He uses for this solemn occasion Sinon's treacherous oath to the Trojans, by means of which that worthy

[1]*Gulliver's Travels* (New York: Random House, 1950), pp. 71, 73.

35

managed to gain admittance for the horse and its concealed burden of Greeks.[2]

I should like to suggest that this book is also such a container, filled with Greeks who are, once introduced, destined to conquer a new Troy, or, translated into "the little language," destined to conquer Lilliput. In other words, I wish to contend that *Gulliver's Travels* is one of the last explicit statements in the famous Quarrel between the Ancients and Moderns and perhaps the greatest intervention in that notorious argument. By means of the appeal of its myth, it keeps alive the classical vision in ages when even the importance of the quarrel is denied, not to speak of the importance of that classical viewpoint, which appears to have been swamped by history. The laughter evoked by *Gulliver's Travels* is authorized by a standard drawn from Homer and Plato.

Prior to entering directly into the contents of the book, I should try to make this assertion somewhat more extrinsically plausible. The quarrel itself is today regarded as a petty thing, rather ridiculous on both sides, a conventional debate between old and new, reactionary and progressive, which later ages have resolved by way of synthesis. Both sides lacked perspective; intellectual history is but one long continuous development. Moreover, the quarrel is looked on largely as a purely literary dispute, originating in the comparison of Greek and Roman poetry with French. Now this understanding is quite different from that of the participants, who, if not always the best judges, must be the first witnesses in any hearing. They understood the dispute over poetry to be a mere subdivision of an opposition between two comprehensive systems of radically opposed thought, one finding its source in ancient philosophy, the other in modern philosophy. The moderns believed that they had found the true principles of nature and that, by means of their methods, new sources of power could be found in physical nature, politics, and the arts. These new principles represented a fundamental break with classical thought and were incompatible with it. The poetic debate was meant, on the part of the advocates of modernity, only to show the superiority of modern thought based on modern talents and modern freedom in the domain where the classics were most indisputably masters and models. The quarrel involved the highest principles about the first causes of all things and the best way of life. It marked a crossroad, one of the very few at which mankind has been asked to make a decisive change in direction. The choice once made, we have forgotten that this was not the only road, that there was another once before us, either because

[2]*Ibid.*, p. 332; cf. Virgil, *Aeneid*, II, 79–80.

we are ignorant of a possible choice or because we are so sure that this is the only road to Larissa. It is only by return to our starting point that the gravity of the choice can be realized; and at the crossroad one finds the quarrel. It is not, I repeat, a quarrel among authors as such, but among principles.

In his own way, Swift presents and contrasts those principles. He characterizes ancient philosophy as a bee whose wings produce music and flight and who thus "visits all the blossoms of the field and garden . . . and in collecting from them enriches himself without the least injury to their beauty, their smell, or their taste." The bee is opposed to a house-building spider, who thinks he produces his own world from himself and is hence independent, but who actually feeds on filth and produces excrement. As the bee says, "So, in short, the question comes all to this; whether is the nobler being of the two, that which by a lazy contemplation of four inches round, by an overweening pride, feeding and engendering on itself, turns all into excrement and venom, producing nothing at all, but flybane and a cobweb; or that which by a universal range, with long search, much study, true judgment, and distinction of things, brings honey and wax."[3]

This description is drawn from one of Swift's earliest writings, *The Battle of the Books. Gulliver's Travels* was one of his latest. Throughout his life Swift saw the Quarrel between the Ancients and the Moderns as the issue in physics, poetry, and politics, and it is in the light of it that he directed his literary career and his practical life. The quarrel is the key to the diverse strands of this various man; his standards of judgment are all classical; his praise and blame are always in accord with that of Plato. He learned how to live within his own time in the perspective of an earlier one. Swift, the Tory and the High Churchman, was a republican and a nonbeliever.

Gulliver's Travels is always said to be a satire, and there is no reason to quarrel with this designation. But it is not sufficient, for satire is constructed with a view to what is serious and ridiculous, good and bad. It is not enough to say that human folly is ridicule what was folly to Aristophanes would not have seemed so to Tertullian, and conversely. If the specific intention of the satire is not uncovered, the work is trivialized. Swift intended his book to instruct, and the character of that instruction is lost if we do not take seriously the issues he takes seriously. But we do not even recognize the real issues in the Quarrel, let alone try to decide which side had the greatest share of truth. In our time, only Leo Strauss has provided us with the

[3]*Gulliver's Travels, op. cit.,* pp. 529–30.

scholarship and the philosophic insight necessary to a proper confrontation of ancients and moderns, and hence his works are the
prolegomena to a recovery of Swift's teaching. Swift's rejection of
modern physical and political science seems merely ill-tempered if not
viewed in relation to a possible alternative, and it is Leo Strauss who
has elaborated the plausibility, nay, the vital importance, of that
alternative. Now we are able to turn to Swift, not only for amusement,
but for possible guidance as to how we should live. Furthermore, Swift's
art of writing explicitly follows the rhetorical rules for public expression
developed by the ancients, of which we have been reminded by Professor Strauss. That rhetoric was a result of a comprehensive reflection
about the relation between philosophy and politics, and it points to
considerations neglected by the men of letters of the Enlightenment.
Gulliver's Travels is in both substance and form a model of the problems
which we have been taught to recognize as our own by Leo Strauss.
It is fitting that this essay be designed to do him honor; its content
is beyond acknowledgment indebted to his learning.

Gulliver's Travels is a discussion of human nature, particularly of
political man, in the light of the great split. In general, the plan of
the book is as follows: Book I, modern political practice, especially
the politics of Britain and France; Book II, ancient political practice
on something of a Roman or Spartan model; Book III, modern philosophy in its effect on political practice; Book IV, ancient utopian
politics used as a standard for judging man understood as the moderns
wished to understand him. By "ancient" Swift means belonging to
Greece and Rome—Greece for philosophy and poetry, republican
Rome for politics. For Swift, Thomas Aquinas is a modern.[4]
There are many indications of both a substantial and a formal
kind, which indicate the order of the parts. For example, Gulliver
takes the same ship, the Adventure, to both Brobdingnag and the land
of the Houyhnhnms. Books I and III are the only ones which are
directly susceptible of an analysis appropriate to a roman à clef: Lilliput
is full of characters clearly identifiable as personages in British politics,
and Laputa is peopled largely by modern philosophers and members
of the Royal Academy. The only clearly identifiable modern elements
in Brobdingnag or the land of the Houyhnhnms are those in England
referred to by the travelling Gulliver. When he is in Lilliput and
Laputa (notice the similarity of the names), he tells nothing of his
world or native country. He need not, for the reader should recognize

⁴Ibid., p. 533.

it; Gulliver is alien, and the interesting thing is the world seen through his eyes. His perspective is that of a man totally outside England; with the Brobdingnagians and the Houyhnhnms, he is all English, and they are usually foils used to bring out the weaknesses in his nature. In the former case, he is used as the standard for strictures against modern England; in the latter, the Houyhnhnms and Brobdingnagians are used as a standard in criticizing him in the role of a modern Englishman. In one sense the book is all about England; in another, it is all about antiquity. The formula is simply this: when he is good, the others are bad; when he is bad, they are good. The bad others are found in Books I and III, which treat of the recognizably modern. The good others are in Books II and IV, which are, at the least, removed from modernity. Parallel to this movement is Gulliver's sense of shame; in Book I he is shameless—he defecates in a temple and urinates on the palace; and in Lilliput, the people care. In Brobdingnag, where they could not care less, he is full of shame, will not allow himself to be seen performing these functions, and hides behind sorrel leaves.[5] We can say that Gulliver is somehow in between—superior to the inferior and inferior to the superior, but never equal. He lacks something of perfection, but from a certain point of view he is superior to his contemporaries.

Gulliver informs us on his return from Brobdingnag that it was not necessary for him to visit Lilliput in order for him to see Englishmen as Lilliputians; it was only necessary for him to have been to Brobdingnag, for when he landed, he thought himself to be the size of a Brobdingnagian. This was not the case; but having shared their perspective, he could forget his real self and see his likes as he was seen by the giants.[6] The English are truly pygmies. The lesson is that one must study Brobdingnag. Gulliver is as a giant in Lilliput because of what he has learned in Brobdingnag; when he is with the Brobdingnagians, however, he returns to his awareness of himself as a real Lilliputian. He recognizes his weaknesses, but he is great because of his self-consciousness or self-knowledge. He learns "how vain an attempt it is for a man to endeavor to do himself honor among those who are out of all degree of equality or comparison with him."[7]

Swift's device in Lilliput and Brobdingnag is to take moral and intellectual differences and project them in physical dimensions. From this simple change everything else follows. In working this transfor-

[5] *Ibid.*, pp. 29–30, 60–61, 103.
[6] *Ibid.*, pp. 168–169.
[7] *Ibid.*, p. 138.

mation, he pursues Aristotle's suggestion that nature intends the differences in men's souls to be reflected in their bodies and that men
whose bodies are greatly superior, resembling the statues of gods, would
readily be accepted as masters.[8] As a literary device, Swift's transformation works wonders; for literature lives on images and sensations,
appealing to fancy and imagination, but there is no way that philosophy can make a direct appeal by means of the arts. When the im-
perceptible differences so suddenly become powerful sensual images,
however, all becomes clear. Gulliver's attempts to take the physical
beauty of the Lilliputians seriously, or the king of Brobdingnag's holding Gulliver in his hand and asking him if he is a Whig or a Tory,
resume hundreds of pages of argument in an instant. And, moreover,
the great majority of men cannot, for lack of experience, understand
the great superiority of soul which is humanly possible. But when that
power is seen in terms of size, all men, if only momentarily, know
what superiority is and recognize the difficulties it produces for its
possessor and those in its immediate vicinity. To tell men of the vanity
of human pretensions may be edifying, but what sermon has the force
of the absurd claim that Lilliput is "the terror of the universe"?

Gulliver's adventures in Lilliput are largely an exposition of the
problems faced by him and the Lilliputians because of his bigness.
With the best of will, neither side can understand the concerns of
the other. They do not belong together, but they are forced together,
if only by their common humanity—a humanity stretched to its limits.
He is imprisoned by them and needs them for his maintenance; they
do not know how to get rid of him (if they were to kill him, the
stench of his decaying body might sicken the atmosphere) and are
torn between fear and distrust, on the one hand, and dazzling hopes
for using him, on the other. Their problem is aggravated by their
vision: The Lilliputians "see with great exactness but at no great
distance." They suffer from a loss of perspective. It is not their fault;
that is the way they are built.

What this entails is best revealed when we see giants through
the eyes of our Cicerone: nothing could be more revolting than the
description of the woman's breast. He sees things which are really
there, but he no longer sees the object as a whole; a thing that from
the human point of view should be beautiful and attractive becomes
in his vision ugly and repulsive. Odors and tastes are distorted; Gulliver
in Brobdingnag experiences the literally dirty underside of life. And
thus we learn that the Lilliputians experienced him as he did the

[8]Aristotle, *Politics*, 1254ᵇ, 27–39.

Brobdingnagians. One Lilliputian even had the audacity to complain of his smell on a hot day, although he was renowned for his cleanliness.[9] They can never grasp him as he really is; the different parts seem ugly; the ugliness of nature, which disappears in the light of its unity, is their overwhelming impression. In them one can understand the maxim "No man is a hero to his valet; not because he is not a hero but because the valet is a valet." I think there can be little doubt that Swift believes the giant's perspective is ultimately proportionate to the true purpose of things; there is not a simple relativity.

Now, many critics have observed that the recent invention of the microscope and the telescope influenced Swift in his satire on pygmies and giants. If this is true, one can assert that Swift meant to show that the increase in knowledge made possible by these instruments is offset by a corresponding loss of awareness of the whole. The Brobdingnagians have a far-reaching sense of order, totally lacking in the Lilliputians. In Brobdingnag, everything is considered in relation to the kind of man who is to be produced, and learning and actions are accepted or rejected in terms of this standard.

Although Gulliver tries to act in good faith with the Lilliputians, he finds it difficult to observe what they observe and to give their opinions the same cosmic significance that they give them. Lilliput is a monarchy, and all life centers on getting certain vain honors and offices; these purely conventional distinctions form the whole horizon of the important persons in the court, and Gulliver is asked to take them as seriously as the courtiers do, as though this nonsense had a natural status. Gulliver earnestly undertakes to live in these terms: although he is a Nardac and hence of higher rank than the Lord-Treasurer, Gulliver does concede him precedence in virtue of his office. Flattery and interest are the only political motives, and these vices play their role on a stage set by conflict of religious belief. Currently, the country is divided by the struggle between the *slamecksan* and the *tramecksan*—the high heels and the low heels. Swift, who devoted his public life to the High Church, represents the difference between Tory and Whig as constituted by the difference between High Church and Low Church, and the substance of that difference he compares to an infinitesimal difference in the heights of heels. Further, recent Lilliputian history has been dominated by the strife between those who break their eggs at the big end and those who break them at the small, and, more importantly, foreign policy is still dominated by it. This dispute rests on the interpretation of sacred texts and the king's

[9]*Gulliver's Travels, op. cit.*, pp. 62, 101, 132–33.

right to determine the canonic interpretation. For such issues wars are fought and nations turned upside down. Gulliver is willing to help his country, but only for its self-defense; he has no crusading fervor.[10]

The nobleman who presents the politico-religious situation to Gulliver concludes by citing the words of the Blundecral: "All true believers break their eggs at the convenient end." "And," he continues, "which is the convenient end, seems in my humble opinion, to be left to every man's conscience, or at least in the power of the chief magistrate to determine." Gulliver's friend proposes a ridiculous solution to a ridiculous problem and resumes, thereby, the range of solutions proposed in the seventeenth and eighteenth centuries to the question posed by the demands of the revealed religions on civil society.

There was first the split between Catholic and Protestant and then that between High and Low Church, each pretending to possess the authoritative view of divine things which must guide political life. Due to the irreconcilability of the two opponents and the wars which were their consequence, there then arose a school which said that the king should decide these issues or, alternatively, and more importantly, that there must be freedom in these matters, that the conscience cannot be forced. This school was strongly supported, if only on prudential grounds, by the minority sects, who saw the basis for their preservation in the doctrine of the freedom of the conscience. This way of thinking was the source of the peculiarly modern libertarianism, which holds that a determination of the supreme ends cannot be a part of the political function and that these are a matter for individual decision. This doctrine, which was in its beginnings a mere compromise in order to avoid civil wars, later became absolute and is certainly familiar to us. In the mouth of this dwarf it sounds ridiculously sententious. His formulation must be compared with that of the king of Brobdingnag, commenting on the same problem. He laughed at Gulliver's "odd kind of arithmetic," as he was pleased to call it, "in reckoning the numbers of our people by a computation drawn from the several sects among us, in religion and politics. He said he knew no reason why those who entertain opinions prejudicial to the public should be obliged to change or should not be obliged to conceal them. And, as it was tyranny in any government to require the first, so it was weakness not to enforce the second; for a man may be allowed to keep poisons in his closet, but not to vend them about for cordials."[11]

[10]*Ibid.*, pp. 51–53, 57–58.
[11]*Ibid.*, p. 147; cf., e.g., Swift, *On the Testimony of Conscience* ("The Prose Works of

This is Swift's own view of the matter and accords with classic traditions. This view presupposes that there is a sensible understanding of the politically beneficial that a ruler may acquire and that there is no reason to compromise the understanding conducive to the general welfare with the freedom of fanatical minorities. Although this is the reasonable position, it does not imply that, given particular circumstances, other doctrines might not be momentarily necessary or helpful; the only thing insisted on is that party and sect are in themselves noxious and that a good regime must be rid of them. The king of Brobdingnag could speak with relative ease in these matters, for there was no history of religious difference or warfare in his realm. The only political problem was the classic and natural one among king, nobility, and people, and that had been solved long before by the establishment of a balanced regime.[12]

Swift himself lived at a time when his nation had long been split by differences of belief which issued in political parties. He took a strong party stand, for he believed that only through the parties could any political goals be achieved in his age. He tried to choose the most reasonable alternative, the one which would best provide the moral basis for a decent regime and the production of good men and good citizens. But there is no doubt that he regarded his situation as defective. Far better would be a regime not vexed by such disputes and habits of belief, one in which the rulers could be guided by reason and faction could be legitimately suppressed without the suppression having the character of one fanatical half of the nation imposing its convictions on the other equally fanatical half. But more of this later. For the moment it is sufficient to say that religion is the central problem of modernity for Swift; and in his utopias the problem is either handled in a pagan way or is totally suppressed. A large part of Gulliver's difficulties in Lilliput are due to a failure to understand this problem or to take a stance in relation to it.

The kinds of compromises that must be made by the prudent man in politics are indicated in Chapter VI of Book I. This chapter is usually regarded as a later, inharmonious addition, in which Swift exposes his own view about the political good. The chapter is introduced on the pretext of presenting the ancient institutions of Lilliput, which have become corrupted. It is often argued that these are not consonant with what has preceded and are only a vehicle for Swift's

Jonathan Swift," Vol. IV [London: George Bell, 1898]), pp. 120–22; *The Sentiments of a Church of England Man, ibid.*, III, 55.
[12]*Gulliver's Travels, op. cit.*, p. 156.

expression of opinion. However, even a superficial reading of this section would show that the institutions are not the same as those used by the Brobdingnagians or the Houyhnhnms, who are clearly and explicitly stated to be the models. These institutions are undoubtedly an improvement of Lilliput's actual government, as Gulliver states. But they are just as undoubtedly a compromise with the best institutions, based on the real practices and principles of eighteenth-century England. Swift proposes a reform, but not that of an idealist. He knows that root and branch changes are impossible; one must begin from the character of those who are to be reformed.

There is much of John Locke in what Gulliver relates. Fraud is one of the greatest of crimes in the kingdom, for without trust credit is destroyed. Rewards for virtue as well as punishments for vice are established; the rewards consist of sums of money. Commerce and money—essentially selfish interest—are used as the basis for reform, and the motivation for decent conduct is gain. Moreover, the system of education separates parents from children, allowing the children to be raised by the state because "they will never allow that a child is under any obligation to his father for begetting him, or to his mother for bringing him into the world, which considering the miseries of human life, was neither a benefit in itself, nor intended so by his parents, whose thoughts, in their love encounters, were otherwise employed." The parents cannot be trusted to educate their children because they are naturally completely selfish. Thus the children are to be trained to citizenship by the state; the formula repeats the teaching of Locke on filial obligation. These three crucial heads of the reform rest on a principle of egotism. A fourth is that all Lilliputians must believe in a divine Providence, but on purely political grounds. Their kings claim to be deputies of Providence; hence their authority would be undermined by disbelief. There are other possible bases for respect for authority, but given the English situation, this is the only viable one. The specific content of the belief is not made precise. It is consistent with a plurality of sects. Gulliver outlines a set of institutions which would be good for Lilliputians, given their specific character; a wise man could support them with a good conscience, but with full awareness that other institutions might be more admirable, given a better people. This might make him seem to be in contradiction with himself, but he would only seem so.

Gulliver's disaster in Lilliput occurs because he is too big for the Lilliputians; the specific charges against him are only corollaries of that fact. The outcome was inevitable. Civil society cannot endure such disproportionate greatness; it must either submit itself to the one best man or ostracize him. The condemnation of this comic Socrates is not to be blamed on the prejudices of the Lilliputians; it is a necessity that no amount of talk or education will do away with. The four major charges against Gulliver are as follows. (1) He urinated on the royal palace, even though there was a law against urinating within its confines. (2) He refused to subdue Blefuscu, to utterly destroy the Big-Endian exiles, to force the Blefuscudians to confess the Lilliputian religion, and to accept the Lilliputian monarch. (3) He was friendly to the Blefuscudian ambassadors who came to treat for peace and helped them in their mission. (4) He had the intention of paying a visit to Blefuscu.[13]

If we generalize these charges, they would read as follows. (1) He does not accept the judgments of the Lilliputians about what is noble and what is base. He does what is necessary to preserve the palace, using means indifferent in themselves but repulsive to the queen; from her point of view, of course, what was done was pretty disagreeable. Swift's humor in defense of the crown, which displeased Queen Anne, has been compared to the acts cited in this charge. It is also reminiscent of Aristophanes' Dung-beetle, who, because he goes low, can go high. But the chief thing to underline is the fact that, because of their different situations, Gulliver cannot have the same sentiments as the Lilliputians about what is fair and what is ugly. He identifies the fair or noble with the useful—a rational procedure, but one which can hardly be accepted by civil society which lives on the distinction between the two. (2) He does not share the religious prejudices of the nation and is unwilling to be inhuman for the sake of what can only appear as senseless dogma to him. He cannot see the importance of the faith or of the ambition of the king. Big end, small end—they all appear human to him. (3) He does not accept the distinction between friend and enemy defined by the limits of the nation. Once again, common humanity is what he sees. At the same time, from the Lilliputian standpoint, how can a foreigner who consorts with the enemy be trusted—especially a foreigner of such exceptional power? They can only attribute to him the motivations which they already know; they cannot see the interior workings of his soul, and, if they could, they would not understand them. By any canons, Gulliver's behavior is suspicious, no matter how innocent it may actually be. How can the Lilliputians see he has no ambition to subdue both kingdoms and make himself ruler of the known world? How could they believe that what seems so important to them is too

---

[13]*Ibid.*, pp. 74–76.

petty even to be considered by Gulliver? (4) Gulliver is not satisfied
in his new home; he thinks there is much to be learned elsewhere.
He may find what pleases him more in another land. His loyalty is
questionable; he has the dubious taste for being away from home.

Gulliver is condemned because the Lilliputians discovered in the
palace fire that his moral taste was not the same as theirs. He did not
behave as a good citizen; he did not identify what is good with what
is Lilliputian. The court jealousies and hatreds were only predisposing
factors in the ultimate crisis. Given the uses which could be made of
him, he was bound to be an object of flattery and conspiracy, as he
appeared to incline to one side or another. The proposal for resolving
the Gulliver crisis is the standard for civil society's use of genius: he
is to be blinded, for thus he would retain his power but could be used
more easily by the civil authority. He is to be a blind giant—blind
to the ends which he serves, adding only might to the means which
are to achieve them.[14] This is an intolerable solution for him, but the
alternative would be for the Lilliputians to alter themselves to fit him.
The disproportion is too great. Finally, the high hopes deceived, the
kings of both Lilliput and Blefuscu are heartily glad to be rid of him.
This is Swift's description of his own situation and that of other great
men.

This interpretation of Lilliput depends, of course, on the information supplied by the voyage to Brobdingnag. Gulliver's superiority
to the Lilliputians is as the Brobdingnagians' superiority to him.
Against the background of Brobdingnag, Gulliver's moral perspective
comes into focus. The Brobdingnagians are great because they are
virtuous; they are, particularly, temperate. Political life is not a play-
thing of their lusts. There is neither faction nor Christian controversy
(they are polytheists).[15] Hence there is no war, for they have no
neighbors and no civil strife—not because of the victory of one part
of the body politic over the others, but because of the judicious blend-
ing of all three parts. They maintain themselves in a state of constant
preparedness, simply for the sake of preserving the advantages stemming from military virtue. Theirs is entirely a citizen army. Their
concentration is on obedience to law, not interpretation of it. Law is
powerful so long as it is respected, and respect implies assent. The
mind should not be used to reason away the clear bases of duty. No
commentaries are allowed on the laws. There is no political science.
Their learning is only such as will produce good citizens, or, put
otherwise, their studies are made to produce not learning, but virtue.

[14]Ibid., pp. 76–77.
[15]Ibid., p. 127.

They know morality, history, poetry, and mathematics, and that is all.[16]

The vices that Gulliver finds in the common people are at worst summed up in an excess of thrift, and most are simply a result of his peculiar perspective; he assumes ill-intention where there is probably only indifference or inattention. The Brobdingnagians are a simple, decent people whose state exists, not for the pursuit of knowledge or the cultivation of diversity, but for the sake of well-known, common-sense virtues. Brobdingnag is a sort of cross between Sparta and republican Rome; it concurs in almost all respects with the principles of Aristotle's *Ethics*. Swift was an enemy of the Enlightenment, its learning and its politics.

We can make only a short visit to Laputa.[17] Gulliver goes there, after having seen modern politics, to see modern science and its effects on life. He finds a theoretical preoccupation, which is abstracted from all human concerns and which did not start from the human dimension. On the flying island the men have one eye turned inward, the other toward the zenith; they are perfect Cartesians—one egotistical eye contemplating the self, one cosmological eye surveying the most distant things. The intermediate range, which previously was the center of concentration and which defined both the ego and the pattern for the study of the stars, is not within the Laputian purview. The only studies are astronomy and music, and the world is reduced to these two sciences. The men have no contact with objects of sensation; this is what permits them to remain content with their science. Communication with others is unnecessary, and the people require a beating to respond to them. Rather than making their mathematics follow the natural shapes of things, they change things so as to fit their mathematics; the food is cut into all sorts of geometrical figures. Their admiration for women, such as it is, is due to the resemblance of women's various parts to specific figures. Jealousy is

[16]*Ibid.*, p. 153.
[17]For the interpretation of the details of the voyages to Laputa and Lagado, cf. Marjorie Nicolson, *Science and Imagination* (Ithaca: Cornell University Press, 1956), pp. 110–154; *Voyages to the Moon* (New York: Macmillan, 1948); with Nora Mohler, "The Scientific Background of Swift's Voyage to Laputa," *Annals of Science*, II (1937), 299–334; "Swift's Flying Island in the Voyage to Laputa," *ibid.*, pp. 405–30.

The unifying theme of all of Swift's criticism of the new science is not the external absurdity of its propositions, or its impious character, or its newness, but its partialness and abstraction from what is known about human things. Modern science represented a complete break with classical principles and methods, and Swift believed that there was a whole range of phenomena it could not grasp but which it would distort. The commitment to it, if absolutized, would destroy the human orientation. This contention remains to be refuted.

unknown to them; their wives can commit adultery before their eyes
without being noticed. Above all, they lack a sense for poetry. This
is a touchstone for Gulliver; no mention is made of poetry in Lilliput
and Laputa, although both the Brobdingnagians and the Houyhnhnms
have excellent poetry, of a Homeric kind.[18] Poetry expresses the
rhythm of life, and its images capture the color of reality. Men without
poetry are without a grasp of humanity, for the poetic is the human
supplement to philosophy—not poetry in our more modern sense, but
in that of the great epics which depict the heroes who are our models
for emulation. Modern science cannot understand poetry, and hence
it can never be a science of man.

Another peculiarity of these men is described by Gulliver as
follows. "What I chiefly admired, and thought altogether unaccountable, was the strong disposition I observed in them towards news and
politics, perpetually inquiring into public affairs, giving their judgments in matters of state, and passionately disputing every inch of a
party opinion. I have indeed observed the same disposition among
most of the mathematicians I have known in Europe, although I could
never discover the least analogy between the two sciences."[19] Gulliver,
we see, has recovered his old superiority. On this theme of science
and politics, so important today, Swift's perspicacity is astonishing.
He not only recognizes the scientists' professional incapacity to understand politics, but also their eagerness to manipulate it, as well as
their sense of special right to do so. The Laputians' political power
rests on the new science. Their flying island is built on the principles
of the new physics founded by Gilbert and Newton. Swift saw the
possibility of great inventions that would open new avenues to political
endeavor. This island allows the king and the nobles to live free from
conspiracies by the people—in fact free from contact with them—
while still making use of them and receiving the tribute which is
necessary to the maintenance and leisure of the rulers. They can crush
the terrestrial cities; their power is almost unlimited and their responsibilities nil.[20] Power is concentrated in the hands of the rulers;
hence they are not forced even by fear to develop a truly political
intelligence. They require no virtue; everything runs itself, so there
is no danger that their incompetence, indifference, or vice will harm
them. Their island allows their characteristic deformity to grow to the
point of monstrosity. Science, in freeing men, destroys the natural
conditions which make them human. Here, for the first time in history,

[18]*Gulliver's Travels, op. cit.*, pp. 153, 311; cf. p. 184.
[19]*Ibid.*, p. 185.
[20]*Ibid.*, p. 194.

is the possibility of tyranny grounded not on ignorance, but on science. Science is no longer theoretical, but serves the wishes and hence the passions of men.

Gulliver is disgusted by this world; he represents common sense, and he is despised for it. This he finds disagreeable, and he seeks to return to earth, where he can be respected. But in Lagado, he finds things even worse; everything is topsy-turvy because what works has been abandoned in favor of projects. Here Gulliver's critique, although funny, impresses us less than it does elsewhere. He seems to have seriously underestimated the possible success of the projects. But perhaps some of the reasons supporting this posture are still intelligible to us. The transformations planned by the projectors are direct deductions from the principles used in Laputa; they are willing to give up the old life and the virtues it engendered for the sake of a new life based only on wishes. If the new life succeeded it might produce some comforts; but they do not know what that way of life will do to them. This transformation and this incertitude induce Gulliver to be conservative. He distrusts the motives of the projectors and wonders if they do not represent a debasement of the noble purposes of contemplation. If Gulliver is not right in ridiculing the possibilities of applied science, he may nevertheless be right in doubting its desirability. At any rate, there is today in America a school of social criticism which is heavy-handedly saying the same thing. And as for education and politics, Gulliver looks as sound as ever when he ridicules substitutes for intelligence and study, or when he outlines Harold Lasswell's anal science of politics. Gulliver's attack on modern science and projecting foresaw the problem which has only recently struck the popular consciousness: what does the conquest of nature do to the conquerors?

The visit to Glubdubdribb allows Gulliver to see modern historical science as it really is, because he is able to evoke the shades of those with whom it deals. History is of particular importance, because from it one can understand what has been lost or gained and the direction in which one is going. We learn that this science is most inaccurate. It has embellished modern men and misunderstood the ancients; even our knowledge of the Greek language has decayed to the point of incomprehensibility. Gulliver most admires Homer, Aristotle, and the heroes who opposed tyranny. There is only one modern—Sir Thomas More—among these latter. All the later interpreters of the poets and the philosophers misunderstood and denatured them. An effort to recover them must be made; and the result of that study will be the recognition of the unqualified superiority of classical antiquity. "I desired that the senate of Rome might appear before me in one large chamber, and a modern representative, in counterview, in another. The first seemed an assembly of heroes and demigods; the other, a knot of pedlars, pick-pockets, highwaymen and bullies."[21]

The fourth and last stop which we must make in the voyage to Laputa is Luggnag. Here Gulliver has his interlude on immortality. Death is feared in all other nations, but not in Luggnag, where immortality is constantly present in the form of the Struldbrugs. The desire for immortality, or the fear of death, leads men to all kinds of vain hopes and wishes. Gulliver is to some extent released from this anxiety by his experience with the Struldbrugs, who never die but grow ever older. They are repulsive and have no human traits. "They were not only opinionative, peevish, covetous, morose, and talkative, but incapable of friendship and dead to all natural affection. . . . Envy and impotent desires are their prevailing passions."[22] They hate all that is young. No doubt, most men would prefer to be dead than to live this living death. However, it has often been remarked that to the extent one can imagine immortality, one can imagine perpetual youth. Gulliver himself imagines perpetual youth when he discovers the existence of the Struldbrugs and learns that they are not advisers at court, but are banished. He is surprised. These particular immortals grow old and decrepit; the criticism of man's desire for immortality applies only to the versions of it which do not include perpetual youth.

Now, why has Swift presented his case in this way? One might suggest that he was reflecting on the only example in our world of an institution that claims immortality, namely, the Church. I gather this from Gulliver's concluding remark about the Struldbrugs, who are not allowed to hold employment of public trust or to purchase lands: "I could not but agree that the laws of this kingdom relative to the Struldbrugs were founded upon the strongest reasons and such as any other country would be under necessity of enacting in the like circumstances. Otherwise, as avarice is the necessary consequent of old age, those immortals would in time become proprietors of the whole nation, and engross the civil power, which, for want of abilities to manage, must end in the ruin of the public."[23]

This merely echoes the views prevailing in England after the Reformation on the importance of limiting church lands, especially those of the Roman Catholic Church. Modern times are characterized

---

[21]*Ibid.*, p. 223.
[22]*Ibid.*, p. 242.
[23]*Ibid.*, p. 244. Although Swift defended the property of the Church of Ireland, he did it only within severe limits and for the sake of preserving an important civil institution. He well knew the dangers of the higher clergy's possible avarice, and he also was perfectly aware of the political difficulties caused by the property and influence of the Roman Church prior to the Reformation.

by an immortal body inhabiting, but not truly part of, civil society—
a decrepit body with a dangerous tendency to aggrandize itself. Death
is preferable to the extension of life represented in the Church; and
civil society is safe only so long as that body is contained by law.

The voyage to the Houyhnhnms is of particular significance in
our cross-examination of Lemuel Gulliver, for this was his last trip
and the one that most affected him; it is under the influence of seeing
Houyhnhnms contrasted with Yahoos that he wrote this book, which
had as its explicit end the reform of all human vices. In Lilliput and
Laputa he learned nothing and found nothing to admire; in Brobdingnag he admired; but among the Houyhnhnms he imitated. Any
reform must be in the direction of their practices. The Houyhnhnms
are not human beings; man's standard is now a nonhuman one. What
Swift has done in the land of the Houyhnhnms is to elaborate a utopia,
a utopia based on Plato's *Republic*; but it is a super *Republic*, for the
problem which made the construction of the best city so difficult for
Socrates has disappeared—the Houyhnhnms lack the passionate part
of the soul. The whole difficulty in the *Republic* is to make the three
orders take their proper role in relation to one another. Punishment
and rhetoric are necessary; the book is full of the struggle between
the rational and the appetitive; and the irascible or spirited, intended
as reason's ally, shows a constant tendency to turn against it. The
passionate and the spirited are in perfect natural harmony with the
rational in the Houyhnhnms. Swift has taken everything that was
connected with the passionate or erotic nature and made a kind of
trash heap from it, which he calls the Yahoos. Or, in another and
more adequate formulation, Swift has extrapolated the Houyhnhnms
from man as depicted by Plato, and the Yahoos from man as depicted
by Hobbes.

It is not correct to say that this section is a depreciation of man
in general in favor of animals, for the animals are very particular
animals, possessing certain human characteristics of a Platonic order,
and the men are a very particular kind of passionate men. Man has
a dual nature—part god, part beast; Swift has separated the two parts.
In reality they are in tension with one another, and one must decide
which is in the service of the other. Are the passions directed to the
service of reason, or is reason the handmaiden of the passions? If the
latter, then the Yahoo is the real man; if the former, then the Houyhnhnms represent man as he really is. The separation effected by
Swift leads to clarity about the ends.

Nature is the standard, and the Houyhnhnms are "the perfection
of nature," which is what the name means. Nature is Parmenidean;

being is; the changeable has no meaning. The Houyhnhnms speak and speculate only about what is, for only what is can be said. There is not even a word for opinion, nor do the Houyhnhnms have those passions which partake of nonbeing. There is nothing in them that can take account of what is not or can partake of what is not; hence they cannot say what is not. They need not lie, for like Plato's gods, they need not deceive, nor do they have friends who need to be deceived. Virtue for them is knowledge. They see what must be done and do it; there is no need of moral habituation. They always reason like philosophers; when they recognize what a phenomenon is, they say so—otherwise they say nothing. This is why Gulliver is such a problem: is he a Yahoo or is he not?[24] He is and he is not. This, by the way, perhaps indicates a weakness in the Houyhnhnms' understanding; they cannot adequately grasp this composite being.

Gulliver, who in the first stages of his relationship with his master tried to obscure his Yahoo nature, is finally forced to undress himself. He makes a sort of girdle "to hide my nakedness," echoing Adam before the Lord. Gulliver again feels shame, as he did in Brobdingnag. The Houyhnhnms are shameless; no part of the body is any more or less beautiful than another.[25] Gulliver feels shame because he is a lustful being and cannot control desires which he understands to be bad. He is a sinner and a repenter, whereas the Houyhnhnms are like Aristotle's gentleman who never blushes because he has nothing to be ashamed of. This is the indication which allows us to see the Yahoos as peculiarly modern man. They are a sort of cross between man as Augustine describes him and as Hobbes describes him. They have the uncontrollably corrupted nature of Augustinian man, with particular concentration on sexual lust. And the relation of Yahoos to one another is one of Hobbesean war. The Yahoos have infinite desires, and most of all they hate to see anyone else taking possession of anything at all. They are needy beings with a constant sense of scarcity. They hoard and have an unlimited desire for gold without any idea of what they want to use it for. They know of no natural limits, so they are never satisfied. They are strong, but fearful; and they set a leader over themselves to govern them.[26] If one conceives of the real life of man as in the passions, this is the kind of picture one must have of him. There is absolutely no suggestion in Swift's view of the Houyhnhnms that a being who senses his own corruption and tries to improve himself, or who yearns for salvation, is desirable.

[24]Ibid., pp. 267, 272, 304, 313, 319, 261, 263, 266–70, 274–75, 291.
[25]Ibid., p. 269.
[26]Ibid., pp. 296–304.

There can be little doubt that the land of the Houyhnhnms is a
perfection of the *Republic*. A glance at the list of similarities is convincing; the changes are all based on the Houyhnhnms' superiority.
There is hardly any need for politics because the citizens are so orderly
and accept their roles. The needs that cause war are absent. The rulers
are free to converse. They are philosophers; in one example of their
reasoning—the explanation of the origin of Yahoos—they reason
exactly like pre-Socratic philosophers. At all events, this is a land
ruled by philosophers.

The Houyhnhnms live simply, and their wants are provided by
the community. There is no money. Because they live simply and
naturally, there is no need for the arts of medicine or of forensic
rhetoric. There is a class system, but one based entirely on natural
differences. They do not fear death nor do they mourn those who
depart. They regard the land as their first mother. They belong to the
land as a whole and have no special, private interests.

To come to the paradoxes treated in Book V of the *Republic*,
there is also among the Houyhnhnms equality of women and virtual
community of wives and children. Marriages are arranged on grounds
of reason; *eros* does not play a role. They separate into couples and
have private houses, but when necessary they break up families, service
one another, and switch children—all this in the name of the community as a whole. Friendship and benevolence are their virtues and
the themes of their conversation. Their poetry, which has all the
power of Homeric epics, supports their character. There is, therefore,
no need for any of the elaborate devices mentioned in the *Republic*
for the censorship of poetry or the destruction of the family interest.
There is no distinction between public and private, between the good
and one's own. They do not love their children; they take care of
them for the sake of the common good.[27]

The contrast in Book IV is between Plato and Hobbes, between
the perfected political animal and man in the state of nature. The
Yahoos have tyrants; the Houyhnhnms are republicans who need no
subordination because they have sufficient virtue to govern themselves. Swift took refuge in animals because nothing in the conception
of man indicated the possibility of such a regime in state or soul. He
conceived a hatred of the Yahoos; for only by this self-contempt could
he cultivate that in himself which was akin to the Houyhnhnms.

It has been asked, Why, with all their virtues, do the
Houyhnhnms have no god? But this clearly follows from their prin-

[27]*Ibid.*, pp. 304–17. Note the reference to Socrates and Plato at the beginning of this
passage.

ciple. They cannot say the thing which is not. They can see only the permanent, eternal, unchanging being. In England, Yahoos have a religion; their sacred issues cannot even be rendered in the Houyhnhnm language.[28] These Trojan horses contain more than they appear to. In Books I and II, size is the illustrative device. Here the meaning is projected by difference of species.

Gulliver's Travels has often been called a misanthropic book. Indeed, it does not present a very flattering picture of man. But we should ask ourselves what a misanthrope is. If anything, he is a hater of humanity—one who had great expectations of others and has been deceived. Above all—if we can believe Molière—he is a man who tries to live according to the highest standards of virtue and finds they are unacceptable in human society; he is a man who always tells the truth and acts according to principle. Rousseau, who left society to return to nature, was a misanthrope; and Kant taught the absolute morality of the misanthrope. Gulliver, in his letter to Sympson, doubtlessly speaks in the tones of a misanthrope. He has renounced all hopes of human reform, because he gave his countrymen six months since the publication of his book, which is surely more than sufficient, to improve—and they have not improved a bit.

But we also know that Gulliver is a liar and admires successful liars like Sinon. A liar can hardly be a misanthrope; he cares enough about his fellow men to respect their prejudices; noble lies are acts of generosity. They are based on the truth of becoming and the existence of opinion; they prove an understanding of this world, an understanding not possessed by Houyhnhnms. Finally, and above all, misanthropes are not funny; this world and morality are too serious for that. I do not know about Gulliver, but Swift is surely one of the funniest men who ever lived. His misanthropy is a joke; it is the greatest folly in the world to attempt to improve humanity. That is what it means to understand man. And, after all, perhaps we are not serious beings. In the jest, there is a truth; we glimpse the necessity of the distinction between what we are and what we ought to be. But this leaves us with a final impression of fond sympathy for poor mortals. To understand is to accept; Gulliver's Travels makes misanthropy ridiculous by showing us the complexity of our nature and thereby teaching us what we must accept.

[28]Ibid., p. 279. These issues are called "difference in opinions." Cf. the Houyhnhnms' view of opinion, p. 304.

Political Philosophy and Poetry

I

THE CIVILIZING and unifying function of the people's books, which was carried out in Greece by Homer, Italy by Dante, France by Racine and Molière, and Germany by Goethe, seems to be dying a rapid death. A Marlborough could once say that he had formed his understanding of English history from Shakespeare alone; such a reliance on a poet today is almost inconceivable. The constant return to and reliance on a single great book or author has disappeared, and the result is not only a vulgarization of the tone of life but an atomization of society, for a civilized people is held together by its common understanding of what is virtuous and vicious, noble and base.

Shakespeare could still be the source of such an education and provide the necessary lessons concerning human virtue and the proper aspirations of a noble life. He is respected in our tradition, and he is of our language. But the mere possession of his works is not enough; they must be properly read and interpreted. One could never reestablish the Mosaic religion on the basis of a Bible read by the Higher Critics, nor could one use Shakespeare as a text in moral and political education on the basis of his plays as they are read by the New Critics.

There has been a change in the understanding of the nature of poetry since the rise of the Romantic movement, and it is now considered a defiling of art's sacred temple to see the poem as a mirror of nature or to interpret it as actually *teaching* something. Poets are believed not to have had intentions, and their epics and dramas are said to be *sui generis*, not to be judged by the standards of civil society or of religion. To the extent that Shakespeare's plays are understood to be merely literary productions, they have no relevance to the important problems that agitate the lives of acting men.

55

But when Shakespeare is read naïvely, because he shows most vividly and comprehensively the fate of tyrants, the character of good rulers, the relations of friends, and the duties of citizens, he can move the souls of his readers, and they recognize that they understand life better because they have read him; he hence becomes a constant guide and companion. He is turned to as the Bible was once turned to; one sees the world, enriched and embellished, through his eyes. It is this perspective that has been lost; and only when Shakespeare is taught as though he *said* something can he regain the influence over this generation which is so needed—needed for the sake of giving us some thoughtful views on the most important questions. The proper functions of criticism are, therefore, to recover Shakespeare's teaching and to be the agent of his ever-continuing education of the Anglo-Saxon world.

The poetic, according to the modern argument, transcends the base public concerns of politics; the artist is closer to the antipolitical bohemian than to the political gentleman. As soon as one speaks of a political interpretation of poetry, one is suspected either of wanting to use poetry as an ideological weapon or of trying to import foreign doctrines—such as those of Marx or Freud—and making Shakespeare their unconscious precursor, all the while forgetting the plays themselves.

It is certainly true that the political teachings which underlie the modern state are prosaic—intentionally so. And, if the bourgeois, the man "motivated by fear of violent death," is the product of political life, the poetic must seek another field for its activity, since such a man, characterized only by the self-regarding passions, is not a proper subject of poetry. But political life was not always conceived in this way; it was classically thought to be the stage on which the broadest, deepest, and noblest passions and virtues could be played, and the political man seemed to be the most interesting theme of poetry. It is at least plausible that, by taking our present notions of politics as eternal, we misinterpret the poetry of the past. In that case, we would be guilty of a grave historical error, an error which could be corrected by an open-minded study of the plays themselves.

Shakespeare devotes great care to establishing the political setting in almost all his plays, and his greatest heroes are rulers who exercise capacities which can only be exercised within civil society. To neglect this is simply to be blinded by the brilliance of one's own prejudices. As soon as one sees this, one cannot help asking what Shakespeare thought about a good regime and a good ruler. I contend that the man of political passions and education is in a better position to understand the plays than a purely private man. With the recognition of this fact, a new perspective is opened, not only on the plays but also on our notions of politics.

If politics is considered antithetical to poetry, philosophy is thought to be even more so, for poetry deals, it is said, with passions and sentiments, whereas philosophy bases itself on reason. The poet is the inspired creator, whereas the philosopher understands only what is. To this, again, it can only be responded that much of modern philosophy certainly seems to take no account of poetry, but it is not so clear that this is necessarily the case or that a poet cannot also be a thinker.

There is some question whether it would be possible for a man who had not thought a great deal about human nature to write a convincing drama. It is only an assumption that Shakespeare did not have a consistent and rational understanding of man which he illustrated in his plays; only a final and complete interpretation of them all could demonstrate that this is so. On the face of it, the man who could write *Macbeth* so convincingly that a Lincoln believed it to be the perfect illustration of the problems of tyranny and murder must have known about politics; otherwise, however charming its language, the play would not have attracted a man who admittedly did know. The contemporary antagonism between philosophy and poetry is a child of our age; it might serve most profitably to remind us of another kind of philosophy, one which could talk sensibly about human things, and of another kind of poetry, one which could unite the charm of the passions with the rigor of the intellect.

II

Shakespeare wrote at a time when common sense still taught that the function of the poet was to produce pleasure and that the function of the great poet was to teach what is truly beautiful by means of pleasure. Common sense was supported by a long tradition which had a new burst of vitality in the Renaissance. Socrates had said that Homer was the teacher of the Greeks, and he meant by that that those who ruled Greece had their notions of what kind of men they would like to be set for them by the Homeric epics. Achilles was the authentic hero, and his glory was that against which all later heroes up to Alexander competed. A man who knew Homer was a Greek. If we follow Herodotus, Homer, along with Hesiod, also invented the gods in the forms in which they were worshiped by later generations.

He was the true founder of his people, for he gave them what made them distinctive, invented that soul for which they are remembered. Such are the ambitions of the great poet. Goethe understood this:

> A great dramatic poet, if he is at the same time productive and is actuated by a strong noble purpose which pervades all his works, may succeed in making the soul of his plays become the soul of the people. I should think that this was well worth the trouble. From Corneille proceeded an influence capable of forming heroes. This was something for Napoleon, who had need of a heroic people, on which account he said of Corneille that, if he were still living, he would make a prince of him. A dramatic poet who knows his vocation should therefore work incessantly at its higher development in order that his influence on the people may be noble and beneficial.[1]

As Napoleon knew, it is *only* a poet who can give a people such inspiration.

Poetry is the most powerful form of rhetoric, a form which goes beyond ordinary rhetoric in that it shapes the men on whom the statesman's rhetoric can work. The philosopher cannot move nations; he speaks only to a few. The poet can take the philosopher's understanding and translate it into images which touch the deepest passions and cause men to know without knowing that they know. Aristotle's description of heroic virtue means nothing to men in general, but Homer's incarnation of that virtue in the Greeks and Trojans is unforgettable. This desire to depict the truth about man and to make other men fulfill that truth is what raises poetry to its greatest heights in the epic and the drama. Poetry takes on its significance, in both its content and its uses, from the political nobility of the poet. Poetry is not autonomous; its life is infused by its attachment to the same objects which motivate the best of acting men.

The poet's task is a double one—to understand the things he wishes to represent and to understand the audience to which he speaks. He must know about the truly permanent human problems; otherwise his works will be slight and passing. There must be parallelism between what he speaks of and the most vital concerns of his audience; without that, his works will be mere tributes to the virtuosity of his techniques. In the great work, one is unaware of the technique and even of the artist; one is only conscious that the means are perfectly appropriate to the ends. The beauty of the words is but a reflection of the beauty

[1]Johann Peter Eckermann, *Conversations with Goethe*, April 1, 1827.

of the thing; the poet is immersed in the thing, which is the only source of true beauty. And he must know what to touch in his audience. A photograph of a man does not usually convey his character; that is grasped in certain traits which may rarely be seen. The painter can abstract all that is not essential to that impression, and he knows how the eye of the viewer will see the man. Certain illusions are often necessary to see the man as he really is; the sense of reality is transmitted in a medium of unreality. So the poet, too, must know how to play on his audience, how to transform its vision while taking it for what it is. That audience is a complex animal made up of many levels. To each he must speak, appealing to the simple souls as well as to the subtle. Thus his poem is complex and has many levels, just as does the audience; it is designed first for the conventional order composed of aristocracy and commoners, but more profoundly for the natural order composed of those who understand and those who do not. The poet knows the characters of men from both looking at them and speaking to them. That is why the intelligent man takes him seriously; he has a kind of experience with men that the practitioner of no other art or science possesses.

The poet is an imitator of nature; he reproduces what he sees in the world, and it is only his preoccupation with that world which renders him a poet. He is not creator, for that would mean that he makes something from nothing; were he to look only within himself, he would find a void—a void destined by nature itself to be filled with knowledge of the essential articulations of things. What distinguishes a good poet from a bad one is whether he has seen things as they are and learned to distinguish the superficial from the profound. In particular, poetry imitates man, and this means—according to the classical tradition which I am elaborating—his virtues and his vices. A man is most what he is as a result of what he does; a man is known, not simply by his existence, but by the character of his actions— liberal or greedy, courageous or cowardly, frank or sly, moderate or profligate. Since these qualities produce happiness or misery, they are of enduring interest to human beings. Hence they are the specific subject matter of poetry. Passions, feelings, and the whole realm of the psychological are secondary. This is because feelings are properly related to certain kinds of action and to the virtues which control such action; they are formless when considered by themselves. Jealousy and ambition have to do with love and politics and gain their particular qualities from the particular objects to which they are directed and the particular men who feel them; therefore, the primary concern of the poet is with the various kinds of human action. The plot, the story of a series of actions which leads to prosperity or misfortune, is the soul of the play and that which guides all else, including the portrayal of psychological affections.

Human virtues and vices can be said to be defined primarily in political terms. Civil society and its laws define what is good and bad, and its education forms the citizens. The character of life is decisively influenced by the character of the regime under which a man lives, and it is the regime that encourages or discourages the growth within it of the various human types. Any change in a way of life presupposes a change in the political, and it is by means of the political that the change must be effected. It is in their living together that men develop their human potential, and it is the political regime which determines the goals and the arrangement of the life in common. Moreover, it is in ruling and being ruled, in the decisions concerning war and peace, that men exercise their highest capacities. There may be situations in which men have no chance to be rulers, but, to the degree to which they are excluded from political life, they are less fully developed and satisfied. In political life, not only are the ordinary virtues projected on a larger screen, but totally new capacities are brought into play. The political provides the framework within which all that is human can develop itself; it attracts the most interesting passions and the most interesting men. Hence, the dramatist who wishes to represent man most perfectly will usually choose political heroes. Because of his artistic freedom, he can paint his figures more characteristically, less encumbered by fortuitous traits, than can a historian.

What is essentially human is revealed in the extreme, and we understand ourselves better through what we might be. In a way, the spectators live more truly when they are watching a Shakespearean play than in their daily lives, which are so much determined by the accidents of time and place. There could be a theater dealing totally with the private life, the cares of providing for a living and raising a family. But men who never got beyond that life would be cut off from their fullest human development, and a theater which acquiesced in that view of human life would be only a tool in increasing the enslavement to it.

This is a popular account of the traditional view of the drama, that which was current in Shakespeare's time; it is more likely that he shared it than that he held anything like the modern view. It is not necessary to argue that he himself had reflected on it; it was in the air, and he would come naturally to think about things in these terms. But, in fact, it seems clear on the basis of the evidence provided by the history plays that Shakespeare did, indeed, elaborate his intentions and consciously wanted his works to convey his political wisdom. In these plays, he tried to develop a sensible view of what the English regime is and how it should be accepted and revered by succeeding generations of Englishmen. He was successful in this attempt, for the English do understand their history and what it represents much as he depicted it. Here his intention was clearly political, and his understanding of what is both beautiful and exciting to his audience is based primarily on the concerns of civil society. Is it plausible to say that this was just a series of good stories? They are, indeed, good stories, but they are that precisely because of the kind of interest they evoke. Can one reasonably say that he dashed off the historical plays because he needed money or that he was ignorant of the essential facts of English history because he had never studied? This would be as much as to say that Jefferson, with no consideration of political principle, wrote the Declaration of Independence because he wanted to be well-known and that its success is due to its being an excellent Fourth of July oration.

What is so manifestly true of the histories could well be true of the tragedies and comedies, too. Shakespeare's humanity was not limited to England or to making Englishmen good citizens of England. There is a whole series of fundamental human problems, and I suggest that Shakespeare intended to depict all of them and that the man who, *per impossibile,* could understand all the plays individually would see the consequences of all the possible important choices of ways of life and understand fully the qualities of the various kinds of good soul. But that takes me beyond the scope of this introduction; I allude to it only to indicate the range of Shakespeare's genius. For the moment, it is sufficient to suggest the possibility that, for the other plays, just as for the histories, Shakespeare may have seen politics as, at the least, very important, that he had a pedagogic intention, and that his learning was sufficient to make him aware of the fundamental alternatives, theoretical and practical.

If this is so, political philosophy would be essential to our interpretation of his works. However wrong Shakespeare may have been about the real nature of poetry as discovered by modern criticism, in understanding him we would have to use his framework instead of trying to squeeze him into our new categories. Every rule of objectivity requires that an author first be understood as he understood himself; without that, the work is nothing but what we make of it. The role of political philosophy in Shakespearean criticism would be to give a discursive account of the goals of the passions depicted in the plays.

When Sextus Pompeius is given the choice of murdering his guests and becoming emperor of the universe or remaining within the pale of decency and being done away with himself, we are confronted with a classic problem of political morality, one that is presented with detail and precision in *Antony and Cleopatra*. We must recognize it as such, and we must further have some knowledge of the kinds of men who desire to rule and of what this desire does to them. It is only in philosophic discussion that we find a development of these problems, and from that we can help to clarify the problems of which Shakespeare gives us models. In our day, we are particularly in need of the history of political philosophy, for we are not immediately aware of the various possible understandings of the political and moral phenomena and must seek those which most adequately explain what Shakespeare presents to us.

Shakespeare has set his plays in many nations and at various times in history. This is a good beginning for the investigation of his teaching, for various nations encourage various virtues in men; one cannot find every kind of man in any particular time and place. Just the difference between paganism and Christianity has an important effect on the kinds of preoccupations men have. To present the various possibilities, the typical men have to be in an environment in which they can flourish. The dates and places of Shakespeare's plays were chosen with a view to revealing the specific interests of the heroes. It was only in Venice that Othello and Shylock could act out their potentials; they were foreigners, and only Venice provided them freedom and a place in the city. Only in Rome could one see the course of political ambition free of other goals which mitigate it. It would be a worthwhile project to spend a lifetime studying the settings of the plays in relation to the plots, trying to see what are the typical problems of what time and what nation. All this would be with a view to distinguishing what Shakespeare thought the best kinds of men and what advantages and disadvantages go with what ways of life. We are in need of generations of criticism—naïve criticism which asks the kinds of question of Shakespeare that Glaucon and Adeimantus once posed to Socrates. How should we live? Is it best to be a ruler or a poet? Can one kill a king? Should one's parents be disobeyed for the sake of love? And so on endlessly.

Schiller pointed out that modern times are characterized by abstract science on the one hand and unrefined passions on the other and that the two have no relation. A free man and a good citizen must have a natural harmony between his passions and his knowledge; this is what is meant by a man of taste, and it is he whom we today seem unable to form. We are aware that a political science which does not grasp the moral phenomena is crude and that an art uninspired by the passion for justice is trivial. Shakespeare wrote before the separation of these things; we sense that he has both intellectual clarity and vigorous passions and that the two do not undermine each other in him. If we live with him awhile, perhaps we can recapture the fullness of life and rediscover the way to its lost unity.

On Christian and Jew:
The Merchant of Venice

VENICE IS a beautiful city, full of color and variety. To this day it represents the exotic and the exciting to the minds of those who know it—a port with all the freedom that the proximity to the sea seems to encourage and with the presence of diverse kinds of men from diverse nations, races, and religions brought by the hope of adventure or gain to its shores. The prosperous merchants of Venice lavishly adorned it in a romantic taste, combining the styles of East and West, between which it was the link. Add to this the sun of Italy and the attractiveness of its people and you have that city which remains the setting of dreams of pleasure and happiness.

Shakespeare, in his two Venetian plays, *Othello* and *The Merchant of Venice*, admirably captures the atmosphere of Venice. It is not surprising that he chose this locale in which to present his most exotic heroes; Othello and Shylock are the figures who are the most foreign to the context in which they move and to the audience for which they were intended. In a sense, it is Shakespeare's achievement in the two plays to have made these two men—who would normally have been mere objects of hatred and contempt—into human beings who are unforgettable for their strength of soul. For the first time in European literature, there was a powerful characterization of men so different; Shakespeare, while proving his own breadth of sympathy, made an impression on his audiences which could not be eradicated. Whether they liked these men or not, the spectators now knew they

This essay is based on a lecture given at the Hillel Foundation of the University of Chicago in January 1960. I wish to dedicate it to the memory of Rabbi Maurice B. Pekarsky, the director of that organization for seventeen years. He was a wise and good man who inspired men of many faiths with respect for Judaism; he appealed on the highest grounds to both heart and mind.

were men and not things on which they could with impunity exercise their vilest passions. Venice offered the perfect setting for the actions of Shylock and Othello because it was the place where the various sorts of men could freely mingle, and it was known the world over as the most tolerant city of its time. In this city, those men who, it was generally thought, could never share a common way of life seemed to live together in harmony.

Shakespeare, however, does not depict Venice with the bright colors which one would expect, given its beauty and its promise. When one thinks of Othello or Shylock, one can only remember their somber fates. In both cases, I believe, their unhappy destinies were in some measure a result of their foreignness, or, in other words, Venice did not fulfill for them its promise of being a society in which men could live as men, not as whites and blacks, Christians and Jews, Venetians and foreigners. To understand why Shakespeare has thus presented Venice, we must for a moment consider what it meant to enlightened men in the sixteenth and seventeenth centuries.

I

Venice was a republic—one of the few successful examples of such a political organization in its time. It had for several hundred years guarded its independence. It had an orderly form of government in which a large proportion of the citizens could take an active part. It was prosperous and had even become powerful enough, in spite of its size, to cherish some imperial ambitions. During the Renaissance, there was a revival of the republican spirit among thoughtful men; it was thought that the proper practice of political life had deteriorated since the fall of the Roman Republic. For whatever reasons, the political—the condition of human dignity—had become indifferent to men, and they lived under monarchs. The independence and pride that are a result of self-government had vanished; the political virtues praised by the ancients had no opportunity for exercise and withered away. One can find this point of view developed most completely in Machiavelli, but it was shared by many eminent thinkers. Nonetheless, public-spirited men also looked for examples of the possibility of republics in modern times, and Venice was the most fitting one. From the end of the sixteenth century to the middle of the seventeenth, Venice was constantly admired and written about as the model of a good political order in modernity. It preceded Amsterdam as the model and Harrington and Spinoza—to name only two of its most illustrious

advocates—drew liberally on it in the elaborations of their teachings.
It was, indeed, a modern state and hence different from Rome in many
crucial respects. It is in these respects that it was of most interest to
modern theorists, because it seemed to provide an answer to their
central problems.

Along with the taste for republicanism came a certain depreciation of the biblical religions, partly because their otherworldliness
seemed to be the source of the disinterest in the political and partly
because they were at the root of the religious fanaticism which issued
in such occurrences as the religious wars and the Inquisition. These
religious attachments, it was believed, led men away from their political interests and divided them on the basis of opinions. Modern
republicanism had to overcome the religious question, to attach men
to the here and now rather than to the hereafter. The state had to
become tolerant to be able to embrace in a stable order men of widely
differing beliefs. This was a problem not directly addressed by ancient
political thought, and its resolution is the most characteristic aspect
of later political thought. It was believed that only by directing men's
interest to something which could subordinate their religious attachments would it be possible to establish a way of life in which religious
doctrines and their intransigence would not play the leading part. It
was not thought possible to educate men to a tolerant view or to
overcome the power of the established religions by refuting them; the
only way was to substitute for the interest and concern of men's
passions another object as powerfully attractive as religion.

Such an object was to be found in the jealous desire for gain.
The commercial spirit causes men to moderate their fanaticism; men
for whom money is the most important thing are unlikely to go off
on Crusades. Venice was above all a commercial city and had indeed
succeeded in bringing together in one place more types of men than
any other city.[1] The condition of Shylock's living in Venice was its
need of venture capital for its enterprises. The laws which would not
be respected for themselves were obeyed because they were the foundation of the city's prosperity. As the Merchant himself says:

> The Duke cannot deny the course of law:
> For the commoditie that strangers have

[1]For a typical and influential pre-Shakespearean evaluation of Venice, cf. Jean Bodin,
Les Six livres de la République (Paris: 1577), pp. 726, 790. For the general understanding
of Venice at the period, cf. Cardinal Gaspar Contareno, The Commonwealth and
Government of Venice (London: 1599). Although the translation did not appear until
five years after the production of The Merchant of Venice, the book appeared in Italian
in 1543, had been translated into French much before 1594, and was well-known.

> With us in Venice, if it be denied,
> Will much impeach the justice of the state
> Since that the trade and profit of the city
> Consisteth of all nations.[2]

The Jews in Venice were well off and enjoyed the full protection of the law in the fifteenth and sixteenth centuries; the Venice Jewish community was relatively privileged among the Jewish communities in the Diaspora. Shylock's claim against Antonio rests entirely on that law, and he is perfectly aware of its commercial roots. Venice was a model city for the new political thought; it was tolerant, bourgeois, and republican. This solution to the political problem is the one which became dominant in the West and is only too familiar to us.

It behooves us, therefore, to examine Shakespeare's view of that city which contained the germ of what is today generally accepted. He did in that city, as I have said, present his view of the relations among men who are foreign to one another. This is the link between the two Venetian plays. He understood the hopes based on the Venetian experiment, and, as the fates of his heroes show, he was pessimistic about the possibilities of its success. This is not to say that he did not approve of what Venice stood for; but he tried to understand the human consequences of the legal arrangements, and he found that friendship between such unlike personages is very difficult, if not impossible. Laws are not sufficient; they must be accompanied by good dispositions on the part of those who live under them. Shakespeare presents the depths of souls as no man has ever done, and through his divine insight we can catch sight of the difficulties which stand in the way of human brotherhood—difficulties which are real and cannot be done away with by pious moralizing.

II

Shylock and Antonio are Jew and Christian, and they are at war as a result of their difference in faith. It is not that they misunderstand each other because of a long history of prejudice and that enlightenment could correct their hostility; rather, their real views of the world, their understanding of what is most important in life, are so opposed that they could never agree. When confronted with each

[2]III, iii, 31–36; cp. IV, i, 39–43. All citations are to the Furness Variorum edition (Philadelphia: J. B. Lippincott Co., 1888).

other in the same place in relation to the same people, they must necessarily quarrel. Their difference as to whom and on what terms one should lend money is the most external sign of this root-and-branch opposition. To do away with their hostility, the beliefs of each would have to be done away with—those beliefs which go from the very depths to the heights of their souls. In other words, their being would have to be changed, for men are constituted most essentially by their understanding of the most important things. The law of Venice can force them to a temporary truce, but in any crucial instance the conflict will reemerge, and each will try to destroy the spirit of the law; for each has a different way of life which, if it were universalized within the city, would destroy that of the other. They have no common ground.

Antonio and Shylock are, however, not merely individuals who differ; Shakespeare, rightly or wrongly, has presented them as types, representatives of Judaism and Christianity. Each acts according to the principles of his faith. They do not differ because they are men who have idiosyncrasies, but because their principles are opposed; those principles are not their own, but are derived from their respective religions. Of course, we do not see them in the purity of their worship; they act in the corrupt world of private and political life. But we do see the extension of their principles in that world. Antonio and Shylock are each depicted as models of their heritage; each is even a parody of a remarkable biblical figure, not as those figures were but as they might be in the context of Venice. Shakespeare views them from outside without considering the truth of either.[3]

Shylock holds that respect for and obedience to the *law* is the

[3]Shakespeare, unlike the earlier dramatists who presented Jews, seems to have gone to the Bible to find his characterizations rather than use a traditional image. His Jew is Jewish in his profession of faith; his principles are recognizable. It is similar with the Christian. Shakespeare seems to have taken a certain side of the Old Testament and added to it the criticism of the Jews made in the Pauline Epistles. One might look especially to Romans 9–11; the opposition between Shylock and Antonio might well be characterized as that between "a vessel of anger and a vessel of mercy." Or, more generally stated, the issue is precisely the quarrel between the Old Law and the New Law, each presenting its own evaluation of what is the most important element in piety and the morality consequent on piety. The two laws are related, but inimical. Shakespeare is, I believe, far more interested in Antonio's principles than in Shylock's. The Jews were not a problem in England; there were none, or practically none, and his audience was Christian. But Antonio's origins are somehow in Shylock's law, and he can only be seen in terms of those origins and his opposition to them. This is parallel to the New Testament's treatment of Jesus. The confrontation of the two is a reenactment of the original confrontation, but altered and embittered by the unhappy history of fifteen hundred years. Cf. the dialogues between Antonio and Shylock (I, iii, 40–187; III, iii, 3–28; IV, i, 39–124).

condition for leading a decent life. Throughout the play, law is his only appeal and his only claim. Righteousness is hence the criterion for goodness; if a man obeys the law to its letter throughout his life, he will prosper and do what is human. No other consideration need trouble him. Justice is lawfulness; Shylock is a son of Moses. Along with this goes a certain positive temper; Shylock lives very much in this world. Money is a solid bastion of comfortable existence, not for the sake of pleasure or refinement, but for that of family and home. The beggar is contemptible and was probably not righteous. This earth is where man lives, and justice and injustice reap the fruits of reward and punishment on it. Decent sobriety is the rule of life, each man living for himself according to the rule. A certain toughness and lack of far-ranging sympathies characterize him.[4]

Moreover, shrewdness concerning the things about which the law does not speak is perfectly legitimate and even desirable. To live well on this earth, one must have some amount of substance, without which life is miserable; given the nature of men, one is likely to lose what properly belongs to one, if one is not careful. Shylock's model is Jacob, who had to deceive his father to attain his succession and who used tricks to get a fair wage from Laban.[5] So he is a moneylender; he does not cheat men—he only takes advantage of their need. If a man wants money for his business or his pleasures, he can make use of what Shylock possesses. Shylock does not care for the man or his interests, but through them he can profit himself. What he does is neither noble nor generous, but it is not unjust. Why should he concern himself with Bassanio's prodigality or his hopes to make a good match for himself? Would it not be folly to waste one's sympathy and one's substance on the vices of others? Shylock lives privately in his "sober home" with his daughter, and this way of life is protected by his shrewdness and the money which he earned with it.

Antonio, on the contrary, bases his whole life on generosity and love for his fellow man. For him, the law, in its intransigence and its indifference to persons, is an inadequate guide for life. Not that one should ignore the law, but it is only a minimum condition. Equity and charity are more important virtues than righteousness. Antonio has money; it is, however, not for his own enjoyment, but rather for his friends. He lends his money but not for profit. Life on this earth is but a frail thing and only gains whatever allure it has in seeing others made happy. Antonio is sad, and life does not mean much to

---

[4]IV, i, 150, 94–108; II, v, 30–40.
[5]I, iii, 74–100.

him. Life is but a stage, and our actions take on meaning only in a
larger context. Antonio is perfectly willing to die for his friend to
prove how much he loves him. Calm calculation is beyond him. He
makes promises he cannot keep, and his hopes are based on ships that
are yet to come in. The restraint and the coldness of the Jew are not
his; his sympathies go out to all men, and he cares much for their
affection. He is full of sentimentality. He has no family, and we hear
nothing of his home; he is a bachelor.[6]

Antonio and Shylock are not made to understand each other.
When Shylock sees Antonio approaching, he says, "How like a fawn-
ing publican he looks," echoing the sentiments of the Pharisee in the
Gospel who prides himself on his own righteousness and despises the
publican's abasement before the Lord.[7] Antonio in his turn has, in
imitation of Jesus, driven the moneylenders from the Rialto. He has
spit on Shylock, for his sympathy cannot extend to a man who denies
the fundamental principle of charity.[8] That is the limit case. Neither
can regard the other as a human being in any significant sense because
in all that is human they differ. It is very well to tell them to live
together, but in any confrontation of the two they are bound to quarrel.
What is prudence for one is robbery for the other; what is kindness
for one is mawkish sentimentality to the other. There is no middle
ground, since they see the same objects as different things; common
sense cannot mediate between them. If there is to be harmony, one
must give in to the other; pride, at least, if not conviction, precludes
this. But the two men need each other; they are linked by money.
Antonio must borrow from Shylock. They have a contract, but one
that is not bound by good faith.

In this not-very-funny comedy, the most amusing figure is the
clown, Launcelot Gobbo. He is so amusing largely because he represents the ridiculousness of the man who tries to live in the worlds
of Antonio and Shylock at the same time; everything is so different
that he is like someone who wants to stand on his head and his feet
at the same time. He works for the Jew, but his conscience tells him
that the Jew is the Devil; so he wants to leave the Jew, but his
conscience tells him that he must do his duty. His conscience, that
great instrument of moral guidance, tells him that he must go and
stay at the same time. Launcelot is utterly confused. Ultimately, he

[6]I, i, 5–11, 98–109, 164–70; iii, 133–40; II, viii, 38–52; III, ii, 309–14; IV, i, 75–
88, 120–124.
[7]Mark 18:10–14. Shylock's righteousness in general parallels that of the Pharisee.
[8]I, iii, 110–40.

follows the only thing he knows surely, his stomach. Shylock's parsimony has left him hungry; also, Bassanio gives pretty uniforms, a thing unthinkable in the home of the austere Jew. There seem to be no rules of moral conduct which can govern the relationship between men so diverse. Launcelot draws out the paradox of the situation when he discusses Jessica's conversion with her. She can, he says, only be saved if her father were not her father; but, if her sin of being the Jew's daughter is removed, she will inherit the sin of her mother's adultery. She is damned if she does and damned if she doesn't. Besides, Launcelot, on his gastroeconomic grounds, is against conversion because it will make the price of pork go up.[9]

Shylock states his principle for relating to the Christian community in which he lives as follows: "I will buy with you, sell with you, talke with you, walke with you, and so following: but I will not eate with you, drinke with you, nor pray with you."[10] What is most important to him he cannot share with his neighbors. When men do not agree about what is most important, they can hardly be said to constitute a community. *Othello* is about a man who tried to assimilate and failed. In *The Merchant of Venice*, we see the soul of a man who refused to assimilate. He is consequently distrusted and hated. He reciprocates, and his soul is poisoned.

III

Shylock makes one compromise with his principle. He goes to dinner at Bassanio's. Punishment is swift and harsh. During the dinner, he loses his daughter plus a considerable sum of money. Everything that he has held most dear is gone; he becomes a monster intent only on revenge. It is no longer principle which guides him, for he has compromised his principle by disobeying the law. He can only think that Antonio arranged the dreadful deed, although Antonio apparently knew nothing of it.[11] Shylock recognizes that no one cares for

---

[9]II, ii, 2–29; III, v, 1–25. Launcelot carries his confusion further in his relations with his father, whom he respects and despises, thus mixing the responses of Portia and Jessica. His father, in this play which has so much to do with fathers, is blind. Launcelot, moreover, also parodies the loves between foreigners in this complicated world (III, v, 36–41).

[10]I, iii, 33–39. Shylock's faith cuts him off from others; moreover, it gives him a different notion of the things that really count.

[11]What causes Shylock to change his mind and go to eat with the Christians is unclear and can only be a subject of conjecture (II, v, 14–21). There is no indication that

him, that his sorrows are the joys of others. No humiliation could be more complete; as a man with dignity, he can only make others suffer for what he suffers. Others have counted him out of the pale of humanity, and he will show them that they were right in doing so. Formerly, he was bitter, but he had his little life in which he could practice his faith and enjoy his home. Now this is all gone. He has a certain grandeur in the depth of his rage, but he has become terrible. The strong impression he makes is based only on that which is negative in him. How could he forgive when he would only be despised for his forgiveness? If he cannot be loved, he can at least gain the respect of fear. But now his life is carried on only in response to the Christians whom he hates; it has no solid content of its own. In this portrayal, Shakespeare to some extent gives justification to the Christian reproach that the Jews had lost the one most important thing and carried on only the empty forms of their law.

Shylock is not a comic figure. There is no scene in the play in which he is meant to be laughed at in person. He does appear comic in the eyes of some of the Christian actors, but this only proves that Shakespeare did not agree with them and is as much a commentary on them as on Shylock. He is most comic to Salerio and Solanio, who burlesque his screaming after his ducats, his daughter and his ducats.[12] Shylock is reproached, as were the Jews in general, for materialism, a materialism which made it impossible to make proper distinctions between things. This is borne out by Shylock's conduct, but in no ignoble way. For him, as we have said, life is an earthly thing, and his money is connected intrinsically with his existence. His affection for his daughter is based on the fact that she is his flesh and blood.[13] The so-called spiritual ties do not exist for him; everything he has belongs to him in the same intimate way that his body belongs to him. There is no distinction between spirit and matter; the relation of souls alone without the other bonds is impossible; therefore, a universal humanity is excluded. Kinship is the source of love; hence, his real loves are his family and his "sacred nation."

When Shylock talks to Tubal about his daughter and his money,

---

Antonio knew of the abduction (II, vi, 69–75). But Shylock takes it as a conspiracy known to and supported by the whole Christian world (III, i, 22–23).
[12]II, viii. This scene not only describes a comic Shylock, but also gives a description of the parting of Bassanio and Antonio. This, too, in its way, has elements of the comic, although they are not intended by the speakers. It also reveals the pretense in Antonio's selflessness; Bassanio is reminded of the risks his friend is taking for him when Antonio tells him to forget them. The scene cuts in both directions.
[13]III, i, 32–34.

he does indeed express the sentiments attributed to him by his ridiculers, but they appear very differently to us.[14] He would like to see his daughter dead with the jewels in her ear. We are shocked by the distortion of the sentiment, but we also see that his daughter is more a part of him than his money, that this is an expression of the depth of his loss. Jessica does not belong to him anymore; all he can count on now is his money. She has broken the law and defied him. She is no more, and he must forget her, for she existed as a human for him only as long as she was faithful. It is a hard code, but the passion and discipline that are required to obey it are a measure of what it means to Shylock. As Jessica was hated with intensity when she left the fold, so she would have been loved if she had remained within it. Shylock's daughter is dead to him, but part of him has also died. The feeling of which Shylock is capable is seen in the admirable response he makes when he hears that Jessica has bartered for a monkey the turquoise he gave his wife. "I would not have given it for a wilderness of monkies."[15] This is the expression of a man practiced to a parsimony of sentiment, but whose sentiments for that reason are deep and unutterable. It differs from the effusiveness of Antonio's expressions of love, but is it not equal?

The most quoted speech in *The Merchant of Venice* is the one which best of all shows the plight of Shylock:

> I am a Jew: Hath not a Jew eyes? hath not a Jew hands, organs, dementions, sences, affections, passions, fed with the same foode, hurt with the same weapons, subject to the same diseases, healed by the same meanes, warmed and cooled by the same Winter and Sommer as a Christian is: if you pricke us doe we not bleede? If you tickle us, doe we not laugh? if you poison us doe we not die? and if you wrong us shall we not revenge? if we are like you in the rest, we will resemble you in that.[16]

Shylock justifies himself by an appeal to the universality of humanity. Behind this harsh but touching complaint is a plea for the exercise of the Golden Rule. Men can only be men together when they mutually recognize their sameness; otherwise they are like beings of different species to one another, and their only similarity is in their revenge. But, sadly, if one looks at the list of similar characteristics on which Shylock bases his claim to equality with his Christian tor-

[14]III, i, 75–123.
[15]III, i, 115–16.
[16]III, i, 47–66.

mentors, one sees that it includes only things which belong to the body; what he finds in common between Christian and Jew is essentially what all animals have in common. The only spiritual element in the list is revenge.[17] Like Antiphon the Sophist, Shylock asserts that the brotherhood of man can only come into being on the basis of the lowest common denominator, and that common denominator is very low indeed. It is the body; all the higher parts of the soul must be abstracted from, because they express men's opinions and beliefs about what is good and bad, virtue and vice. These, men do not share; these beliefs make men enemies. Shylock appeals to a humanity which all men can recognize, but in so doing he must discount what all noble men would regard as the most important.

Shylock stands for Judaism, and his life has gained its sense from that fact, not from the fact that he eats, drinks, and feels; Christianity has played a similar role in the lives of his opponents. They would have to transform their beings in order to become unified. The choice seems to be a hostile diversity on a high level or a common humanity on the level of the beasts—a common humanity grounded on an indifference to the opinion about the nature of the good. The four Jewish names in *The Merchant of Venice* seem to be drawn from two successive chapters, 10 and 11, of Genesis. Chapter 11 has as its theme the Tower of Babel; perhaps this is part of Shakespeare's meaning. "Let us go down and there confound their language, that they may not understand one another's speech." Men's separateness is an act of divine providence.[18]

---

[17]Shylock characteristically mentions laughter as a result of tickling. He and Antonio would not laugh at the same jokes.

[18]Tubal, 10:2; Chus, 6; Jessica (Jesca), 11:29. The last two names are spelled otherwise in the King James version, but appear as they are here in the translations which follow the Greek of the Septuagint, and they were so spelled in translations at Shakespeare's time (cp. Note 30). "Shylock" poses a greater problem, and its origin can only be conjectured. But in the same passage is a name which comes closer to it than any other and is repeated six times (10:24; 11:12–15); it occurs both before and after the account of the Tower of Babel. This name appears as "Salah" in the King James, but is spelled "Shelah" (the last syllable is pronounced *ach*) in Hebrew, and so it appears in the English version of 1582. This is very close indeed and the Hebrew spelling of this name is almost the same as that of the only other biblical name which has been suggested as a possible source: "Shiloh" (Genesis 19:10). Given that "Shelah" occurs in the same passage with the other names, it seems probable that he is Shylock's ancestor.

IV

Whether or not Shylock originally intended to exact the pound of flesh if possible, after the loss of Jessica his whole hope was to be able to gain revenge within the limits of the law. The drama of Shylock and Antonio would have come to a disastrous end if it had not been for Portia. The contrast between Portia and the other two major figures is sharp, and the difference in atmosphere between Belmont and Venice is striking. Portia brings with her a love of gaiety, satisfaction, subtlety, and, above all, common sense that is entirely lacking in Venice. While scenes of hate are being unfolded in Venice, at Belmont Portia presides over a feast of love—love, not in the sense of Antonio's spiritual love for Bassanio, but of the erotic love between man and woman. Portia is the master of this world of Belmont, and her own satisfaction is the highest law of the land. She has no doctrines, and she is willing to appear to be anything to achieve her ends. She rules, and rules for her own good, while always keeping up the appearances of propriety and justice. Belmont is beautiful, and there we enter the realm of the senses. It is pagan; everyone there speaks in the terms of classical antiquity. Religion is only used there, and it even has a temple for the Moor. The themes of conversation and the ideas current in Belmont have an ancient source. Portia has the tastes of a Roman and is compared to one whose name she shares.[19]

Belmont, too, is a cosmopolitan place, but the attraction there is not money but love. Men from all over the world come to woo the fair Portia, and she is able to see and evaluate what the wide world has to offer. She is no cloistered little girl. She presents a typology of national characteristics in going over the list of her suitors—the horse-loving Neapolitan, the severe Pole, the drinking German, and so forth. She judges them each in relation to the commodity of a pleasant shared existence. Her candor when she is alone with her servant is shocking to some and exasperating to others, but it can also appear to be the clear vision of one who is liberated and has spurned the unhappy depths of tragedy. Portia rejoices in the beauties of the surface, and certainly no one can assert that her hedonism leads to vulgarity. She chooses for her husband a fellow countryman after having seen all that is exotic and strange. She is the opposite of the shy, untutored Desdemona. She opts for the familiar, not only because

---

[19]I, i, 175–76. The temple is mentioned at II, i, 50; Portia's use of religion is indicated in III, iv, 29–35. Portia would seem to be representative of classical *eros*. All myths and examples cited in Belmont are drawn from classical antiquity.

it is the familiar, but also because it represents most adequately what is agreeable and appropriate to her; Bassanio is a sort of mean in relation to the other suitors, just as is his nation speaking geographically.

The test of the three caskets shows the principles implied in Portia's choice as well as it prefigures the technique she will use in the trial. Portia is apparently not the mistress of her fate; she is ruled by the will of her father, who has decreed that the man who is to win her must first pass a seemingly foolish test of character. Portia professes dissatisfaction with this arrangement, but, as a good daughter, she intends to abide by the restriction. She does not, like Desdemona or Jessica, defy conventions to gain the object of her wishes; she has a great respect for the forms, if not the substance, of the conventional. The test is, moreover, not entirely disagreeable, because its conditions drive off many an undesirable suitor who might otherwise be importunate. She uses her traditional duty to satisfy her desires, but, as becomes clear, does not become its victim.

The first suitor who risks the choice is a Moor, who begins his wooing with the request: "Mislike me not for my complexion." He is in certain respects like Othello, but rendered comic in the atmosphere created by Portia. He is a great warrior and a passionate lover, full of noble words. This hasty man of the South chooses the golden casket because of its appearance. He is a slave of his senses. Portia, who has treated him with elaborate politeness, dismisses him from her thoughts with, "Let all of his complexion choose me so." She is no Desdemona who "saw Othello's visage in his mind."[20] She makes no effort to transform her immediate sensual impressions. She knows the sort of man who would be to her taste.

As the Moor was immediate, sensual, and passionate, Aragon is the cool, reflected gentleman of the North. He is a pious moralizer, full of the most correct commonplaces. He chooses the moderate silver, and the basis of his judgment is the text. He chooses to have his just desert, but is angry when his deserving turns out to be less than what he conceives.[21] Aragon is a fool who thinks that the accents of virtue constitute its essence. Portia sees in him only a bore. The Moor chose by images; Aragon, by texts. Neither is right. Portia seeks a man who can combine feeling and thought in a natural grace of sentiment. The South is barbaric; the North, cold and sententious. True civilization implies a mixture of developed understanding and reflection with a

[20]*Othello*, I, iii, 280.
[21]II, ix, 1–86.

full capacity to perceive; one must both see things as they are and react to them appropriately. Texts and images must go together as a natural unity.

Portia wants Bassanio. She is aware that he is not a hero, that he is not her equal. She knows his weaknesses and even the fact that he hopes to recoup his fortunes by marriage. But she also sees that he is a nice man, a man of refined sentiments, and a true gentleman. He does not sermonize, and he is balanced and graceful in his judgments. He is neither primitive nor overcivilized. He has no eminent virtues, but he pretends to none, and he has no marked vices. He is a mean; he is both handsome and cultivated. Bassanio is also no fanatic. He is the only one of the Venetians who does not instinctively hate Shylock. He always treats him like a man, indifferent to the doctrines which separate them. He is surprised and shocked at Shylock's conduct; he does not expect it, and even encourage it, as does Antonio. Bassanio is humane and simple. Like Portia, he approaches the world with no preconceptions, but lets impression and taste guide him; but his is an educated taste. He loves Portia, and Portia wants him. So she cheats and lets Bassanio know how to choose by the song she sings. It depreciates the senses, and its meaning is clear. Moreover, the first rhyme is "bred" with "head," which also rhyme with "lead." Bassanio's own reflections are very just and show a capacity to put text and image together, but he is assured of choosing aright by the song. Portia does this delicately; but, by using the convention which seems to limit her, she becomes the master of her fate. She breaks her faith, but in such a way that the appearances are saved, thus preserving the principle without being a victim of the principle. The law is only a means to an end with her.[22]

V

Portia goes off to Venice to save Antonio, not out of any principle of universal humanity, but because he is her husband's friend, and

[22]The authority of the father is like that of the law and is supported by it. Both are binding and unmoving, and law gets its authority from the ancestral, from the fact that it was given by the fathers. Hence, Portia's experience with her father's law and what it means to her prepares her for dealing with the law in general—not as a lawyer, who by profession is committed to the law, but as one who stands outside the law and sees its relation to life and happiness. Shylock, on the other hand, simply takes his authority and his law for granted, or, otherwise stated, he identifies the law with the good.

Bassanio is involved in the responsibility for his plight. She leaves on the pious pretext of going to a nunnery to prepare herself for marriage and takes on a new appearance, that of a boy.[23] She becomes a representative of the law and interjects herself as such between the warring Jew and Christian. The situation between them has become intolerable; only senseless bestiality can be the consequence. Shylock lives only for revenge; the law supports him. He desires the flesh of Antonio, although it can profit him in no way. There is no compromise possible.[24] Shylock knows that he is hated and that he can never have respect from the others. He has no private life to which he can retreat with dignity; that is all gone. He would seem weak or cowardly if he gave in. Antonio, on the other hand, is not entirely averse to martyrdom. It fits well with his general melancholy, and he can prove his great love by dying for Bassanio. He can make an ever-living memorial for himself in the guilt of his friend, whom he expects to write an epitaph for him.[25] Only by altering the law can this absurd situation, which law never intended, be avoided. But the essence of the law is its fixity. Only a Portia, indifferent to the law but aware of its power, can manipulate it.[26]

Portia understands Shylock's intention quickly; she knows that law is what counts for him. So she presents herself at the beginning as the severest interpreter of the law, which wins Shylock's confidence. First, in a most direct and frank way, she tries to settle the case without chicanery. Shylock must be merciful. She does not appeal directly to his simple humanity; she knows that Shylock is a Jew and that she must begin from there. She tries to suggest a common ground on which Jew and Christian can meet, and not the low one of animal nature. She tries to show that both have the Scripture in common, that they pray to the same god with the same prayer, the Lord's Prayer. Christian and Jew do share on a high level, and neither need step out of his faith to experience the unity. And the present case is covered

[23]III, iv. It is a man's world, but men are no longer able to control it, so the woman must become a man and restore the balance.
[24]IV, i, 20–74. There is a strong resemblance between this scene and the accounts of the Crucifixion in the Gospels, with the role of the Duke paralleling that of Pilate (cf. Matthew 27:17–23; Mark 15:8–15; Luke 23:13–25). Shylock's insistence that Antonio die and his unwillingness to say why are parallel to the Jews' conduct in relation to Jesus. Without Portia, the conclusion would have also been similar.
[25]IV, i, 120–24. Antonio seeks martyrdom; Portia will not allow it to him.
[26]Portia gives the appearance of total indifference to persons which is proper to the law: "Which is the Merchant here? And which the Jew?" (IV, i, 181). But she has prepared her case, and it is a discriminatory one. Shylock transfers his devotion from the religious law to the civil law: law as law is respectable to him. This is Portia's great insight.

by the community of faith. "Forgive us our debts as we forgive our debtors." Equity and mercy stand above the law.[27] But this noble attempt does not succeed, at least with Shylock. The interpretation of the meaning of the same Scripture differs too much between the two. The law, and only the law, is still the highest for Shylock.

Portia tries a second mode of reconciliation through the mean motive of profit. This, too, fails, and now Portia starts using her wiles. First she gains Shylock's acceptance of her adjudication by the appearance of strict interpretation of the law. He puts himself completely into her hands—"a Daniel, come to judge me." Then, by a series of steps which we need not recount, she turns the tables on Shylock and deprives him of his revenge, his fortune, and his Judaism. Her means are contrary to all good legal proceeding. Portia, in demanding that the flesh be cut to the exact weight and that no drop of blood be spilled, makes it impossible to achieve ends that have been agreed to be legitimate. With particular reference to the blood, she asks for a miracle: flesh must have the qualities of nonflesh. That would be as great a miracle as the reverse. Shylock's faith in the righteousness of his cause apparently does not go so far as to count on divine intervention. The age of miracles is past.

Portia has maintained the appearance of the law, and the case is settled. Shylock suffers terribly; with the loss of his revenge, he has lost everything. Someone had to suffer in this terrible affair, and Shylock was the one who in justice should do so. He insisted on the inhuman. The war of Shylock and Antonio could not go on, and Portia decides in favor of Antonio. Venice is a Christian city, and Antonio her husband's friend. If the cancer of civil discord must be rooted out, then Shylock is the one to go.

Conversion is no solution.[28] We can all see that Shylock is now a dead man. Justice has not been done to him in any complete sense. Shakespeare wishes to leave a doleful impression of the impossibility of the harmonious resolution of such problems. He does this with the unforgettable picture of Shylock's grandeur and misery. But Shylock is not a nice man.

It has been remarked that Shylock's reduction to nothingness is too quick and too improbable. Is it plausible that Shylock, who has evinced such pride, would give in to Portia in such a cowardly way?

[27]IV, i, 207–11. "Therefore Jew . . . we do pray for mercy." The Lord's Prayer (Matthew 6:9) is meant to be a distillation of common Jewish teachings. The specific teaching about mercy is frequently referred to Ecclesiasticus 28.
[28]IV, i, 397–419.

This would make him like those Jews of the earlier literature who were only devices of plot. I believe that those who make this objection have missed the genius of the trial scene. It is not by cowardice that Shylock is reduced, but by respect for the law. He was proud and resolute because of his conviction of his righteousness; when he no longer has the law on his side, he collapses. He has accepted Balthasar as a second Daniel, and, whatever she reveals the law to be, is law for him. "Is that the law?" he questions.[29] Shakespeare has maintained the unity of the character. As the law was Shylock's heart and soul, it is the cause of his destruction, and in this he attains to the dignity of tragedy. He is a dupe of the law. He has never reflected that the law might be a means to an end and hence only an instrument which might be variable in relation to that end or that laws depend, at least in some measure, on human frailty. Portia has taken on the name of Balthasar; that was the name of Daniel in the court of Nebuchadnezzar.[30] She is a lawgiver who mediates between Belmont and Venice and harmonizes justice with law. She, according to Shakespeare, understands the limits of law. This is the poet's picture of the Jews—a people great by its devotion to the law but deceived by it.

Antonio, too, suffers from Portia's victory. She is aware that the ties which bind Bassanio to Antonio are strong. If Antonio had died, those ties would have poisoned Bassanio's life. She frees Bassanio from that onus, and then, with her deception concerning the rings, she forces Bassanio to admit explicitly the superiority of his love for Portia over everything else. She substitutes her lusty, gay, physical love for the gloomy, spiritual love that united Bassanio and Antonio. And Antonio is forced to speak up as guarantor for the new fidelity, which he had earlier challenged.[31]

VI

The conclusion of the trial is too unhappy a theme on which to end a comedy. Venice is an unpleasant place, full of ugly passions and unfulfilled hopes. It must be remembered that Portia only plays the role of a *deus ex machina*; the ugly truth remains that, if her improbable appearance had not been made, revenge and blood would have been

[29]IV, i, 329.
[30]Daniel 1:7. In the King James version, the name is Belshazzar, but it was frequently spelled "Balthasar," following the Greek (cp. Note 18, *supra*).
[31]V, i, 273–80; cp. IV, i, 296–303, 469–71. The obviously erotic symbolism of the rings contrasts the basis of Portia's power over Bassanio with that of Antonio's.

the result. She has done nothing in principle to resolve the problems which led to the war of Shylock and Antonio. And there is no resolution. We can only hasten to Belmont to forget them.

Belmont is the seat of love; but it does not exist; it is a utopia.[32] What is not possible in Venice is possible here. The only love affair that takes place in Venice is a sordid one. Jessica, without the slightest trace of filial piety, remorselessly leaves her father and robs him. She is one of the very few figures in Shakespeare who do not pay the penalty for their crimes; and disobedience to one's parents, be they good or bad, is a crime for Shakespeare; so is robbery. But somehow the atmosphere of Belmont changes all this. It is a place where there are no laws, no conventions, no religions—just men and women in love.

Jessica escapes to this never-never land with her Christian lover and is saved.[33] Here the past is transformed in the glow of Eros; the duties of everyday life appear the concerns of drudges; duty is not the fulfillment of virtue, but the burden of necessity. There is, indeed, a harmony in the world; it is the harmony of the eternal order. In Venice, we forget this, but Lorenzo reminds us in his great Platonic speech.[34] We participate in one cosmos, and every soul is a reflection of that cosmos. This is the harmony to which all men as men can attain. But, because we are "grossly closed in" by a "muddy vesture of decay," we cannot hear the music of the spheres. It is only through the effect of music that we touch from time to time on that higher world; and many men no longer have any music in their souls. We are all human on a high level and can have complete unity. But the accidents of life force men into customs that cause them to forget the whole and the immortal part of themselves; the nations have no time for music. The ultimate harmony of men is a harmony, not on the level of their daily lives, but on that of a transcendence of them, an indifference to them, an assimilation to the movements of the spheres. Hence, humanity is attainable by only a few in rare circumstances, but it is potentially in all of us, and that is what makes us humans.

---

[32]It is literally nowhere; it is unknown in Italy. I take it to be the elaboration of men's prayers; that best place which indicates the perfection which is unattainable in ordinary life, with its accidents and necessities. Etymologically, it is "beautiful mountain." Could it be Parnassus?

[33]V, i, 1–22. On the first level, it is clearly Jessica's conversion that saves her. But other difficulties are overcome by the magic of the place. At the beginning of their scene in the garden, Jessica and Lorenzo recite a list of unhappy lovers whose loves were either forbidden by parents or divided by nation.

[34]V, i, 63–98. Cf. Plato, *Republic*, x, 616[d]–617[d], and John Burnet, "Shakespeare and Greek Philosophy," *Essays and Addresses* (London: Chatto & Windus, 1926).

The realization of Belmont does not solve the problems of Venice; it only mitigates their bleakness for those who understand. Portia, the goddess of love, can orchestrate a human harmony for a few.

Shakespeare does not understand Judaism, for he saw it from the outside; he looked at it, as no man rightfully can, from a purely political point of view. But he was personally less interested in the question of Judaism than in man's attempt to become man and man alone. He was of the conviction that it is the nature of man to have varying opinions about the highest things and that such opinions become invested in doctrine and law and bound up with established interests. When confronted with one another, these opinions must quarrel. Such is life, and that must be accepted with manly resolution. In Venice and modern thought, there was an attempt to cut the Gordian knot and unite men, not on the level of their truly human sameness, but on that of the politically beneficial—a unity expressed in men's universal desire for gain. The consequences of this must be either conflict or a bastardization of all that is noble and true in each of the separate points of view. Venice had the adorned beauty of a strumpet. Shakespeare was not willing to sacrifice for this illusion the only true beauty, which lies somewhere beyond the heavens for the happy few.

RICHARD II

SHAKESPEARE NOT ONLY presents us with the spectacle of a man becoming a god (Julius Caesar) but in *Richard II* also permits us to witness a god becoming a man. As a consequence of what one might call political logic, Richard was thought to be, and thought himself to be, somehow divine: to have the right and the capacity to rule men a king ought to have a superior nature, must be a god or the representative of a god; because he must be, he is. The play tells the tale of Richard's unkinging and his agony as he faces the human condition for the first time.

Richard II is also the tale of Henry Bolingbroke's grasping of the crown and thereby his loss of innocence. He thought he would purge the throne of a stain left on it by Richard's having committed the sin of Cain, but he is constrained to commit the same sin in order to found his rule. Instead of becoming a god, he becomes a murderer. The king he became could never be the king Richard was.

Thus these two tales join to tell a third tale, that of kingship in its divine claims and criminal foundations.

I

In spite of what some critics say, there can be little doubt that Shakespeare teaches us that Richard is a sort of legitimate tyrant who deserves to be deposed. Moreover, he chooses to present the divine right of kings as the underpinning of Richard's rule and thereby teaches that the principle is responsible for his tyrannical deeds. Richard never understands the real conditions of rule and believes that he is unaccountable. This does not mean that Shakespeare holds there to be

83

nothing divine in kingship; nor does it mean that Shakespeare believed that once Richard's undisputed title to rule vanishes, there could ever be an unproblematic legitimacy in this world. But that is precisely the burden of the play: legitimacy is a problem, and Richard, God's vicar, is an artificial contrivance which disguises rather than resolves the problem.[1]

Similarly, the fact that Bolingbroke's accusations are true does not mean that his motives are good or that he understands what he is about. He entertains the baseless certainty of a tribunal beyond the king's to which he can appeal, which will vindicate him and give him ground on which to stand. And he wants rule; his accusations are pretexts for supplanting the king. He does not wish to reform Richard but to replace him. Strangely, though, Shakespeare seems to have more sympathy with Henry's ambition than his indignation, for the perfect justice demanded by the latter passion has no foundation in politics and the quest for it is even pernicious, while the former passion is an expression of the manliness so lacking in this regime and so necessary to political virtue. Such manliness—to be found in the Roman heroes and in Henry's son Henry—rebels against rule by others and, properly educated and channeled, is the surest foundation of freedom. Richard becomes manly only for a moment at the very end when it is too late. And Henry, who began by being manly, loses his nerve when he realizes the consequences of what he has done. He cannot bear to accept the responsibility, tries to return to the old pieties and becomes humble. But his pride has set in motion tendencies which are to culminate in a wholly new world, one in which the pride of noble men will have its place and rule will require prudence and courage as well as birth.

In keeping with the purely conventional character of a regime where the ruler is absolute and his title is only birth supported by a

---

[1]Henry IV does not affect us as a usurper whose crime is the cause of his misery. The presentation of Richard and Henry is too carefully banked with extenuating considerations to allow for simple blame of the latter or respect for the former. The play's impact is not such as to induce reverence for the king (either the old one or the new); rather, there is a subversive element in the detachment it induces. We pity the toothless descendant of Richard the Lion-Hearted; he is shown to possess neither divine nor human strength, and he no longer inspires awe. We experience no horror at what Henry does, but on the other hand, he does not inherit Richard's former sacredness. Moreover, the reader of the Histories as a whole can hardly believe that Shakespeare thought John or Richard to be rulers superior to Henry V or Henry VIII. Shakespeare's view of kingship and legitimacy is subtle and cannot be reduced either to reverence for tradition or bald rationalism. But one thing is certain: Henry V and Henry VIII face up to their priests as neither John nor Richard II does; and this seems to be at the core of the teaching of these plays.

fiction of divine right, the atmosphere of *Richard II* is suffused with artificiality of speech and deed. This artificiality is particularly to be remarked in the relationships among human beings. At the outset it is taken for granted that the just man is to be proved in trial by combat and that God, just as He is immediately present in the king, will directly indicate where the truth lies by the victory in arms. Divine action and brute force preempt entirely the field properly governed by prudence. God is just and provides a law behind which He stands, but human reason cannot penetrate to His reasons and plays no role in the system of justice. Richard, despite his fears that the result of the combat will inculpate him, is constrained by the rules of honor to permit it. But this aborted combat on St. Lambert's day in the lists at Coventry is the last trial by combat England will ever see. When Richard II recognizes that the risks are too great for him and halts it, he unwittingly brings the era of chivalry, the era of Christian knights inaugurated by the first Richard, the Lion-Hearted, to its end. By Act IV the challenges of the lords have become empty bluster and a parody of what they had been. They will never be committed to a test. New ways of settling disputes and determining the right will have to be found.

Thus at the outset we see "medieval" England, but we also see that it is moribund. A criminal king against whom there is no recourse is opposed to an ambitious potential successor who comes ever closer to challenging the sacred person of the king himself. And the supports of the old order—represented by the dukes of Lancaster and York— are themselves old and have lost conviction. Lancaster passively leaves the issue to heaven and dies, while York, who is really a comic figure, provides the transition to the new order. The principle of the old order is enunciated by Gaunt in his discussion with the Duchess of Gloucester (I, ii), and he embodies its dignity. One must bear with insults and apparent injustices in this world in the conviction that they are expressions of God's infinite goodness. Unswerving loyalty and faith against all the evidence of the senses and merely human reason is the subject's proper posture.

> God's is the quarrel; for God's substitute,
> His deputy anointed in his sight,
> Hath caus'd his death; the which if wrongfully
> Let heaven revenge, for I may never lift
> An angry arm against his minister.   [I, ii, 39–43]

But the duchess represents the problem in Gaunt's principle and the countervailing principle. Her husband has been murdered, and he was

Gaunt's brother. Outraged family feeling ought to seek vengeance.
The ordinary sentiments, directly experienced by all normal human
beings, are suppressed in favor of a purely arbitrary duty to obey the
king. Whereas all the principal men in *Richard II* are artificial, and
none particulary admirable, the three women in the play (Richard's
queen and the Duchess of York in addition to the Duchess of Gloucester) are all both natural and admirable. They love their husbands and
their children. Humanity, banished by the men, seems to have taken
refuge in the women. For varying but related reasons these women
cannot depend on the men in their families; and in their sufferings
they do not appear to hope in God. They endure, and in their fortitude
they provide a measure for the failings of the men to whom they are
most nearly related—the Duchess of Gloucester to Gaunt, the queen
to the king, the Duchess of York to the Duke of York. In the scene
under discussion the audience cannot but side with the Duchess of
Gloucester against Gaunt, nor can one help but feel that if Gaunts
are the subjects, the rulers will be Richards. Disarming good men is
equivalent to arming evil men.

Moreover, there is no doubt that the first two acts are intended
to establish Richard as an evil king who deserves to lose his throne.
He is shown to be a murderer, a thief, a wastrel surrounded by flatterers,
lacking in all the familial pieties—a monarch without care or conscience. He is convicted before our eyes of all the accusations made
against him, and this portrait is relieved by no charming features.
Bolingbroke's schemes are thereby given the color of justice. By the
end of Act II power and loyalty have slipped away from Richard as a
rightful consequence of his crimes. But even if Bolingbroke is right
in deposing Richard, that fact alone does not suffice to make him
king. He has justice on his side, as well as the talent to govern in
these troubled times, a secondary title of inheritance,[2] the consent of
the nobles, and the adherence of the people. But all of this does not
quite add up to Richard's indisputable family title and the sense of
divine right apparently attached to it.

Henry's problem is posed and solved in comic fashion by York,
the last remaining son of Edward III and the last remaining fragment
of the old regime. Although he has reproved his nephew Richard for
depriving Henry of his inheritance, as Lord Governor in Richard's
absence he loyally forbids Henry entry into England and treats him
as a rebel. But he possesses no power and certainly lacks the energy

[2]Bolingbroke is next in line to the succession after the infant Earl of March, grandson
of the Duke of Clarence, Edward III's second son. Cf. *Richard II*, I, i, 120–21; iv,
36–37, New Variorum edition, ed. Black (Philadelphia: Lippincott, 1955).

or the conviction to be a martyr to Richard's cause. So he declares himself neuter and invites the rebels to spend the night at his place. York's neutrality symbolizes the exhaustion of the old order. He solves his own problem by ending up a fanatic adherent of the new king, acting as though Henry were the old king. The example of Henry's change from subject to ruler teaches a lesson which York desperately tries to suppress, one from which other subjects will nonetheless profit.

II

Suddenly, at the beginning of Act III, Richard, who is no longer really king and is beginning to realize it, becomes interesting. As he descends to the estate of mere man, his soul is inspired by the poetic muse. It is as though Shakespeare wished to tell us that the most divine in man is man. He provides Richard with the play's most beautiful lines to allow him to voice questions about what he might really be when he discovers he is not what convention told him he is. He never succeeds in finding himself, but we see the articulation of his soul as he gropes toward his goal. We do not find that Richard is ever good, but we do find him touching.

Richard returns to England from the Irish wars to find his neglected country torn by rebellion. He speaks confidently to the earth of England which he takes to be animate and loyal, reminding it of his expectation that its flora and fauna will take up the cause of its rightful king. When chided by his episcopal adviser Carlisle, who tells him that God helps those who help themselves, he responds by comparing himself to the sun and announces that for every rebel soldier God provides Richard with a fighting angel. But when he hears that his Welsh troops have departed, he becomes disconsolate, only to regain confidence when he thinks of his uncle York's troops. Again his mood wavers when he expects to hear bad news from Scroop. Now he takes the tack of resignation. Of what value are human things? They are nothing when seen in the perspective of God's power or in that of the bleakness of death. All men are equal in both perspectives. Richard is ready piously to accept the vicissitudes of life. Being a king was nothing but a care to him. As he was confident in being everything, he professes himself resigned to being nothing. But, suddenly, he suspects that he has been betrayed by his friends, and now he is the man-God, Jesus, abandoned by all, surrounded only by Judases. And finally, when he learns that the man about to become king has executed his close associates, Richard collapses in despair:

> let us sit on the ground
> And tell sad stories of the death of kings.
>   (III, ii, 158–59)

Then once more he responds to the chidings of Carlisle and remembers York's troops. But when he learns that York is with Henry, he knows he is no longer king and abandons all hope. He had hoped in God's arms, the Welsh arms, and York's arms. He has no arms of his own, nor does he imagine trying to get them. Richard is night, Henry day. A new sun has risen.[3]

As is evident, Richard's moods are mercurial. But what is most striking about them is that they move between two poles and never point to another alternative. He is either hopeful or despairing, arrogant or humble, the glorious king or the poor man menaced by death. There is no middle ground.

> I'll give my jewels for a set of beads
> My gorgeous palace for a hermitage,
> My gay apparel for an almsman's gown,
> My figur'd goblets for a dish of wood,
> My sceptre for a palmer's walking staff,
> My subjects for a pair of carved saints,
> And my large kingdom for a little grave,
> A little little grave, an obscure grave.
>   (III, iii, 155–62)

The little piece of time between the two eternities—God and death—that comprises human life has no status for Richard. Yet it is only in this interval that political life is to be found, somewhat independent, and perhaps a bit forgetful, of God and death. The statesman must not be overwhelmed by the power and glory (not to mention the high moral demands) of God nor disheartened by the shadow cast over his concerns by death. He must trust in his own efforts and take seriously the goals of life, liberty, and glory. He must respect this world. But just as Richard's reign is founded on the God of the Christians, he has a Christian view of the world. He is either like God, or like Jesus, or like a monk or a hermit. He is never a political man. He is imprisoned in Julius Caesar's tower[4] but has no other connection with such men.

Richard has frequently been compared to Hamlet, for both possess histrionic natures. They are also alike in that Hamlet too views things in extremes, extremes which derive from a Christian's perspective.

---

[3]III, ii.
[4]V, i, 4.

The Hamlet who is unwilling to kill the usurper while at prayer for fear that his soul will be saved and who thus loses his chance to right things in the realm is akin to Richard. They are both actors of their parts rather than being what they are, and they see this world through the optic of another world and thus transform it. And these two characteristics are probably effects of a single cause.[5]

Richard, like Gaunt, is able to see only divine justice or brute force, God's pastorate or a tyrant's arbitrariness. A world in which men are responsible for the defense of justice and provide for its rewards and punishments is unknown to him. This is underlined in III.iv, which immediately follows the two scenes on which the foregoing reflections are based. Richard's sweet queen wanders in the Duke of York's gardens and overhears the conversation of the gardener and his assistant. They are humble men; but for that very reason, in a world where everything high is conventional and artificial, Shakespeare makes them speak the language of nature and reason. They, like the women in this play, help to supply what cannot be gotten from the high-born, convention-ridden men. These two artisans compare their garden to the state and explain what should have been done by Richard and why his failing to do it has caused his downfall. They ascribe to an absence of art what others understand to be a result of God's will and men's sins. One cannot help being reminded of *Prince* XXV, where Machiavelli interprets what men call fortune or God's action in politics as a lack of prudence or foresight. Floods, he says, injure men not because they are sinners but because they did not build dams. These two workers suggest that art, in cooperation with nature, can make states as well as gardens grow. The founding of political science requires only a clear vision of things. But it is precisely that natural vision which is hard to achieve, for the prospect is clouded over by myths which must first be dispelled. The queen angrily reproaches the gardeners for committing the sin of Adam, for eating of the fruit of the tree of knowledge and thus bringing about a second Fall. The only defense she can contrive for her husband is to view this not as nature's garden, given over to the control of rational men who can make it

[5]Mowbray is an interesting example of the political man living in this kind of world. He is a scoundrel, capable of all kinds of crimes. But he is also a believing Christian, praised as a defender of the faith against the infidels. He is a Christian knight from the times of the Crusades. He is a great sinner and a great repenter. He has a conscience and confesses. Although he takes political things seriously, they are for him apparently low. His Christianity affects him primarily, if not solely, insofar as it debases his view of human life and politics. All the great things are somewhere else, beyond this sphere, but he is still involved in politics. He is treacherous without any of the great justifications one finds in great political men. And his treachery is compromised by his conscience. (I, i, 83–150; IV, i, 91–100.)

produce fruit for their sustenance, but as God's garden, the Garden
of Eden, ruled directly by God, producing what God wills without the
cooperation of man, whose inquiries into the mysterious ways of the
ruler would be a sin. As gardeners should not put their hands to God's
garden, rational subjects should not question Richard's state. This
vision makes political science impossible and renders the attempt to
establish it a sin, the sin of disobeying the ruler and of attempting to
replace him. Piety, not art, is the foundation of Richard's state, and
the emancipation of art requires the overturning of that state.

The case for Richard's rule is made by the finest or at least the
most disinterested man among the principals, the Bishop of Carlisle.
(It goes without saying that Richard's touching eloquence does not
make a case for his remaining as king. It only gives witness to the
noble aspect of what makes him unfit to be a king.) Carlisle stands
up before Henry and warns him not to depose the king. With his
". . . if you rear this house against this house,"[6] he accurately pro-
phesies the horrors of the Wars of the Roses. The overturning of one
monarch provides argument for the overturning of another. There
must be established authority and agreed-upon legitimacy. He believes
that only divine right can establish such legitimacy, and an attack on
the king is an attack on God. The dire consequences of such an attack
Carlisle evidently attributes to God's wrath, although civil war would
appear to follow naturally from the absence of a recognized sovereign.
We would conclude that if Richard's rule is a failure, then some other
source of legitimacy must be sought for. The king in his nation,
according to Carlisle, is the image of God in the world. And everything
that Richard is or is not derives from that vision of the whole. God's
rule of the whole is the source of Richard's rule in England, and the
latter seems to be the necessary consequence of the former. If there
is something wrong with the order in England, it is probably related to something wrong with the cosmic order on which it is
modeled.

This order is one in which prophecy takes the place of foresight,
and Carlisle's prophecy is the supplement to Gaunt's earlier prophecy.[7]
Gaunt treats England as a living being, its constitution, like that of
a body, inseparable from it and unchangeable. Richard will be purged
like a disease. Gaunt's indignation does not lead to rebellion, and
none seems possible. Country and constitution are identical; rulers
are produced out of its womb; one is oneself a part of one's country
and one must love it. Carlisle, on the other hand, sees England's

[6]IV, i, 115–50.
[7]II, i, 33–70.

Christianity as something separable from it and knows the possibility of rebellion and change. Christianity is universal, and a nation can either participate in it or not. His loyalty is to Christianity. For him Christianity is represented by Richard. If England is to be purged of Richard, an element of that purgation must be a change in the nation's relation to Christianity, most specifically to God's representatives, the king and the priests. Carlisle forces us to correct Gaunt's vision. If England is to be free from the danger of Richards, there must be a change in the constitution and the spirit informing it. To render England unto itself the elements of the nation must be separated out and certain alien matter be removed. Only at the end of the history plays is there a king, Henry VIII, who is himself really the high priest and interprets the divine in such a way as to serve England. The eighth Henry is truly at home; Richard was only a stranger; and this he learns when he looks at himself in the mirror. A long and bloody path leads from Richard to Henry VIII, a path on which Englishmen learn that kingship is founded on nobles and commoners as well as on God. This mixture is perilous but through it wisdom can at least occasionally peep without being sinful or causing civil war. Carlisle shows us both the greatest dignity and the greatest weakness of the old order. God is supposed to rule; Richard actually rules. Without his faith that God protected him, he would have taken more care.

III

In the final act, York completes his comedy, Richard completes his tragedy, and Henry begins his career as a guilt-ridden, world-weary man, insecure and plotted against, distrusting even his own son.

Old York, the crumbling pillar of both the old and new order, tries madly to persuade himself that they are identical by accusing his son of treason and demanding his death. His son was loyal to Richard and thus is disloyal to the usurper. York abandons Richard and, aping a Roman citizen, demands his own son's death as a punishment for disloyalty. The Roman's deed inspires awe because it proves firmness of soul and is done for the unquestioned common good and in the name of the most ancient and unquestioned authority. But after what has already transpired, nothing York could do would prove his firmness of soul. And Aumerle's adherence to Henry would imply the abandonment not only of his sovereign but his friend. It is ridiculous to suppose that Henry can command instinctive loyalty. That is exactly his problem. Attachment to him must be born of his wisdom, beneficence, and strength, for he is beginning afresh without the sanctions which were available to Richard. York's conduct merely puts that problem in relief and strikes us as horrible or absurd. The Duchess of York wins the sympathy of everyone, including the new king, with her defense of her son, springing as it does from a mother's natural affection. Such sentiments are taken more seriously now that the old structure of obligations has collapsed, and they must become part of the new structure if it is to hold. Henry's clemency is a start in that direction.[8]

Richard, despised and abandoned, having suffered the insults of the crowd, no longer looks to his divine Father for special protection. He surveys his situation and finds only his loneliness and vulnerability. He compares his prison to the world and populates it with his thoughts representing the different alternative lives, none of which can satisfy him. The life lived in the hope of the afterlife is contradicted by the demands of greatness on this earth. The king's glory and wealth are opposed by the commandments of humility and poverty. The Christian king imitates God while God calls the "little men." Being a king seems to preclude hopes for eternal bliss. The life of ambition cannot succeed, for it demands powers beyond those available to man. And the life of Stoic contentment does not work. Richard does not quite say why, but he indicates that such a posture only makes the best of a bad business and would be abandoned once out of misfortune: there is no true self-sufficiency. This is the popular view of philosophy, as expressed when one says, "He's taking it philosophically," a phrase never used when good things happen. Of the three alternatives it is fair to say that Richard has only thought through and experienced the first. Here at least he breaks out of its constraints but gives only a hasty glance at the other two. It is too late to consider them seriously. Richard's life and fall are marvelously illustrative of the first, which is the Christian alternative and is the one which dominated his world. Others would have to investigate the other ways of life, for Richard himself immediately slips back into his old choice between being a king or a beggar, or the synthesis of the two—nothing. At the last moment, tired of acceptance and drawing on an instinct of which he has hitherto been unaware, he rises to his own defense and fights his attackers. He dies like a man and as a man.[9]

When Henry learns that his wishes are fulfilled, that his rival, the question mark after his legitimacy, has been slain for him, just as Gloucester was slain for Richard, he is stricken with remorse. He

[8]V, ii–iii.
[9]V, v.

accuses himself of the sin of Cain, as he had accused Richard, and vows to go on a crusade. He salves his conscience by trying to return to the chivalric tradition which he has just uprooted. This crusade will never take place because business at home is too pressing. His conscience takes his heart away from home, but home preempts his action. He is split. He cannot bear to face the possibility that the sin of Cain, as Machiavelli teaches, may play a role in the establishment of earthly justice. In deposing Richard he was halfway to the realization that he was committing a crime but that such crimes are sometimes necessary for the common good. However, so strong is his faith or his fear of hell-fire, he prefers to brand himself a guilty man and cripple his political sense and dedication rather than admit what his deed has shown.[10] His son returns to his father's original impulse and with healthy self-assurance abandons crusades in favor of unjust wars with France which serve the evident interests of England instead of serving his conscience, using the priests as his political ministers rather than as the masters of his beliefs. He thus unifies England and himself. The Henriad as a whole shows the limits of conscience. Henry V provides a contrast to his predecessors not unlike the contrast between Hamlet and Fortinbras in a play that seems to bear a similar message. The exquisitely refined souls do not belong to the best political men.

There are two sins mentioned in *Richard II:* the sin of Adam and the sin of Cain. They seem to be identical, or at least one leads to the other. Knowledge of political things brings with it the awareness that in order for the sacred to become sacred terrible deeds must be done. Because God does not evidently rule, the founder of justice cannot himself be just. He cannot be distinguished from the criminal by his justice or anything else accessible to vulgar eyes. This capital problem was addressed long ago by Sophocles who showed that the hero who solved the riddle of the Sphinx and thereby discerned man killed his father and slept with his mother. Machiavelli later repeated the teaching, perhaps in perverting it. I do not suggest that here Shakespeare stopped, but here he surely began. The universal problem of kingship is played out in the particular events of England by Shakespeare, who in his histories could be more philosophic than the historian because he was a poet. He gave England a mirror in which it could recognize itself as it ought to be, one which England would not have to smash as Richard smashed the mirror which reflected his image.

---

[10]V, vi.

HIPPARCHUS OR THE PROFITEER

TRANSLATED BY STEVEN FORDE

SOCRATES; A COMRADE

225a SOCRATES: So what is profit? Just what can it be, and who are the profiteers?

COMRADE: In my opinion, they are those who think it worthwhile to make a gain from worthless things.

SOCRATES: But do they, in your opinion, know these things are worthless, or do they not know? For if they don't know, you are saying the profiteers are fools.

b COMRADE: I say they're not fools but villains and evildoers who are overcome by profit. They know that the things from which they dare to make a profit are worth nothing, yet they still dare to be profiteers through shamelessness.

SOCRATES: Then do you say that the profiteer is of this sort, like a man who is a farmer, who plants knowing his plant[1] is worth nothing and raises it thinking it worthwhile to make a profit from that? Do you say he is of that sort?

Hipparchus was the son of the Athenian tyrant Peisistratus (see n. 8 below). According to popular Athenian tradition Hipparchus inherited the tyranny of Athens on his father's death (527 B.C.) and ruled until he was assassinated, when the tyranny passed to his brother Hippias.

"Profiteer" in Greek is the word *philokerdēs*, meaning literally "lover of gain." The construction of the word gives rise to all sorts of talk in the dialogue concerning love of other things, so it should be noted that "love" here is *philia*, the same word that applies to friendship. The other Greek word for love, *eros*, or "erotic passion," appears only once in this dialogue (at 229d).

[1]The verb "to plant" (*phyteuein*) and the noun "plant" (*phyton*) have the same root as the Greek word for "nature" (*physis*).

COMRADE: The profiteer, Socrates, thinks he ought to make a profit from everything.

c SOCRATES: Don't answer me so aimlessly, as though you had suffered some injustice from someone, but pay attention to me and answer as though I asked you again from the beginning: don't you agree that the profiteer knows about the worth of this thing from which he considers it worthwhile to make a profit?

COMRADE: I do, indeed.

SOCRATES: Now, who knows about the worth of plants, in what seasons and soils it is worth planting them—if we too may throw in one of those wise phrases with which people who are clever in the law courts beautify their speeches?[2]

d COMRADE: I suppose the farmer.

SOCRATES: And do you say that thinking it worthwhile to make a profit is anything but thinking one ought to make a profit?

COMRADE: That's what I say.

226a SOCRATES: Then don't try to deceive me, an older man now, you being so young, by answering as you did now with what you yourself don't think, but speak truly. Is there any farmer, do you think, who knows he plants a worthless plant and thinks to make profit from it?

COMRADE: By Zeus, not I!

SOCRATES: And what about this: do you think that a horseman who knows he is giving his horse worthless food doesn't know that he is harming the horse?

COMRADE: I don't.

b SOCRATES: Then *he* doesn't think that he is making a profit from worthless food.

COMRADE: No.

SOCRATES: What about this: do you think that a pilot who furnishes his ship with worthless sails and rudders doesn't know that he will suffer loss[3] and will run the risk of being destroyed himself and destroying the ship and everything he is carrying?

COMRADE: I don't.

SOCRATES: So *he* doesn't think that he is making a profit from worthless equipment.

c COMRADE: No indeed.

SOCRATES: Furthermore, does a general who knows that his army has

[2]Socrates' beautiful phrase is a sentence ending with the rhyming words *hora* and *chora*—"season" and "soil"—in a pair.

[3]The Greek words for "to suffer loss," which appear frequently in this dialogue, can also mean "to be punished" and "punishment," respectively.

worthless arms think to make a profit from them or consider it worthwhile to make a profit from them?

COMRADE: Not at all.

SOCRATES: Or does an aulos player with worthless auloi,[4] or a citharist
with a lyre, or an archer with a bow, or, in short, any one of the
artisans at all, or any of the other men with intelligence, think to
make a profit with tools or with any other equipment whatever that
is worthless?

d COMRADE: It doesn't appear so, at least.

SOCRATES: Then just who do you say are the profiteers? For I suppose
that they are not the ones we have just gone through but[5] those who,
knowing the worthless things, think they ought to make a profit from
them. But in that case, as you say, you surprising fellow, there is not
one profiteer among human beings.

COMRADE: But I, Socrates, want to say that the profiteers are those
who, out of greed, are always striving preternaturally for insignificant

e things of little or no worth in loving profit.

SOCRATES: Surely not knowing, best one, that they are worth nothing,
for the argument just proved against us that that is impossible.

COMRADE: So it seems to me.

SOCRATES: And if they don't know it, clearly they are ignorant, thinking that worthless things are worth a great deal.

COMRADE: Apparently.

SOCRATES: Now, do not the profiteers love profit?

COMRADE: Yes.

SOCRATES: And do you say that profit is the opposite of loss?

227a COMRADE: I do.

SOCRATES: Is there anyone for whom it is good to suffer loss?

COMRADE: No one.

SOCRATES: Is it bad instead?

COMRADE: Yes.

SOCRATES: Human beings then are harmed by loss.

COMRADE: They are.

SOCRATES: Loss therefore is bad.

COMRADE: Yes.

SOCRATES: And profit is the opposite of loss.

COMRADE: The opposite.

[4]The aulos (plural auloi) was a musical instrument.
[5]The word "but" does not appear in the manuscripts here, but something like it
appears to be required for the sense. Another possible emendation would read "those
who, knowing the worthless things, do not think they ought to make a gain from
them."

SOCRATES: Then profit is good.

COMRADE: Yes.

b SOCRATES: So you call those who love the good, lovers of profit.

COMRADE: So it seems.

SOCRATES: At least you don't say the profiteers are madmen, comrade. But you yourself, do you love or not love whatever is good?

COMRADE: I do.

SOCRATES: Is there anything good that you don't love, or is it the bad instead?

COMRADE: By Zeus, not I!

SOCRATES: Perhaps you love all good things.

COMRADE: Yes.

c SOCRATES: Now ask me too if I don't as well; for I will agree with you that I too love the good things. But aside from you and me, don't all human beings seem to you to love the good things and to hate the bad?

COMRADE: So it appears to me.

SOCRATES: Didn't we agree too that profit is good?

COMRADE: Yes.

SOCRATES: Then everyone turns out in this way to be a lover of profit, but according to what we said earlier, no one is a lover of profit. Now, which of these arguments should one use to avoid error?

d COMRADE: I think, Socrates, that one would have to conceive the profiteer correctly. Is it correct to suppose that he is a profiteer who is serious about those things and that he thinks it worthwhile to make a profit from them which the decent[6] wouldn't dare to profit from.

SOCRATES: But you see, sweetest one, that we have already agreed that to make a profit is to be benefited.

COMRADE: Well, what of it?

SOCRATES: Just this, that we agreed in addition that everyone wants the good things always.

COMRADE: Yes.

SOCRATES: Furthermore, the good want to have all profits, if these are good at least.

e COMRADE: Not, Socrates, profits from which they are going to suffer harm.

SOCRATES: Do you say that suffering harm is suffering loss or something else?

COMRADE: No, I say it is suffering loss.

---

[6]The word *chrēstos*, "decent," can also mean "useful." I have translated "decent" throughout, but the ambiguity of the Greek should be borne in mind.

SOCRATES: Is it by profit that human beings suffer loss or by loss?

COMRADE: By both: because they suffer loss both by loss and by evil profit.

SOCRATES: Well, does anything decent and good seem to you to be evil?

COMRADE: Not to me.

228a SOCRATES: And we agreed a little while ago that profit is the opposite of loss, which is bad?

COMRADE: I assent.

SOCRATES: And that being the opposite of bad it is good?

COMRADE: We agreed to that.

SOCRATES: So you see, you are trying to deceive me, purposely saying the opposite of what we agreed to before.

COMRADE: No, by Zeus, Socrates, you on the contrary are deceiving me, and I don't know how you are managing to turn everything upside down in the argument!

b SOCRATES: Hush![7] It wouldn't be right of me not to obey a good and wise man.

COMRADE: Who is that? What are you talking about?

SOCRATES: A fellow citizen of yours and mine, the son of Peisistratus[8] of Philaidae, Hipparchus, who was the oldest and wisest of Peisistratus' children. His wisdom was displayed in many fine deeds; in particular, he first brought the Homeric epics to this land and compelled the rhapsodes at the Panathenaea[9] to recite them in relays, one after

c another, as they still do now. He also sent a fifty-oared ship for Anacreon of Teos,[10] to bring him to the city, and always had Simonides

[7]The word is *euphēmein*, which literally means "speak well" and was used especially in connection with sacred rites, during which an ill-spoken or improper word could taint the performance of the ritual and anger the god. In order to ensure that no improper word was spoken inadvertently during a ceremony, therefore, the practice was to maintain absolute silence; hence the word came to denote silence, especially the pious or awed silence in the presence of the god.

[8]Peisistratus first established tyranny at Athens, rising to the position of tyrant in 560 B.C. He was expelled from the city twice thereafter and returned twice, eventually passing tyranny on to his sons. Hipparchus and Hippias were sons of Peisistratus by his wife, but he had at least two other children by another woman as well. According to Thucydides (VI, 54, 55), Hippias, not Hipparchus, was Peisistratus' oldest son. The most likely construction of Socrates' reference to Philaidae is that it indicates the deme of Peisistratus' origin; according to the scholiast, Philaidae was a deme of the tribe of Aegeus.

[9]The Panathenaea was a great summer festival at Athens, which included horse races and musical contests and culminated in a great festive procession, on what was supposed to be the birthday of Athena, up to the Acropolis. This procession is depicted on the famous frieze of the Parthenon.

[10]Anacreon was a lyric poet born at Teos, a Greek city in Asia Minor. He consorted

of Ceos[11] around him, persuading him by means of great pay and gifts. He did these things, wishing to educate the citizens, so that he would rule over people who were the best possible; being a gentleman, he thought that no one should be begrudged wisdom. Now when the

d citizens from the city itself had been educated by him, and marveled at him for his wisdom, he, contriving to educate the people in the country as well, set up Hermae[12] for them along the road in the middle of the city and of each deme.[13] Then from his own wisdom, which he got both from learning and from his own discovery, he selected the things that he thought were wisest, put them himself into elegiac

e form, and inscribed them, his own poetry and examples of his wisdom, on the figures. This he did in the first place so that his citizens would not marvel at the wise Delphic inscriptions, "Know thyself," "Nothing in excess," and the like but would rather think the words of Hipparchus wise; but also so that in traveling back and forth they would read and get a taste of his wisdom and would come out of the countryside to

229a complete their education. The inscriptions are two in number: on the left side of each Hermes it is inscribed that the Hermes stands in the middle of the city or of the deme, while on the right it says:

b <blockquote>This is a memorial of Hipparchus:
Walk thinking just thoughts.</blockquote>

There are many other beautiful pieces of his poetry inscribed on other Hermae. In particular there is one on the Steiria[14] road, on which it says:

---

first with the tyrant Polycrates of Samos and then with the Peisistratids at Athens. His poetry, even in his old age, sang mostly of love and wine.

[11]Simonides was a lyric poet born on Ceos, an island in the Aegean. He had a long and illustrious career at Athens during the rule of the Peisistratid tyrants and afterward, but later consorted with the tyrant Hiero of Syracuse. He was generally noted for his greed.

[12]The Hermae were figures representative of the god Hermes, generally consisting only of a square pillar with a phallus attached, and culminating in a head of the god. The worship of Hermes as the god of travelers was quite ancient, as was the practice of putting these figures on the streets and squares of towns. They sometimes bore inscriptions. Athens had an unusually large number of them on the streets and at the entrances to houses, and Attica, the territory of Athens, was somewhat unusual as well for having them on the country roads. There may be reason to link some of the Athenian Hermae to the Peisistratids (cf. Fustel de Coulanges, *The Ancient City*, IV, 7.1).

[13]The Greek word *dēmos*—"deme"—refers either to a country district or to a town or village in the country. In Attica demes were legal or administrative districts outside "the city," Athens itself.

[14]Steiria was a town on the southeast coast of Attica, in a deme of the tribe of Pandion.

> This is a memorial of Hipparchus:
> Don't deceive a friend.

Now, since I am your friend I would surely not dare to deceive you
and disobey such a one as this. After his death his brother Hippias
ruled as tyrant over the Athenians for three years, and you would
have heard from all the men of old that only for those three years was
there tyranny in Athens and that during the rest of the time the
c Athenians lived almost as in the time when Cronos was king.[15] Indeed,
it is said by the more cultivated human beings that his death came
about not in the way that the many think, on account of a sister's
being dishonored in the ritual basket carrying—since that is silly—
but because Harmodius was the favorite[16] of Aristogeiton[17] and was
educated by him; thus Aristogeiton prided himself on educating human
d beings and supposed himself to be a rival of Hipparchus. Now during
the same time Harmodius himself happened to be a lover of one of
the beautiful and well-born youths of that period—they do say what
his name was, but I don't remember it—and this youth for a while
marveled at Harmodius and Aristogeiton for their wisdom, but later,
after associating with Hipparchus, he despised them. They, being
greatly pained by this dishonor, killed Hipparchus for that reason.

COMRADE: Well then, Socrates, it seems that either you don't consider
e me your friend, or if you do, you aren't obeying Hipparchus. For that
you are not deceiving me in this argument—though I've no idea
how—I will never be persuaded.

SOCRATES: But on the contrary, I am willing, as in a game of draughts,
to let you change anything you want of what was said in the argument
so that you won't think you are being deceived. Should I make this
change for you, that the good things are not desired by all human
beings?

---

[15]The "reign of Cronos" in Greek mythology was an ancient period when Cronos,
the father of Zeus, ruled perfectly and dispelled all human ills (Hesiod, *Works and
Days*, 109–26; Plato, *Laws*, 713b–714a; *Statesman*, 269a–273e). On this analogy to
the rule of the Peisistratids, see Aristotle *Constitution of Athens*, XVI, 7. Thucydides
says (VI, 54) that the rule of Peisistratus and his sons was generally mild and salutary
and became harsh only after the assassination of Hipparchus.

[16]The word *paidika* is derived from the word for "boy." One of its uses was, in the
terminology of pederasty, to denote the beloved, hence "darling" or "favorite."

[17]Aristogeiton was a man of the middle class, according to Thucydides (VI, 54), who
was in love with the young and beautiful Harmodius. The two of them together
plotted against the tyranny and killed Hipparchus. Harmodius and Aristogeiton were
celebrated by the Athenian democracy of the fifth century as tyrannicides and cham-
pions of democracy. For the details of the story of Harmodius and Aristogeiton to
which Plato alludes here, see Thucydides' account.

COMRADE: No, no.

SOCRATES: Or that suffering loss, or loss, is not bad?

COMRADE: No, no.

SOCRATES: Or that profit and making profit are not opposite to loss and suffering loss?

230a COMRADE: Not that either.

SOCRATES: Or that making profit, as the opposite of bad, is not good?

COMRADE: It isn't always; change that for me.

SOCRATES: Then it is your opinion, it seems, that some profit is good, and some bad.

COMRADE: It is.

SOCRATES: Then I'll change that for you: Let some profit be good and some other bad. And neither of them is more profit than the other, neither the good nor the bad, is it?

COMRADE: Just what are you asking me?

SOCRATES: I'll explain. There is some food that is good and some that is bad?

b COMRADE: Yes.

SOCRATES: Well, is one of them more food than the other, or are they both similarly this same thing, food, and in this respect at least no different at all one from the other inasmuch as they are food but only inasmuch as one of them is good and the other bad?

COMRADE: Yes.

SOCRATES: And so for drink and everything else that exists, when some things that are the same come to be good and others bad, the
c one does not differ from the other in that respect whereby they are the same? Just as with human beings, I suppose, one is decent and another is evil.

COMRADE: Yes.

SOCRATES: But neither of them, I think, is more or less a human being—not the decent more than the evil nor the evil more than the decent.

COMRADE: What you say is true.

SOCRATES: Then are we not of this mind too about profit, that both the evil and the decent sort are equally profit?

COMRADE: Necessarily.

SOCRATES: So then he who gets a decent profit doesn't make any more
d gain than he who gets an evil one; it appears rather that neither one is more profit, as we agree.

COMRADE: Yes.

SOCRATES: For "more" or "less" is not attached to either one.

COMRADE: No, indeed.

SOCRATES: And how could anyone ever do or suffer anything either more or less with something like that, to which neither of these things is attached?

COMRADE: It is impossible.

SOCRATES: So now, since both are equally profit, and profitable, we have to consider, on account of what you call both alike profit: what

e do you see in both of them that is the same? Just as if you were to ask me, about the previous examples, on what account I call both good food and bad food equally food, I would say to you that it is because both are dry nourishment for the body—simply on account of that. You would also agree, I suppose, that that is what food is, wouldn't you?

COMRADE: I would.

SOCRATES: And concerning drink the answer would be of the same

231a manner, that the wet nourishment of the body, whether decent or evil, has this name, drink, and similarly for the others. Try therefore to imitate me by answering in the same way. When you say that decent profit and evil profit are both profit, what do you see to be the same in both—the thing that is actually profit? If you are unable yourself to answer again, consider what I say next: do you call a profit every possession that one has obtained either by spending nothing or by spending less and getting more?

b COMRADE: Yes, I think I would call that profit.

SOCRATES: Are you referring to some such things as this, where one is treated to a feast, spending nothing while being regaled, but then becomes sick?

COMRADE: By Zeus I am not!

SOCRATES: Becoming healthy instead from the feast, would he be getting a profit or a loss?

COMRADE: A profit.

SOCRATES: Then this at least is not profit, obtaining just any possession.

COMRADE: No, indeed.

SOCRATES: And it is not a profit whenever it is bad? Or will one not obtain a profit by obtaining just any good thing?

COMRADE: Apparently one will if it is good.

c SOCRATES: While if it is bad, will not one suffer a loss?

COMRADE: So it seems to me.

SOCRATES: Do you see then, how you are coming round to the same thing? Profit appears to be good, and loss bad.

COMRADE: Well, I don't know what to say.

SOCRATES: Not unjustly are you bewildered. But still, answer this also:

if one obtains more than one has spent, do you claim that is a profit?

COMRADE: Not if it is bad, I say, but if one gets more gold or silver than one has spent.

d SOCRATES: Then let me ask you this: if one spends half a measure of gold and gets double in silver, has he got a profit or a loss?

COMRADE: A loss, surely, Socrates, for then his gold is only worth double instead of twelve times as much.

SOCRATES: Still, he has obtained more. Or isn't double more than half?

COMRADE: Not in worth, comparing silver and gold.

SOCRATES: So then it seems necessary to add the consideration of worth to profit. For now you are saying that silver, although more than gold, is not worth gold, while you say that gold, although less, is of equal worth.

e COMRADE: Absolutely; that's the way it is.

SOCRATES: Worth, then, is what is profitable, whether it is small or great, and the worthless what brings no profit.

COMRADE: Yes.

SOCRATES: Do you say that worth is worth anything except when it is possessed?

COMRADE: Yes, only when it is possessed.

SOCRATES: Furthermore, do you say that worth is the possession of what is disadvantageous or advantageous?

COMRADE: Surely what is advantageous.

SOCRATES: Now, isn't the advantageous good?

COMRADE: Yes.

232a SOCRATES: Well then, most courageous one, haven't we once again, for the third or fourth time, come to the agreement that the profitable is good?

COMRADE: So it seems.

SOCRATES: Do you remember from what point this discussion of ours began?

COMRADE: I think so.

SOCRATES: If you don't, I will remind you. You disagreed with me, arguing that the good do want to gain not from every profit but only from those profits that are good, not from the evil.

COMRADE: That's right.

b SOCRATES: And now doesn't the argument compel us to agree that all profits, small and large, are good?

COMRADE: For my part, Socrates, it has compelled rather than per-suaded me.

SOCRATES: Well, perhaps later it will persuade you as well. Now, though, whether you are persuaded or however you are disposed, you do at least agree that all profits are good for us, both small and large?

COMRADE: Yes, I agree.

SOCRATES: Do you agree too that all decent human beings want all good things or not?

COMRADE: I agree.

c SOCRATES: And you yourself said that the evil for their part love profit, whether small or large.

COMRADE: Yes, I did.

SOCRATES: Then according to your argument, all human beings would be profiteers, both the decent and the evil.

COMRADE: Apparently.

SOCRATES: Then if someone reproaches another with being a profiteer, it is not a correct reproach; for it so happens that the one making this reproach is himself of the same sort.

THE POLITICAL PHILOSOPHER
IN DEMOCRATIC SOCIETY:
THE SOCRATIC VIEW

IN AN AGE in which not only the alternatives of action but also those of thought have become peculiarly impoverished, it behooves us to search for the lost, profound possibilities of human life. We are in need of a comprehensive reflection on the ends of politics, but we are confronted with a host of objections which make that enterprise seem impossible. A return to the origins of political philosophy—that is, a return to Socrates—is requisite if we are to clarify the nature of political philosophy and elaborate its intention and possibility. This attempt to recapture the original project of the political philosopher is a difficult one because we are searching without knowing quite what we are looking for; hence it is hard to know when we have found it. The best beginning is to focus our attention and efforts on those works which have least in common with our mode of treating problems and which were once taken seriously by serious men but are hard for us to take seriously. Writers like Isocrates and Xenophon have fallen into disfavor, but it is precisely from their rhetoric and restraint that we could learn of the taste of Thucydides and Plato and of the capital importance of the virtue of moderation in the political thought of the ancient authors. When we do not understand Isocrates and Xenophon, we do not understand Thucydides and Plato. We see in these latter concerns of our own, and they lose their liberating effect. Our horizon is protected from attack by a habit of not noticing what is not comprehended by it. As a result, what is unknown and important takes on the guise of the commonplace or trivial for us.

One of the best antidotes for this kind of myopia is the study of the smaller Platonic dialogues. They are short, which in one sense makes them easier; for it is almost impossible to devote the appropriate attention to every line, every word, of a book the length of the *Laws*;

our eye skips over what ought to be perplexing; time does not permit
the attention to the incredibly elaborate detail, nor are our intelli-
gences ordinarily competent to the survey of such a large, complex
whole. A dialogue which is a few pages long permits one to wonder
over every detail, to ask innumerable questions of the text, to use on
it every resource of intellect, passion, and imagination. In another
sense, though, these small dialogues are much more difficult, for they
are so strange. With the *Republic*, for example, a long tradition of
philosophy tells us what the issues are; we know that the question is
justice and the best regime. When we read the sections on the good
and knowledge, we feel at home because we see them as parts of a
great discussion which has been going on in Western thought for two
and a half millennia, a discussion participated in by Locke, Kant, and
Nietzsche, who use the same terms as does Plato. This sense of familiarity may be spurious; we may be reading the text as seen by the
tradition rather than raising Plato's own questions, interpreting all of
the foreign elements in the book in the light of questions posed to it
by later thinkers. This is, of course, the danger; for if we cannot
understand dialogues which do not contain the well-known themes,
it means that we do not really know what Plato was about or what
the dialogue form is and means. Still and all, we do feel at home in
the big, famous dialogues. But when we come to a dialogue like the
Ion, what are we to say about Socrates' meeting with a stupid reciter
of the Homeric poems whom Socrates treats like an oracle, to whom
he attributes divine inspiration, and who, at the end, in desperation
at his incapacity to define himself in the face of Socrates' sophistic
arguments, insists that he is Greece's greatest general? It all seems too
mad. What is the philosophic significance of all this? Each of the
smaller dialogues has this strange character. The scholarly reaction to
such curious works has been to ignore them, to consider them spurious
because Socrates would never have engaged in such discussions nor
Plato recorded them, or to treat them as logical exercises, propaedeutic
to real philosophy.

I would suggest that the big dialogues cannot be understood without understanding the little ones first, for the former are responses to
problems elaborated in the latter, responses which become meaningful
only against the background of those problems. Plato was more interested in posing the proper questions than in providing answers.
Perhaps the most important question of all is what is philosophy, how
is it possible, and why is it necessary? Philosophy emerges late in
human history; it was still new in Socrates' time. It is not coeval with
man as families, cities, and the useful arts seem to be. It could not

be taken for granted. It also was suspected, ridiculed, and hated. It not only had to constitute itself; it had to defend itself. The little dialogues characterize Socrates', and hence philosophy's, confrontation with the opinions or conventions out of which philosophy emerged, the confrontation with the authoritative views of the pious, the poets, the statesmen, the people at large, etc. In other words, these dialogues sketch out the images on the wall of the cave, reveal their inadequacy, and point toward the road upward; they present the first, the commonsense horizon of man, the horizon which must be transcended but which must first be known in order to be transcended. Every explanation of the world presupposes a rich apprehension of the phenomena of the world; otherwise that explanation will be as impoverished as is the awareness which it seeks to clarify. Plato elaborates the commonsense horizon in the little dialogues. Each of the interlocutors represents an archetypical prejudice. Their arguments are always poor, but they are poor because something in their souls attaches them to falsehood. Thus, if we see the reasons for the poor arguments, we learn of the complexity of the soul as well as of the various views of what is most important to believe and know. These dialogues canvass the types of human soul and the most powerful prephilosophic opinions about the true and the good. They appear mad, because the common sense of this world is always somehow self-contradictory or askew; if pushed to its conclusion it leads to absurdity in thought and action, and it is precisely this character of common sense that necessitates philosophy and makes its emergence difficult. Philosophy, unlike the prejudices it seeks to replace, must be aware of its origins and its reason for being. The smaller dialogues are necessary to us because they unambiguously force us to learn Plato's mode of interpretation of the world and because they are almost indispensable aids to the enrichment of our consciousness so vital to any nonabstract pursuit of clarity about the most important questions.

Now the *Hipparchus* is one of two dialogues Socrates carries on with an unnamed companion. The other is the *Minos*. Because the dialogue is acted out directly, we can learn nothing of the setting, the occasion for the meeting of the two men or any other detail which might reveal its intention. Both the *Hipparchus* and the *Minos* begin with the most profound Socratic question "What is . . . ?," the *Minos* investigating the nature of law and the *Hipparchus* that of profit, and both culminate in a provocative, extravagant, and unsubstantiated praise of a man usually thought to be an enemy of Athens, after whom the dialogue is named. A foreign oppressor is involved with respect to the law, a domestic tyrant with respect to profit. The similarities

between the two dialogues make their differences interesting and revealing. Minos is the son of a god and has intercourse with him;
Hipparchus is the son of a human being and no mention of the gods
is made in the dialogue except for four oaths of the companion. Perhaps
connected with the foregoing observations is the fact that Socrates is
peculiarly brutal to his companion in the *Hipparchus*. This fact is
certainly related to the further fact that Hipparchus, the man praised,
was a tyrant.

The *Hipparchus*, like the *Minos*, has a double title; it is "Hipparchus or The Profiteer" (I translate *philokerdēs* as "profiteer," for that
about matches the moral tone of the Greek). Perhaps the two are
meant to be identical; if so, the praise of Hipparchus would be most
revealing.

As already stated, the first words of the dialogue put the Socratic
question, and it is put by Socrates himself. He is trying to learn from
the companion, asking what kind of a thing profiteering is. It is a
naïve question, one that makes Socrates look like the unworldly inhabitant of the thinktank Aristophanes put him into, now venturing
forth into the world to find out about the human things known to
everyone else. We obviously enter a conversation that has already
begun, and we do not know the reason Socrates puts his question to
his companion, who is quite willing to instruct him, but we may
suppose that the companion had said something denigrating about
profiteers and Socrates wanted to know what was wrong with them.

"What is profiteering?" is indeed in the form of an authentic
Socratic question, but it is really ill put, or a secondary question, for
the answer to it depends on a prior answer to the question "What is
profit?" The neglect of the more fundamental question results in the
totally unsatisfactory character of the whole discussion, for the companion and the Socrates clearly mean different things, and the companion is unaware of even the possibility of such a difference. But this
is not what we would today call a difficulty of communication, for it
would clearly be beyond the capacity of the companion to grasp what
Socrates holds to be profitable; if Socrates were to explain that to
him, the companion would merely hear words. Although the discussion in that case might not arrive at its ultimate impasse, their agreement would be merely formal, for the companion would still continue
prizing the things he had always prized. The difficulty in speech reveals
a difficulty in the soul of the companion; the insufficiency of the
conversation is a condition of a sufficient representation of that soul
which necessarily holds self-contradictory opinions. The interesting
thing about the conversation is its development of the views typically

held by a man such as the companion and particularly the relation of those views to the life of Socrates.

The companion holds that money, or what it represents, is what is good. The word "profit" for him means what it means today to most men in commercial societies. They might be aware of a broader sense of the term, but that sense is not what they primarily mean when they use the term. The attachment to money is really identical to the attachment to life and comfort and, according to Socrates, is the motivation of the great majority of men. The companion, hence, belongs to, and represents, that lowest class of the *Republic* which Socrates calls the money-loving or profiteering class, even though the companion professes to berate profiteers. His exclusive concern for money is made explicit only at the end of the discussion, but it motivates his responses from the beginning. The discussion never moves beyond the companion's understanding of profit. It would have been easy to make it do so, for few men are willing in speech to admit that they care solely for safety and comfort; something forces them to recognize that there are nobler objects, but in deed most men care more for the useful than the noble. The *Hipparchus* investigates the moral taste of such men; Socrates facilitates this intention by not mentioning the companion's motive and only questioning its consequences, for in this way that motive operates unabashedly, unaffected by the shame exposure would cause.

225   Socrates asks a double question: what is profiteering and who are
a–b   the profiteers? The companion chooses to tell who the profiteers are, proving that he is less interested in the nature of the thing than in attacking a certain kind of man. He formulates it with rhetorical elegance: profiteers are those who think it is worth profiting from what is worthless. His meaning is immediately obvious—he means cheaters, those who sell useless things by deceit, the most common type of fraudulent business operators—but that meaning is not obvious to Socrates. He naïvely asks whether they know that the things are worthless, adding that they would be fools if they did not. Socrates, Candide-like, apparently does not know that there are men who would deceive others about the worth of things, and the companion is eager to inform him of the hard ways of the world, expecting to gain an ally in his war against the vicious. The companion in his assurance as to Socrates' meaning and his haste to make his condemnation of the profiteers fails to notice the ambiguity of Socrates' question. He takes it that Socrates wants to know if the profiteers make a profit by selling something the value of which they mistakenly overestimate; this would mean they could not be blamed; one must know one is

committing a crime if one is to be considered responsible for it; since
the companion wishes to blame the profiteers, he must insist on their
full knowledge. But Socrates' question could, and should, be interpreted to mean that if something is simply worthless, one cannot profit
from it, and only a fool would try to. There are two senses of worth
here, worth for making profit and worth for the buyer. Socrates begins
to play on their double sense, not to confuse the companion but
because it represents a real, unresolved problem in the companion's
own thought. The companion believes the profiteers actually do get
something good, although he himself may be hurt by their doing so.
He concentrates on the harm done to others, including himself, by
profiteers, whereas Socrates seems indifferent to that and seems to
concentrate on the efficacy of the profiteers' quest for profit. The
companion, in reassuring Socrates that the profiteers certainly do know
what they are doing, manifests a certain envy of the profiteers, calling
them wicked and villains. Of course, he who makes a quick killing is
no fool; he gets his own good at the expense of others. The companion
believes, as do all those who speak in this way, that he knows what
is profitable and that there is a conflict between private and public
good, and he condemns the pursuit of private good in order to protect
the public good. The profiteer is daring; he is shameless. Shame, fear
of the opinion of others, prevents men from being profiteers; but shame
or no shame, it remains that what the profiteer gets is truly profitable
to him. The more advantageous the profiteer's dealings are, the more
intense is the blame. Socrates, however, does not share the companion's ambivalence. Rather than looking naïve, he might on closer
examination appear shameless himself; he is not shocked at men's
profiting from the worthless; he is merely curious as to whether it can
be done. He attempts to indicate this to the companion by citing the
example of a farmer. Would a farmer think it is worth profiting from
planting a worthless plant? The companion, not responding to Socrates' hint, answers that a profiteer supposes he should profit from
everything.

The example, to which the companion paid no attention, is
actually quite revealing. The farmer and the profiteer both aim at
increase; if a farmer's plants are worthless, they will not grow; if the
profiteer sows worthless seeds of profit, they will not grow into profits.
Judging from the point of view of the farmer and the profiteer, no
worthless means can achieve their ends. The companion would readily
admit this for the farmer, but he does not see the analogy between
farmer and profiteer. The farmer's harvest is produced by nature and
has a natural use value, whereas the profiteer harvests a crop of con-

ventional money. It is precisely the disproportion between the natural or use value of things and what people will pay for them that the profiteer exploits and the companion complains about. But the companion is a lover of money and takes its pursuit to be natural. Thus he would really have to accept the comparison between a farmer's planting and a profiteer's investing and hence have to evaluate the worth of the means in relation to the achievement of the ends. Money, as Aristotle and Marx also saw, is ambiguous: it can represent the natural value of things, or it can be valuable in itself; in the former case it would be measured by the things, in the latter the things would be measured by it. Thus money can become an end in itself and can be desired in infinite amounts, divorced from any possible use, as opposed, say, to artichokes. The love of money, beginning from a natural desire for future power, gradually makes a man a prisoner of conventional value and alienates him from even the consideration of natural worth. The companion loves money and, at the same time, wants those who sell to him to be more concerned with natural worth or usefulness than money. The companion, in order to avoid contradiction, would have to distinguish between worth in money to the seller and worth in use to the buyer and elaborate the consequences of that distinction. But he is hopelessly confused about it, and this confusion is vitally linked to his whole view of men and things.

225b–
226a
Socrates responds brutally to the companion's assertion that the profiteer supposes he should profit from everything. He tells him to stop answering aimlessly like a man who has suffered some injustice at someone's hands. The sense of injustice suffered causes a man to make irrelevant answers, according to Socrates; he implies that indignation, at least in the companion's case, is only a form of selfish revenge and high principles only a form of self-protection. Indignation, outrage at injustice, only cloud serious consideration of important questions. Socrates, most uncharacteristically, banishes considerations of justice in favor of those of profit. At this point in the discussion he appears to deny the companion the possibility of saying that the profiteer is bad because he harms others, implying that the arguments against profiteering are merely made to protect one's own profit from cleverer seekers of profit. He treats the companion like an enemy, part of a conspiracy to deny him his own profit. He heightens this impression by making a contemptuous reference to the "wise phrases" clever men use in the courts of justice and mocking the rhetorical style of the companion's definition of profiteers. This moralism is a lot of high-flown talk designed to give a veneer of decency to a compact between men who do not believe in justice but wish to avoid suffering

injustice, a compact made to inhibit a man from knowing what his true profit is. The courts are the instruments of this conspiracy. Socrates accuses the companion of wilfully trying to deceive him. As the companion feared deception in money matters, so Socrates fears it in speeches. It would seem that to avoid the deceptions of the profiteer there is a tendency to deceive potential profiteers about the nature of profit. What in another context might have been identified as considerations of justice Socrates here qualifies as the contrivances of hypocrisy. Socrates charges the companion with wanting Socrates to believe what the companion does not himself believe. Presumably for the sake of self-protection, he wants to convince Socrates of the badness of the profiteers; thus the companion could rely on him.

226
a–d   By thus browbeating the companion, Socrates turns the conversation away from the blame of profiteering and does not permit him to introduce considerations of justice or the effect of profiteering on others. He takes the companion's assertion that the profiteers know that they are profiting from worthless things and converts it into the assertion that a profiteer is a knower, like all the artisans who know things. The farmer, the horse trainer, the pilot of a ship, and the general would never knowingly choose worthless means to gain their end; the end of each of the arts mentioned is clear, and the worth of the means is determined by the end of the art. One would never, for example, judge of the worth of the manure used in farming by the discomfort it causes passersby. Similarly the profiteer's means would properly be judged in relation only to his end, which is profit, and not to the effects of those means on others. He would certainly not use worthless things for profit in this sense, for it would be both contrary to the nature of the knower and impossible. And thus it turns out that according to the companion's definition no one is a profiteer; he blames men who do not exist.

We are of course outraged by this terrible argument, but it really does the companion full justice in the deeper sense. He is selfish; he loves money overmuch, but at the same time he wishes to restrict the pursuit of money so that a community, the precondition of his making money, can exist. It is somewhat like Locke's solution to the political problem. In this perspective not the pursuit of profit but the means used are blamed. But that community has no dignity; it is no different from a band of robbers. Such a community's laws can hardly compel a man of superior power to abandon his pursuit of profit. The moral prohibitions become empty, mere attempts to dupe him. In the most radical way, Socrates' argument concludes that the ends justify the means. It is a dangerous conclusion. The only way for the companion to avoid its dangerous consequences is for him to reconsider the ends.

226d–
227c This he now tries to do but in a fainthearted way, for neither his thought nor his tastes make him capable of discussing the hierarchy of goods—since he does not really believe there is one. He merely suggests that due to incontinence or insatiability men cling to things that are worth little or nothing. Thus he tries to find his way out of the maze by saying that profiteers are always worried about profit, meaning money, even when the gains are very small; uncontrolled passion causes them to be that way. This definition is an attack no longer on lack of shame but on lack of moderation. A man who controlled his passions would not want or need so much profit. The profiteer is motivated by a desire for gain which is not quite worthless but which is not worthwhile enough to justify his efforts. There is a praise of moderation implied in all of this, but there is no indication in the name of what; it is clear only that moderate men would not be likely to need to take advantage of other men, but what good moderation would be to its practitioners the companion in no way indicates. In order to salvage his condemnation of profiteers he now does speak of their ends and says that they are of very small weight; he is almost forced to say that profit is not important. Shame would cause a man to care about others and was a sufficient motivation for the comrade to encourage when he thought Socrates would share his concern; now he must argue that continence is good for the individual or that profit is not good. He can hardly believe this definition as he did the first, and Socrates easily overturns it. He rather illegitimately argues from their agreement about the means that the profiteers cannot know their ends are worthless. If they are ignorant, they cannot be blamed; they would need education. Men only pursue what they think to be good, so that, for the discussion, all that remains of the second definition is that profiteers have a passion for profit. Socrates establishes that profit is good, or even *the* good, by the negative road of getting the companion to admit that all loss is bad. The companion may have his doubts about profit for reasons of shame or fear, but loss he cannot accept. However, if profit is the opposite of loss, profit must be good. The companion and Socrates and all men love all good things and wish to possess them. Therefore all men are profiteers, and again profiteers cannot be blamed. The companion could only defend himself if he were to say that men should be judged on the basis of the adequacy of their understanding of the good, but he cannot, for he believes that the good is really known and its pursuit is shared by all men.

Socrates is gradually disarming the companion and breaking down all the barriers to selfish conduct to which the companion holds. He

has tantamount to defended shameless daring in the use of the means
to profit and immoderation in the pursuit of the end of profit.

227c–
228b

The companion makes a last effort to defend his condemnation
of profiteers. This he does by setting as a standard the conduct of
decent men, or gentlemen, and applying it to the consideration of
the ends and means of profit. He no longer insists that these ends or
means are worthless; he has learned he cannot argue that. Instead he
distinguishes between two kinds of men, the decent and the wicked,
and asserts that the profiteer is among the wicked, for he is serious
about things which no gentleman would be serious about and thinks
it is worth profiting from things no gentleman would dare to profit
from. If we can enter into the companion's world for a moment, we
can see what he is trying to do. He knows that there are some admirable
men, men faithful in their contracts, men whom one can trust. Such
men are somehow superior; they are proof against the temptations
ever present in human dealings. We blame profiteers because they do
not behave as such men do, whether it is from shamelessness or
extreme passion. The decent men, as it appears to the companion,
are not motivated by profit; their conduct cannot be understood in
terms of utility; decency and profit are irreducible, and if profit alone
were pursued, there would be no decency left in the world. The
companion thus both wishes profit and despises it in admiring those
who are superior to it. Although he tries to maintain the notion of
moral dignity, his view is in some sense low because he sees no profit
in decency. He is forced to say that there are good goods and bad
goods, and bad goods are those which are profitable but not such as
are pursued by decent men. But decency is then without motivation;
astonishingly, the companion's morality is like Kant's. Socrates, on
the other hand, insists that all desire and action must be motivated
by desire to possess the good; good and bad men are not distinguished
from one another by the latters' caring for their own good while the
former do not. On the companion's level, Socrates' teaching must
appear corrupt, for as he understands it, that teaching encourages men
to do whatever they want, or more specifically, to pursue money
without restraint. Only by denying that increase of money is profit
could that consequence be avoided, and this the companion will never
do, at least in his heart of hearts. And Socrates thus has put his finger
on the internal contradiction in the ordinary view of decency: it is
not held to be profitable itself, hence it is either useful for some other
goal or it is without ground and its practice folly. Profit has been
conceded by the companion to be good, but he must also say it is
bad, and so must anyone who is aware that there is a tension between

profitable conduct and decent conduct. Socrates, in his pursuit of the good, must again accuse the companion of deceiving him because the companion tries to stop him from his pursuit by saying that the good is bad.

Now the companion has been told by Socrates that any way of profiting is good, that we should pursue profit insatiably and that good men to not differ from bad ones in this decisive respect; and thus he, with an oath, must counter by accusing Socrates of deceiving him. The arguments seem to have removed all restraints on what the companion must assume to be Socrates' desire to do him harm; and Socrates is destroying the horizon without which the companion cannot orient himself. The companion learns about a new kind of cheating, the use of worthless arguments which he cannot understand. He wishes to repress the profiteering of the man who seeks knowledge that might be damaging to him just as much as he wishes to repress the profiteering of the man who seeks monetary gains that might be damaging to him. Socrates, since he has apparently destroyed all grounds for the companion's trusting him, must hasten to reassure him.

228b–
229d
Socrates adopts a fantastic mode of reassuring the companion. He tries to show him that he is a disciple of a man who did not believe in deceiving others, or rather, friends. In doing so he must also show that his master is a man to be admired, and thus, in this backhanded and implausible way, Socrates introduces the hero of the dialogue, Hipparchus. Only this digression, which disrupts the surface movements of the discussion and is apparently irrelevant to it, permits us to see its true intention. Socrates' procedure is odd from any point of view, for in making Hipparchus his authority, he refers to a man who is popularly considered to have been a tyrant, the most extreme example of what the companion has been attacking, the ultimately successful profiteer who has gained possession of the city and everything in it. Rather than identify himself with what is respectable and thereby prove his own respectability, Socrates has the insolence to choose the greatest villain known to the Athenian democracy, praise him, and expect to be respected for it. He modestly introduces Hipparchus as "our fellow citizen." Socrates suggests that the profiteer will indeed be beyond the law, will take advantage of others, will not want to accept the rule of equality which is dear to the companion; but he further suggests that such a profiteer is a superior man and that, if the companion will only let himself be taken advantage of, he will profit from being ruled by him. Hipparchus is, above all, motivated by the love of wisdom; as money is profit for the companion, so is wisdom profit for Hipparchus, who was willing to spend money lavishly on

procuring and displaying wisdom; he is a profiteer, a *philokerdēs*, but in his case this is identical with being a lover of wisdom, a *philosophos*. This is a new kind of profiteering, unknown to the companion, an insatiable thirst, one which defies the laws of equality but the satisfaction of which does not depend on taking from others but rather provides plenty for others without loss to itself. This is what Socrates was referring to when he spoke of profit, and here we get a hint of his side of a discussion in which we have thus far seen only the companion's side. In this perspective, Socrates' conclusions, which seemed so sinister to the companion, are not only innocent but salutary. But the companion would condemn this form of profiteering just as he did the other. It does not obey the rules so essential to the companion's self-protection; his condemnation of the low form of profiteering includes a condemnation of the high form, and Socrates' apparent defense of the low form is really a defense of the high to a man who cannot even imagine its existence. This explains Socrates' anger with the companion; the companion, in all his apparent respectability, is the enemy of philosophy.

But in order to clarify all this, we must investigate the Hipparchus story and particularly Thucydides' account of it. In this way, we can see what Socrates is doing against the background of reality. The Athenians believed that Hipparchus was an unjust tyrant and that he was assassinated by Harmodius and Aristogeiton out of a noble love of freedom. They were thus in the deepest sense the founders of Athenian democracy and were sacrificed to as divine beings. The goodness and necessity of Athenian democracy were proved by the terribleness of the alternative to it; the attachment to the democratic regime was strengthened by this belief, and anyone diverging from the principles of the democracy could be accused of tyrannical ambitions. The fear of tyranny, grounded in alleged Athenian experience, was a valuable tool for demagogues. Thucydides, in the context of the Athenian condemnation of Alcibiades after the mutilation of the Hermae, takes the occasion to subject this essential part of the Athenian tradition to closer scrutiny. He shows that the rule of the Peisistratid family was excellent prior to the assassination of Hipparchus and that the bad behavior of the tyrants was a result of the tyrannicides' deed. The whole Athenian account belongs to the realm of political myth. All of the details are wrong. Hippias was the tyrant; the plot against Hippias failed and only his younger brother Hipparchus was killed. Harmodius and Aristogeiton were motivated not by love of freedom but by revenge in a tawdry, subpolitical erotic scandal. The two lovers had only the remotest connection with the establishment of democracy. They rather caused the tyranny to become tyrannical; it was the Spartans, foreigners, who deposed the Peisistratids, and it is not at all clear that Harmodius' and Aristogeiton's deed had any part in producing this result. Thucydides in this correction of the popular account implicitly asks the question whether a tyranny is the worst possible alternative; he shows the unreasoning element in the treatment of Alcibiades. He makes it possible to think what is unthinkable and allows one to see out beyond the walls built in the mind by Athenian prejudice.

Socrates takes a different route to a goal not dissimilar to Thucydides'. In discussion with an Athenian, he accepts the story that Hipparchus was the ruler. He simply denies that the description of Hipparchus is accurate. Hipparchus is the victim of a calumny of the democrats, and if one were to understand the facts, one would wish to be ruled by him again, for his was the golden age and the Athenians lived as in the time of Cronos.

Socrates makes his own myth to counterpoise the Athenian one and thus liberates from Athenian prejudice, finding within Athens and its tradition a model for the regime and the man he understands to be good.

The salient aspects of the description of Hipparchus are the following: he was a lover of wisdom and was motivated by the desire to be admired for his wisdom. He therefore had to become an educator in order to make his subjects good enough to admire his virtues. There was a perfect proportion between his selfish interest and the common good. In order to be admired for his own wisdom he had to become an opponent of the prevailing wisdom, which was the Delphic wisdom, expressed best in the two phrases "Know thyself" and "Nothing too much." In response to these he set up Hermae throughout Attica, engraved with such examples of his wisdom as these: "Walk thinking just thoughts" and "Don't deceive a friend."

These two wise sayings do not appear to rival those of the Delphic oracle, but reflection may at least help to give some indication of what might be considered wise in them. A hint is provided by the *Charmides* where the potential tyrant Critias in discussing moderation interprets the two Delphic utterances as meaning the same thing; a man who knows himself does nothing in excess; the Delphic teaching is one of moderation. And in combating it Hipparchus carries forward the criticism of moderation which dominated the first part of the dialogue. It was precisely the refutation of the arguments for vulgar moderation that forced Socrates to try to find a substitute for it that can guarantee decent human intercourse, and Hipparchus' sayings are supposed to

be that substitute. Following Critias' lead, we might suggest that Hipparchus' two sayings are also identical: justice is not deceiving friends.
To put it otherwise, a man should behave decently toward others not
because he has restrained his passions or given up his satisfaction but
because they are friends, because his satisfaction comes from benefiting
them. There are two opposed notions of justice, the one conceiving
of justice as unprofitable duty, the other as the satisfaction of giving
their deserts to those whom one loves. The former, a more political
view, concentrates on men's opposition of interests and provides what
is necessary for a community; the latter, more fitting to the private
life, concentrates on what men can have in common and the mutual
satisfactions of worthy men. Hipparchus' dictum is the principle by
which Socrates guided his life.

If one is not to deceive a friend, he must know the truth, and
he must find other men who are capable of learning it from him. The
real solution to the companion's impasse is not "Don't deceive a friend"
but philosophy, which that exhortation implies. It is the only way of
life which is both of profit to its practitioner and of benefit to those
with whom he associates. This is of course not a political solution,
for it implies a community composed only of the wise or the potentially
wise, which is impossible. But Socrates' description of Hipparchus'
politics contains a justification of his own life.

In order to support this praise of Hipparchus, Socrates must explain why he was assassinated and convert the conventional praise of
Harmodius and Aristogeiton into blame. He accepts without question
that the motives were erotic, but this is in no sense blameworthy in
his eyes. Eros seems to constitute the core of life, and Hipparchus
founded a regime in which eros can enjoy its full rights. Education is
understood as an erotic activity or at least as closely bound up with
it, and Hipparchus' ruling is only education. The true story, according
to Socrates, is that Aristogeiton was a rival educator (perhaps of
Delphic persuasion) and had loved and educated Harmodius, who in
turn had loved a well-born boy. This boy began by admiring the older
men's wisdom but had come to despise them after meeting Hipparchus.
Because they were enraged at this dishonor, they slew Hipparchus. In
this account, Hipparchus was not the unrequited lover who insulted
the sister of Harmodius; Harmodius is the unrequited lover and Hipparchus an object of love. He was lovable because he was wise and
was slain because his wisdom alienated the affections of the best of
the young.

I submit that this tale of Hipparchus is nothing but a description
of Socrates, and the intention of telling it is only to explain why

Socrates was later put to death. Both Hipparchus and Socrates met death as a result of the envy of democrats who claimed that the youth were corrupted by their teachings. Socrates, like Hipparchus, was a lover of wisdom who benefited his friends by educating them and who competed with the Delphic oracle. He leads those who listen to him away from respect for the community and its leaders; he teaches them the immoderate pursuit of the good. Anytus, the major accuser of Socrates, was in later times said to have been a frustrated lover of Alcibiades, who himself said that he became a lover of Socrates. At all events, Anytus appears in Socrates' trial as the defender of the Athenian young against the Socratic seductiveness. I would suggest that as Socrates equals Hipparchus, Anytus equals Harmodius, and Alcibiades equals the nameless youth. Just as Harmodius turned to Aristogeiton, Anytus turns to his educator and lover, the Athenian *dēmos*, for aid in revenging himself on Socrates for stealing Alcibiades away. Just as Hipparchus and Aristogeiton were the real enemies there, Socrates and the *dēmos* are the real enemies here. Alcibiades despised the justice of the *dēmos*, and this was blamed, not totally without basis, on Socrates. Socrates silently exculpates himself by expressing reverence for the Hermae Alcibiades was accused of mutilating. But in spite of that, those Hermae were not meant to be protectors of the democracy, and Hipparchus is no friend to it. The little story of Hipparchus reiterates a well-known Socratic teaching: the wise should rule and should certainly never be ruled by the many.

Now how does all of this relate to the companion and his argument? Very simply: the companion wants to impose the morality of the *dēmos* on Socrates and would ultimately be willing to destroy him if he does not accede. That morality consists in the restraint, according to the rules necessary to the existence of a community, of the pursuit of certain profitable things which are scarce and can be the sources of strife among men; it is the morality of private property. As revealed in the first section of the dialogue, Socrates cannot accept this morality, and his own teaching undermines it, at least in principle. One can say that the companion really holds that men are equal, in the sense that they all equally desire money and the things represented by it. The distinction among them is only in the way they pursue the satisfaction of that desire; the good men are those who play by the rules, the bad ones are those who do not. Men who pursue profit without restraint are enemies, and this is what Socrates does. It is a different kind of profit that the companion means, to be sure, but his net catches philosophers as well as bandits or embezzlers. Socrates' students would not be reliable citizens of a democracy, and Socrates

himself does not hold that the lovers of wisdom should accept the way
of life set down by the lovers of money. They want democracy; he is
apparently a proponent of monarchy.

The first two parts of the dialogue present two kinds of lovers of
profit, the lover of money and the lover of wisdom, and their necessary
conflict. With the praise of Hipparchus, Socrates has revealed himself
and manifested the source of the difficulty in the first part. The companion is really a praiser of Harmodius and Aristogeiton, for he can
flourish in the regime of which they are the founders, just as Socrates
would have flourished in the regime founded by Hipparchus. The first
and second parts elaborate the conflict between the two men; the
third is meant to be a resolution of sorts.

229d–   Not surprisingly, Socrates fails to persuade the companion of the
230a   validity of his earlier arguments by his invocation of Hipparchus. The
companion says that either Socrates does not consider him to be a
friend or he is not persuaded by Hipparchus. It would be hard for
Socrates to disprove him on either count. Socrates' speeches seem to
the companion to be like those of a profiteer; he deceives in argument,
as do profiteers in business matters, but he is unable to find out quite
where or how Socrates does it. He distrusts the cleverer, unconven-
tional arguer. So Socrates inducts him into the art of dialectic to see
whether he can learn and whether argument can persuade him. The
companion is given the opportunity, as in chess, to change any of his
earlier moves. Quite appropriately he returns to the attempt to distinguish between good and bad profit; he wishes to revoke his agreement that all profit is good. He appears to be thinking of something
like the difference between money made in honest trade and that
acquired in a bank robbery. He has steadily resisted the impetus of
the argument tending to regard the one as just as legitimate as the
other.

230a–   Socrates begins the examination of the companion's assertion by
231c   making explicit a general rule implied in that assertion: a thing is as
much what it is whether it is good or bad; good does not relate to the
being of a thing, it is rather something a thing undergoes, an accident
of being. Bad food, drink, or men *are* as much as good food, drink,
or men. This may be a questionable rule, but it certainly reflects the
companion's view: the money in itself is still money—and desirable—
no matter how acquired. He accepts it readily. The next step is to
define profit. At last this most essential question is posed. Socrates
suggests an answer. Profit is spending nothing or little and getting
back more. This is, of course, also readily accepted by the companion.
Then Socrates suggests an example: a man gets a free dinner and then

gets sick from it. Is that a profit? By Zeus, no! (The companion's oaths always reinforce his powerful awareness of his own self-interest.) The companion is brought back from the world of money to that of nature; he sees that he must define profit not in terms of more or less money but in terms of its human effects. Health is naturally good and food must be judged in relation to it. Having begun from the premise that a thing does not exist more or less due to its goodness or badness, we now end with the companion's asserting that a thing does not exist if it is not good. The good, originally taken to be irrelevant to nature, comes back as the cause of being. There can be no such thing as bad profit.

In order to see the deeper sense of this curious result, we must apply it to one of the examples mentioned, apparently casually, by Socrates—man. It was admitted that a man is a man whether he is good or bad; now it would appear that if he is not good, he is not a man. Socrates defined food and drink in terms of their function, as nourishment of the body. If they do not perform that function, they are not food and drink but mere shadows. It would follow that a man who did not fulfill his function as a man is not a man.

Such a conclusion would have profound political consequences. What has the shape of a man but does not fulfill the function of a man would not be treated in the same way as one who does. Just as the companion does not want to admit a hierarchy of profits, he does not want to admit a hierarchy of men. This understanding of man is democratic: all men are equal and have equal rights in the political community, the only distinction among them being made on the basis of their obeying the rules of that community. But Socrates, in the same way he has forced the companion to deny the equality of profits, or that much of what appears to be profit is profit, silently forces him to deny the equality of men, or that many who appear to be men are men. Food was judged in relation to health of the body; men would be judged in relation to health of the soul. Socrates' understanding is profoundly aristocratic or even monarchic. The companion may have thought he was protecting the principle of equality in all of its forms in accepting the general rule; further probing resulted in his being forced to abandon the principles on which he bases his life.

231c–
232b At this reversal of his position the companion confesses himself at a loss, in an *aporia*, or, as I would like to translate, without means. No amount of money or power can help him out here. Socrates tells him that it is not unjustly that he is without means, applying a new standard of justice, and reiterates the earlier definition of profit, spending less and getting more. The companion testily replies that he does

not mean that getting more of something bad is profitable, but it is profitable if one gets more gold or silver. Socrates asks if it is a profit to spend a certain weight in gold and get twice that weight in silver. The companion eagerly replies that it would be a great loss. It is clear that it is not more or less that determines profit but worth. Gold is worth more than silver. One must know worth first of all; one wants more of what is worth something. The companion throughout has thought that determination of worth is a simple matter; everybody knows the worth of things measured in money. But how is it determined that gold is worth more than silver? That is merely a convention which has no relation to the human benefits connected with each, and it is the human benefits Socrates has been talking about. The companion is hopelessly conventional.

Money is what is worthwhile, according to the companion; the only way of distinguishing among men, then, is in their way of pursuing it, their means. For Socrates there are various levels of worthwhile things, and the primary way of distinguishing among men is in what they pursue as worthwhile, their ends. The political consequence of this is that, for the companion, the purpose of law would be to regulate the means of pursuing profit in such a way as to ensure the possibility of the existence of civil society, which, in its turn, is necessary for the pursuit of profit. Law would inevitably be the will of the community of lovers of money expressing their self-interest. For Socrates the primary standard for a law would be that which conduces to the benefit of the members of the community of true human beings. One can see why the companion and Socrates are at war.

The companion, because he is torn between his belief that everything can be measured and bought with money and his awareness that there are natural goods like health, does again have to agree that profit is benefit and consequently that the profitable is always good, thus contradicting himself. He does not really see that it is the value of money that is called into question; he believes that it is the basis of morality that has been placed in doubt by Socrates. That would indeed be the result of Socrates' teaching for a man who believed money to be profit, since men should pursue the good and profit is good. It is hence a dangerous teaching.

232   The companion must now accept that good men want all possible
b–c   profit, whether great or small. He can no longer blame the profiteers. But he must if he is to protect his vital interests. He can see no unbridled pursuit of profit which would not be dangerous. Socrates tells him that the argument has compelled them to accept that the good men are profiteers. The companion responds that he is compelled

but not persuaded. That does not seem to disturb Socrates; for if a man's passions prevent him from responding to the persuasion of reason, if his limitations, intellectual and moral, make it impossible for him to care for truth rather than gain, he should not be allowed to rule those who are capable of reason. He must be compelled, at least to the extent he impinges on the life of the others. Socrates is introducing a new tyranny, based on the force of argument. This accounts for his praise of Hipparchus and his tyrannical tone with the companion. If he cannot rule the companion, the companion will rule him. He tells the companion that his blame of profiteering is only hypocrisy inasmuch as he himself is a profiteer. His blame is his way of protecting his own profit at Socrates' expense. To compromise with him would be to compromise the higher with the lower, true profit with sham profit. Although this can in no sense result in a practical political proposal, the analysis of the companion and his thought indicates that he should not be treated with the concern or respect due a human being. The *Republic* is an attempt to find a regime in which philosophers are not ruled by such men, and the observations made by Socrates in this dialogue have a profound effect on the way he lives his life in democratic Athens, which is not the *Republic*. Maimonides sums up the teaching of the *Hipparchus* when speaking of the way in which a philosopher should live among his fellows: "He should . . . regard all people according to their various states with respect to which they are indubitably either like domestic animals or like beasts of prey. If the perfect man who lives in solitude thinks of them at all, he does so only with a view to saving himself from the harm that may be caused by those among them who are harmful if he happens to associate with them, or to obtaining an advantage that may be obtained from them if he is forced to it by some of his needs." This is the resolution, provided in the third part, of the antagonism presented in the first two parts of this very radical statement of the ancient view of the relation between the wise man and civil society.

ION

OR ON THE ILIAD

TRANSLATED BY ALLAN BLOOM

SOCRATES; ION

530a SOCRATES: Ion, welcome. From where do you come to visit us now? From your home at Ephesus?

ION: Not at all, Socrates, but from the festival of Asclepius at Epidaurus.

SOCRATES: You don't mean to say that the Epidaureans dedicate a contest of rhapsodes to the god, too?[1]

ION: Indeed they do, and also for the other parts of music.

SOCRATES: Tell me, did you compete for us? And how did you do in the competition?

b ION: We carried off first prize, Socrates.

SOCRATES: You speak well,[2] and see to it that we conquer at the Panathenaia,[3] too.

ION: But it will be so, god willing.

SOCRATES: Well now, I have often envied you rhapsodes, Ion, for your art. For that it befits your art for the body to be always adorned and

---

[1] Athletic and musical competitions were held in Epidaurus (a town in the Peloponnese not far from Athens) in honor of its patron Asclepius, god of healing. Ephesus was a Greek city in Asia Minor.

[2] Literally, "you speak well" (*eu legeis*). The idiom—"good" would be a more colloquial translation—is a common one, but the literal sense seems to acquire thematic importance in this dialogue; cf. 531c–532a, 536d. It is related to the expressions "you speak correctly or rightly" (*orthōs legeis*), "you speak truly" (*alēthē legeis*), and above all, "you speak finely, nobly, or beautifully" (*kalōs legeis*), all of which occur frequently in the dialogue.

[3] The great Panathenaia was a festival celebrated every four years at Athens in honor of its patron goddess, Athena. There was also a small Panathenaia celebrated every year.

for you to appear as beautiful as possible, and that, at the same time, it is necessary to be busy with many good poets and above all with Homer, the best and most divine of the poets, and to learn his thought
c thoroughly, not just his words, is enviable. Because one could never be a good rhapsode if he did not understand the things said by the poet. The rhapsode must be the interpreter of the thought of the poet to the listeners, but to do this finely is impossible for the one who does not recognize what the poet means. All these things, then, deserve to be envied.

ION: You speak truly, Socrates. For me, at any rate, this part of the art requires the most work, and I suppose that I speak most finely of
d all human beings about Homer—that neither Metrodorus of Lampsacus nor Stesimbrotus the Thasian nor Glaucon[4] nor anyone else who has ever lived has had so many fine thoughts to speak about Homer as I.

SOCRATES: You speak well, Ion. And it is evident that you won't begrudge me a display.

ION: It is surely worth hearing, Socrates, how well I have adorned Homer—so that I suppose I deserve to be crowned with a golden crown by the Homeridae.[5]

SOCRATES: And I shall surely yet find the leisure to listen to you. But
531a now answer me this much: are you clever[6] about Homer alone or about Hesiod and Archilochus, too?[7]

ION: Not at all, but only about Homer, for that seems sufficient to me.

SOCRATES: And is there any matter about which both Hesiod and Homer say the same things?

ION: I suppose there are—many.

SOCRATES: About these matters, then, would you give a finer explanation of what Homer says than of what Hesiod says?

ION: A similar one, about those matters, at least, about which they say the same things.

---

[4]Metrodorus of Lampsacus, a friend of the philosopher Anaxagoras, had interpreted Homer allegorically, understanding the various deities as representations of natural phenomena. Stesimbrotus of Thasos was another early practitioner of allegorical interpretation and apparently composed a book on Homer. Of Glaucon nothing is known.
[5]Originally a guild of poets claiming descent from Homer but generally applied to his admirers (cf. *Republic,* 599e).
[6]*Deinos:* literally, "terrible." The word was commonly applied to an effective speaker.
[7]Hesiod's *Theogony* is an early systematization of Greek theology; it was considered only slightly less authoritative than the Homeric poems themselves. Archilochus was generally regarded as the originator of iambic or lyric poetry.

b SOCRATES: But what about those matters about which they do not say the same things? For example, both Homer and Hesiod say something about divination.

ION: Certainly.

SOCRATES: Well then, of the things these two poets say about divination that are similar and those that are different, would you give a finer explanation or would one of the good diviners?

ION: One of the diviners.

SOCRATES: If you were a diviner would you not, if indeed you were able to explain the things said similarly, know also how to explain the things said differently?

ION: It's plain that I would.

c SOCRATES: Why, then, are you clever about Homer but not about Hesiod or any of the other poets? Or does Homer speak about other things than what all the other poets speak about? Didn't he tell about war for the most part, and about the associations with one another of good human beings and bad ones, and private ones and those in public works, and about gods' associating with one another and with human beings—how they associate—and about the events in the

d heavens and those in Hades and the begettings of both gods and heroes? Are not these things about which Homer has made his poetry?

ION: You speak truly, Socrates.

SOCRATES: And what of the other poets? Don't they make poetry about these same things?

ION: Yes, but, Socrates, they have not made poetry in a way similar to Homer.

SOCRATES: How then? Worse?

ION: Very much.

SOCRATES: Homer is better?

ION: Better indeed, by Zeus!

SOCRATES: Dearest Ion, when there are many men speaking about number and someone speaks best, won't there be someone who recognizes the one who speaks well?

ION: I should say so.

e SOCRATES: Does this same man also know the one speaking badly, or is it someone else?

ION: The same one, surely.

SOCRATES: And isn't this the one who has the arithmetical art?

ION: Yes.

SOCRATES: What of this? In a situation where many are speaking about what sorts of foods are healthy and a single person speaks best, will it be one man who recognizes that the person speaking best does speak best while another recognizes that the person speaking worse does speak worse? Or will it be the same man?

ION: Plainly, to be sure, the same man.

SOCRATES: Who is he? What name is there for him?

ION: Doctor.

SOCRATES: Let us say then, in summary, that the same man will always 532a recognize who speaks well and who speaks badly when there are many speaking about the same things. Or if he does not recognize the one who speaks badly, it is plain that he will not recognize the one who speaks well, at least about the same thing.

ION: That is so.

SOCRATES: Then the same man turns out to be clever about both?

ION: Yes.

SOCRATES: Don't you affirm that both Homer and the other poets, among whom are Hesiod and Archilochus, speak about the same things but not similarly, the former speaking well and the others worse?

ION: And I speak truly.

SOCRATES: Then if you really recognize the one who speaks well, you
b would also recognize that the ones who speak worse do speak worse.

ION: It's likely, at any rate.

SOCRATES: Then, my excellent fellow, we won't go wrong when we say that Ion is similarly clever about Homer and the other poets, too, since he himself agrees that the same man will be an adequate judge of all who speak about the same things and since very nearly all the poets make their poems about the same things.

ION: Then whatever is the cause of the fact that when someone speaks
c about another poet, I neither pay attention nor am able to contribute anything at all worthy of mention but simply[8] doze? But when someone makes mention of Homer, I wake up immediately, pay attention, and have plenty to say?

SOCRATES: That, at least, is not hard to guess, comrade, but it is entirely clear that you are unable to speak about Homer by art and knowledge. For if you were able to do so by art, you would also be able to speak about all the other poets too. For presumably the poetic art is a whole, isn't it?

ION: Yes.

d SOCRATES: Then when someone grasps any art whatsoever as a whole, for all the arts, the same manner of inquiry holds. Do you have any need to hear me explaining what I mean when I say this, Ion?

---

[8]*Atechnōs:* literally, "artlessly." The play on this idiom is almost certainly conscious; cf. 534d, 541e.

ION: Yes, by Zeus, Socrates, I, for one, do. I take pleasure in listening to you wise men.

SOCRATES: I only wish you spoke the truth, Ion. But presumably you are wise, you rhapsodes and actors and those men whose poems you sing. As for me, I speak nothing but the truth, as is fitting for a private

e human being. Now see how what I asked you about just now is an ordinary and private thing and how it belongs to every man to rec-ognize what I said—that, when somebody grasps an art as a whole, the inquiry is the same. Let us grasp this by speech: there is an art of painting as a whole, isn't there?

ION: Yes.

SOCRATES: And there are and have been many painters good and poor.

ION: Certainly.

SOCRATES: And did you ever know anyone who is clever at showing what Polygnotus the son of Aglaophon[9] paints well and what he does

533a not but is incapable of doing so concerning the other painters—so that when someone makes a display of the works of other painters, he dozes, is at a loss, and has nothing to contribute, but when he is required to give a judgment about Polygnotus, or any other single painter you please, he wakes up, pays attention, and finds plenty to say?

ION: No, by Zeus, surely not.

SOCRATES: What of this? In regard to sculpture, did you ever know anyone who ᴜ clever at explaining what was well made by Daedalus

b the son of Metion, or Epeius the son of Panopeus, or Theodorus of Samos,[10] or some other single sculptor but before the works of other sculptors is at a loss, dozes, and has nothing to say?

ION: No, by Zeus, I haven't seen this either.

SOCRATES: Indeed not, as I for one suppose; nor in regard to aulos playing, cithara playing, singing to the cithara, or rhapsody, you never saw a man who is clever at explaining Olympus, or Thamyras, or

c Orpheus, or Phemius the Ithacan rhapsode[11] but is at a loss about Ion and has nothing to contribute about what in rhapsody he does well and what not?

[9]Polygnotus was the most celebrated painter of the fifth century.
[10]Daedalus is the legendary inventor of carpentry, statues that walked, and wings for man; Epeius, the builder of the Trojan horse; Theodorus, a famous sculptor and architect of the sixth century.
[11]Olympus is the legendary musician and aulos player, said to have been taught by the satyr Marsias (see Minos, 318b); Thamyras and Orpheus were celebrated in legend for their abilities with the cithara; Phemius is Ion's counterpart in the Homeric poems (Odyssey, XXII, 330ff.).

ION: I have nothing to say in response to you, Socrates, about this, but I myself know well that I speak most finely of human beings about Homer, and I have plenty to say, and everyone else affirms that I speak well about him, but about the others this is not the case. Now then, see what this is.

SOCRATES: I do see, Ion, and I am going to show you what it seems
d to me that this is. For it is not art in you that makes you able to speak well about Homer, as I just said, but a divine power which moves you, just as in the stone which Euripides named Magnesian[12] but which the many call Heraclean. For this stone not only draws iron rings to itself but puts a power in the rings as well to do the same thing the
e stone does—to draw other rings to them, so that sometimes a very long chain of iron rings is strung hanging one from the other. But in all of them the power depends on this stone. In this way also the Muse makes some men inspired herself, and through these inspired men, others are gripped with enthusiasm and form a chain. All the good epic poets speak all their fine poems not from art but by being inspired and possessed, and it is the same for the good lyric poets. Just as those carried away by Corybantic frenzy[13] are not in their
534a right minds when they dance, so also the lyric poets are not in their right minds when they make these fine songs of theirs. But when they launch into melody and rhythm, they are frantic and possessed, like Bacchic dancers who draw honey and milk from rivers when they are possessed but cannot when they are in their right minds. And the soul of the lyric poets works in this way, as they themselves say. For the poets tell us, don't they, that culling their songs from fountains
b flowing with honey and certain gardens and glens of the Muses they bear them to us just like bees, flying as they do. And they speak the truth. For the poet is a light thing, winged and sacred, unable to make poetry before he is inspired and out of his mind and intelligence is no longer in him. For as long as this is his possession every human being
c is unable to make poetry or oracular utterance. Since they make poems and say much that is fine about things, just as you do about Homer, not by art but by divine dispensation, each is able to do finely only

[12]From a district in Asia Minor where magnetized iron could readily be found: Euripides, fr. 567.
[13]The words for "inspired" (*entheoi*) and "gripped by enthusiasm" (*enthousiazontes*) are closely related, both suggesting the notion of "a god within." The Corybantic rites were mystery rites that included frenzied dancing in which the worshipers were guided and inspired by certain demons called Corybantes. There may have been some connection between these Corybantic rites and similar ecstatic forms of worship associated with the god Bacchus (Dionysus). Cf. *Laws*, 790d; *Phaedrus*, 228d and 234d.

that to which the Muse has impelled him—one making dithyrambs,
another encomia, another choral chants, another epics, another iambic verses—while with regard to the rest, each of them is ordinary.
For they say these things not by art but by divine power. For if they
knew how to speak finely by art about one of them, they would be
able to do so about all the rest. On this account the god takes
d away their intelligence and uses them as servitors along with sooth-
sayers and diviners of the gods so that we hearers may know that these
men, who are without intelligence, are not the ones who say things
worth so much but that god himself is the speaker and gives utterance
to us through them. The greatest proof of the argument is Tynnichus,
the Chalcidean, who never composed any poem worth remembering
other than the poem which everybody sings and which is very nearly
e the finest of all songs, being simply, as he himself says, "a discovery of
the Muses." In this man the god especially shows us, it seems to me,
so that we need not be in doubt that these fine poems are not human
nor belonging to human beings, but divine and belonging to gods,
and the poets are nothing but interpreters of the gods, possessed by
the one who holds each. To show this, the god on purpose sang the
535a finest lyric through the most ordinary poet. Do I seem to you to speak
the truth, Ion?

Ion: Yes, by Zeus, to me you do. For somehow you lay hold of my
soul with these speeches, Socrates, and I believe that the good poets
are interpreters of these things from the gods through divine dispensation.

Socrates: Now, don't you rhapsodes, in turn, interpret the things of
the poets?

Ion: You speak the truth in this, too.

Socrates: Then are you interpreters of interpreters?

Ion: Entirely so.

b Socrates: Wait now, and tell me this, Ion, and don't hide from me
whatever I ask you about. When you are speaking epics well and most
amusing the spectators, singing of Odysseus leaping on the threshold,
revealing himself to the suitors and pouring out the arrows before his
feet,[14] or of Achilles chasing Hector,[15] or of one of the pitiful stories
c about Andromache, or Hecuba, or Priam,[16] are you then in your right
mind? Or do you become beside yourself, and does your soul think it
is at the scene of the deeds of which you speak in your inspiration,
either at Ithaca, or Troy, or wherever the epic takes place?

[14]*Odyssey*, XXII, 2ff.
[15]*Iliad*, XXII, 131ff.
[16]See particularly *Iliad*, XXII, 33ff.; XXIV, 477ff.

ION: How vivid is this proof of yours to me, Socrates! For I shall tell without hiding anything from you. When I speak of something pitiful, my eyes fill with tears, and when of something frightening or terrible, my hair stands on end from fear and my heart leaps.

d SOCRATES: What then, Ion? Shall we asssert that this man is then in his right mind who, adorned with rich raiment and golden crowns, cries in the midst of sacrifices and festivals, although he has lost none of these things, or who is frightened while standing before twenty thousand friendly human beings, although no one is stripping or harming him?

ION: No, by Zeus, certainly not, Socrates, to tell the truth.

SOCRATES: Do you know then that you work these same effects on most of the spectators?

e ION: Indeed I do know it very finely. For I look down on them each time from the platform above as they are crying, casting terrible looks and following with astonishment the things said. I must pay the very closest attention to them, since, if I set them to crying, I shall laugh myself because I am making money, but if they laugh, then I shall cry because of the money I am losing.

SOCRATES: You know, then, that this spectator is the last of the rings which I said get their power from one another through the Heraclean 536a stone? And you the rhapsode and actor[17] are the middle, and the top is the poet himself, but the god through all these draws the soul of human beings wherever he wishes, transmitting the power from one to the other. And just as from this stone, a very great chain is formed of dancers, choral masters, assistant masters, suspended sideways from the rings hanging from the Muse. And one poet is suspended from b one Muse, another from another. And we name this "being possessed," and it is very nearly that, for he is held.[18] And from these first rings, the poets, other men are suspended—some from one, some from another—and gripped by enthusiasm. Some are suspended by Orpheus, some by Musaeus.[19] But the many are possessed and held by Homer. You are one of them, Ion, and are possessed by Homer, and when someone sings from another poet, you fall asleep and are at a loss for something to say, but when someone utters a song of this poet, c you wake up immediately and your soul dances and you have plenty to say. For you say what you say about Homer neither by art nor by knowledge but by divine dispensation and possession. Just as those

---

[17]Or "interpreter" (*hypokritēs*).

[18]The word meaning "to be possessed" (*katechesthai*) is derived from *echein*, "to have or hold."

[19]Musaeus is the legendary inventor of poetry; oracular verses circulated under his name as well as under that of Orpheus (cf. *Protagoras*, 316d; *Republic*, 363c–64c).

carried away by Corybantic frenzy perceive sharply only that song which belongs to the god by whom they are possessed and have plenty of figures and phrases for that song but pay no heed to others, so you,

d too, Ion, have plenty to say when someone mentions Homer but are at a loss with the others. And the cause, for which you ask me, of your having plenty to say about Homer and not about the others is that you are a clever praiser of Homer not by art but by divine dispensation.

Ion: You speak well, Socrates. But I should be surprised if you could speak so well as to persuade me that I am possessed and am mad when I praise Homer. Nor do I believe I would appear so to you if you heard me speaking about Homer.

Socrates: And I am certainly willing to hear you, though not before

e you answer me this: about which one of the things about which Homer speaks do you speak well? For surely you don't speak well about them all.

Ion: Know well, Socrates, that I do about them all.

Socrates: But surely not about those things you don't happen to know and about which Homer speaks?

Ion: And what sort of things are those that Homer speaks of and I do not know?

537a Socrates: Doesn't Homer in many places have many things to say about the arts—for example, about charioteering? If I can remember the verses, I'll tell them to you.

Ion: I'll do it, for I remember.

Socrates: Tell me, then, what Nestor says to his son Antilochus when he urges him to be careful at the turn in the horse race in memory of Patroclus.

Ion: "And lean yourself," he says, "in the well-polished chariot a little

b to the left of them. And calling aloud to the horse on the right, give him the goad; give him free rein with your hands, and let the left horse go near to the turning posts so that the nave of the well-wrought wheel seems to graze it, but beware of touching the stone."[20]

c Socrates: That's enough. And who would judge better whether Homer speaks these words rightly or not, Ion, the doctor or the charioteer?

Ion: The charioteer, surely.

Socrates: Because this is his art or for some other reason?

Ion: Because this is his art.

Socrates: Then each of the arts has been assigned by the god the power of knowing some work, has it not? For presumably we won't know by medicine what we know by piloting, will we?

[20]Iliad, XXIII, 335–40.

ION: No indeed.

SOCRATES: Nor will we know by carpentering what we know by medicine.

d ION: No indeed.

SOCRATES: Isn't it so with all arts—that what we know by one art we do not know by another? But answer this for me first: do you affirm that one art differs from another?

ION: Yes.

SOCRATES: I find evidence of this in my calling one art different from another when one is knowledge of some things and the other knowledge of others. Do you also?

e ION: Yes.

SOCRATES: For if it were ever a knowledge of the same things, in what respect would we assert one to be different from the other, inasmuch as the same things could be known by both? Just as I know that these fingers here are five and you too know the same about them as I, and if I should ask you whether you and I know the same things by the same art—the art of arithmetic—or a different one, you would surely say by the same.

ION: Yes.

538a SOCRATES: Now, tell me what I was going to ask you a moment ago. Does it seem to you to hold for all the arts that the same things must of necessity be known by the same art and that by a different art the same things are not known but that, if it is really different, it is necessary that it also know different things?

ION: It seems so to me, Socrates.

SOCRATES: Then whoever does not have a certain art will not be able to know in a fine way the things of that art which are finely said or done, will he?

b ION: You speak truly.

SOCRATES: Would you or a charioteer, then, know in a finer way about whether the verses you just recited were finely said by Homer or not?

ION: A charioteer.

SOCRATES: For you, presumably, are a rhapsode but not a charioteer?

ION: Yes.

SOCRATES: And the rhapsode's art is different from the charioteer's?

ION: Yes.

SOCRATES: And if it is different, it is a knowledge of different things.

ION: Yes.

SOCRATES: And what about when Homer tells how Hecamede, Nes-
c tor's concubine, gives a potion to the wounded Machaon to drink. It goes something like this: "In Pramneian wine," he says, "she grated

goat cheese with a bronze grater, and beside it set an onion as relish
for the drink."[21] Is it for the doctor's art or the rhapsode's to ascertain
in a fine way whether Homer says these things rightly or not?

ION: The doctor's.

d SOCRATES: And what about when Homer says: "She went down into
the deep like a lead sinker which, set on the horn of a field-ox, comes
in haste bearing woe to ravenous fishes,"[22]—would we assert it is for
the fisherman's art rather than the rhapsode's to judge of what he is
saying and whether he says it finely or not?

ION: Plainly, Socrates, it is for the fisherman's art.

SOCRATES: Consider, then. Suppose you were questioning and asked
e me: Socrates, since for these arts you find in Homer the things appropriate for each to judge, come now and find for me the sort of
things with regard to which it is appropriate for the diviner and the
diviner's art to be able to ascertain whether they are done well or
badly—consider how easily and truly I shall answer you. For in many
places in the Odyssey he speaks of it; for example, in what Theocly-
539a menes, the diviner of the Melampid line, says to the suitors:
"Wretches, what evil is this you suffer; covered over with night are
your heads and faces and your limbs below; and wailing is kindled;
your cheeks are bathed in tears. Full of ghosts is the porch, and full
b the hall, hastening to Erebus under the darkness. The sun has perished
out of heaven and evil mist hovers over all."[23] And he speaks of it
many places also in the Iliad, for example in the Battle at the Wall
where he says: "A bird came over them as they were eager to cross
c over, a high-flying eagle, skirting the host on the left, bearing in his
claws a bloody red snake, a monstrous one, alive and still struggling,
nor had it forgotten its battle joy. For it bent back and struck its
captor on the breast by the neck; and the bird cast it from him to the
d ground, smarting with pain, and threw it in the midst of the throng.
And he with a loud cry followed the windy blast."[24] I assert that these
things, and others like them, are appropriate for a diviner to consider
and judge.

ION: And you speak truly, Socrates.

SOCRATES: And you, Ion, you speak truly in saying so. But come now,
just as I have selected for you from the Odyssey and the Iliad the sort
of things that belong to the diviner, the sort that belong to the doctor,
e and the sort that belong to the fisherman, since you are more expe-

[21]Ibid., XI, 630, 639.
[22]Ibid., XXIV, 80–82.
[23]Odyssey, XX, 351–57.
[24]Iliad, XII, 200–207.

rienced in Homer than I, so you select for me the sort of things that belong to the rhapsode and the rhapsode's art, those that it is appropriate for the rhapsode above all other human beings to consider and judge.

ION: I assert all things, Socrates.

SOCRATES: But you don't assert all, Ion—are you so forgetful? And yet it is not fitting for a man who is a rhapsode to be forgetful.

540a ION: What am I forgetting, then?

SOCRATES: Don't you remember that you asserted the rhapsode's art is different from the charioteer's?

ION: I remember.

SOCRATES: And since they are different, do you agree they will know different things?

ION: Yes.

SOCRATES: Then according to your account the rhapsode's art will not know everything, nor the rhapsode either.

ION: Everything, except, perhaps, such things, Socrates.

b SOCRATES: By "such things" you mean pretty much the things belonging to the other arts. But what sort of things will he know, if not everything?

ION: The things that are appropriate, I for one suppose, for a man to say, and the sort for a woman,[25] and the sort for a slave and the sort for a free man, and the sort for one who is ruled and the sort for one who is ruling.

SOCRATES: Do you mean that the rhapsode will know in a finer way than the pilot what sort of things it is appropriate for a ruler of a ship caught in a storm at sea to say?

ION: No, the pilot will know that, at any rate.

c SOCRATES: And does the rhapsode know in a finer way than the doctor what sorts of things it is appropriate for a ruler of a sick man to say?

ION: Not that either.

SOCRATES: Then do you mean such as are appropriate for a slave?

ION: Yes.

SOCRATES: Do you mean that the rhapsode will know, but not the cowherd, what things it is appropriate for a cowherd who is a slave to say to calm angry cattle?

ION: No, not at all.

SOCRATES: Then, such as are appropriate for a spinning woman to say about the working of wool?

d ION: No.

SOCRATES: Well then, will he know such things as are appropriate for a man who is a general to say when exhorting his troops?

[25]Or "for a husband to say, and what sort for a wife."

ION: Yes, the rhapsode will know such things.

SOCRATES: What? Is the art of rhapsody generalship?

ION: I would certainly know such things as are appropriate for a general to say.

SOCRATES: For perhaps you are an expert at generalship, too, Ion. And if you happened to be at once an expert at horsemanship and an expert at the playing of the cithara, you could know whether horses
e were being well or badly ridden. But if I asked you, "Through what art, Ion, do you know well-ridden horses? Is it the one by which you are a horseman or the one by which you are a citharist?" what would you answer me?

ION: The one by which I am a horseman, I would answer.

SOCRATES: If, then, you are ascertaining those who played the cithara well, you would agree that you ascertain this through the art by which you are a citharist and not through the one by which you are a horseman.

ION: Yes.

SOCRATES: Since you know military matters, do you know them through the art by which you are an expert at generalship or the one by which you are a good rhapsode?

ION: For me, at least, there doesn't seem to be any difference.

541a SOCRATES: What? You say there is no difference? Do you say that the art of rhapsody and the art of generalship are one or two?

ION: To me, at least, it seems to be one.

SOCRATES: Whoever is a good rhapsode, therefore, happens also to be a good general?

ION: Surely, Socrates.

SOCRATES: And whoever happens to be a good general is also a good rhapsode?

ION: No, that doesn't seem so to me.

SOCRATES: But that does seem to you to be the case—whoever is a good rhapsode is also a good general?

b ION: Certainly.

SOCRATES: Aren't you the best rhapsode among the Greeks?

ION: By far, Socrates.

SOCRATES: Then are you also the best general among the Greeks, Ion?

ION: Know it well, Socrates, and these things I learned from Homer.

SOCRATES: Then why, by the gods, Ion, when you are the best at both among the Greeks—general and rhapsode—do you go about being a
c rhapsode for the Greeks and not a general? Or does it seem to you that the Greeks have great need of a man crowned with a golden crown and none of a general?

ION: Socrates, our city is ruled by your people and commanded by your generals and needs no general. But neither your city nor that of the Lacedaemonians would choose me as general, for you suppose you are sufficient.

SOCRATES: Ion, my excellent fellow, don't you know Apollodorus of Cyzicus?

ION: What's he?

SOCRATES: A man whom the Athenians have chosen many times for
d their general although he is a foreigner. And also Phanosthenes of Andros and Heracleides of Clazomenae,[26] for all that they were foreigners, were elevated to generalships and other offices by Athens when they had demonstrated that they were worthy of mention. Why, then, will she not choose Ion of Ephesus as general and honor him if he should appear worthy of mention? Weren't you Ephesians originally
e Athenians, and isn't Ephesus a city inferior to none? But Ion, if you speak truly when you say you are able to praise Homer by art and knowledge, you do me injustice. For you profess to have knowledge of many fine things about Homer and say you will make a display, but you are deceiving me. You are so far from making a display that you are not even willing to tell what things you are clever about, although I have been entreating you for a long time. You are simply like Pro-
542a teus,[27] assuming all sorts of shapes, twisting this way and that until finally you escape me in the guise of a general, in order not to display how clever you are in the wisdom concerning Homer. If, then, you are expert at the art, as I just said, you deceive me in promising to make a display about Homer, and you are hence unjust. But if you are not expert at the art but are by divine dispensation possessed by Homer and, knowing nothing, you say many fine things about the poet, you are not unjust. Choose, then, whether you want to be held by us to be an unjust man or a divine one.

b ION: There is a great difference, Socrates. For to be held to be divine is far finer.

SOCRATES: Then this finer thing you may have from us, Ion, to be a divine praiser of Homer, not one expert at the art.

---

[26]Phanosthenes was the commander of an expedition against Andros in 406–405 B.C. (Xenophon *Hellenica*, I,v, 18); Heracleides raised the fee paid citizens attending the assembly, probably in about 393 B.C. (Aristotle, *Athenian Constitution*, XLI 3). Ephesus detached itself from Athenian hegemony in about 420–415 B.C.
[27]*Odyssey*, IV, 455ff.

An Interpretation of Plato's *Ion*

In Xenophon's *Banquet* Antisthenes asks, "Do you know any tribe more stupid [or simple] than the rhapsodes?" This question, obviously rhetorical, leads the reader of the *Ion* to the further question, "Why in the world does Socrates choose to speak to a man like Ion, a typical member of the tribe of rhapsodes?" Even though Socrates claims that he investigates men with respect to their knowledge and ignorance, it is hard to see why he should think it important to test Ion. Moreover, their conversation is private, so that it cannot be Socrates' intention to show Ion off, or up, to others. Socrates in the dialogues exposes the important kinds of human souls and their characteristic errors. To make this particular discussion a worthwhile enterprise for him, the empty reciter of Homer's poems must represent something beyond himself.

Socrates seems most anxious to have this conversation, since it is he who apparently stops Ion, who shows no particular interest in Socrates or desire to talk to him. Thus the first four exchanges occur entirely at Socrates' initiative, Ion responding in a way which would end the dialogue if Socrates did not return to the charge. Ion is a self-satisfied man who feels no need to render an account of himself or his activity; he knows who he is and what he does; and he knows both himself and his activity to be important. He is as far from the radical self-doubt of philosophy as a man can be. He is willing to talk about himself and accept praise; he has, however, little curiosity about others, for he does not sense a pressing need to learn from them. In order to engage Ion and induce him to reveal himself, Socrates must attract him and become respectable for him. Ion is vain, and he is first attracted by flattery and then captured when his self-esteem is threatened.

138

Socrates begins by expressing the greatest interest in Ion's achievements, making it clear that he is one of Ion's admirers. We learn from Socrates' first questions about Ion's recent doings that Ion is a man who travels from city to city and is admired in the cities he visits. He is not bound by the ordinary limits of citizenship: he is a cosmopolitan (or more properly a Hellenapolitan, for his universality will prove to be counterfeit, based on Greek convention rather than anything universally human). His rhapsody is his passport, and he finds proof for his worth in the prizes the peoples award him. He knows himself in relation to the unquestionable acclaim he evokes from others. Above all, Ion is needed to partake in the festivals dedicated to the gods whom all Greeks honor. He is a servitor of the Greeks, and his authority is somehow connected with the gods of the Greeks; this is the ground of his pious vanity.

530
b–c
Socrates, who apparently knows Ion's character, prevents him from breaking off the conversation by praising him. Once Ion has taken Socrates' bait, he will soon be at his mercy—begging Socrates for a justification for his way of life. Socrates professes envy of the rhapsodes, and he goes on to specify what arouses that ugly but flattering passion in him. The rhapsodes are among the knowers; they possess an art—a skill or a kind of know-how. That art is divided into two apparently unrelated parts of widely divergent dignity: its practitioners adorn their bodies so as to look most beautiful, and they occupy themselves with the thought of the good poets, especially the divine Homer, the teacher of the Greeks. Socrates has to explain what he means by the second part of the art, which is apparently not as clear as the first. To be a good rhapsode, one must understand what a given poet says, for the rhapsode is a spokesman or interpreter of the poet's thought to the listeners. Hence, the rhapsode must know what the poet means. Knowledge of what the poet thinks and fidelity in conveying his thought to an audience constitute the core of the rhapsode's art. He is an intermediary whose sole authority emanates from the poet.

c–d
Ion readily accepts this description of what he does, not considering its broad implications. He has not reflected on art in general nor on the particular requirements of an art of Homeric thought. He does not see that the conversation has really moved from a discussion of himself and of rhapsody to a testing of the interpreters of Homer. Ion's adequacy as an interpreter is about to be put to the test, and thus the received interpretation of Homer, the interpretation by the most popular and typical of his interpreters, is to be called into question.

In response to Socrates' assertions about Ion's art, Ion avows that Socrates has hit the nail on the head and that it is precisely to understanding the thought of Homer that he devotes the greatest energy. He is delighted to participate in the prestige generally accorded to Homer, but he also covertly tries to strike out on his own; he puts the accent on his contribution to Homer, on what is his own rather. than Homer's. His speech, not Homer's, is particularly beautiful; he has more fair thoughts about Homer than anyone. He is not simply Homer's faithful servant. Socrates recognizes that Ion would like to give a display of his talents; this is Ion's work, and he counts on charming his auditors, charming them in such a way that they ask no further questions. Ion insists that he is really worth hearing; he reminds us of the forgotten first part of the rhapsode's art; he has *adorned* Homer and for that he deserves to be adorned with a golden crown by the devotees of Homer. He uses Homer to his profit. Socrates, however, does not permit Ion's disloyalty to Homer; he has no interest in an Ion independent of Homer. The ever idle Socrates says he has no leisure to listen to the performance of Greece's greatest rhapsode; he wants the answer to only one question.

531a   That question is as follows: is Ion clever only about Homer or about Hesiod and Archilochus too? This apparently naïve query leads to the heart of the matter, for Socrates knows that Ion will respond that Homer is sufficient for him. And the fact that Ion has no curiosity about the teachings of the other poets is symptomatic of what he is— the most conventional agent of what is most conventional. It is a thing to be wondered at—though far from uncommon—that a man would be willing to live his life according to principles which are merely given to him, while he would not purchase so much as a cloak without looking into the alternatives. Socrates investigates such a man in this little conversation, one who accepts Homer's view of the gods, the heroes, and men without any need to see whether what the other poets say about these things is in any way useful. Even more, Ion is the one who transmits the Homeric view. In a word, he represents tradition. He accepts the orthodox view, and he teaches it. He does not seek reasons why this particular tradition should be accepted rather than any other. If there are a number of conflicting accounts of the world, men must make a choice among them. But Ion and his kind can give no reasons why their particular source should be preferred. They can merely assert the superiority of their text. In this respect, Homer's book resembles the Bible. It has adherents who rely on it utterly but who can provide no argument in its favor when confronted with other books. And if the book cannot be defended, neither can the way of life grounded in it. Ion relies on Homer, which would be sufficient if he had no competitors. But there are always other poets in addition to the official ones. The Greeks learn the poems of Hesiod and Archilochus as well as those of Homer, and any man who questions must wonder which of them he should follow, for his happiness depends on the right answer. For Ion, Homer is sufficient, but for the sole reason that it is for reciting Homer's poetry that golden crowns are awarded.

531
a–b
    Socrates presses the question about Ion's competence with the other poets in a comprehensive fashion; he does not leave it at Ion's insistence that the rhapsode need know only Homer. Where Homer and Hesiod say the same thing, Ion must be an equally competent exegete of both. So Ion turns out to be an expert on a part of Hesiod as well as on the whole of Homer. Now they must test Ion's expertise on the remainder—the part of Hesiod which is not the same as Homer. It is not so easy to determine this part as the other, and a new step must be introduced into the argument. Socrates begins to forge the link between what Homer and Hesiod say differently by pointing to a subject matter about which they both speak: divining. Now, divining plays a great role in the *Ion*, but here it is brought in innocuously as an example of a common theme of the poets. When the poets say the same thing, the poets' words are enough; when they say different things, one must turn away from the words to the things the words are about. Both Hesiod and Homer mention divining, and their words about it take on meaning from the object to which these words relate. And it is the diviner who can comment on what both Hesiod and Homer say about divining, not because he is a student of the words of Hesiod and Homer, but because he knows divining.

    Knowers draw their knowledge from the great book of the world, and the poet, whether he is a knower or not, is dependent on and speaks about that world. No written book is sufficient unto itself; every book is essentially related to something beyond itself which acts as a standard for it. Socrates has gradually narrowed the discussion and focused on the poet as a source of knowledge and on the rhapsode as a knower of that knowledge. Ion does not notice that it is the diviner, not the rhapsode, who is the expert on Homer in this case. The consequences of that fact will become clear to him later. Now the argument has established only that a man can speak well about Homer because he knows the subject matter about which Homer speaks. It thus becomes necessary to determine what Homer speaks about, since Ion must be a knower of that in order to be a competent interpreter of Homer. If Homer speaks about the same things as Hesiod, Ion's claim to be incompetent about Hesiod will not be able to stand, whether or not Homer and Hesiod agree about those things.

c   What is it, then, that Homer speaks about and the knowledge of which Ion must be presumed to possess? The answer is, simply, everything—everything human and divine. Homer speaks about the whole, and if he speaks truly, he reveals to men those things which they most want and need to know if they are to live well. At this point Socrates hints for the first time at the reason for his choosing to speak to this slight man who is never himself aware of the import of the discussion. Homer presents the authoritative view of the whole according to which Greeks guide themselves: he is the primary source of knowledge or error about the most important things. Every group of men begins with some such view of the whole by which its members orient themselves and which acts as a framework for their experience. They are educated by and in it from earliest childhood. No one starts afresh, from nothing. In particular there is always an authoritative view belonging to the community, and it constitutes the deepest unity of that community. It purports to be the true view, and the man who accepts it is supposed to possess all the knowledge he needs for living rightly and well.

Socrates, then, is testing the Greek understanding of things, particularly of the gods. At least symbolically, he shows the beginning point of philosophic questioning. Every man starts from a more or less coherent view of the whole which has been instilled in him by a tradition. Somehow that rare individual who possesses a philosophic nature becomes aware that the tradition is not founded in authentic knowledge but is only an opinion, and he is compelled to seek beyond it. The philosophic quest implies a prior awareness of the inadequacy of traditional opinion, and the problems of philosophy come to light as a result of the investigation of that traditional opinion which appears unproblematic to most men. Socrates treats Ion as the purveyor of the Greek tradition which stems from Homer, and therefore he tries to ascertain whether what Ion says about Homer can be understood to have the authority of knowledge. If it does not, the man who seeks for knowledge must start all over again in the interpretation of Homer, unmoved by popular opinion. Ultimately, of course, the same question must be asked of Homer himself: is his speech about gods and men based on knowledge of them? And in the event that it is not, one would have to try to return to the beginnings and start a second time. In the *Ion*, Socrates confronts authority, the authority for the most decisive opinions. He does so with great delicacy, never stating the issue directly, for he knows that the community protects its sacred beliefs fanatically. In spite of his caution he was finally put to death by the community for investigating the things in the heavens and under the earth rather than accepting Homer's account of them. In the failure of Ion to meet the test Socrates puts to him we see the reason why Socrates was forced to undertake a private study of the things in the heavens and under the earth.

As the exegete of Homer, Ion must be the knower of the things of which Homer speaks if he is to be taken seriously. He must, it has been made clear, possess the art of the whole. According to the most famous of Socratic professions, Socrates is ignorant, ignorant about the whole, and his awareness of his ignorance causes him to make a quest for knowledge. He knows what it means to possess knowledge, and in the *Ion* he shows the kinds of things that men must think they know and why they are unable to see the inadequacy of their opinions. As the spokesman of the tradition, Ion has answers to the most important questions, but he does not know that those answers are themselves questionable. Socrates' contribution is only that of questioning the traditional answers and thereby elaborating the essential structure of human alternatives.

Socrates is, therefore, deeply indebted to the tradition, which is the only basis for the ascent to a higher level of consciousness, but he is forced to break with it. In the *Apology* Socrates reports that he examined three kinds of men who were supposed to know: statesmen, poets, and artisans. He chose the statesmen and the poets because they are men whose very activity implies knowledge of the whole. Thus the commands of statesmen imply that they know what the good life is, and the tales of poets tell of gods and men, death and life, peace and war. Socrates discovered that statesmen and poets knew nothing but that the artisans did in fact know something. They could actually do things such as making shoes or training horses, and by their ability to teach their skills to others they proved they possessed knowledge. Nevertheless Socrates preferred to remain ignorant in his own way rather than to become knowledgeable in the way of artisans, for the latters' knowledge was of partial things, and their pride of competence caused them to neglect the human situation as a whole. However, Socrates did learn from the artisans what knowledge is and hence was made aware that those who talk about the whole do not possess knowledge of it. The choice seems to be between men who talk about the whole but are both incompetent and unaware of their incompetence, and men who deal with insignificant parts of the whole competently but are as a consequence oblivious of the whole. Socrates adopts a moderate position; he is open to the whole but knows that he does not know the answers although he knows the questions. In the *Ion*, he applies the standard of knowledge drawn from the arts to the themes treated by poetry, thus showing wherein poetry and the tradition fail and what stands in the way of such knowledge.

d–e   After determining what Homer talks about, Socrates asks whether all poets do not speak about the same things. Ion recognizes that an admission that they do would imply both that he is conversant with all the poets and that Homer is comparable to other poets. While agreeing that other poets do speak about the same things as Homer, Ion, therefore, adds that they do not do so in the same way. He means that Homer cannot be judged by the same standard as other poets, that they do not, as it were, inhabit the same world. Ion does not really accept or understand the position which Socrates has been developing; he wants to interpret the world by the book rather than the book by the world. He is quickly disarmed, however, when Socrates asks whether the difference consists in the others being worse than Homer. Ion cannot resist affirming this suggestion; its corollary, that Homer is better, he reinforces with an oath by Zeus.

"Better" and "worse," Socrates is quick to respond, are terms of relation, and the things to which they apply are comparable. Turning to the standard provided by the arts, the expert—the man who knows an art—is equally competent to judge all speeches that concern the objects of his specialty. To determine that one speech is better, a man must know that another is worse. When someone speaks about numbers, the arithmetician judges whether he speaks well or badly; when someone speaks about healthy foods, the doctor judges whether he speaks well or badly. The two are able to do so because they know numbers and health, respectively. Who is it, then, who can judge of the better and worse speeches of poets because he knows the object about which the poet speaks? The difficulty of responding to this question reveals the problem of the dialogue. The premise of the discussion with Ion is that the rhapsode is the competent judge of the poets' speeches, but rhapsodes are not even aware of the questions, let alone the answers. The very existence of the rhapsodes—these shallow replacements for knowers of the art of the whole—serves to initiate us into a new dimension of the quest for knowledge of the highest things. In investigating Ion, Socrates studies a kind of popular substitute for philosophy. When we reflect on who judges whether Ion speaks well or badly, we recognize that it is not an expert but the people at large. The issue has to do with the relation of knowledge and public opinion in civil society.

The iron-clad necessity of the argument based on the arts thus constrains Socrates and Ion to accept the conclusion that, if Ion is clever about Homer, he is also clever about Hesiod and Archilochus. Socrates urbanely maintains the unquestioned hypothesis of the dialogue, that Ion does in fact know Homer, and concludes from it that Ion is an expert on all poets. This conclusion is excellent and ineluctable except that it is not true. Ion recognizes that he is confronted by a mystery: reason forces him to be expert on all poets and he is not; he cannot give an account of himself. The tables are turned; his confidence is somewhat abated, and now he turns to Socrates, who has established some authority over him, for an explanation. With the poets other than Homer he dozes as do the people, according to Socrates' description in the *Apology*, when they have no gadfly to arouse them. It is this miracle that needs clarification.

532
c–d
Socrates has no difficulty in supplying the answer: he responds that Ion is incapable of speaking about Homer by art and exact knowledge. Ion is not an expert as are other experts. Socrates pursues this result with further and more pointed comparisons to the other arts. At the same time, he takes advantage of his new prestige to make it quite clear to Ion that the latter is now in tutelage. He poses a question in an obscure way and forces Ion to ask for an explanation. Ion who wanted to be heard now must hear instead, and Socrates, by engaging Ion's passions, will be a far more compelling performer for Ion than Ion would have been for him. But Ion, whose vanity is now involved, is not without his own wiles for preserving his self-esteem and humiliating Socrates. He gives gay assent to his instruction with the remark that he enjoys hearing "you wise men." For him, Socrates' argument is to be a display, such as any of the currently popular sophists might give, of technical virtuosity at confuting common sense, a display more notable for form than for substance. If one treats Socrates in this way, he need not be taken too seriously; one can observe him idly as one does any other performer. Socrates, however, does not grant Ion this protection for his vanity. He takes the offensive himself and accuses Ion of being wise along with actors and poets, whereas he, Socrates, speaks only the truth, as befits a private man. The opposition between what is here called wisdom and public men, on the one hand, and truth and private man, on the other, hints at the human situation which forces Ion to be ignorant without being aware of it and points to the precondition of the pursuit of the truth. In order to satisfy their public, the public men must pretend to wisdom, whereas only the private man, who appears to belong to a lower order of being, is free to doubt and free of the burden of public opinion. The private life seems to be essential to the philosophic state of mind.

For example, the private man can think and speak of mean and contemptible things which are revealing but are beneath the exalted level expected of public men.

532d–
533e

After this skirmish for position, Socrates returns to tutoring his new pupil. Arts are wholes, Socrates argues, and the practitioners of an art are thus comparable; the man who can judge one practitioner of an art is in possession of the means to criticize all of its practitioners. He now provides Ion with examples of arts which are much more like rhapsody than either medicine or arithmetic are; he cites imitative painting, sculpture, and flute, harp, and cither playing. (He here covertly insults Ion by appearing to compare his grand art with the relatively trivial ones of flute, harp, and cither playing.) The ostensible purpose of this segment of the discussion is to prove to Ion that the grasp of an art implies competence to deal with all of it; Socrates succeeds in doing this and thus forces Ion to realize that he cannot pretend to the authority of art, as Socrates had first led him to believe he could. However, these examples implicitly raise a further problem that remains unexamined for the moment. What is it that constitutes the unity or wholeness of the arts of painting and sculpture? Two possible answers suggest themselves: their subject matters or their use of materials. Obviously, the things represented are primary in one sense, but the medium is a more distinguishing and clearly separable aspect. The entire thrust of Socrates' argument is toward identifying poetry with its subject matter and not with its medium. He abstracts from the poetic in poetry, from what constitutes its characteristic charm, although in a hidden way he attempts to explain that charm. The duality of style and content, or medium and subject matter, in poetry calls to mind the two aspects of Ion's art mentioned by Socrates at the beginning: the rhapsodes are adorned and they understand the thought of the poet. Socrates seems to forget the beautiful in poetry, just as he has neglected to discuss the rhapsodes' adornment. But while apparently paying attention only to the poets' teaching, he is actually studying the relationship of the true to the beautiful, or the relationship of philosophy to poetry, from the point of view of philosophy or truth. Socrates is perfectly aware of the uniqueness of poetry, and he is examining the role poetry plays in establishing the false but authoritative opinions of the community. The need for poetry is one of the most revealing facts about the human soul, and that need and its effect on the citizens constitute a particular problem for Socrates' quest. Ion's total confusion about the difference between speaking *finely* and speaking *well*, between the charming and the true, is exemplary of the issue Socrates undertakes to clarify.

The examples of practitioners of arts used by Socrates, in the context of showing Ion that he must know all the poets, help to make an amusing, covert point. There is one painter, a contemporary; there are three sculptors, only one of whom is a contemporary, while the other two are mythical personages. Five rhapsodes are named; the only contemporary is Ion himself, and the others are all mythical. Of the mythical rhapsodes at least two of the first three met violent death as a result of their singing. The fourth, Phemius, served the mob of suitors running riot in Ithaca during the king's absence. He was saved from suffering death for it only by begging for mercy at the feet of the wise Odysseus. Perhaps there is a hidden threat in Socrates' speech; at least Ion asks for Socrates' succor, finally yielding completely. What does it mean that he who knows he speaks most *finely* or *beautifully* of all men about Homer and of whom all others assert that he speaks *well*, is unable to do so about other poets?

The dialogue has three major divisions. Ion's plea to Socrates ends the first, which has concluded that a knower of Homer must be a knower of the whole art of poetry and, implicitly, of the whole.

The central section of the *Ion* has, in turn, three parts, two long speeches on divine possession surrounding an interlude of discussion. The explicit intention of this section is to find some source of Ion's power other than art. This attempt at first succeeds but is finally rejected by Ion, and the final section of the dialogue is an effort to resuscitate his reputation as the possessor of an art. In this dramatic context Socrates' teaching about divine possession must be interpreted. It is presented as *the* alternative for giving dignity to Ion's speech about Homer; it proves unsatisfactory, but since the other alternative is no less unsatisfactory, it helps to reveal the nature of Ion's claim and appeal.

533c–
535a

Ion insists that Socrates try to explain why Ion is so good about Homer and not about the other poets. In response, Socrates provides Ion with a respectable and flattering answer—divine possession. Moreover, he takes the opportunity to do what Ion himself had for so long wished to do; he offers a poetic display and gives a long speech, beautifully adorned, telling of gods and men and their relations. And the speech has the effect on Ion that poetry is supposed to have. "Yes, by Zeus . . . the speeches somehow lay hold of my soul." Socrates plays the poet, not to say the god. It remains to be seen whether he himself is divinely possessed or whether he self-consciously and rationally constructs a tale designed to appeal to Ion's needs and wishes.

The tale Socrates tells does satisfy Ion's demands. It explains why he can only interpret Homer and at the same time gives his interpretations a dignity perhaps greater than those based on an art would have, for there is no dignity greater than that of the gods. Socrates seemingly succeeds where Ion has failed: he establishes a special place for Homer, one that transcends the limits of rational comparison; the comparison between Homer and others would be akin to the comparison between the Bible and another book made by a believer rather than the comparison between two technical treatises. There is a source of wisdom which does not depend on the rational study of nature (a word which does not occur in the Ion), so that art is not the only road to wisdom. It must be stressed that art and divine possession are not merely two ways to arrive at the same result, alternative ways of understanding the same thing. They are exclusive, each implying a different and contrary view of the whole. An art requires a subject matter which is permanent and governed by intelligible rules. Divine possession implies the existence of elusive and free gods who are not to be grasped by reason, who govern things and who can only be known if they choose to reveal themselves. In the latter case the highest and most decisive things are to be known only by the word rather than the word being judged by the thing. Ion, as the spokesman of a god, and not the artisan, would be the one who would know the truth. Socrates not only describes the well-known and undeniable phenomenon of passionate, frenzied insight but backs up the description by asserting that the source of that insight is really a god and that, hence, it is of the highest status. Reason (noûs) is delusive and must be denigrated.

Socrates takes *enthusiasm*, literally the presence of a god within, as the archetype of the poetic experience. The unreasoning and unreasonable movement of the soul which expresses itself in the orgiastic dances of the Corybantes is an example of the kind of condition in which this revelation is likely to be found. This is the state of soul in which men foretell the future, become diviners and oracles. Religious excitement and fanaticism constitute the ambiance in which Ion and his poetry move. Socrates compares the god to a lodestone which both moves and lends its power to move to other things. Reason, perhaps a source of rest or of self-motion, must be out of a man for him to be affected fully by this source of motion. Poetry, as presented here, ministers particularly to that part of the soul which longs for worship of the sacred, and Ion, who sings at the festivals dedicated to the gods, finds himself at home in this atmosphere of man's longing for the divine. Socrates, however, suggests that the stone can be understood in two different ways. One interpretation comes from Euripides, a poet, who calls it the Magnet, implying it is only a stone, and the other comes from the vulgar, who call it the Heraclean, implying that only the presence of the divine can account for its mysterious power. It might be suggested that in this speech Socrates adopts the account of the vulgar to explain Ion's mysterious attractiveness, lending to that attractiveness a significance commensurate with his and his audiences' wishes.

Upon Ion's enthusiastic reception of his speech, Socrates questions him. He does so ostensibly to tighten the links of his argument but with the real effect of revealing finally the nature of Ion's soul, this little Ion as opposed to the great interests he represents. At the same time Socrates elaborates the character of the religious experience which has been suggested. The poet is the spokesman of a god, and the rhapsode is the spokesman of a poet and hence the spokesman of a spokesman. As a part of this great chain, Ion is asked to tell frankly of his experiences on the stage. Is he not possessed when he tells the fearful tales of the avenging Odysseus and Achilles, or the piteous ones of the sufferings of Hecuba and Priam? When he recites, is he not out of his mind and does he not suppose his soul transported to the place of these events? Ion confesses freely to this rapture, this total sympathy with his subject. When he tells of the piteous, his eyes fill with tears, and when he tells of the fearful, his hair stands on end and his heart jumps. Ion's world is that of the passions connected with tragedy; he arouses pity and fear, and he purveys that most curious of pleasures, the pleasure experienced in the tears shed for the imaginary sufferings of others. Men desire and need the satisfaction found in contemplating the mutilation and death of noble men. This satisfaction is provided in beautiful poetry and is presided over by fair gods. Socrates points out how unreasonable Ion's noble sentiments are in the real circumstances in which he finds himself—he, adorned with golden crowns, cries when he has not lost his crowns and is frightened when his friendly audience does not attack him. Ion's tears, Socrates implies, would be only for his golden crown, and his terror only for his life and comfort. He may be the spokesman for the grandest beings and sentiments, but he is a very ordinary mortal. His tragedy would be the loss of the means of display and self-preservation. He is, in the deepest sense, an actor. Ion readily accepts Socrates' characterization of his situation, without sensing his own vulgarity in doing so.

Finally, after establishing that the poet is possessed by a god, and Ion by the poet, Socrates completes his argument by asking Ion to confirm that the spectators are possessed by Ion. Thus the spectators would constitute the last link in a chain of attractions originating in the god. Ion asserts that the spectators do indeed share his experiences. He knows this because he is always looking at them and paying the closest attention to them. He reassures Socrates that this is so by explaining that he laughs when they cry, for he will get money, and he cries when they laugh, for he will lose money. This man possessed, living with the gods and the heroes, is at the same time counting the box-office receipts. He is at war with the spectators—when they cry, he laughs, and when they laugh, he cries—but there may be a deeper kinship in that Ion's low interest in the money which preserves life is not totally alien to the fear of death which is at the root of the spectator's interest in the tragic poems. At all events, we can see that the real magnet is the spectators and that Ion gives them what they want. He can best be understood by comparison to the Hollywood stars, who are nothing in themselves, are only fulfillments of the wishes of their fans, but who, in order to satisfy them, must appear to be independent, admirable, even "divine." The spectators must deceive themselves, absolutize their heroes, who exist only in terms of their tastes. It is a kind of self-praise; what the people love must be rooted in the best and highest; what appears to go from gods to men really goes in the other direction. Ion senses the vox dei in himself, but it is only the vox populi. He may think himself superior to the people, laugh at them, thinking he is duping them, but he is their flatterer and their creature; his self-esteem depends on their prizes; he does what he does at their bidding. The nature of the people and Ion's relation to them perhaps comes most clearly to light when we recognize that, if what the people most wanted were comedy, Ion would not have to deceive them and could be at one with them. He would laugh when they laugh. This may help to explain Socrates' earlier opposition between truth and public men and cast some light on his dictum that the city is the true tragedy.

535e–
536d   A second long speech is designed to complete the argument about divine possession and perfect the new view of Ion's calling designed for him by Socrates. But this speech, similar to the first one in its poetic qualities, is no longer successful, and Ion, far from being possessed, rejects it. The form is the same, so we must look elsewhere to account for the failure of this speech to persuade. The simple answer is that it no longer flatters Ion as did the first. Socrates gives with the first speech an example of successful poetry and with the second an example of unsuccessful poetry, slyly suggesting thereby that the essence of popular poetry is its capacity to flatter the aspiration of its

audience. This second speech tells Ion that not only are the poet and the rhapsode possessed but the audience too is possessed. Everyone is possessed; possession is not a special honor or a title to wisdom; possession explains nothing. The story of divine possession is merely a description of the entire set of activities and attractions involved in poetry. Moreover, Socrates now stresses that the various poets are equally possessed, and Homer is in no sense superior in this decisive respect. It just happens that some men are more attracted to Homer than to any other poet. Divine possession provides no basis for believing what Homer says any more than what Orpheus or Musaeus says. And Ion's speeches about Homer suffer correspondingly. As a matter of fact, each of the various conflicting sayings of the poets has equal divine sanction. Ion is now a helpless instrument of a blind power. Finally, Socrates implies not only that the poets and their votaries are at odds but that there are different gods revealing contrary ways. There is no cosmos, only a chaos; and the truth of Ion's and Homer's speech, which was the original theme, becomes impossible to determine. Such are the consequences of the teaching about divine possession when further elaborated.

536d   Ion, dimly aware of the unsatisfactory character of Socrates' explanation of his activity, refuses to admit that he is possessed and mad; he makes a last attempt to possess Socrates by making a display. Socrates, however, again puts him off, asking for an answer to yet another question. Ion is to be forced to support his claim that he possesses an art. He will, of course, fail in this attempt. The conclusion of the first section was that Ion knew all the poets; the conclusion of this one will be that he does not even know Homer. The first section shows the universality of Ion's proper concern, the third his incapacity to fulfill the requirements of that concern. Given the disproportion between the claim and the fulfilling of it, Ion will be forced back upon divine possession in order to salvage his reputation. But that divine possession will be nothing more than an idle, self-justificatory boast.

536e–   Socrates begins by asking Ion about what particular thing in
537c Homer he speaks well. Ion responds quite properly that there is nothing in Homer about which he does not speak well. But what about those things he does not know, that is, those arts of which Ion is not himself a practitioner? Without giving Ion time to respond, Socrates searches for a passage in Homer that is technical in character. Ion is caught up in the artifice and eagerly asks to recite the passage. At last he gets to perform, if only on a dull set of instructions for a chariot race. Socrates tells him what to recite and tells him when to stop. Socrates

is now Ion's master and gives a demonstration of how he should be used. The passage recited belongs more to the domain of a charioteer than to that of a doctor. It deals with the details of a chariot race, but one might wonder whether such a poetic presentation could be properly interpreted by a charioteer either. Socrates relentlessly pursues the issue of expertise. Between doctor and charioteer Ion sees no choice, although he probably thinks he himself could best comment on the verses. But Socrates did not ask that; his goal is to get Ion to admit that in this instance the charioteer is more competent than the rhapsode. But before he can compel Ion to do so, Socrates must come to a further agreement with him.

537c–
538a
    This agreement concerns the relation of arts to their subject matters. There is a variety of different kinds of things in the world, and to each of these kinds is assigned an art whose business it is to know that kind. One subject matter, one art, and what we know from one art we cannot know from another. The difference in names of arts comes from this difference in subject matter; there can be only one kind of expert for each kind of thing. Therefore, if the charioteer is expert on a passage in Homer, the rhapsode, as rhapsode, cannot be. Once this rule is accepted, Ion, who does not particularly care about this passage anyway, is prepared to admit that it is of the domain of the charioteer rather than the rhapsode. But this admission leads inevitably to the consequence that there is no passage in Homer about which Ion is competent, for the world is divided up among the well-known special arts. And even though there were some segment of Homer which dealt with rhapsody, Ion would be only one of many experts called in to interpret Homer. But, if rhapsody is anything at all, it must somehow be competent to deal with all of Homer. The helpless Ion, in order to be something, must look for some specific subject matter which he alone knows. He finally emerges in the guise of a general.

    This segment of the discussion is particularly offensive to anyone who loves poetry. Its consequence is not only that Ion is deprived of a claim to his profession but also that Homer is reduced to a mere compendium of technical information drawn from the arts. Nothing could be more antipoetic. After all, a poem is a whole, one which may use material drawn from the arts but which puts them together in a unique way which cannot be derived from the arts.

    Socrates knows what poetry is; the argument is intended to be defective. The very verses cited prove this. For example, the passage assigned to the fisherman could not be interpreted by a fisherman as such, for it is a simile, comparing a fisherman's line falling through the water to the plunge of a goddess. The man who can understand this passage must know the gods as well as fishing tackle. Then, too, the verses about the healing of Machaon's wounds are more appropriately judged by the statesman who knows what kind of medicine is good for the character of citizens than the doctor (cf. *Republic*, 408). Even the first example, which on the surface looks like a straightforward account of the way to handle a chariot, is not unambiguously technical. Examination of the context of the passage reveals that Nestor is actually telling his son how to use somewhat unsportsmanlike tactics in the race; the judgment of the propriety of such advice does not evidently fit too well into the charioteer's sphere of competence. The insufficiency of this argument is clear; it does not do justice to the poem or to Ion. But Socrates wishes to compel us to see precisely wherein it fails and thereby to see a real and profound problem which Ion, and, for that matter, most men, do not sufficiently grasp. They, in their lives, are caught up in it unawares. This argument merely reflects a contradiction in the most common understanding of things.

The problem would be most immediately perceived by modern men as that of specialization. If one looks around a modern university, for example, one sees a variety of independent, seemingly self-sufficient disciplines. Physics, astronomy, literature, and economics teach competences which are thought to be unquestionable. Now where is the unity? They are parts of the university but there is no one who is expert about the knowledge present in the university as a whole. There is always a central administration, to be sure, but it does not have an intellectual discipline of its own; it merely provides the wherewithal of survival to the disciplines and accepts their intellectual authority. There are men who talk about the whole domain of knowledge and who are even applauded for doing so. But no one thinks of crediting them with knowledge of the same solidity or certitude as that of the specialists. One finds competent specialized speech or bloated, unconvincing general speech. It is this very problem that Socrates is approaching here, the problem alluded to in the *Apology* when Socrates tells of his examination of the artisans as well as of the poets and statesmen. He does not deny that Homer constitutes a unity, which is more than the result of the mere addition of parts. The question is the status of that unity. Does Homer's general view have the character of knowledge, or is it an adorned deception which satisfies men's longings and which they can dupe themselves into taking seriously by calling "divinely inspired"? Men in Socrates' time, as at present, believed that the arts are the only sources of simply persuasive knowledge.

But if that is the case, then men's general views can never be knowledge.

If one examines the principle of specialization posited by Socrates somewhat more carefully, one becomes aware that it is wrong. And Ion's acceptance of that principle is the source of the dissolution of poetry's unity. Socrates asserted that each subject matter is dealt with by one art and that no other art can speak precisely about that subject matter. But this is not so. What is forgotten is the master arts. The horseman, for example, speaks of the saddlemaker's art with great competence and precision. As a matter of fact, he may speak of it with even greater authority than the saddlemaker himself, for he sets the latter in motion. He alone can judge the good and bad saddles, for he is their user, but he is surely not a saddle maker. The best model of the master artisan is the architect who rules the specialized artisans who build a house. Socrates' argument forgets that each of the arts treats of a subject matter which is part of a whole which is itself the subject of a more sovereign art. None of the specialties is really independent, although it may seem to be.

This leads us back to the art of the whole, the necessity of which emerged early in the discussion. The subject matter of poetry turned out to be the whole, and if poetry is to be based on knowledge, or to be discussed knowledgeably, there must be knowledge, or an art, of the whole. But somehow men do not see this art and do not see the whole presupposed in each of its divisions. They have a view of the whole, but it seems to stem from altogether different sources than their view of the parts. The helmetmaker's art seems somehow altogether different from the statesman's art, which in war directs the wearers of the helmets. The parts seem rationally intelligible, but the whole of which they are parts does not seem to be so. The discovery of the possibility of a rationally intelligible whole may be called the discovery of nature, and that discovery is the origin of philosophy. It has already been remarked that the word *nature* does not occur in the *Ion*; it comes as no surprise, then, that the word *philosophy* is also nowhere to be found. In this dialogue Socrates examines the prephilosophic soul which knows neither of nature nor of the master art which seeks the first principles of nature. This art is the quest for that universal and unifying knowledge which is neither special nor spurious, that knowledge of which Ion could not conceive and we can no longer conceive. Ion's world knows of special arts which are highly developed and even awe-inspiring; such arts are almost coeval with man, and reflection on them leads to the notion of a permanent and comprehensible order which is the cause of the intelligibility of the parts.

But that reflection is not a part of Ion's world; instead there is a dazzling poetry telling of gods and heroes, a precursor of philosophy but its bitterest enemy. The *Ion* is a representation of the emergence of philosophy out of the world of myth.

538e–
539   It is not only ignorance that prevents the discovery of nature; man's most powerful passion sides with poetry and is at war with his love of wisdom. Socrates reveals this in his final examples drawn from Homer. With great emphasis he recites passages from the *Iliad* and the *Odyssey* dealing with divining, presumably to show once again the kind of thing in Homer with which a specialist should deal. However, he has already amply made his point, and the peculiar solemnity of his presentation forces one to search further for his intention. It can be found in his desire to call particular attention to the art of divining. This art has been mentioned several times in the dialogue and has been connected with rhapsody throughout, suffering the same fate as it. In the first section, divining was treated as an art; indeed, it was the first example mentioned of an art. In the central section, it was one of the examples of divine possession, and now it has again become an art. Although not obviously similar to rhapsody or poetry, divining is used by Socrates to point up their character. By reflecting on divining we can penetrate what Socrates wishes to teach us about rhapsody and poetry.

Diviners exist because men wish to know the future, because they are worried about what will happen to them as individuals. There can be such knowledge only if there is providence; if the fate of individuals is but a matter of chance, this fond wish would have to remain unfulfilled. Providence implies the existence of gods who care for men. If divining is to be considered an art, it is strange in that it must profess to know the intentions of the gods; as an art, it would, in a sense, seem to presuppose that the free, elusive gods are shackled by the bonds of intelligible necessity. Divining partakes of the rational dignity of the arts while supposing a world ruled by divine beings who are beyond the grasp of the arts. It belongs somehow both to the realm of the arts and to the realm of divine possession. Moreover, divining is a most peculiar art in that it treats of the particular while other arts speak only of the general. The unique, the special, is the only concern of divining, while the particular is taken account of by other arts only to the extent that it partakes in the general rules. And finally, although divining is a pious art, the knowledge derived from it is to be used to avoid the bad things and gain the good ones. On the one hand, it presupposes a fixed providence; on the other hand, it ministers to man's desire to master his destiny rather than accept it.

Socrates' view of the proper use of divining has been preserved for us by Xenophon. In the context of defending Socrates' piety—he had been accused of impiety—Xenophon tells that Socrates

advised them [his companions] to do necessary things in the way they thought they would be best done. As for things the consequences of which are unclear, he sent them to inquire of diviners whether they should be done. He said that those who are going to manage households and cities in a fine way had need, in addition, of the art of divining. With respect to becoming skilled at carpentry, skilled at metalworking, skilled at farming, skilled at ruling human beings, skilled at investigating such deeds, skilled at calculating, skilled at household management, or skilled at being a general, he held that such studies can be acquired by human thought. However, he said that the gods reserved the most important parts of them for themselves and of these parts nothing is clear to human beings. For it is surely not clear to the man who plants a field in a fine way who will reap it; nor is it clear to the man who builds a house in a fine way who will live in it; nor is it clear to the general whether it is beneficial to exercise command; nor is it clear to the statesman whether presiding over the city is beneficial; nor is it clear to the man who marries a beautiful girl for his delight whether she will prove a misery to him; nor is it clear to the man who makes alliances of marriage with men powerful in the city whether he will as a result be driven from the city. He said that those who suppose that nothing of such things belongs to the domain of the divine but all are within the capacity of human thought are possessed by madness. But they are also possessed by madness who inquire of diviners concerning things that the gods have given to human beings to judge on the basis of study; for example, if someone were to ask whether it is better to get a charioteer for a chariot who has knowledge or one who does not have knowledge? Or whether it is better to get a pilot of a ship who has knowledge or one who does not have knowledge? Or to ask about what can be known by counting, measuring, or weighing. Those who inquire about such things from the gods he believed do what is forbidden. He said that what the gods have given human beings to accomplish by study must be studied; what is not clear to human beings should be inquired about from the gods by means of divining; for the gods give a sign to those who happen to be in their grace. [Memorabilia, I, i, 6–9]

Art can tell a man how to sow, but whether he will reap what he sows is beyond the power of art to know, for chance is decisive in determining whether that man will live or die. But the man who sows does so only because *he* wants to reap. What he cares about most as a living, acting man is not guaranteed by art. Socrates reasonably prescribes that men should obey the rules of art where they apply, and, in what belongs to chance, consult the diviner. In other words, he urges men not to let what is out of their control affect their action. They should separate out their hopes and fears from their understanding and manfully follow the prescriptions of what true knowledge they possess. They must not let their passionate aspirations corrupt that knowledge.

But such a solution is not satisfactory to most men; they must see the world in such a way that their personal ambitions have a cosmic status. The fate of an individual man is no more significant to the knower of man than is the fate of a particular leaf to the botanist. The way of the knower is unacceptable for the life of men and cities. They must see a world governed by providence and the gods, a world in which art and science are inexplicable, a world which confuses general and particular, nature and chance. This is the world of poetry to which man clings so intensely, for it consoles and flatters him. As long as human wishes for the signifcance of particular existences dominate, it remains impossible to discover nature, the intelligible and permanent order, for nature cannot satisfy those wishes. Ion cannot imagine an art of the whole because, as rhapsode, he most of all serves the longing for individual immortality, and he uses his poetry to that end.

The effect of this longing for immortality on the soul is illuminated by Socrates' comparison of the enthusiastic diviners and rhapsodes with the Bacchic or Corybantic dancers (534a–b). In the *Laws* (790d–791b) the Athenian Stranger speaks of Corybantism as an illness resulting from excessive fear, which gets its relief and cure in the frantic dances. The hearts of the Corybantic dancers leap, just as does Ion's, and they dance wildly; carried away by powerful internal movements which they translate into frenzied external movements, they dedicate their dance, and themselves, to a protecting deity. The fear of death, the most profound kind of fear and the most powerful of passions, moves them until they are out of their minds, and they can be healed only in the fanatic religious practice. In the *Ion*, Socrates points to the most important source of religious fanaticism and suggests that the function of that kind of poetry which is taken most seriously is to heal this fear and console man in his awareness of his threatened existence. This poetry irrationally soothes the madness in all of us. It is a useful remedy but a dangerous one. Fanaticism is often its result. The man who most believes the poets' stories is likely to be most intolerant of those who do not. Socrates, the philosopher who tests the stories as well as those who tell them, is a menace to the sense of security provided by them. It is precisely overcoming this concern with oneself, in all its subtle and pervasive forms, that is *the* precondition of philosophy and a rational account of one's own life. Poetry, as Ion administers it to suffering man, gives a spurious sense of knowledge while really serving and watering the passions hostile to true knowledge.

539d–
540d

Socrates, who has taken over from Ion and has himself been reciting from Homer, showing his own rhapsodic gifts, now demands that Ion select the passages that belong to the rhapsode. Ion must look for some special segment which speaks about rhapsody. But, oxlike, he asserts that all of Homer belongs to him. He does not seem to have followed the argument. It is not only stupidity, however, but self-interest that makes him so dense. He loses his title to respect if he is not the interpreter of the whole, and besides, he clearly recites all of the *Iliad* and *Odyssey* and not just individual passages. Socrates forbids him, however, to say that he is an expert on all of Homer. Their earlier agreements about the practitioners of arts who can judge parts of Homer bind Ion. Socrates chides Ion for being forgetful. It is not appropriate for a rhapsode, of all people, to be forgetful. Socrates implies that the rhapsode is really only a memory mindlessly repeating the ancestral things. Ion believes he can abide by the agreements and emerge relatively intact. As he sees it, the parts of Homer dedicated to these petty, uninteresting arts are of no real importance to the whole. Ion can be the expert on what really counts: the human things. In particular he knows what is fitting for men and women, slave and free, ruled and ruler, to say; he knows the proprieties of civil, as opposed to technical, man.

Socrates does not allow Ion to leave it at this general statement of his competence in what men should say. Homer never presents man in general; his personages are always particular kinds of men doing particular kinds of things. There is a free man who is a ruler of a ship; he is the pilot; what he would say in a particular difficult situation is known to the practitioner of the pilot's art. The same is true of the man who is a doctor treating a sick patient. Ion must answer "no" when Socrates asks him whether he knows the proprieties of such speech. What about the things it is fitting for a slave to say? To this Ion answers "yes." But Socrates will not even let him remain a slave or be a woman. Both must be artisans, too. Then Socrates asks whether Ion would know what it is fitting for a man who is a general to say in exhorting his troops. In a last desperate attempt, Ion seizes on this alternative, his final hope of salvaging his dignity. Socrates interprets Ion's assertion that he knows what a general should say to mean Ion possesses the general's art; he who knows the speech of a general must be a general. Socrates began by talking to a rhapsode and ends by commissioning him as a general. Socrates rejects the distinction between speech and deed which Ion suggests but cannot defend.

Now, there is clearly a possibility of discussing man in general without knowing all the particular activities which he can undertake. Similarly, there is a capacity to speak about deeds, and to understand them, without performing them. Ion is caught in a sophistic argument. But Socrates does not do him an injustice, for if he were able to present a defense of the dignity of speech, if he had any justification for his own life, which is devoted to speech alone, he could extricate himself from the difficulty. He makes a living from speech but does not really respect it or understand it. Ion, apparently following Homer, admires the heroes and their deeds; they are more important than the speeches which glorify them. Speech follows on deed, and the life of action is the best kind of life. Or rather, there is no theoretical life; for only if there is a theoretical life can speech be regarded as anything more than a means. Thus Ion sings the poems not for their own sake but for the sake of money.

Only in a world in which thought could be understood to be highest, in which there are universals—which means essentially intelligible beings—can there be significant general speech. Without such universals, only particulars exist. That is why Ion is unable to stop Socrates' progressing from the man in general Ion said he knew about to slaves guarding sheep, pilots in a storm, and so on. Only if he knew of human nature could he speak of man; but we have already seen why he cannot even conceive of nature. For him, all speeches are distillations of the deeds of doers, and the poets and rhapsodes are but incompetent imitators of the competent. The splendor and authority of poetry would seem to indicate that speech can be higher than deed, but the poets and rhapsodes do not explain how that can be. In order for that explanation to be given, there would have to be a total revolution in their view, a revolution which can only be effected by philosophy. When poetry can celebrate the speeches of Socrates, the poet—in this case Plato—has found a ground for the life devoted to speech.

540d–   All of this becomes clearer in the further elaboration of Ion's
541b   generalship. Socrates permits Ion to masquerade in this comic garb,
although he could easily have shown that this position cannot be
defended either. This role for the actor is apparently too appropriate
to be denied him. Ion now knows what he must do to defend himself,
so he is willing to assert that there is no difference between the
rhapsode's and the general's art and that all rhapsodes are generals
(although he cannot bring himself to go so far as to argue that all
generals are rhapsodes). There is a hidden madness in all unselfconscious human lives, and Socrates, in dissecting this soul, brings
its peculiar madness to light. Ion's choice of the general's art is appropriate for many reasons. It is a particular practical art, one which
is pervasive in Homer, one which is needed and admired beyond most
other arts.

But more profoundly one can see that the propriety of Ion's
becoming a general has something to do with the whole view of the
world peculiar to Ion and his understanding of Homer. In the beginning, when Socrates listed the things the poets talk about, the first
item was war, and it was the only one which stood alone, not coupled
with an appropriate companion as were the others. The obvious complement to war, peace, is missing in the poets. Superficially this means
that the great poems tell of warlike heroes and the struggles between
and within cities. In a deeper sense it means that they tell of a world
ruled by gods who also struggle and who refer back to an ultimate
chaos. The only harmony is to be found in the rational cosmos, which
is grasped not by the practical man but by the theoretical man.

541b–   Socrates pursues this theme by asking Ion why he goes around
542b   Greece being a rhapsode instead of a general. Adopting Ion's own
hidden prejudice, Socrates, who never does anything but talk, ridicules
the notion that the Greeks need a man wearing a golden crown more
than a general. Instead of arguing that the interpretation of poetry is
a better and nobler thing than leading men in war, Ion offers an excuse
for doing second best. He is a citizen of a subject city and would not
be used as a general by either Athens or Sparta. Ion would apparently
be willing to adapt himself to the service of either of these warring
cities. Perhaps this is also just what he does with his poetry: he adapts
what is apparently universal to the needs of opposing heres and nows.
His poetry provides the gods which Athenians and Spartans invoke
as guarantors of their causes when they march out to slay one another.
Ion's cosmopolitanism is only a sham with roots in nothing beyond
the needs of the cities, giving particular and passing interests a universal significance. He is a servant who must appear to be master in

order to satisfy his masters. While a philosopher is truly a citizen of the world, in that his pursuit is essentially independent of the opinions or consent of any group of men, the political man needs a country and a people to serve. Ion has no satisfactions which are not dependent on the approval of his spectators. He needs the cities as they need him. For political men the accident of where they are born is decisive in limiting their possibilities of fulfillment.

Socrates tries to act as though these limits of politics did not exist: he treats politics as though it were as cosmopolitan as any of the arts, for example, arithmetic. He abstracts from the peculiar atmosphere of chance and unreason surrounding political life, expressing astonishment at Ion's unwillingness to act like any other man of knowledge; he thereby provides a measure of the difference between the life of reason and that of cities. It is the city to which Ion belongs, and his irrationality only points to the city's. Socrates names a few obscure, not to say unknown men, alleging that they were chosen as generals by Athens. On this rather dubious basis, he asserts that not being a citizen is no hindrance to political participation. Ion, Socrates concludes, must be insisting that it is a hindrance only in order to avoid giving that wondrous display which Socrates has been so eager to hear for so long. Ion, suggests Socrates, must be an unjust man, since he does not fulfill his promise. Or as an alternative, perhaps he is really divinely possessed. Socrates gives Ion a choice: he can be either divine or unjust. Perhaps the two are ultimately the same.

Socrates compares Ion to the slippery Proteus and thus implicitly compares himself to Menelaus, who sought for guidance about the gods from Proteus so he could save himself. But this Proteus cannot help the new Menelaus. So they part, Ion humiliated but wearing a new, divine crown, Socrates in search of more authoritative knowledge of the gods.

ARISTOPHANES AND SOCRATES:
A RESPONSE TO HALL*

[Plato in the Republic] *sought and made a city more to be prayed for than hoped for . . . not such that it can possibly be but one in which it is possible to see the meaning [*ratio*] of political things.*
—Cicero, Republic *II 52*

I am grateful to Professor Hall for a number of reasons, especially for the seriousness with which he has taken my interpretation of the *Republic*. That he disagrees with it is secondary. We do agree on the fundamental thing: it is of utmost importance to understand Plato.

The issues raised by Hall are enormous, and an adequate response to his arguments would require volumes, but what we really disagree about is how to read Plato. He asserts that I read my prejudices into the text. I respond that he does not pay sufficient attention to the text. In looking at a few of his central criticisms, I shall attempt to prove my contention and show the characteristic errors of his approach to the Platonic dialogue.

I

In the first place, Hall presupposes that he knows the Platonic teaching and reads his understanding of it into the text. Arguing against my contention that the best regime of the *Republic* is not a serious proposal, he tells us, "Socrates is explicit that his *polis* is

*Dale Hall, an English political scientist, *Political Theory*, Vol. 5, No. 3, August 1977, pp. 293–313.

natural." I search in vain for Socrates' statement to that effect. Indeed, I know of no assertion anywhere in the Platonic corpus that the city is natural or that man is by nature a political animal. Whatever the *ideas* may be—and they are the highest and most elusive theme to which we must ascend very carefully and slowly from the commonly sensed particulars—there is not the slightest indication that there is an *idea* of the city or of the best city, as there is said to be an *idea* of the beautiful or an *idea* of the just. What the omission means is debatable, but one must begin by recognizing that it is so. Obviously, from the point of view of the *ideas*, the naturalness of the city must have a status very different from that of, for example, man. The kallipolis cannot participate in an *idea* which is not. While there are many men and an *idea* of man, the city does not exist as a particular or as a universal; it is neither sensed nor intellected.

Careful observation of what the text says about this question of naturalness would have helped Hall. In his discussion of the three waves of paradox in Book V, Socrates says (a) the same education and way of life for women as for men is possible because it is natural (456b–c); (b) the community of women and children is not against nature (466d)—however, now Socrates shifts the criterion of possibility from naturalness to coming into being (many things which are not natural, and even against nature, can come into being); (c) the coincidence of philosophy and rule is just that, coincidence or chance (473c–d). All the attention is given to the possibility of that highly improbable coincidence. Cities, let alone the best city, do not come into being as plants and animals do. Some men are by nature fit both to philosophize and to rule the city, but it is not said that it is natural that they do so. If they actually do both, the cause is art, human making, not nature. If I were to use against Hall the methods he uses against me, I would say that, with respect to the naturalness of the city, he has read Aristotle's *Politics*, not Plato's *Republic*. He does not see that the city is more problematic for Plato than for Aristotle.

Just as Hall reads in, he reads out. In trying to argue that for Plato there is no significant distinction between the theoretical and the practical life, he says that Plato "does not suggest that philosophising and ruling are unrelated functions." Compare that to the text: "each of [the philosophers] will go to ruling as a necessary as opposed to a good thing . . . if you discover a life better than ruling for those who are going to rule, it is possible that your well-governed city will come into being. . . . Have you another life that despises political offices other than that of true philosophy? . . . But men who aren't lovers of ruling [they love something other: wisdom] must go to it"

(521a–b). The philosophers won't be willing to act [engage in *praxis*] (519c). There could be no more radical distinction made between the practical and theoretical lives than that drawn in Books V–VII and IX of the *Republic* (cf. especially 476a–b). The separateness of the forms is strongly asserted, as are the possibilities of a reason using only forms without admixture of the senses and a life lived in contemplation of the forms purely. This latter life is the best life, the only good life. It is precisely the difference between it and the life of ruling that is the artifice that is supposed to make the city work. Deed and speech are also radically distinguished, and the latter is said to be absolutely superior.[1] I really find it hard to imagine how Hall is able to say the things he does in the face of the evidence to the contrary. I challenge him to find a single statement in the *Republic* that indicates that the philosophic life requires ruling or that the activity of ruling in any way contributes to philosophizing.[2] What is striking about the *Republic* is the distance Socrates puts between the theoretical and practical lives, a distance belied by things he says elsewhere and by his own life. But that is what he does here, and, as Hall says, "we are accustomed to taking Socrates seriously." There is simply not a scintilla of proof that the making, painting, or "creating" activity of the founders of the city is a part of the philosopher's life as such. Hall piles abstraction on abstraction, unrelated to the text, in order to *construct* a case for the sameness of the two lives, but he has no evidence. The most striking aspect of the last half of his paper is its almost entirely personal character and almost total absence of reference to text. It is true, as he says, that the potential philosophers must be compelled to leave the cave as well as return to it. But once out, they recognize how good it is to be out. They never see a reason to go back, and compelling them to go back is said to be good for the city, not the philosophers. If they thought it good to go back, they would not be good rulers. It is only by going out that they become aware that the kallipolis is a cave, nay Hades, and to be in it is to be a shade (516d; 521c; cf. 386c). In the midst of his complex prestidigitatory activity,

[1]471e–473b; 475d–480a; 485a–b; 510a–511d; 514a–519c; 532a–b; 540a–b. Plato surely makes a distinction between the practical and theoretical lives. Hall only introduces a red herring when he says I took the distinction from Aristotle. There is a difference between them concerning the distinction between *phronesis* and *sophia*, but that is irrelevant here. Everything I said was based on Plato. Hall, on the other hand, comes dangerously close to saying that knowing is making, a view to be found only in modern thought.
[2]The statement at 497a, an intermediary stage in the discussion of philosophy and the city, need mean nothing more than that the philosopher would find more encouragement in such a city than elsewhere. Cf. 528b–c.

Hall announces that it is because I am a modern political scientist that I cannot see that Platonic ruling is really philosophizing. I would like to accept that testimonial to impress some of my colleagues who have their doubts about the genuineness of my credentials as a political scientist, but unfortunately the explanation does not work. Again, one must look at the text. Rulers, in the best city, provide for food, clothing, and shelter, and they lead the soldiers to war. Above all, Hall forgets the reasons the philosophers are invoked: they are primarily matchmakers or eugenicists who have to spend a great deal of time and subtlety on devising "throngs of lies and deceptions" designed to get the right people to have sexual intercourse with one another (458d–460b). Is that a philosophic activity?

Displaying the same tendency to neglect what is really in the text, Hall spins a subtle web of reasonings about a Platonic notion of happiness which is frankly beyond my comprehension, a notion evidently intended to overcome the tensions between philosophy and ruling. In this context he insists that "Plato, clearly, does not define *eudaimonia* in terms of felt satisfaction . . . and the personal happiness of the philosophers is not his primary desideratum." Now, the culmination of the whole dialogue—the judgment concerning the happiness of the unjust man versus that of the just man, which was demanded by Glaucon at the beginning of the dialogue and was its explicit motive—concerns, if I understand what Hall means by *personal* happiness, the personal happiness of the philosopher (576b–588a). The terms of the comparison have been quietly changed during the course of the dialogue from the unjust man versus the just man to the tyrant versus the philosopher. Three tests are made, all three of which are won by the philosopher. The first test is self-sufficiency: the philosopher can get the good things he desires without needing or depending on other men while the tyrant lives in fear and is full of unsatisfiable desires because of his dependency on men. The other two tests prove that the philosopher is the expert *par excellence* in pleasure and that he experiences the purest and most intense pleasures. Socrates calculates that the philosopher's life is 729 times more pleasant than the tyrant's. Is this not "felt satisfaction" of a wholly personal kind? Philosophy is presented as choiceworthy on the ground that it provides permanently accessible pleasures for the individual, and the philosopher here is not presented as ruling or in any way concerned with the city.

In addition to making Plato answer his own questions rather than discovering what Plato's questions are and distorting the phenomena by casting a gray web of abstraction around them rather than letting them come to light in their fullness and complexity, Hall moralizes, not open to the possibility that justice is not preached in the *Republic* but rather questioned and investigated. For example, so sure is he that benefiting one's fellow man is an imperative of Plato's thought that he does not take note of the fact that the city has no concern for other cities and is even willing to harm and stir up factions in them, supporting the inferior elements, solely to keep them from threatening it. Best would be isolation, and next best is crippling one's neighbor; never would it try to improve them (422a–423a). Since the soul is said to be like the city, would not it, too, be concerned only with itself? The vulgar standards of just conduct to which the well-ordered soul is said to conform are all negative—things it does not do, such as stealing, lying, and committing adultery (442e–443a). As we indicated early on, Socrates' just man does no harm; he is not said to do good, to be a benefactor (335d). And the reason why the well-ordered soul does not do harm becomes clear when it is revealed to be the philosophic soul. The philosopher's abstinences are not due to goodwill, a Kantian "settled and sincere disposition to behave justly," but to a lack of caring for the vulgar things on which the vulgar standards are founded. His passionate love of wisdom makes him indifferent to, for example, money (485d–486b). This is no more praiseworthy than a eunuch's abstinence from rape. There is no "moral" motive involved.[3] It escapes Hall that of the three classes in the city, two have no concern for the common good at all—the artisans are in it for gain or out of fear, and the philosophers are there because they are compelled to be—while the dedicated class, the warriors, are dedicated only because they believe in a lie and are deprived of any possibility of privacy. There is, on the evidence of the *Republic*, no enlightened, nonillusionary love of the common good. The virtues of the warriors are finally said to belong more to the body than to the soul, to be mere habits (518d–e). The only authentic virtue is that of the mind contemplating its proper objects. It is not I who Aristotelianize. The *Republic* is not the *Ethics*; there are no moral virtues in it.

I have chosen to mention these points because they help to illustrate what is required to read a Platonic dialogue; and Plato intended to make the requirements for reading him identical to those for philosophizing; his little world is the preparation for the big world. In fine, what is needed is an openness to things as they appear unaided

---

[3]At 487a justice appears in the list of virtues belonging to the philosopher. By 536a it has dropped out.

by the abstractions which so impoverish things that they can no longer cause surprise or wonder and a freedom from a moralism which forbids us to see what in nature defies convention and refuses to console us in our hopes and fears.

II

My difference with Hall can be summarized by saying that he does not take the form of the dialogue seriously, that he does not begin where it fairly cries out for us to begin, with the story or the drama, with those pictures of life on the basis of which we might generalize about life and which are so much more accessible to us than are "Plato's metaphysics" or the *ideas*. If I may be permitted an Aristotelian expression, but one which is of Platonic inspiration, we must begin from the things which are first according to us in order to ascend to the things which are first according to nature. We must talk about shoemakers and pilots and dogs and such things, the Socratic themes so despised by his less wise interlocutors. I can appreciate Hall's opinion that there is something mad in the assertion that a work of political philosophy which argues that philosophers should be kings actually means that philosophers should not be kings. But if we were to suppose for a moment that this is not precisely a book of political philosophy, at least such as we know books of political philosophy to be, but is a drama at one moment of which one of the characters makes an unusual proposal that is designed to affect the action, as are so many speeches in dramas, then the paradoxical character of my interpretation disappears. The tale would go roughly as follows: Socrates visits the Piraeus in the company of a young man whom, according to Xenophon, he is trying to cure of excessive political ambition as a favor to his brother, Plato (Mem. III, vi). There they meet a group of men among whom is a famous intellectual who argues that justice is abiding by laws set down in the interest of the rulers. It is, therefore, in one's interest to be ruler or, put otherwise, to be tyrant. Glaucon, evidently motivated by more than idle curiosity, asks Socrates to show him that justice (understood as concern for equality or law-abidingness) is a good outweighing all the obvious good things (pleasures and honors) which tyranny (understood as the peak of injustice) can procure. Socrates never precisely shows Glaucon that justice as Glaucon conceives it is good. Rather, in the course of founding a city and, thus, learning the nature of justice, Socrates introduces, as a political necessity, the philosophers. Glaucon learns that to be a ruler in the city he has founded he must be a philosopher. Then, when he is shown what philosophy is, he learns that it is the best life and is essentially independent of political life. From the point of view of philosophy—which Glaucon had not considered and, thus, had not considered as a good thing—the city looks like a cave or a prison. The movement from rulers simply to philosophic rulers is a step in Glaucon's liberation from the desire to rule. The dialogue has the character of an ascent, like the ascent from the cave to the region of the *ideas*. At the peak of that ascent Socrates reveals himself to be the happy man. He does not persuade Glaucon that he should not pursue his own good. He only makes him aware of goods to which the tyrant cannot attain and the pursuit of which takes away the temptation to meddle in politics and, hence, to be unjust as a tyrant is unjust. At the end of the comparison between the tyrant's and the philosopher's lives, close to the end of his education, Glaucon recognizes that the philosopher's city exists only in speech, and that no longer disturbs him. Socrates tells him it makes no difference whether it exists, for it can exist in the soul and that is enough (592a–b). A man can be happy being a good citizen of the city of philosophy without its existing. Timocrats and timocratic cities exist; democrats and democratic cities exist; tyrants and tyrannical cities exist; but, although there are no philosophical cities, philosophers exist. The tyrannical man who does not rule a city is not fully a tyrant (578b–c); the philosopher is a philosopher whether or not he is a king in a city. And there is, at this final stage, no suggestion that Glaucon should work to establish this city or that he should even long for its establishment. Glaucon has moved from the desire to be a ruler to the desire to be a ruler-philosopher to the desire to be a philosopher. The conceit of philosopher-kings was the crucial stage in his conversion. In the last word of the *Republic*, Odysseus—the archetype of the wise man—cured of love of honor or ambition and, having seen all the human possibilities, chooses the life of a private man who minds his own business. The *Republic*, while demonstrating Socrates' concern for justice, culminates in providing a foundation not for justice but for moderation.

Hall rightly concentrates on the statement that "unless philosophers rule as kings or those now called kings . . . philosophize . . . there is no rest from ills for the cities." That there will be no rest from ills for the cities is the teaching of the *Republic*, and this is what distinguishes ancient from modern philosophical politics. Socrates, moreover, does not suggest that there are ills of philosophy that would be cured by the union of wisdom and politics. The proposal is for the sake of the city, and not the philosopher. The distinction made in the discussion with Thrasymachus between justice as devotion to a community (be it a band of thieves), which is only necessary, a means to an end (351c–d; 352c–d), and justice as perfection of the soul, which is good in itself (352d–354a), persists throughout. The philosophers' service to the community is necessary, while their life of contemplation on the Isles of the Blessed is good (540b). The two senses of justice are never resolved into a single coherent one.

Hall's failure to read the dialogue as a dialogue, his unawareness of its movement, causes him to give undue weight to isolated phrases or passages torn from their contexts. His greatest error is to take the discussion of *logismos*—calculation or deliberation—in Book IV as providing a definition of the "natural function" (both words are Hall's, not Plato's) of reason rather than as a provisional statement corresponding to the incomplete stage of the argument and of the interlocutors' awareness. Following the parallel of the rulers in the city, who deliberate about the affairs of the city, reason first comes to light in the *Republic* as the element of the soul which calculates about the desires, deciding which should and which should not be indulged. This description is a consequence of the analogy between city and soul which is being pursued in the discussion. What has first been determined about the city is applied to the soul (although Socrates points out that the discussion is inadequate, 435c–d). What we get in Book IV is a plausible account of reason's activity in the affairs of daily life, an activity akin to that of rulers who deliberate about public affairs, one that supports the view that man and city are in perfect harmony. But after the emergence of philosophy in Book V, a totally different account of the rational part of the soul is given, one which shows that the parallel between city and soul breaks down. The highest reaches of the soul are said to long only to *see* what *is* (437c–487a; 509c–511e; 514a–518b; 532a–534d). Deliberation or calculation (*logismos*), which was the only attribute of the rational part of the soul given in Book IV, is no longer even mentioned. The opposition between desire and calculation which was the defining characteristic of calculation in the earlier passage is overcome, and philosophy is described as a form of *eros* (485c; 499b). The contemplative activity of the soul is simply something entirely different from the deliberative activity of a ruling class in a city (533b). Such contemplation is alien to the ruler's ends, and as a body they possess no organ for it. What the soul really is is both a revelation and a surprise in Book V, and its almost accidental discovery changes everything. The philosophic part of the soul has no use for action, and deliberation is not part of its function (527d–528e); it does not calculate. One must look to the difference between *logismos* and *noûs* to appreciate the significance of this development. *Logismos* is for action; *noûs* is for itself. The rulers of the city are highest because they are most useful to the city and its nonphilosophic ends. Reason in the soul is highest because it is the end of man and should be the end of the city. Unless one reads the *Republic* as a drama, one does not see that it has a reversal and a discovery, that there is a peripety. Platonic books are closer in form to dramas than to treatises.

III

I have put off until the end discussion of what is only a subsidiary part of Hall's criticism—what he says about Plato's relation to Aristophanes. But this issue seems to me central to our differences. The elusive texture of Platonic thought—so different from our own—can, I believe, only be approached when one becomes aware of its peculiar combination of what we take to be poetry and philosophy. Or, put otherwise, Platonic philosophy is poetic, not merely stylistically but at its intellectual core, not because Plato is not fully dedicated to reason, but because poetry points to problems for reason that unpoetic earlier and later philosophy do not see and becuases poetic imagination properly understood is part of reason. The Socrates of the *Clouds*—an account of the early Socrates substantially confirmed by the Platonic Socrates (*Phaedo*, 96ff.)—was unpoetic, and this had something to do with his incapacity to understand political things. The Platonic Socrates can in some sense be understood as a response to the Aristophanic Socrates, or, more strongly stated, Socrates may have learned something from Aristophanes. The *Republic*, in one of its guises, is the proof that philosophers are not unpolitical (and it must not be forgotten that, according to all serious testimony, in particular that of Aristotle and Cicero, there was no political philosophy prior to Socrates), that they know the political things best and are most necessary for politics. Socrates, who in the *Clouds* stands aside, is neutral, in the dispute between the just and the unjust speeches, in the *Republic*—in a reference which is clearly to Aristophanes—presents himself as an unconditional partner of the just speech (*Clouds*, 896–7; *Republic*, 368b–c). And in the *Symposium* Aristophanes is Socrates' only serious competitor in the contest for the best praise of *eros:* only these two have some inkling of what *eros* really is. Socrates the philosopher shows that his valid interlocutor is Aristophanes the comic poet, and that he is Aristophanes' superior in politics and erotics. Until we can take Aristophanes seriously and Plato comically, we shall not understand either. It is only our stiff pedantry that causes us to ignore Plato's countless allusions to Aristophanes. For us academics they simply cannot be important. Professor Plato must talk only to his fellow professors. My response is that we must look where Plato tells us to look and not where we think we should look.

Now Hall says he sees nothing funny in Book V. My assertion that there is something ridiculous about the sexes exercising naked together is tossed off lightly by Hall by reference to a passage in Xenophon which does not exist. Hall really means Plutarch, and a glance at the appropriate passage will prove to him that boys and girls in Sparta did not exercise naked together. He, further, fails to understand me. I know that there was homosexuality in Greece. What I meant is that a legislator can consistently forbid homosexual relations and condemn the attractions connected with them (as did the Athenian and Spartan legislators), but he cannot do the same for heterosexual relations. Socrates explicitly says that those who exercise naked together, because they do so, will be sexually drawn to one another (458c–d). Senses of humor, I am aware, do differ, but imagination suggests that the external signs of those attractions on the playing fields might provide some inspiration for tasteless wits.

Similarly, Hall says that Socrates does not appeal to absurd premises in Book V. I do not think it is just my ethnocentrism which gives me the impression that it is absurd for Socrates to found his argument on the assertion that the difference between male and female is no more to be taken into account than the one between bald men and men with hair.

But, to speak meaningfully about the *Republic*'s debt to the *Ecclesiazusae* (*The Assembly of Women*), we must say a few words about the meaning of that play. I shall not enter into the discussion as to whether Socrates really refers to Aristophanes' play. It is too evident to need discussion, and only lack of attention or the desire to quibble could cause one to deny the relation. To support the denial one has to invent schools of thought the existence of which has no basis in historical fact, or to invert all probabilities based on dates as well as capriciously to neglect the text. Socrates calls his new projects the *female drama* (451b–c), just as Aristophanes' play is his female drama *par excellence.* Socrates speaks repeatedly of comedy and laughter with respect to his proposals (e.g., 452a–b; 473c; 518a–b). One need only compare Praxagora's speech putting forth her revolutionary plan with Socrates' own speech to see the great similarities in tone and content

(*Ecclesiazusae*, 583–709; *Republic*, 458–466a). There are several quotes
from the *Ecclesiazusae* in the *Republic*, two of which I shall mention
in what follows. It behooves us to follow the simple procedure of
seeing what this means on the basis of the evidence presented to us
instead of fabricating ancient beliefs about which we know nothing
to explain what we have not yet understood. The *Ecclesiazusae* and
the *Republic* both show female rulers who establish total communism,
i.e., communism of property and women and children. They are the
only writings which ever presented this particular combination. The
writer of the *Ecclesiazusae* is deemed worthy of a response in both the
Apology and the *Symposium*. Why not in the *Republic?* It is improbable
that the response is in the reverse direction because all of Aristophanes'
mentions of Socrates are as an unpoetic, unpolitical, unerotic man,
whereas Plato's Socrates is always countering those charges.

So let us look at the *Ecclesiazusae*. Hall tells us that "for Aristophanes' satire of such social arrangements to have had point, others
must have recommended them quite seriously." On the basis of such
reasoning we would be forced to say that someone must have seriously
proposed that the birds be made gods or that a dung beetle be used
to get to heaven and bring back Peace for Aristophanes to have
invented such conceits. Why should these schemes not have been
among the imaginative poetic novelties on which Aristophanes prided
himself? Surely the hilarious schemes which animate every comedy of
Aristophanes ridicule, or show the ridiculous aspect of, something
important. But the explicit project of the heroes does not reveal the
intended object; it must be sought in an understanding of the effect
of the play as a whole. In the *Ecclesiazusae*, the point is really quite
clear: Aristophanes extends the principle of Athenian democracy to
the extreme and shows that it is absurd, and thereby shows the limits,
or the problem, of that regime. Athens is ridiculed, not some anony-
mous political projector. The Athenians want equality or to abolish
the distinction between rich and poor, have and have-not. Athens is
in trouble, and it is popularly thought that salvation can be achieved
only by reforms which realize the goals of its popular regime. New
rulers, women, propose communism, the utter destruction of privacy,
in order to insure dedication to the common good and allow all to
share equally in all good things, in order to make the city one. This
will be a city which comprehends everything and satisfies all human
longings. Praxagora's reform is subjected to searching criticism in two
great scenes: (a) Chremes in good faith gives all his property to the
city when it is perfectly clear that other men will not. He appears as
a decent fool because the roots of private property go too deep to be

torn out. Hence, inequality and selfishness would seem to be necessary concomitants of any political order. (b) A beautiful young man is forced to have sexual intercourse with a succession of ugly old hags. This is the application of the most radical, but also most necessary, reform connected with communism. What seems to be most private and most unequal by nature must become subject to the public sector, or there will be have-nots in the most extreme and important sense, and the young and the beautiful will have profound reservations in their commitment to civil society. This powerful and unsurpassedly ugly scene lays bare the absurdity of trying to make politics total, of trying to make an equal distribution of all that is rare, special, and splendid, of allowing nothing to escape or transcend the political order. It reveals the tension between *physis* and *nomos*, nature and civil society. By hypothesizing a perfect social union, Aristophanes lets his audience see for itself that it would be a hell, that some things must remain private and that men must accept the inconsistencies of a community which leaves much to privacy. The actualization of the Athenian goal is not to be desired.

Socrates adopts the premise of the *Ecclesiazusae*: for there to be a community, everything must be made public; above all there must be a community of women and children. In a passage that is all but a direct quote from the *Ecclesiazusae* (461c–d; *Ecclesiazusae*, 634–9), Glaucon asks how the citizens would recognize their close kin, to which Socrates responds, as did Praxagora, that they will not. Neither of these great reformers is worried about incest, the prohibition against which is most sacred and seems to be the backbone of both family and city. Their reform is far-reaching indeed.

But this defiance of *nomos* in Plato's picture does not turn out to be ugly or ridiculous, and we should therefore conclude that Plato thought Aristophanes to be wrong about the intransigent character of *nomos*, the impossibility of perfect communism and the transpolitical nature of *eros*. Aristophanes' hostility to philosophy made him miss the crucial point: philosophers, those consummate liars, could make it all work. Because he did not understand philosophy, Aristophanes thought the political problem to be insoluble. The focus of the issue for both Praxagora and Socrates is sexual affairs, and Socrates acts as though he can handle them as Praxagora could not. Useless philosophy proves to be most useful. Socrates as the replacement for Praxagora to turn failure into success is the Platonic improvement on Aristophanes' female drama.

Now it must be noted that Socrates is not introducing some grave, ponderous scholar as ruler. Philosophers as types were as yet essentially unknown and hardly respectable. The public model of the philosopher is that silly little fellow in the basket who makes shoes for gnats in the Clouds. Socrates dares to say that he is the perfect ruler. The comedy consists partly in Socrates' bringing together two of Aristophanes' plays, the Clouds and the Ecclesiazusae, using the ridiculous character of the one to solve the ridiculous problem of the other. The philosophers will see to it that the beautiful sleep with the ugly for the public good and do so without disorder or dissatisfaction.

So all is well. But now Socrates adds his scene, akin to those of Aristophanes. We get a glimpse of the relation of the philosopher to the multitude. Socrates follows Aristophanes' procedure. He makes the proposal and then lets his audience see it in action, letting them judge its actualization for themselves. Socrates uses the same language about the philosopher's relation to the multitude that one of the old hags uses to the beautiful young man: their intercourse is a Diomedean necessity (Ecclesiazusae, 1028–29; Republic, 493c–494a). The multitude can never know or properly use the beautiful, but it will make the beautiful its slave. Aristophanes' comic scene is repeated on a higher level. The impossible and undesirable thing is the forced intercourse of philosophy and the city. The city, which once looked beautiful, has become ugly, and it compels what has now come to light as the truly beautiful. Hag is to boy as city is to philosopher. The privileged eros is philosophic eros. The differences between Aristophanes and Socrates have to do with the old war between philosophy and poetry, and here we can do no more than mention it and point out that it is what we must study. They agree about the limits of the city with respect to the highest things. Socrates uses Aristophanes' mad conceits to highlight both of these points. The political result of the inquiry of the Republic is revealed in the Laws, Plato's discussion of an actualizable regime. There the fundamental compromise is made: private property is accepted. It follows immediately that gentlemen, not philosophers, rule, that women are educated differently and lead very different lives from men, and that the family is retained.

Another perspective on the similarities of the reforms of Praxagora and Socrates is to be found in adopting the point of view of the founders. The question cui bono can be usefully posed about foundings as well as about crimes. In the case of Praxagora, it is clear that her whole institution is an elaborate device to profit her. She is a young woman married to an old man. To satisfy her natural longings she has in the old order to commit adultery, to break the law. Under the new dispensation a young woman who sleeps with an old man—which

Praxagora already does—has the right to make love to a young man. Praxagora's desires have thus become legitimate. Similarly, Socrates, in the Apology, says that he deserves to be fed at public expense in the prytaneum like the Olympic victors (Apology, 36c–e; Republic, 465c–d). The Republic is an outline of the only regime where he would be guaranteed dinner in the prytaneum and be delivered of his persistent domestic problems; or, to put it less poetically, this is the only regime in which philosophy would be respected. Philosophy, like adultery, is illegal in Athens, for the philosophers do not believe in the gods of the city and corrupt the young. In the kallipolis philosophy would no longer be a crime; the farmers would produce food for the philosophers and the auxiliaries would protect them. Praxagora and Socrates both attempt to make their profoundest longings legal. In order to do so they have to make reforms so sweeping as to deny the essential demands of political life (e.g., the prohibition against incest). There is no regime which can serve them, and they must continue to make do as criminals.

Now, what precedes is nothing but a series of hints. An adequate articulation of the issues involved in Socrates' playful competition with Aristophanes is the work of a lifetime. The real questions will only come to light by looking at the texts in full consciousness that we do not now know what the real questions are, let alone the answers to them. Plato's way is to think about the seemingly trivial or outrageous proposals of a Praxagora. We must imitate that way if we are to understand not only ancient thought but the permanent human problems, problems no longer quite visible to us.

CONCLUSION

My differences with Hall come down to whether philosopher-king is a compound formula, joining two distinct activities and, thus, violating the rule of justice, one man–one job, as I insist, or whether philosopher and king are two words for the same thing, as Hall insists. I believe Hall produces no evidence for his belief. Socrates' irony, which he claims I invoke as a deus ex machina, is to be found in the relation of his speeches to his deeds and his treatment of his various companions. It is present to every eye, and only by looking the other way can the problems I say need explaining be ignored or denied. As I pondered what separates me from Hall, I came to the conclusion that he misunderstands how political I take Socrates to be and how much attention I think he paid to particulars (as opposed to ideas).

In other words, he does not pay attention to what I say about the cave or to the cave itself. The philosopher, of course, begins, as do all men, in the cave; and, to go Hall one better, he pays the strictest attention not only to particular or individual things but to their shadows. But the difference between him and other men is that he learns that they are only shadows—shadows which give us access to the truth—whereas they believe the shadows are the real things and are passionately committed to that belief. That is what cave-dwelling means. The cave must always remain cave, so the philosopher is the enemy of the prisoners since he cannot take the nonphilosopher's most cherished beliefs seriously. Similarly, Socrates does care for other men, but only to the extent that they, too, are capable of philosophy, which only a few are. This is an essential and qualitative difference, one that cannot be bridged and that causes fundamental differences of interest. Only they are capable of true virtue (518b–519b). To the extent that the philosopher turns some men to the light, he robs the cave-dwellers of allies. It is not because he lives in the sun, out of the cave, that I say the philosopher is at tension with the city; his problem is due precisely to the fact that he is in it, but in a way different from that of other men. This, however, should be the theme for an ongoing discussion. I only hope that it is clear that Hall's criticism has not settled the issue.

EMILE

In the *Discourse on the Origins of Inequality* Rousseau summons men to hear for the first time the true history of their species.[1] Man was born free, equal, self-sufficient, unprejudiced, and whole; now, at the end of history, he is in chains (ruled by other men or by laws he did not make), defined by relations of inequality (rich or poor, noble or commoner, master or slave), dependent, full of false opinions or superstitions, and divided between his inclinations and his duties. Nature made man a brute, but happy and good. History—and man is the only animal with a history—by the development of his faculties and the progress of his mind has made man civilized, but unhappy and immoral. History is not a theodicy but a tale of misery and corruption.

Emile, on the other hand, has a happy ending, and Rousseau says he cares little if men take it to be only a novel, for it ought, he says, to be the history of his species.[2] And therewith he provides the key to *Emile*. It is, as Kant says,[3] the work which attempts to reconcile nature with history, man's selfish nature with the demands of civil society, hence, inclinations with duty. Man requires a healing education which returns him to himself. Rousseau's paradoxes—his attack on the arts and the sciences while he practices them, his praise of the savage and natural freedom over against his advocacy of the ancient

[1] In *Oeuvres complètes de Jean-Jacques Rousseau*, ed. Bernard Gagnebin and Marcel Raymond, 4 vols. (Paris: Gallimard, 1959–1969, Bibliothèque de la Pléiade), Vol. 3, p. 133; *The First and Second Discourses*, ed. R. Masters (New York: St. Martin's, 1964), pp. 103–4.
[2] P. 416.
[3] "Conjectural Beginning of Human History," in *On History*, ed. Lewis Beck (Indianapolis, Ind.: Bobbs-Merrill, 1963), pp. 60–61.

city, the general will, and virtue, his perplexing presentations of himself as citizen, lover, and solitary—are not expressions of a troubled
soul but accurate reflections of an incoherence in the structure of the
world we all face, or rather, in general, do not face; and *Emile* is an
experiment in restoring harmony to that world by reordering the emergence of man's acquisitions in such a way as to avoid the imbalances
created by them while allowing the full actualization of man's potential. Rousseau believed that his was a privileged moment, a moment
when all of man's faculties had revealed themselves and when man
had, furthermore, attained for the first time knowledge of the principles
of human nature. *Emile* is the canvas on which Rousseau tried to paint
all of the soul's acquired passions and learning in such a way as to
cohere with man's natural wholeness. It is a *Phenomenology of the Mind*
posing as Dr. Spock.

Thus *Emile* is one of those rare total or synoptic books, a book
with which one can live and which becomes deeper as one becomes
deeper, a book comparable to Plato's *Republic*, which it is meant to
rival or supersede.[4] But it is not recognized as such in spite of Rousseau's own judgment that it was his best book and Kant's view that
its publication was an event comparable to the French Revolution.
Of Rousseau's major works it is the one least studied or commented
on. It is as though the book's force had been entirely spent on impact
with men like Kant and Schiller, leaving only the somewhat cranky
residue for which the book retains its fame in teacher training schools:
the harangues against swaddling and in favor of breast feeding and
the learning of a trade. Whatever the reasons for its loss of favor (and
this would make an interesting study) *Emile* is a truly great book, one
that lays out for the first time and with the greatest clarity and vitality
the modern way of posing the problems of psychology.

By this I mean that Rousseau is at the source of the tradition
which replaces virtue and vice as the causes of a man's being good or
bad, happy or miserable, with such pairs of opposites as sincere/insin-
cere, authentic/inauthentic, inner-directed/other-directed, real self/
alienated self. All these have their source in Rousseau's analysis of
amour de soi and *amour-propre*, a division within man's soul resulting
from man's bodily and spiritual dependence on other men which rup-
tures his original unity or wholeness. The distinction between *amour
de soi* and *amour-propre* is meant to provide the true explanation for
that tension within man which had in the past been understood to
be a result of the opposed and irreconcilable demands of the body and

[4]*Emile*, tr. Bloom 1979 (New York: Basic Books), p. 40.

the soul. *Emile* gives the comprehensive account of the genesis of *amour-propre*, displays its rich and multifarious aspects (spreads the peacock's tail, as it were), and maps man's road back to himself from his spiritual exile (his history) during which he wandered through nature and society, a return to himself which incorporates into his substance all the cumbersome treasures he gathered en route. This analysis supersedes that based on the distinction between body and soul, which in its turn had activated the quest for virtue, seen as the taming and controlling of the body's desires under the guidance of the soul's reason. It initiates the great longing to be one's self and the hatred of alienation which characterizes all modern thought. The wholeness, unity, or singleness of man—a project ironically outlined in the *Republic*—is the serious intention of *Emile* and almost all that came afterward.

Emile is written to defend man against a great threat which bids fair to cause a permanent debasement of the species, namely, the almost inevitable universal dominance of a certain low human type which Rousseau was the first to isolate and name: the *bourgeois*. Rousseau's enemy was not the *ancien régime*, its throne, its altar, or its nobility. He was certain that all these were finished, that revolution would shortly sweep them away to make room for a new world based on the egalitarian principles of the new philosophy. The real struggle would then concern the kind of man who was going to inhabit that world, for the striking element of the situation was and is that a true theoretical insight seems to have given rise to a low human consequence. What I mean by this is that the *bourgeois*, that debased form of the species, is the incarnation of the political science of Hobbes and Locke, the first principles of which Rousseau accepted. We can see this with particular clarity in Tocqueville's *Democracy in America*, the scheme of which is adopted from Rousseau. Equality, Tocqueville tells us, is now almost a providential fact; no one believes any longer in the justice of the principles on which the old distinctions between ranks or classes were made and which were the basis of the old regime. The only question remaining is whether freedom can accompany equality or universal tyranny will result from it. It is to the formation of free men and free communities founded on egalitarian principles to which both Rousseau and Tocqueville are dedicated.

Now, who, according to Rousseau, is the *bourgeois*? Most simply, following Hegel's formula, he is the man motivated by fear of violent death, the man whose primary concern is self-preservation or, according to Locke's correction of Hobbes, comfortable self-preservation.

Or, to describe the inner workings of his soul, he is the man who, when dealing with others, thinks only of himself, and on the other hand, in his understanding of himself, thinks only of others. He is a role-player. The *bourgeois* is contrasted by Rousseau, on the one side, with the natural man, who is whole and simply concerned with himself, and on the other, with the citizen, whose very being consists in his relation to his city, who understands his good to be identical with the common good. The *bourgeois* distinguishes his own good from the common good. His good requires society, and hence he exploits others while depending on them. He must define himself in relation to them. The *bourgeois* comes into being when men no longer believe that there is a common good, when the notion of the fatherland decays. Rousseau hints that he follows Machiavelli in attributing this decay to Christianity, which promised the heavenly fatherland and thereby took away the supports from the earthly fatherland, leaving social men who have no reason to sacrifice private desire to public duty.

What Christianity revealed, modern philosophy gave an account of: man is not naturally a political being; he has no inclination toward justice. By nature he cares only for his own preservation, and all of his faculties are directed to that end. Men are naturally free and equal in the decisive respects: they have no known authority over them, and they all pursue the same independent end. Men have a natural right to do what conduces to their preservation. All of this Rousseau holds to be true. He differs only in that he does not believe that the duty to obey the laws of civil society can be derived from self-interest. Hobbes and Locke burdened self-interest with more than it can bear; in every decisive instance the sacrifice of the public to the private follows from nature. They produced hypocrites who make promises they cannot intend to keep and who feign concern for others out of concern for themselves, thus using others as means to their ends and alienating themselves. Civil society becomes merely the combat zone for the pursuit of power—control over things and especially over men. With enlightenment the illusions are dispelled, and men learn that they care about their own lives more than about country, family, friendship, or honor. Fanaticism, although dangerous and distorting, could at least produce selfless and extraordinary deeds. But now fanaticism gives way to calculation. And pride, although it is the spur to domination, is also allied with that noble indifference to life which seems to be a precondition of freedom and the resistance to tyranny. But quenched by fear, pride gives way to vanity, the concern for petty advantages over others. This diminution of man is the apparent result of his enlightenment about his true nature.

In response to this challenge of the new philosophy Rousseau undertakes to rethink man's nature in its relation to the need for society engendered by history. What he attempts is to present an egalitarian politics that rivals Plato's politics in moral appeal rather than an egalitarian politics that debases man for the sake of the will-of-the-wisp, security. In imagination he takes an ordinary boy and experiments with the possibility of making him into an autonomous man—morally and intellectually independent, as was Plato's philosopher-king, an admittedly rare, and hence aristocratic, human type. The success of such a venture would prove the inherent dignity of man as man, each and every ordinary man, and thus it would provide a high-level ground for the choice of democracy. Since Rousseau, overcoming of the *bourgeois* has been regarded as almost identical with the problem of the realization of true democracy and the achievement of "genuine personality."

The foregoing reflections give a clue to the literary character of *Emile.* The two great moral-political traditions that were ultimately displaced by the modern natural right teachings—that is, the biblical and the classical—were accompanied by great works of what may be called poetry. This poetry depicts great human types who embody visions of the right way of life, who make that way of life plausible, who excite admiration and emulation. The Bible, on the highest level, gives us prophets and saints; and in the realm of ordinary possibility it gives us the pious man. Homer and Plutarch give us, at the peak, heroes; and, for everyday fare, gentlemen. Modern philosophy, on the other hand, could not inspire a great poetry corresponding to itself. The exemplary man whom it produces is too contemptible for the noble Muse; he can never be a model for those who love the beautiful. The fact that he cannot is symptomatic of how the prosaic new philosophy truncates the human possibility. With *Emile* Rousseau confronts this challenge and dares to enter into competition with the greatest of the old poets. He sets out to create a human type whose charms can rival those of the saint or the tragic hero—the natural man—and thereby shows that his thought, too, can comprehend the beautiful in man.

Emile consists of a series of stories, and its teaching comes to light only when one has grasped each of these stories in its complex detail and artistic unity. Interpretation of this "novel," the first *Bildungs-roman*, requires a union of *l'esprit de géométrie* and *l'esprit de finesse*, a union which it both typifies and teaches. It is impossible here to do more than indicate the plan of the work and tentatively describe its general intention in the hope of indicating the nature of this work

whose study is so imperative for an understanding of the human possibility.

I

Emile is divided into two large segments. Books I–III are devoted
to the rearing of a civilized savage, a man who cares only about himself,
who is independent and self-sufficient and on whom no duties that
run counter to his inclinations and so divide him are imposed, whose
knowledge of the crafts and the sciences does not involve his incor-
poration into the system of public opinion and division of labor. Books
IV–V attempt to bring this atomic individual into human society and
into a condition of moral responsibility on the basis of his inclinations
and his generosity.

Rousseau's intention in the first segment comes mostly clearly to
light in its culmination, when Jean-Jacques, the tutor, gives his pupil
the first and only book he is to read prior to early adulthood. Before
presenting his gift, Jean-Jacques expresses to the reader the general
sentiment that he hates all books—including, implicitly but especially, the book of books, the guide of belief and conduct, the Bible.
Books act as intermediaries between men and things; they attach men
to the opinions of others rather than forcing them to understand on
their own or leaving them in ignorance. They excite the imagination,
increasing thereby the desires, the hopes, and the fears beyond the
realm of the necessary. All of Emile's early rearing is an elaborate
attempt to avoid the emergence of the imagination which, according
to the Discourse on the Origins of Inequality, is the faculty that turns
man's intellectual progress into the source of his misery. But in spite
of this general injunction against books and in direct contradiction
of what he has just said, Rousseau does introduce a book, one which
presents a new teaching and a new mode of teaching. The book is
Robinson Crusoe, and it is not meant to be merely a harmless amusement for Emile but to provide him with a vision of the whole and a
standard for the judgment of both things and men.[5]

Robinson Crusoe is a soliary man in the state of nature, outside
of civil society and unaffected by the deeds or opinions of men. His
sole concern is his preservation and comfort. All his strength and
reason are dedicated to these ends, and utility is his guiding principle,
the principle that organizes all his knowledge. The world he sees

[5]Op. cit., p. 184ff.

contains neither gods nor heroes; there are no conventions. Neither the memory of Eden nor the hope of salvation affects his judgment. Nature and natural deeds are all that is of concern to him. *Robinson Crusoe* is a kind of Bible of the new science of nature and reveals man's true original condition.

This novel, moreover, provides a new kind of play for the first activity of the imagination. In the first place, the boy does not imagine beings or places which do not exist. He imagines himself in situations and subject to necessities which are part of his experience. Actually his imagination divests itself of the imaginary beings that seem so real in ordinary society and are of human making. He sees himself outside of the differences of nation and religion which cover over nature and are the themes of ordinary poetry. Second, he does not meet with heroes to whom he must subject himself or whom he is tempted to rival. Every man can be Crusoe and actually is Crusoe to the extent that he tries to be simply man. Crusoe's example does not alienate Emile from himself as do the other fictions of poetry; it helps him to be himself. He understands his hero's motives perfectly and does not ape deeds the reasons for which he cannot imagine.

A boy, who imagining himself alone on an island uses all of his energy in thinking about what he needs to survive and how to procure it, will have a reason for all his learning; its relevance to what counts is assured; and the fear, reward, or vanity that motivate ordinary education are not needed. Nothing will be accepted on authority; the evidence of his senses and the call of his desires will be his authorities. Emile, lost in the woods and hungry, finds his way home to lunch by his knowledge of astronomy. For him astronomy is not a discipline forced on him by his teachers, or made attractive by the opportunity to show off, or an expression of his superstition. In this way Rousseau shows how the sciences, which have served historically to make men more dependent on one another, can serve men's independence. In this way the Emile who moves in civil society will put different values on things and activities than do other men. The division of labor which produces superfluity and makes men partial—pieces of a great machine—will seem like a prison, and an unnecessary prison, to him. He will treasure his wholeness. He will know real value, which is the inverse of the value given things by the vanity of social men. And he will respect the producers of real value and despise the producers of value founded on vanity. Nature will be always present to him, not as doctrine but as a part of his very senses. Thus *Robinson Crusoe*, properly prepared for and used, teaches him the utility of the sciences and makes him inwardly free in spite of society's constraints.

Here then we have Rousseau's response to Plato. Plato said that all men always begin by being prisoners in the cave. The cave is civil society considered in its effect on the mind of those who belong to it. Their needs, fears, hopes, and indignations produce a network of opinions and myths, which make communal life possible and give it meaning. Men never experience nature directly but always mix their beliefs into what they see. Liberation from the cave requires the discovery of nature under the many layers of convention, the separating out of what is natural from what is man-made. Only a genius is capable of attaining a standpoint from which he can see the cave as a cave. That is why the philosopher, the rarest human type, can alone be autonomous and free of prejudice. Now, Rousseau agrees that once in the cave, genius is required to emerge from it. He also agrees that enlightenment is spurious and merely the substitution of one prejudice for another. He himself was born in a cave and had to be a genius to attain his insight into the human condition. His life is a testimony to the heroic character of the quest for nature. But he denies that the cave is natural. The right kind of education, one independent of society, can put a child into direct contact with nature without the intermixture of opinion. Plato purified poetry so as to make its view of the world less hostile to reason, and he replaced the ordinary lies by a noble lie. Rousseau banishes poetry altogether and suppresses all lies. At most he gives Emile Robinson Crusoe, who is not an "other" but only himself. Above all, no gods. At the age of fifteen, Emile has a standpoint outside of civil society, one fixed by his inclinations and his reason, from which he sees that his fellow men are prisoners in a cave and by which he is freed from any temptation to fear the punishments or seek the honors which are part of it. Rousseau, the genius, has made it possible for ordinary men to be free, and in this way he proves in principle the justice of democracy.

Thus Rousseau's education of the young Emile confines itself to fostering the development of the faculties immediately connected with his preservation. His desire for the pleasant and avoidance of the painful are given by nature. His senses are the natural means to those ends. And the physical sciences, like mathematics, physics, and astronomy, are human contrivances which, if solidly grounded on the pure experience of the senses, extend the range of the senses and protect them from the errors of imagination. The tutor's responsibility is, in the first place, to let the senses develop in relation to their proper objects; and, secondly, to encourage the learning of the sciences as the almost natural outcome of the use of the senses. Rousseau calls this tutelage, particularly with reference to the part that has to do with the senses, negative education. All animals go through a similar apprenticeship to life. But with man something intervenes that impedes or distorts nature's progress, and therefore a specifically negative education, a human effort, is required. This new factor is the growth of the passions, particularly fear of death and *amour-propre*. Fed by imagination and intermingling with the desires and the senses, they transform judgment and lead to a special kind of merely human, or mythical, interpretation of the world. Negative education means specifically the tutor's artifices invented for the purpose of preventing the emergence of these two passions which attach men to one another and to opinions.

With respect to fear of death, Rousseau flatly denies that man does naturally fear death, and hence denies the premise of Hobbes's political philosophy (as well as what appears to be the common opinion of all political thinkers). Now Rousseau does not disagree with the modern natural right thinkers that man's only natural vocation is self-preservation or that man seeks to avoid pain, but Rousseau insists that man is not at first aware of the meaning of death, nor does man change his beliefs or ways of life to avoid it. He argues that death, as Hobbes's man sees it, is really a product of the imagination; and only on the basis of that imagination will he give up his natural idle and pleasure-loving life in order to pursue power after power so as to forestall death's assaults. The conception that life can be extinguished turns life, which is the condition of living, into an end in itself. No animal is capable of such a conception, and, therefore, no animal thus transforms his life. Rousseau suggests that a man can be kept at the animal's unconscious level in regard to death long enough for him to have established a fixed and unchanging positive way of life, a way of life in which he will be accustomed to pain as well as knowledgeable enough not to be overwhelmed by the fact of death when he becomes fully aware of it. Ordinarily fear of death leads to one of two possible responses: superstition or the attempt to conquer the inevitability of dying. The first gives hope that gods will protect one in this life or provide one with another life. The second response, that of the Enlightenment, uses science to prolong life and establish solid political regimes, putting off the inevitable and absorbing men in the holding action. Neither faces the fact of death, and both pervert consciousness.

This leads us to what Socrates meant by the dictum that philosophy is "learning how to die." All men die, and many die boldly or resolutely; but practically none does so, however, without illusion. Such illusion constitutes the horizon of the cave whose conventions are designed to support human hopes and fears. Thus to know how to die is equivalent to being liberated from the cave. And Rousseau, who argues that there is no natural cave, therefore also concludes that men naturally know how to die. "Priests, doctors and philosophers unlearn us how to die."[6] He does not suggest that every savage or every baby has meditated on death as did Socrates. He means that, naturally, every man is without the illusions about death that pervert life and require the Socratic effort. The tutor's function is to forestall the ministrations of priests, doctors, and philosophers which engender and nourish the fear of death. The simple lesson is that man must rely on himself and recognize and accept necessity; Rousseau shows how this can be achieved without requiring the exercise of the rarest virtues.

Although fear of death makes it difficult to accept necessity, amour-propre is what makes it difficult to recognize necessity. This is the murky passion that accounts for the "interesting" relationships men have with one another, and it is the keystone of Rousseau's psychological teaching. The primary intention of the negative education is to prevent amour de soi from turning into amour-propre, for this is the true source of man's dividedness. Rousseau's treatment of this all-important theme is best introduced by his discussion of the meaning of a baby's tears.[7]

Tears, he tells us, are a baby's language and naturally express physical discomfort and are pleas for help. The parent or nurse responds by satisfying a real need, feeding the baby, for example, or removing the source of pain. But at some point the child is likely to recognize that his tears have the effect of making things serve him through the intermediary of adults. The world responds to his wishes. His will can make things move to satisfy his desires. At this point the baby loses interest in providing himself with things; his inner motive to become strong enough to get for himself the things that others now provide for him is transformed into a desire to control the instrument which provides him with those things. His concern with his physical needs is transformed into a passion to control the will of adults. His tears become commands and frequently no longer are related to his real needs but only to testing his power. He cannot stop it from raining by crying, but he can make an adult change his mind. He becomes aware of will; and he knows that wills, as opposed to necessity, are subject to command, that they are changing. He quickly learns that, for his life, control over men is more useful than adaptation to things.

[6]Op. cit., p. 55.
[7]Op. cit., pp. 64–69.

Therefore, the disposition of adults toward him replaces his bodily needs as his primary concern. Every wish that is not fulfilled could, in his imagination, be fulfilled if the adult only willed it that way. His experience of his own will teaches him that others' wills are selfish and plastic. He therefore seeks for power over men rather than for the use of things. He becomes a skillful psychologist, able to manipulate others.

With the possibility of change of wills emerges the justification for blame and hence for anger. Nature does not have intentions; men do. Anger is caused by intentional wrong, and the child learns to see intention to do wrong in that which opposes him. He becomes an avenger. A squalling brat is most often testing his power. If he gets what he wants, he is a master. If he fails, he is angry, resentful, and likely to become slavish. In either event he has entered into a dialectic of mastery and slavery which will occupy him for his whole life. His natural and healthy self-love and self-esteem (*amour de soi*) give way to a self-love relative to other men's opinions of him; henceforth he can esteem himself only if others esteem him. Ultimately he makes the impossible demand that others care for him more than they care for themselves. The most interesting of psychological phenomena is this doubling or dividing of self-love; it is one of the few distinctively human phenomena (no animal can be insulted); and from it flow anger, pride, vanity, resentment, revenge, jealousy, indignation, competition, slavishness, humility, capriciousness, rebelliousness, and almost all the other passions that give poets their themes. In these first seeds of *amour-propre* as seen in tears, one can recognize the source of the human problem.

Rousseau's solution to *amour-propre*, which would seem inevitably to lead to conflict among men—their using one another as means to their own ends and the need for government and law—is, as with the fear of death, to prevent its emergence at least for a long time. No self-overcomings are required. The child must be dependent on things and not on wills. The tutor and his helpers must disappear, as it were, and everything that happens to the child must seem to be an inevitable effect of nature. Against necessity he will not rebel; it is only the possibility of overcoming necessity or the notion that there is a will lurking behind it which disturbs his unclouded relation to things as they are. It is the mediation of human beings in the satisfaction of need that causes the problem.

Now all of this has even more significance than is immediately apparent, for Rousseau suggests that superstition, all attribution of intention to inanimate things or to the world as a whole, is a result of the early experience of will. In moving things at the child's command the parent gives the child the impression that all things are moved by intention and that command or prayer can put them at man's disposal. Moreover, anger itself animates. The child who is angry at what does not bend to his will attributes a will to it. This is the case with all anger, as a moment's reflection will show. Anger is allied with and has its origin in *amour-propre*. Once it is activated, it finds intention and responsibility everywhere. Finally it animates rivers, storms, the heavens, and all sorts of benevolent and malevolent beings. It moralizes the universe in the service of *amour-propre*.

In early childhood, there is a choice: the child can see everything or nothing as possessing a will like his own. Either whim or necessity governs the world for him. Neither case is true, but for the child the notion that necessity governs his world is the more salutary because nature is necessity and the primary things are necessary. The passions must submit to necessity, whereas necessity cannot be changed by the passions.[8] Before he comes to terms with will, a man must have understood and accepted necessity. Otherwise he is likely to spend his life obeying and fearing gods or trying to become one. Unlike more recent proponents of freedom, Rousseau recognized that without necessity the realm of freedom can have no meaning.

Rousseau's teaching about *amour-propre* goes to the heart of his disagreement with Plato. Plato had argued that something akin to what Rousseau calls *amour-propre* is an independent part of the soul. This is *thymos*, spiritedness, or simply anger. It is the motive of his warriors in the *Republic* and is best embodied in Achilles, who is almost entirely *thymos*. Plato was aware of all the dangers of *thymos*, but he insisted that it must be given its due because it is part of human nature, because it can be the instrument for restraining desire, and because it is connected with a noble and useful human type. Simply, it is *thymos* that makes men overcome their natural fear of death. Rather than excise it, Plato sought to tame this lion in the soul. The education in Books II–III of the *Republic* suggests the means to make it gentle and submissive to reason. However, these warriors do require myths and noble lies. They are cave dwellers. Man naturally animates the universe and tries to make it responsive to his demands and blames it for resisting. Plato focuses on Achilles, who struggles with a river that he takes to be a god, just as Rousseau is fascinated by the madness of Xerxes, who beats a recalcitrant sea.[9] These are the extreme but

[8]Op. cit., p. 219.
[9]Plato, *Republic*, 391a–b.

most revealing instances of the passion to rule. The difference between Plato and Rousseau on this crucial point comes down to whether anger is natural or derivative. Rousseau says that a child who is not corrupted and wants a cookie will never rebel against the phrase, "There are no more," but only against, "You cannot have one." Plato insists that this is not so. Men naturally see intention where there is none and must become wise in order to separate will from necessity in nature. They do, however, both agree that *thymos* is an important part of the spiritual economy, and that, once present, it must be treated with the greatest respect. Herein they differ from Hobbes, who simply doused this great cause of war with buckets of fear, in the process extinguishing the soul's fire. Rousseau gives a complete account of pride and its uses and abuses, whereas other modern psychologists have either lost sight of it or tried to explain it away. Our education does not take it seriously, and we risk producing timid souls or ones whose untrained spiritedness is wildly erratic and seeks dangerous outlets.

Given that the child must never confront other wills, Jean-Jacques tells us that he cannot be given commandments. He would not understand even the most reasonable restriction on his will as anything other than the expression of the selfishness of the one giving the commandments. The child must always do what he wants to do. This, we recognize, is the dictum of modern-day progressive education, and Rousseau is rightly seen as its source. What is forgotten is that Rousseau's full formula is that while the child must always do what he wants to do, he should want to do only what the tutor wants him to do.[10] Since an uncorrupt will does not rebel against necessity, and the tutor can manipulate the appearance of necessity, he can determine the will without sowing the seeds of resentment. He presents natural necessity in palpable form to the child so that the child lives according to nature prior to understanding it.

Rousseau demonstrates this method in a story that shows how he improves on earlier moral teachings.[11] He puts his Emile in a garden where there are no *nos*, no forbidden fruit, and no Fall, and tries to show that in the end his pupil will be healthy, whole, and of a purer morality than the old Adam. He gets Emile to respect the fruit of another without tempting him.

The boy is induced to plant some beans as a kind of game. His curiosity, imitativeness, and childish energy are used to put him to the task. He watches the beans grow while Jean-Jacques orates to him, supporting him in the pleasure he feels at seeing the result of his work

[10]Op. cit., p. 120
[11]Op. cit., pp. 97–100

and encouraging him in the sense that the beans are his by supplying a proper rationale for that sense. The speech does not bore him as a sermon would because it supports his inclination instead of opposing it. Jean-Jacques gives him what is in essence Locke's teaching on property. The beans belong to Emile because he has mixed his labor with them. Jean-Jacques begins by teaching him his right to his beans rather than by commanding him to respect the fruits of others.

Once the child has a clear notion of what belongs to him, he is given his first experience of injustice. One day he finds that his beans have been plowed under. And therewith he also has his first experience of anger, in the form of righteous indignation. He seeks the guilty party with the intention of punishing him. His selfish concern is identical with his concern for justice. But much to his surprise, Emile finds that the criminal considers himself to be the injured party and is equally angry with him. It is the gardener, and he had planted seeds for melons—melons that were to be eaten by Emile—and Emile had plowed under those seeds to plant his beans. Here we have will against will, anger against anger. Although Emile's wrath loses some of its force—inasmuch as the gardener has an even better claim to have right on his side (he was the first occupant), and this according to the very notion of right which Emile uses and which he so eagerly imbibed from Jean-Jacques—the situation could lead to war. But Jean-Jacques avoids that outcome by means of two stratagems. First, Emile's attention is diverted from his beans by the thought of the rare melons he would have enjoyed. Second, a kind of social contract is arranged: in the future Emile will stay away from the gardener's lands if he is granted a small plot for his beans. In this way the boy is brought to understand and respect the property of others without losing anything of his own. If there were a conflict of interest, Emile would naturally prefer his own. But Jean-Jacques does not put him in that position. If Emile were commanded to keep away from what he desires, the one who commanded him to do so would be responsible for setting him against himself and encouraging him to deceive. A luscious fruit in the garden which was forbidden would only set the selfish will of the owner against Emile's nature. Jean-Jacques at least gives Emile grounds for respecting property and brings him as close to an obligation as can be grounded on mere nature. Greater demands at this stage would be both ineffective and corrupting. The tempter is the giver of commandments. Rousseau here follows Hobbes in deriving duties, or approximations to them, from rights. In this way Emile will rarely infringe the rights of others, and he will have no intention to harm them.

It is this latter that constitutes the morality of the natural man and also that of the wise man (according to Rousseau).[12] It takes the place of the Christian's Golden Rule. When Rousseau says that man is by nature good, he means that man, concerned only with his own well-being, does not naturally have to compete with other men (scarcity is primarily a result of extended desire), nor does he care for their opinions (and, hence, he does not need to try to force them to respect him). Man's goodness is identical to his natural freedom (of body and soul) and equality. And here he agrees, contrary to the conventional wisdom, with Machiavelli, who said men are all bad. For Machiavelli meant that men are bad when judged from the standpoint of the common good, or of how men ought to live, or of the imaginary cities of the old writers. These make demands on men contrary to their natural inclinations and are therefore both unfounded and ineffective. If these standards are removed and men's inclinations are accepted rather than blamed, it turns out that with the cooperation of these inclinations sound regimes can be attained. From the standpoint of imaginary perfection man's passions are bad; from that of the natural desire for self-preservation they are good. Machiavelli preaches the adoption of the latter standpoint and the abandonment of all transcendence and with it the traditional dualism. And it is this project of reconciliation with what is that Rousseau completes in justifying the wholeness of self-concern, in proving that the principles of the old morality are not only ineffective but the cause of corruption (since they cause men to deny themselves and thus to become hypocrites), and in learning how to control that imagination which gives birth to the imaginary cities (which, in their opposition to the real cities, are the signs of man's dividedness).

The moral education of the young Emile is, then, limited to the effective establishment of the rule that he should harm no one. And this moral rule cooperates with the intellectual rule that he should know how to be ignorant. This latter means that only clear and distinct evidence should ever command belief. Neither passions nor dependencies should make him need to believe. All his knowledge should be relevant to his real needs, which are small and easily satisfied. In a sense, Rousseau makes his young Emile an embodiment of the Enlightenment's new scientific method. His will to affirm never exceeds his capacity to prove. For others that method is only a tool, liable to the abuses of the passions and counterpoised by many powerful needs. All this is described in the *Discourse on the Arts and Sciences*. But to

[12]Op. cit., pp. 104–5; Plato, *Republic*, 335a–e.

Emile, whose only desire is to know and live according to the necessary, the new science of the laws of nature is a perfect complement.
With a solid floor constituted by healthy senses in which he trusts
and a ceiling provided by astronomy, Emile is now prepared to admit
his fellows into a structure which their tempestuous passions cannot
shake. This fifteen-year-old, who has not unlearned how to die, harms
no one, and knows how to be ignorant, possesses a large share of the
Socratic wisdom.

II

Emile at fifteen cares no more for his father than his dog. A child
who did would be motivated by fear or desire for gain induced by
dependency. Rousseau has made Emile free of those passions by keeping him self-sufficient, and he has thus undermined the economic
foundations of civil society laid by Hobbes and Locke. Since Rousseau
agrees with the latter that man has no natural inclination to civil
society and the fulfillment of obligation, he must find some other
selfish natural passion that can somehow be used as the basis for a
genuine—as opposed to a spurious, competitive—concern for others.
Such a passion is necessary in order to provide the link between the
individual and disinterested respect for law or the rights of others,
which is what is meant by real morality.

Rousseau finds such a solution in the sexual passion. It necessarily
involves other individuals and results in relations very different from
those following from fear or love of gain. Moreover, Rousseau discovers
that sexual desire, if its development is properly managed, has singular
effects on the soul. Books IV–V are a treatise on sex education,
notwithstanding the fact that they give a coherent account of God,
love, and politics. "Civilization" can become "culture" when it is
motivated and organized by sublimated sex.

Sublimation as the source of the soul's higher expressions—as
the explanation of that uniquely human turning away from mere bodily
gratification to the pursuit of noble deeds, arts, and thoughts—was
introduced to the world by Rousseau. The history of the notion can
be traced from him through Kant, Schopenhauer, and Nietzsche (who
first introduced the actual term), and to Freud (who popularized it).
Rousseau's attempt to comprehend the richness of man's soul within
the context of modern scientific reductionism led him to an interpretation which is still our way of looking at things although we have
lost clarity about its intention and meaning. Rousseau knew that there

are sublime things; he had inner experience of them. He also knew that there is no place for the sublime in the modern scientific explanation of man. Therefore, the sublime had to be made out of the nonsublime; this is sublimation. It is a raising of the lower to the higher. Characteristically, those who speak about sublimation since Freud are merely lowering the higher, reducing the sublime things to their elements and losing a hold on the separate dignity of the sublime. We no longer know what is higher about the higher.

These last two books of *Emile* then undertake in a detailed way the highly problematic task of showing how the higher might be derived from the lower without being reduced to it, while at the same time giving us some sense of what Rousseau means by the sublime or noble. It has not in the past been sufficiently emphasized that everything in Books IV–V is related to sex. Yet without making that connection the parts cannot be interpreted nor the whole understood.

Rousseau takes it for granted that sex is naturally only a thing of the body. There is no teleology contained in the sexual act other than generation—no concern for the partner, no affection for the children on the part of the male, no directedness to the family. As a simply natural phenomenon, it is not more significant or interesting than eating. In fact, since natural man is primarily concerned with his survival, sex is of secondary importance inasmuch as it contributes nothing to the survival of the individual. But because it is related to another human being, sex easily mingles with and contributes to nascent *amour-propre*. Being liked and preferred to others becomes important in the sexual act. The conquest, mastery, and possession of another will thus also become central to it, and what was originally bodily becomes almost entirely imaginary. This semifolly leads to the extremes of alienation and exploitation. But precisely because the sexual life of civilized man exists primarily in the imagination, it can be manipulated in a way that the desire for food or sleep cannot be. Sexual desire, mixed with imagination and *amour-propre,* if it remains unsatisfied produces a tremendous psychic energy that can be used for the greatest deeds and thoughts. Imaginary objects can set new goals, and the desire to be well thought of can turn into love of virtue. But everything depends on purifying and elevating this desire and making it inseparable from its new objects. Thus Rousseau, although Burke could accuse him of pedantic lewdness, would be appalled by contemporary sex education, which separates out the bodily from the spiritual in sex, does not understand the problem involved in treating the bloated passions of social man as though they were natural, is oblivious to the difficulty of attaching the indeterminate drive to useful and noble objects, and fails to appreciate the salutary effect of prolonged ignorance while the bodily humors ferment. Delayed satisfaction is, according to him, the condition of idealism and love, and early sat-isfaction causes the whole structure to collapse and flatten.

Rousseau's meaning is admirably expressed by Kant, who, fol-lowing Rousseau, indicated that there is a distinction between what might be called natural puberty and civil puberty.[13] Natural puberty is reached when a male is capable of reproduction. Civil puberty is attained only when a man is able to love a woman faithfully, rear and provide for children, and participate knowledgeably and loyally in the political order which protects the family. But the advent of civilization has not changed the course of nature; natural puberty occurs around fifteen; civil puberty, if it ever comes to pass, can hardly occur before the middle twenties. This means that there is a profound tension between natural desire and civil duty. In fact, this is one of the best examples of the dividedness caused in man by his history. Natural desire almost always lurks untamed amidst the responsibilities of mar-riage. What Rousseau attempts to do is to make the two puberties coincide, to turn the desire for sexual intercourse into a desire for marriage and a willing submission to the law without suppressing or blaming that original desire. Such a union of desire and duty Kant called true culture.

Rousseau effects this union by establishing successively two pas-sions in Emile which are sublimations of sexual desire and which are, hence, not quite natural but, one might say, according to nature: compassion and love.

COMPASSION

In this first stage the young man is kept ignorant of the meaning of what he is experiencing. He is full of restless energy and becomes sensitive. He needs other human beings, but he knows not why. In becoming sensitive to the feelings of others and in needing them, his imagination is aroused and he becomes aware that they are like him. He *feels* for the first time that he is a member of a species. (Until now he was simply indifferent to other human beings, although he *knew* he was a human being.) At this moment the birth of *amour-propre* is inevitable. He compares his situation with those of other men. If the comparison is unfavorable to him, he will be dissatisfied with himself

[13]"Conjectural Beginning of Human History," p. 61, note.

and envious of them; he will wish to take their place. If the comparison is unfavorable to them, he will be content with himself and not competitive with others. Thus *amour-propre* is alienating only if a man sees others whom he can consider happier than himself. It follows that, if one wishes to keep a man from developing the mean passions which excite the desire to harm, he must always see men whom he thinks to be unhappier than he is. If, in addition, he thinks such misfortunes could happen to him, he will feel pity for the sufferer.

This is the ground of Rousseau's entirely new teaching about compassion.[14] Judiciously chosen comparisons presented at the right stage of life will cause Emile to be satisfied with himself and be concerned with others, making him a gentle and beneficent man on the basis of his natural selfishness. Thus compassion would be good for him and good for others. Rousseau introduces a hardheaded softness to moral and political thought.

He asserts that the good fortune of others puts a chill on our hearts, no matter what we say. It separates us from them; we would like to be in their place. But their suffering warms us and gives us a common sense of humanity. The psychic mechanism of compassion is as follows: (1) Once a man's imaginative sensibility is awakened, he winces at the wounds others receive. In an attenuated form he experiences them too, prior to any reflection; he sympathizes; somehow these wounds are inflicted on him. (2) He has a moment of reflection; he realizes that it is the other fellow, not he, who is really suffering. This is a source of satisfaction. (3) He can show his own strength and superiority by assisting the man in distress. (4) He is pleased that he has the spiritual freedom to experience compassion; he senses his own goodness. Active human compassion (as opposed to the animal compassion described in the *Discourse on the Origins of Inequality*) requires imagination and *amour-propre* in addition to the instinct for self-preservation. Moreover, it cannot withstand the demands of one's own self-preservation. It is a tender plant, but one which will bear sweet fruit if properly cultivated.

Emile's first observations of men are directed to the poor, the sick, the oppressed, and the unfortunate. This is flattering to him, and his first sentiments toward others are gentle. He becomes a kind of social worker. And, as this analysis should make clear, the motive and intention of Rousseauean compassion give it little in common with Christian compassion. Rousseau was perfectly aware that compassion such as he taught is not a virtue and that it can lead to abuse

[14]Op. cit., pp. 221ff.

and hypocrisy. But he used this selfish passion to replace or temper other, more dangerous, passions. This is part of his correction of Hobbes. Rousseau finds a selfish passion which contains fellow feeling and makes it the ground of sociality to replace those passions which set men at odds. He can even claim he goes farther down the path first broken by Hobbes, who argued that the passions, and not reason, are the only effective motives of human action. Hobbes's duties toward others are rational deductions from the passion for self-preservation. Rousseau anchors concerns for others in a passion. He makes that concern a pleasure rather than a disagreeable, and hence questionably effective, conclusion.

Rousseau's teaching on compassion fostered a revolution in democratic politics, one with which we live today. Compassion is on the lips of every statesman, and all boast that their primary qualification for office is their compassion. Rousseau single-handedly invented the category of the disadvantaged. Prior to Rousseau, men believed that their claim on civil society has to be based on an accounting of what they contribute to it. After Rousseau, a claim based not on a positive quality but on a lack became legitimate for the first time. This he introduced as a counterpoise to a society based on Locke's teaching, which has no category for the miserable other than that of the idle and the quarrelsome. The recognition of our sameness and our common vulnerability dampens the harsh competitiveness and egotism of egalitarian political orders. Rousseau takes advantage of the tendency to compassion resulting from equality, and uses it, rather than self-interest, as the glue binding men together. Our equality, then, is based less on our fear of death than on our sufferings; suffering produces a shared sentiment with others, which fear of death does not. For Hobbes, frightened men make an artificial man to protect them; for Rousseau, suffering men seek other men who feel for them.

Of course Emile will not always be able to confine his vision to poor men without station. There are rich and titled men who seem to be much better off than he is. If he were brought to their castles and had a chance to see their privileges and their entertainments, he would likely be dazzled, and the worm of envy would begin to gnaw away at his heart. Jean-Jacques finds a solution to this difficulty by making Emile read history and bringing back what had been banished in Book II.[15] This is the beginning of Emile's education in the arts, as opposed to the sciences. The former can only be studied when his sentiments are sufficiently developed for him to understand the inner

[15]Op. cit., pp. 236–44; cf. pp. 110–12.

movements of the heart and when he experiences a real need to know. Otherwise, learning is idle, undigested, excess baggage at best. Emile's curiosity to find out about all of Plutarch's heroes and set his own life over against their lives fuels his study. Rousseau expects that this study will reveal the vanity of the heroes' aspirations and cause revulsion at their tragic failures. Emile's solid, natural pleasures, his cheaply purchased Stoicism and self-sufficiency, his lack of the passion to rule, will cause him to despise their love of glory and pity their tragic ends. The second level of the education in compassion produces contempt for the great of this world, not a slave's contempt founded in envy, indignation, and resentment, but the contempt stemming from a conviction of superiority which admits of honest fellow feeling and is the precondition of compassion. This disposition provides a standpoint from which to judge the social and political distinctions among men, just as Robinson Crusoe's island provided one for judging the distinctions based on the division of labor. The joining of these two standards enables Emile to judge the life of tyrants. Socrates enabled Glaucon and Adeimantus to judge it by comparing it to the life of philosophers; Emile can use his own life as the basis for judgment, for his own soul contains no germ of the tyrannical temptation. The old way of using heroes in education was to make the pupil dissatisfied with himself and rivalrous with the model. Rousseau uses them to make his pupil satisfied with himself and compassionate toward the heroes. The old way alienated the child and made him prey to authorities whose titles he could not judge. Self-satisfaction of egalitarian man is what Rousseau promotes. But he is careful to insure that this satisfaction is only with a good or natural self.

Reading is again the means of accomplishing the third and final part of the education in compassion.[16] This time the texts are fables which contain a moral teaching. They, too, had been banished in Book II, because a child would always identify himself with, e.g., the fox who cheats the crow rather than with the crow who loses the cheese, for a child understands nothing about vanity and a great deal about cheese. At this later stage Rousseau has arranged for Emile to have been deceived by confidence men who play upon his vanity, so that when he reads the fable he will immediately identify with the crow and attain self-consciousness. Satire becomes the mirror in which he sees himself. All this is intended to remind him that he, too, is human and could easily fall victim to the errors made by others. It is

[16]Op. cit., pp. 244–49; cf. pp. 112–16; and Alexis de Tocqueville, *Democracy in America*, Vol. 2, Part 3, Chapter 1.

as though Rousseau had used Aristotle's discourse on the passions as a text and followed Aristotle's warning that those who do not imagine that the misfortunes befalling others can befall them are insolent rather than compassionate.[17] The first stage of Emile's introduction to the human condition shows him that most men are sufferers; the second, that the great, too, are sufferers and hence equal to the small; and the third, that he is potentially a sufferer, saved only by his education. Equality, which was a rational deduction in Hobbes, thus becomes self-evident to the sentiments. Emile's first principle of action was pleasure and pain; his second, after the birth of reason and his learning the sciences, was utility; now compassion is added to the other two, and concern for others becomes part of his sense of his own interest. Rousseau studies the passions and finds a way of balancing them one against the other rather than trying to develop the virtues which govern them. He does for the soul what Montesquieu did for the government: invent the separation and balance of powers.

But for all its important consequences in its own right, compassion within the context of Emile's education is only a step on the way to his fulfillment as husband and father. Its primary function is to make Emile social while remaining whole.

LOVE

Finally Rousseau must tell Emile the meaning of his longings. He reveals sex to the young Emile as the Savoyard Vicar revealed God to the young Jean-Jacques.[18] Although it is impossible to discuss the Profession of Faith of the Savoyard Vicar here, it is essential to the understanding of Rousseau's intention to underline the profound differences between the two revelations. The Vicar's teaching is presented to the corrupt young Rousseau and never to Emile. Moreover, the Vicar teaches the dualism of body and soul, which is alien and contradictory to the unity which Emile incarnates. In keeping with this, the Vicar is otherwordly and guilt-ridden about his sexual desires, which he deprecates, whereas Emile is very much of this world and exalts his sexual desires, which are blessed by God and lead to blessing God. Emile's rewards are on earth, the Vicar's in Heaven. The Vicar is the best of the traditional, and he is only an oasis in the desert which Rousseau crossed before reaching his new Sinai.

[17]Aristotle, *Rhetoric*, II, 8 and 2.
[18]Op. cit., pp. 260–313, 316–34.

Thus at the dawn of a new day, Emile learns that the peak of sexual longing is the love of God mediated by the love of a woman.[19] Sublimation finally operates a transition from the physical to the metaphysical. But before speaking to Emile, Rousseau explains to his readers how difficult it is to be a good rhetorician in modern times. Speech has lost its power because it cannot refer to a world with deep human significance. In Greek and biblical antiquity the world was full of meaning put there by the great and terrible deeds of gods and heroes. Men were awestruck by the ceremonies performed to solemnize public and private occasions. The whole earth spoke out to make oaths sacred. But now the world has been deprived of its meaning by Enlightenment. The land is no longer peopled by spirits, and nothing supports human aspiration anymore. Thus men can only affect one another by the use of force or the profit motive. The language of human relations has lost its foundations. This is, as we would say, a demythologized world. And these remarks show what Rousseau is about. He wants to use imagination to read meaning back into nature. The old meanings were also the results of imaginings the reality of which men believed. They were monuments of fear and anger given cosmic significance. But they did produce a human world, however cruel and unreasonable. Rousseau suggests a new poetic imagination motivated by love rather than the harsher passions, and here one sees with clarity Rousseau's link with romanticism.

With this preface, he proceeds to inform Emile what the greatest pleasure in life is. He explains to him that what he desires is sexual intercourse with a woman, but he makes him believe that his object contains ideas of virtue and beauty without which she would not be attractive, nay, without which she would be repulsive. His bodily satisfaction depends upon his beloved's spiritual qualities; therefore Emile longs for the beautiful. Jean-Jacques by his descriptive power incorporates an ideal into Emile's bodily lust. This is how sex becomes love, and the two must be made to appear inseparable. This is the reason for the delay in sexual awareness. Emile must learn much before he can comprehend such notions, and his sexual energy must be raised to a high pitch. Early indulgence would separate the intensity of lust from the objects of admiration. Rousseau admits that love depends upon illusions, but the deeds which those illusions produce are real. This is the source of nobility of mind and deed, and apart from fanaticism, nothing else can produce such dedication.

Rousseau develops all this with precision and in the greatest

[19]Op. cit., p. 426.

detail. Only Plato has meditated on love with comparable profundity.[20] And it is Plato who inspired Rousseau's attempt to create love. The modern philosophers with whom Rousseau began have notably un-erotic teachings. Their calculating, fear-motivated men are individuals, not directed towards others, towards couplings and the self-forgetting implied in them. Such men have flat souls. They see nature as it is; and, since they are unerotic, they are unpoetic. Rousseau, a philosopher-poet like Plato, tried to recapture the poetry in the world. He knew that Plato's *Symposium* taught that *eros* is the longing for eternity, ultimately the longing for oneness with the unchanging, intelligible *ideas*. Now, Rousseau held that nature is the nature of modern science—matter in motion—that there are no *ideas*; there is no *eros*, only sex. But such a soul, which has no beautiful objects to contemplate and contains no divine madness, Rousseau regarded as ignoble. He set about reconstructing Plato's soul, turning sex into *eros*, by the creation of ideals to take the place of the *ideas*. The philosopher is even more poetic for Rousseau than for Plato, for the very objects of contemplation and longing are the products of poetry rather than nature. The world of concern to man is made by the poet who has understood nature and its limits. So, imagination, once banished, returns to ascend the royal throne.

From imagination thus purified and exalted comes the possibility of Emile's first real relationship with another human being, i.e., a freely chosen enduring union between equals based upon reciprocal affection and respect, each treating the other as an end in himself. This completes Emile's movement from nature to society, a movement unbroken by alien motives such as fear, vanity, or coercion. He has neither been denatured after the fashion of Sparta nor has moral obligation been reduced to a mere product of his selfishness as is the way of the *bourgeois*. He has an overwhelming need for another, but that other must be the embodiment of the ideal of beauty, and his interest in her partakes of the disinterestedness of the love of the beautiful. Moreover it is not quite precise to say that he loves an "other," for he will not be making himself hostage to an alien will and thus engaging in a struggle for mastery. This woman will, to use Platonic language, participate in the *idea* he has of her. He will recognize in her his own highest aspirations. She will complete him without alienating him. If Emile and Sophie can be constituted as a unit and individualism thereby surmounted, then Rousseau will have shown how the building blocks of a society are formed. Individuals cannot be the basis of a real community but families can be.

[20]*La Nouvelle Héloïse*, II, xi, second note.

Now that Emile's dominant motive is longing for an object which exists only in his imagination, the rest of his education becomes a love story within a story. This little prototype of the romantic novel has three stages: the quest for his beloved; his discovery of her and their courtship; their separation, his travels, and their marriage.

The quest. Rousseau uses this time of intense passion to lead Emile into society and instruct him about its ways without fear that he will be corrupted by it.[21] Emile knows what he wants, and Rousseau knows that he will not find it in Paris. Emile's very passion provides him the standard by which he can judge men and women and their relations while being protected from the ordinary charms and temptations. A man in love sees things differently from those who are not so possessed, and he sees their concerns as petty and dull; he is, as well, proof against the attractions of all women other than his beloved. Emile is already in love, but he does not know with whom. He is, therefore, unlike most lovers, an attentive observer, seeking to recognize the one for whom he is looking. In this way Rousseau provides him with the third of four standards for the evaluation of men in society which taken together serve as a substitute for the philosopher's vantage point outside the cave. The first was Crusoe's island, which enabled Emile to understand men's purely material relations in the division of labor and exchange and to maintain his independence while profiting from the progress of civilization in the sciences and productive industries. The second was compassion, which made him aware of mankind in its natural unity and its conventional division into classes. This awareness involved him with his fellows but maintained him in his self-sufficiency. Rousseau separates out into layers what the philosopher grasps together as a whole, and Emile is given an experience, founded in sentiment and imagination, of each of these layers or aspects of man and society. These experiences take the place of the savage's instinct that the civilized man has lost and of the philosopher's rational insight that the ordinary man cannot attain. Thus Emile has principles to guide him in life. They are founded on his deep and strong feelings, and they are his own, not dependent on any authority other than himself.

The third standard or standpoint, that of the lover, puts him in intimate contact with men and their passions. And he is, for the first time, needy. But it does not make him both see and despise the vanities of society and the involvements with others that are not directly related to love. Moreover, in the society of the rich and noble in a great aristocracy Emile associates for the first time with men and

[21]Op. cit., pp. 327–55.

women of high refinement and subtlety of manners. And here he has his first experience of the fine arts which are developed to please such people and constitute their principal entertainment. These arts are always the companions of idleness and luxury and most often are products of vice and instruments of deception as manners are the substitute for virtue. But from them Emile gains an exquisite sensibility and a delicacy of taste in the passions which matches the soundness of his reasoning about things. He has learned the sciences to satisfy his bodily needs; he learns the arts to enrich the transports of love. Poetry for him is not a pastime but the very element in which his sublime longings move. The depth of his feeling is given voice by these great products of civilization and not corrupted by it. He is now a cultivated man, and the motives of his learning have kept him healthy and whole. Rousseau has answered his own objections to the arts and sciences propounded in the *Discourse on the Arts and Sciences*.

Discovery and courtship. Emile's discovery of his Sophie in the country is the occasion for Rousseau's discourse on the differences between the sexes and their proper relations.[22] No segment of *Emile* is more "relevant" than is this one nor is any likely to arouse more indignation, for Rousseau is a "sexist." The particular force of Rousseau's argument for us comes from the fact that he begins from thoroughly modern premises—not deriving from biblical or Greek thought—and arrives at conclusions diametrically opposed to those of feminism. Furthermore, his analysis is unrivaled in its breadth and precision. So persuasive was he to Tocqueville that the latter asserted that the principal cause of America's "singular prosperity and growing strength" was its women, whom he describes as though they had been educated by Rousseau.[23] This analysis will not seem nearly so persuasive today because of the political force of a movement which Rousseau predicted as an almost inevitable result of the bourgeoisification of the world, a tide which he was trying to stem. He saw that rationalism and egalitarianism would tend to destroy the sexual differences just as they were leveling class and national distinctions. Man and woman, husband and wife, and parent and child would become roles, not natural qualities; and as in all play-acting, roles can be changed. The only unaltered fragment of nature remaining, and thus dominating, would be the selfish Hobbesian individual, striving for self-preservation, comfort, and power after power. Marriage and the family would decay and the sexes be assimilated. Children would be burdens and not fulfillments.

[22]Op. cit., pp. 357–63.
[23]*Democracy in America*, Vol. 2, Part 3, Chapter 12.

It is impossible in this place to comment fully on Rousseau's intentions and arguments in this crucial passage. I must limit myself to a few general remarks. In the first place Rousseau insisted that the family is the only basis for a healthy society, given the impossibility and undesirability in modernity of Spartan dedication to the community. Without caring for others, without the willingness to sacrifice one's private interest to them, society is but a collection of individuals, each of whom will disobey the law as soon as it goes counter to his interest. The family tempers the selfish individualism which has been released by the new regimes founded on modern natural right teachings. And Rousseau further insists that there will be no family if women are not primarily wives and mothers. Second, he argues that there can be no natural, i.e., whole, social man if women are essentially the same as men. Two similar beings, as it were atoms, who united out of mutual need would exploit one another, each using his partner as a means to his own ends, putting himself ahead of him or her. There would be a clash of wills and a struggle for mastery, unless they simply copulated like beasts and separated immediately after (leaving the woman, of course, with the care of the unintended progeny). Human beings would be divided between their attachment to themselves and their duty to others. The project undertaken by Rousseau was to overcome or avoid this tension.

Thus the relation between man and woman is the crucial point, the place where the demands of Emile's wholeness and those of civil society meet. If Rousseau can overcome the difficulties in that relation, difficulties which were always present in the past but which have become critically explicit in modern theory and practice, he will have resolved the tension between inclination and duty, nature and society. What he proposes is that the two sexes are different and complementary, each imperfect and requiring the other in order to be a whole being, or rather, together forming a single whole being. Rousseau does not seriously treat a state as an organism, but he does so treat a couple. He tries to show that male and female bodies and souls fit together like pieces in a puzzle, and he does so in such a way as to make his conclusions compatible with natural science, on the one hand, and freedom and equality on the other. In particular, Rousseau argues that woman rules man by submitting to his will and knowing how to make him will what she needs to submit to. In this way Emile's freedom of will is preserved without Sophie's will being denied. Further, Rousseau argues, a woman naturally cares for her children; thus a man, loving her exclusively, will also care for the children. So it is that the family is constituted. None of this is found in the state of nature, but it is in accord with natural potentialities and reconciles the results of civ-

ilization with them. Whatever the success of Rousseau's attempt in
this matter, the comprehensiveness and power of his reasoning as well
as the subtlety of his psychological observation makes this one of the
very few fundamental texts for the understanding of man and woman,
and a touchstone for serious discussion of the matter.

The courtship of Emile and Sophie is merely their discovery of
the many facets of the essential man and the essential woman and
how well suited they are to one another. They reveal to one another
each of the aspects of their respective natures and educations. If these
had been the same, they would not really need each other or know
of love, which is the recognition of an absence in oneself. Each would
be a separate machine whose only function is to preserve itself, making
use of everything around it to that end. The primary aim of the
education of civilized man and woman is to prepare them for one
another. Such education is Rousseau's unique educational innovation
and where he takes most specific exception to Locke and Plato.[24]

Travel. Emile is ready to marry and enjoy the long-awaited con-
summation of his desires.[25] But Jean-Jacques orders him to leave Sophie, thus reenacting both Agamemnon's taking Briseis from Achilles
and God's forbidding Adam from eating of the fruit of the tree of
knowledge. This is the only example of a commandment in *Emile*,
and the only time Emile's inclinations are thwarted by another will.
But Emile, although sorely tried, submits and becomes neither the
wrathful Achilles nor the disobedient Adam. There is no Fall. For
the first time Emile becomes subject to a law and has an inner experience of the tension between inclination and duty. Jean-Jacques's
authority goes back to a promise he extracted from Emile at the time
of the revelation of sex. This is the first and only promise Emile makes
to Jean-Jacques. If his tutor will give him guidance in matters of love,
he will agree to accept his advice. He joins in what might be called
a sexual contract which is the original of all other contracts he will
make in his life; or, to put it more accurately, this first contract
contains all the others. The obligation to Sophie which Emile learns
to fulfill leads to the obligations to the family and these in turn to
those to civil society.

Thus the scene where Jean-Jacques finally asks Emile to keep his
promise encapsulates the whole problem of morality as he envisions
it: why keep a promise? A man makes a promise because he expects
some good to result to him from doing so. But when he finds that it

[24]Op. cit., pp. 357, 362–63, 415–16.
[25]Op. cit., pp. 441–50.

is more advantageous to break his promise, why should he keep it? What is good in itself about keeping faith? If there is no adequate basis for obligation, there is no basis for human society. Throughout *Emile* Rousseau has shown that all previous thinkers had added some kind of reward or punishment—wealth, honor, heaven or prison, disgrace, hell—to faith, thereby reducing it to the calculation of the other palpable goods which have been allied with it. Duty seems always to stem from the will of another, as epitomized in God's prohibition or Agamemnon's command, and society has therefore always demanded an abandonment of natural freedom and an unnatural bending to the needs of community. Spartan denaturing, Christian piety, and *bourgeois* calculation are, according to Rousseau, the three powerful alternative modes of making this accommodation. The first is the only one which does not divide and hence corrupt; but the undesirability of the Spartan example is fully expressed in the word "denaturing." This is why Emile has been subjected to no law but only to necessity and has always been left free to follow his inclinations. His education up to this point has shown just how far one can go in making a man sociable without imposing a law on him. But when it comes to his relation to women, something other than inclination must be involved. Emile must contract with Sophie, and sexual desire will not suffice as a guarantee of his future fidelity. It is instructive to note that the dramatic conflict between Jean-Jacques and Emile concerns the identical problem as do the conflicts between God and Adam and Agamemnon and Achilles. And it would appear that Rousseau resolves the conflict just as his ancient predecessors did, by an act of authority, the imposition of an alien will on his pupil's desires. It seems that Rousseau remains within the tradition which holds that morality is, to use Kantian language, heteronomous. Emile's reluctance to obey Jean-Jacques's command would seem to confirm this.

But the difference in Emile's conflict with Jean-Jacques becomes apparent when we see that Emile does not rebel but acquiesces, and his obedience is not the result of fear. First of all, Jean-Jacques's authority to command is based neither on force, tradition, or age, nor on purported superior wisdom or divine right. Following modern political philosophy, it is based solely on consent. Jean-Jacques commands only because he was once begged by Emile to command. The legitimacy of the contract is supported by the fact that Emile believes that Jean-Jacques is benevolent and interested only in his happiness, in his happiness as he himself conceives of it, not as Jean-Jacques or society might wish it. The promise to obey was intimately connected with the revelation of the greatest imaginable happiness and was in-

tended to secure the only good he did not yet possess—love—and to
avoid the dangers surrounding it. Sophie is to be returned to him,
and there will be no curse of original sin on sexual desire. Everything
speaks in favor of Jean-Jacques's authority.

But still it is authority. If Emile had by himself seen the good in
what was commanded him, it would not have had to be commanded.
The decisive step for Rousseau is to transform the external authority—
however intimate—into an internal one. Jean-Jacques reminds Emile
of his ideal Sophie and tries to show him that his love of the real
Sophie could well undermine it, and with it, love itself. For example,
if Sophie were not faithful, his attachment would remain and drag
him down. Only if he were able to give up Sophie for what Sophie
ought to be could he endure the vagaries of fortune and the human
will. The separation from Sophie is the precondition of accepting life
and of the foundation of the family. Emile's desire for immediate
possession of Sophie rebels against his own will. For the first time he
is forced to make a distinction between inclination and will. The
problem of morality is no longer the conflict between inclination and
duty but between inclination and ideal, which is a kind of equivalent
of the conflict between particular and general will. The dedication to
the ideal, completing the whole education, has been a generalizing
of Emile's soul and his principles of action. The first command occurs
at the moment when he is ready to see that it is not Jean-Jacques who
is commanding but Emile—that he is obeying a law he has in fact set
for himself. Jean-Jacques appears on the scene as an authority just this
once in the course of his twenty-five years with Emile—only in order
to annihilate the influence of authority on him. In this way Emile
can be both free and moral. *Emile* is the outline of a possible bridge
between the particular will and the general will.

The separation from Sophie is used for learning politics.[26] Now
he has a good motive for such learning. When he was unattached,
he was cosmopolitan, staying or leaving as he pleased, able to fend
for himself anywhere, always an inhabitant of Crusoe's island and
hence indifferent to the laws of men. But now, with a wife and
children, he must settle down and become subject to a political regime.
He must know which are most just and most secure, and he must
adjust his hopes to the possible. It is well that he has learned what
subjection to a law is, for politics means laws. But these political laws
rarely if ever conform to the standard of justice, and Emile must reflect
on how he is to come to terms with unjust regimes and their commands.

[26]Op. cit., pp. 450–71.

He knows what perfect duties are, and they will help to guide him in the less than perfect duties imposed on him by civil society. His passion for his future wife and concern for their unborn children, combined with his mature learning, make an abstract presentation of the principles of right accessible to him. He is, in effect, taught the *Social Contract*. (Rousseau thus indicates the kind of reader for whom he intended it.) This provides Emile with his fourth standard, the one which permits him to evaluate the most comprehensive human order, civil society. And his travels enable him, given this focus, to recognize the various alternative "caves" and their advantages and disadvantages.

Finally he is complete and can claim his bride and his happiness. Rousseau has made him intellectually and morally self-sufficient.[27]

[27]Op. cit., pp. 471–80.

ROUSSEAU: THE TURNING POINT

AT THE MOMENT the Framers wrote "We the people of the United States . . . ," the word "people" had been made problematic by Jean-Jacques Rousseau.[1] How do you get from individuals to a people, that is, from persons who care only for their particular good to a community of citizens who subordinate their good to the common good? The collective "we" in the Preamble might well be the voice of a powerful and wealthy few who coerce and deceïve the many and make their consent meaningless. Or the many who consent to the use of "we" may do so innocently, not realizing how much of their "I" they must sacrifice, or corruptly, intending to profit from the advantage of the social contract and evade the sacrifice it demands. It is difficult beyond the belief of early modern thinkers, so Rousseau teaches, to turn men free and equal by nature into citizens obedient to the law and its ministers. "Man was born free. Everywhere he is in chains," he observes. Rousseau's task is not to return man to his original condition but to make the results of force and fraud legitimate, to persuade men that there is a possible social order both beneficial and just.

On the basis of these preliminary remarks, it should be evident that Rousseau begins from an overall agreement with the Framers and their teachers about man's nature and the origins and ends of civil society. Man is born free, that is, able to follow his inclinations and to do whatever conduces to his preservation or comfort, and equal, that is, with no superiors who have a valid claim to command him.

This essay is based on a few relatively short writings of Rousseau: *Discourse on the Arts and Sciences*, *Discourse on the Origins of Inequality*, *Political Economy*, and *Social Contract*. These readings can be supplemented by his longer books: the educational novel *Emile*, the romantic novel *La Nouvelle Héloïse*, and *Confessions*.
[1] *Social Contract*, Book 2, Chapters 8–10.

He has no obligations. Government is, therefore, not natural but a construction of man, and the law is a thing strictly of his making. The natural state is wholly distinct from the civil state, and the only way from the one to the other is consent. All other titles of legitimacy, divine or human, derived from appeals to the ancestral or exclusive wisdom, are neither binding nor believable. In *the state of nature* rights are primary; duties are derivative and become binding only after *the social contract* is freely made.

All this and much more provides the common ground of modernity where Rousseau walks arm and arm with his liberal predecessors and contemporaries. He does not reject the new principles, but he radicalizes them by thinking them through from the broadest of perspectives. In his eyes the epic battle of his Enlightenment fellows against throne and altar, which had lasted for two centuries, had simply been won. Monarchic and aristocratic Europe was, he correctly predicted, on its last legs. There would soon be great revolutions, and it is the visage of the political orders that were to emerge that concerns him. He could even afford a few generous gestures of recognition toward the defeated nobles and kings (though rarely the priests) whose moral and political greatness was hardly recognized by those who had been locked in battle with them. The new world would be inhabited by individuals who know they are endowed with rights, free and equal, no longer treading the enchanted ground where rights and duties were prescribed by divinities, now recognizing no legitimacy with higher sources than their own wills, rationally pursuing their own interests. Might they become the victims, willing or not, of new despotisms? Might they not become as morally questionable in their way as the unthinking patriots or fanatic believers who were the special objects of modern criticism and whose place they were to take?

Rousseau's reflections had the effect of outflanking the Framers on the Left, where they thought they were invulnerable. Their enemies were the old European orders of privilege, supported by the church and monopolizing wealth and the ways of access to it, and their revolution was the movement from prejudice to reason, despotism to freedom, inequality to equality. This was a progress, but not one that was to be infinite, at least in principle. The dangers were understood as coming from the *revanchisme* of throne and altar in various forms. There were many opponents of Enlightenment and its political project—in the name of tradition or the ancestral, in the name of the kings and the nobles, even in the name of the ancient city and its virtue. But Rousseau was the first to make a schism within the party of what we may call the Left. In so doing he set up the stage on which the political drama has been played even until this day. The element that was so much more extreme in the French Revolution than in the American Revolution can be traced, without intermediaries, to Rousseau's influence on its principal actors. And it was by Rousseau's standard that it was judged a failure and only a preparation for the next, and perhaps final, revolution. The camp of radical equality and freedom has very few clear political successes to show for itself, but it contains all the dissatisfactions and longings that put a question mark after triumphant liberalism.

Rousseau gave antimodernity its most modern expression and thereby ushered in extreme modernity. It is a mistake to treat him as only the genius of the Left. His concentration on the people, the corporate existence of individual peoples, provided the basis for the religion of the nation in the nineteenth and twentieth centuries. His assault on cosmopolitan civilization prepared the way for the assertion of national cultures, unique and constitutive of their individual members. His regret of the lost happy unity of man was the source of the romanticism that played at least as much of a role on the Right as on the Left. His insistence on the centrality of religion to the life of the people gave a new content to theology and provided the impulse for the religiosity that is one of the salient traits of the nineteenth and twentieth centuries. The contempt for the new man of liberal society that Rousseau articulated lent itself to the projects of both extremes of the political spectrum, and his Left informed the new Right, which constituted itself on the intellectual shambles of the old Right. His influence was overwhelming, and so well was it digested into the bloodstream of the West that it worked on everyone almost imperceptibly. Even the mainstays of democratic liberalism were affected by Rousseau; they were impressed by his critique of the harshness of the political and economic relations characteristic of the modern state and sought to correct them on the basis of his suggestions. The influence was direct on Alexis de Tocqueville, indirect, by way of Wordsworth, on John Stuart Mill. The Thoreau who for America represents civil disobedience and a way of life free from the distortions of modern society was only reenacting one part of the thought and life of Jean-Jacques.

It is this ubiquity of his presence, often where conservatives or Leftists would least like to recognize him, that makes him the appropriate introduction for this second part of *Confronting the Constitution*. He is the seedbed of all these schools and movements that enrich, correct, defend, or undermine constitutional liberalism. His breadth and comprehensiveness make it impossible to co-opt him completely into any single camp. The schools that succeed him are all isms, intellectual forces that inform powerful political or social movements with more or less singleness of purpose. Rousseau resists such limitation. For him the human problem is not soluble on the political level; and although he, unlike Socrates, suggests practicable solutions, they are tentative and counterpoised by other solutions and temptations. One can always find in him the objections to each school that depends on him. Therefore, Rousseau did not produce an ism of his own, but he did provide the authentically modern perspective. His concern for a higher, nonmercenary morality is the foundation of Kant's idealism. His critique of modern economics and his questions about the legitimacy of private property are at the root of socialism, particularly Marxism. His emphasis on man's origins, rather than his ends, made anthropology a central discipline. And the history of the movement from the state of nature toward civil society came to seem more essential to man than his nature—hence historicism. The wounds inflicted on human nature by this process of socialization became the subject of a new psychology, especially as represented in Freud. The romantic love of the beautiful and the doubt that modern society is compatible with the sublime and pure in spirit gave justification to the cult of art for art's sake and to the life of the bohemian. The longing for rootedness and for community in its modern form is part of Rousseauean sensibility, and so is the love of nature and the hatred for nature's conquerors. All this and much more flows from this inexhaustible fount. He possessed an unsurpassed intellectual clarity accompanied by a stirring and seductive rhetoric.

THE BOURGEOIS

The *bourgeois* is Rousseau's great invention, and one's disposition toward this kind of man determines one's relation to modern politics inasmuch as he is the leading human type produced by it. The word has a strong negative charge, and practically no one wants to be *merely* a *bourgeois*. The artists and the intellectuals have almost universally despised him and in large measure defined themselves against him. The *bourgeois* is unpoetic, unerotic, unheroic, neither aristocrat nor of the people; he is not a citizen, and his religion is pallid and this-worldly. The sole invocation of his name is enough to legitimate revolutions of Left and Right; and within the limits of liberal democracy, all sorts of reforms are perennially proposed to correct his motives or counterbalance them.

This phenomenon, the *bourgeois*, is the true beginning point of Rousseau's survey of the human condition in modernity and his diagnosis of what ails it. The *bourgeois* stands somewhere between two respectable extremes, the good natural man and the moral citizen. The former lives alone, concerned with himself, his preservation, and his contentment, unconcerned with others, hence wishing them no harm. The latter lives wholly for his country, concerned solely with the common good, existing only as a part of it, loving his country and hating its enemies. Each of these two types, in his own way, is whole—free of the wasting conflict between inclination and duty that reduces the *bourgeois* and renders him weak and unreliable. He is the individualist in society, who needs society and its protective laws but only as means to his private ends. This does not provide sufficient motive to make the extreme sacrifices one's country sometimes requires. It also means that he lies to his fellow countrymen, making conditional promises to them while expecting them to abide by their promises unconditionally. The *bourgeois* is a hypocrite, hiding his true purposes under a guise of public-spiritedness. And hence, needing everyone but unwilling to sacrifice to help others reciprocally in their neediness, he is psychologically at war with everyone. The *bourgeois*'s morality is mercenary, requiring a payoff for every social deed. He is incapable of either natural sincerity or political nobility.[2]

The cause of this dominant new character's flaws is that he took a shortcut on the road from the state of nature to civil society. Rousseau's thinking through of the new political science, which taught that man is not by nature political—a thinking through that led much further in both directions, nature and society, than his predecessors had believed necessary or possible—proved to him that natural motives cannot suffice for the making of social man. The attempt to use man's natural passions as the foundation of civil society fails while it perverts those natural passions. A man who never says "I promise" never has to lie. One who says "I promise" without sufficient motive for keeping his promise is a liar. Such are the social contracts proposed by Hobbes and Locke, requiring binding promises from their participants, who are concerned solely with their own well-being and whose contracts are therefore conditional on calculations of self-interest. Such social contracts tend toward anarchy or tyranny.

In essence, Rousseau's *bourgeois* is identical to Locke's rational and industrious man, the new kind of man whose concern with

[2]*Social Contract*, Book 1, Chapter 6, note, and *Emile*, trans. Allan Bloom (New York: Basic Books, 1979), pp. 39–41.

property was to provide a soberer and solider foundation to society. Rousseau sees him differently—from the perspective of morality, citizenship, equality, freedom, and compassion. The rational and industrious man might be an instrument of stability, but the cost of relying on him is human dignity. This contrast between two ways of seeing the central actor in modernity summarizes the continuous political debate of the past two centuries.

Rousseau's earliest formulation of this critique of modernity was in his *Discourse on the Arts and Sciences*, which exploded on the European scene with a force hardly credible to us today. In it he made the first attack on the Enlightenment based on the very principles that motivated Enlightenment. Simply put, he argued that the progress and dissemination of the sciences and the arts, their emancipation from political and religious control, are noxious to decent community and its foundation, virtue. By virtue he appears to mean the republican citizen's self-forgetting devotion to the common good, a common good established and preserved by freemen, which protects the equal concern for and treatment of all the citizens. In this definition of virtue, Rousseau follows Montesquieu, who calls virtue a passion and says it was the principle, or spiritual mainspring, of ancient democracies, as fear is of despotism or honor of monarchies. Virtue, of course, was not a passion in any ancient account of it, and it was certainly not especially connected to democracy. Rousseau apparently accepts Montesquieu's account of virtue because he, like the rest of the moderns, believed that passion is the only real power in the soul and that there is nothing else in it capable of controlling the passions. Passion must control passion. Virtue must be understood as a special kind of complex passion. However that may be, Rousseau comes out squarely in defense of those ancient "democracies," early republican Rome and especially Sparta, in opposition to Montesquieu, who in harmony with the general tendency of Enlightenment favored the commercial republic or monarchy (with some indifference as to the choice between the two) because he thought the price for ancient virtue too high. Rousseau chooses patriotism, a motive tinged with fanaticism, because it alone can counterpoise the natural inclination to prefer oneself over everyone else, an inclination much intensified and perverted by man's social condition, where men are interdependent and self-love turns into *amour-propre*, the passion to be first among them, to be esteemed by them as he esteems himself. Patriotism is a sublimated form of *amour-propre*, seeking the first place for one's country. Without such a counterpoise society turns into a struggle for primacy among individuals or groups who unite to manipulate the whole.

Thus it is as the solvent of patriotism that Rousseau objects to Enlightenment. The fabric of community is woven out of certain immediate habits of sentiment. They are vulnerable to reason, which sees clearly only calculations of private interest. It pierces veils of sentiment and poses too powerfully the claims of preservation and comfort. Reason individualizes. In this Rousseau picks up the old assertion of classical political philosophy that there is a tension be-tween the theoretical and practical lives that renders their coexistence at best uneasy. Or, to put it otherwise, Enlightenment proposed a parallelism between intellectual and moral or political progress, which the ancients regarded as very doubtful, a doubt recapitulated and reinforced by Rousseau, who expresses the opposition in the contrast between Sparta and Athens. He, of course, categorically preferred the former. Enlightenment wished to convert the selfishness of man in the state of nature into the enlightened self-interest of man capable of joining civil society rationally on the basis of the natural and dependable natural passions. It is this conversion Rousseau regarded as noxious and the source of moral chaos and the misery of man. He first comes to light as the defender of the old moral order against the spirit of philosophy to a degree unparalleled by any previous philos-opher, doing so perhaps because modernity had more systematically attacked the moral order than had any previous thought. Rousseau is the first philosopher to appear as morality's defender *against* reason. He insisted that the movement from the natural state to the social one could not be made in the direct and almost automatic way En-lightenment claimed.

More concretely, the arts and sciences can flourish only in large and luxurious countries, which means from the outset that they require conditions contrary to those required by the small, austere, tightly knit communities where moral health prevails and the individuals have no objects of aspiration beyond those of the community. For some to be idle, others must work to provide the surplus necessary for them. These workers are exploited for the sake of the few privileged who no longer share their condition or their concerns. The fulfillment of unnecessary desires, begun as a pleasure, ends up being a necessity; the true necessities are neglected and their purveyors despised. Desire emancipated becomes limitless and calls forth an economy to provide for it. The pleasures are exclusive and are pleasant in large measure because they are exclusive. The sense of superiority follows from the practice of the arts and sciences and is also part of the reason they are pursued. Following from the general principles of modernity, it may be doubted that the intellectual pleasures are natural rather than affects of vanity. They almost always have some of the latter mixed in with them, which suffices to render them antisocial. The spirit of Enlightenment philosophy, perhaps of all philosophy, is to denigrate the simple feelings of common humanity that cause men to forget their self-interest.

In fine, the arts and sciences tend to increase inequality and fix its throne more firmly within society. They give more power to the already powerful and make the weak ever more dependent on the powerful without any common good uniting the two parties. The effective freedom of the state of nature, where man could choose what seems to him good for himself, has been replaced by the imposition of arbitrary authority over him, which has no concern for his good. Freedom was the first and most important of the natural goods, as means to live as one pleases, also as an end in itself. Equality meant that in right nobody can command another and in fact nobody wished to do so because men were independent and self-sufficient. The civil condition means, in the first place, mutual dependence, physically and spiritually, but without order, each struggling to maintain the original freedom, failing to do so as relations of force or power take the place of freedom. The purpose of life becomes trying to find an advantageous place in this artificial system. Freedom is lost, not only because there is mastery and slavery but mostly because it becomes absorbed in commanding or obeying, in moving the wills of others rather than in fulfilling the objects of one's own will. The loss of freedom is best expressed in the fact of inequality, that some men are strong, others weak, some are rich, others poor, some command, and others obey. The primary fact of the state of nature as described by all teachers of the state of nature is that men are free and equal. But the *bourgeois* state, which in speech affirms the primacy of natural freedom and equality, in practice does not reflect that primacy. Natural right, as opposed to merely conventional right, demands the continuation or restoration of the original equality of men.

In this all regimes fail, but Rousseau judges that the ancient city came closest of all to real equality and collective freedom. Although the ancient city looks, with all its restraints, traditions, austerity, harsh duties, and so on, to be much further away from the natural state than does a liberal society where men apparently live pretty much as they please, it comes close to the essence of what really counts for man. The study of the state of nature permits Rousseau to see that essence, but such study cannot result in a plan for building a civil

state that protects that essence. That must be a purely human invention, and the easy solutions that seem to preserve or to be most faithful
to nature are specious. Rousseau's analysis leads to a much stricter
insistence on freedom and equality within civil society than the
thought of Locke or Montesquieu. Against their moderation, Rousseau
adds a dose of extremism to modern politics from which it cannot
easily recover. What began as an attempt to simplify politics ends up
as a program for reform more complex and more imperative than
anything that had preceded.

Rousseau introduced the taste for the small, virtuous community
into the modern movement toward freedom and equality. Here freedom becomes less each doing what he pleases than each equally taking
responsibility for making and preserving the law of the city. Ancient
politics used freedom as the means to virtue; Rousseau and his followers
made freedom, the natural good, the end and virtue the means to it.
But, in any event, virtue, morals, and character become central again
to politics and cannot, as the moderns would have it, be peripheral
to the machinery of government, to institutions that channel men's
passions instead of educating, reforming, or overcoming them.

PROPERTY

This point is made most forcefully in Rousseau's reflections on
economics, or, to put it more precisely, on property, the cornerstone
of modern politics. "Ancient political writers spoke constantly about
morals and virtue; ours speak only about commerce and money."[3] A
man's attachment to his property, always threatened by the poor and
the rapacious, is the special motive used by Locke and his followers
to get his consent to the making of a social contract and the reestab-
lishment of government. This is the means of achieving mutual recognition of property rights as well as protection for them from a whole
community capable of punishing aggressors. The rational and the
industrious who provide for themselves by labor rather than by war
are the foundations of civil society, and its purposes are elegantly
defined and limited by their needs. They preserve themselves com-
fortably, following their most powerful inclinations, and produce peace
and prosperity for the whole. Their wills assent to the arrangement
that their reasons determine best for their interest. This is so manifestly

[3]*Discourse on the Origins of Inequality*, Part 2. Compare *Social Contract*, Book 1, Chapter
9.

superior to the condition of war that prevails before the contract that it fully engages the hearts and minds of those who profit from it.

The right to property is society's golden thread, the right that emerges as the ground of consensus of the free and equal. "Work and you shall enjoy the fruits of your labors." For Hobbes, whose civil society emerges out of fear of death alone, property rights are left to the prudence of the sovereign, who can arrange them in whatever way seems fitting for the most secure establishment of peace. But for Locke, who taught that property is the true means to peace, property rights are more absolute, and the economic system governing the increase of property, what is now called the market, must as much as possible be respected by the sovereign. Government protects the in- dividual best by protecting his property and leaving him as free as possible to care for it. The naturalness of property and government's special concern for the protection of the pursuit of it are Locke's novelties and become the hallmark of the serious projects for the reform of governments.

For all of the plausibility and even practical effectiveness of this scheme, Rousseau observes, there is something immediately shocking about the assertion that equal men should freely consent to great inequalities of property. The rich have lives that are so much freer, so much easier, so much more open to the enjoyment of life. They are so much more powerful. They can buy the law, and they can buy men. Why should the poor accept this willingly? No, the poor must have been forced to agree, or they must have been deceived. This is not natural right. The property relations that prevail in the nations are so many acts of violence against the poor, which they are too weak to prevent. There is no legitimacy here. The opposition between Locke and Rousseau is measured by the fact that the establishment of private property is for Locke the beginning of the solution to the political problem while for Rousseau it is the source of the continuing misery of man.[4]

This does not mean Rousseau is a communist or that he believed that it is possible or desirable to do away with private property. He is far too "realistic" to follow Plato's Republic and abandon the sure motive of love of one's own things. It does mean, however, that he strongly opposes the emancipation of acquisitiveness and that he argues against laissez-faire. For him the business of government is to supervise the pursuit of property in order to limit the inequality of fortunes, to

[4]Discourse on the Arts and Sciences, in Roger and Judith Masters, eds., Two Discourses (New York: St. Martin's Press, 1964), p. 51.

mitigate the harshness of economic competition, and to moderate the increase of desire among the citizens. Adam Smith's book *The Wealth of Nations*, which is very much in the spirit of Locke, is in large measure a presentation of the iron laws of the increase of property. Rousseau's book *Political Economy* is a treatise devoted to moral education. A modern reader who picks up *Political Economy* finds himself at sea, wondering what in the world this has to do with economics. The science of economics as we know it is predicated on the emancipation of desire, an emancipation Rousseau is concerned to prevent. In no point does Rousseau's analysis of the meaning of freedom and equality differ so much from Locke's as in the property question. The most practically radical opposition to liberal constitutionalism comes from this direction. The property right, which Locke wished to establish solidly, becomes the most doubtful of all things.

Again, though, this difference begins in an initial important agreement between Locke and Rousseau. Property is in its most primitive form that with which a man has mixed his labor. Neither God nor nature gives man directly what he needs. He must provide for himself, and his appropriation of things necessary for preservation is an extension of the original property that all have in their own body. The man who has planted beans and wishes to eat them is universally recognized to have a better right to do so than the one who without planting takes away the other's beans. There is an original of simple justice here, accessible to men of good sense. And Locke follows it through its fullest development and most complicated expressions in commercial societies. The reciprocal recognition of this right to what one has worked for constitutes property, and this solution unites self-interest with justice. The ancient view that property is constituted by a combination of what one has worked for with what one can use well is reduced to the single principle, for the classical formula implies that property is based on political determinations that can be regarded as subjective and arbitrary.

Rousseau parts company with Locke on the question of scarcity. The man who has no beans concerns him. The economist responds, "He didn't plant any, so he doesn't deserve them." But his hunger obliterates his recognition of the property right of the other, and the essence of the right is in the recognition. This malcontent can be controlled by the union of those who have provided themselves with beans, or who have inherited them, and wish to live in security from the attacks of him and his kind. So force must be introduced to compel the idle and contentious to keep away from others' property and to work to provide for themselves. The civil union is really made up of two groups: those who freely recognize one another's property rights and those who are forced to comply with the rule of the property owners. The latter are used for the collective private interest of the former. *Class* is decisive in civil society, and there is no common good without radical reform.

Thus the liberal view is that society consists in the opposition between, to repeat, the rational and industrious and the idle and quarrelsome. The former produce peace and prosperity for all, while the latter produce penury and war. Rational men must recognize and consent to the order that favors the dominance of the propertied. Rousseauean economics, however, views the social opposition as existing between the selfish, avaricious rich, exploiting nature and men for the sake of the increase of their personal wealth, and the suffering poor, unable to provide for their needs because the land and the other means of production are monopolized by the rich. As the perspective shifts, those who were once objects of execration become objects of pity.

Locke found the source of prosperity in the transformation by labor of the naturally given. This labor is motivated by need, by desire for comfort, and by anxiety for the future. For the satisfaction of all that man might possibly want, there is never enough. Once the imagination has opened out beyond the merest physical need, the desire for acquisition becomes infinite. Rousseau concludes from this that those who are ablest at getting land and money end up possessing all the means of gaining wealth. They produce much wealth, but they do not share. For those who do not succeed, there is ever greater scarcity, and they must live their lives at the mercy of the rich. In the beginning their simple needs did not require much for their satisfaction, but that little disappears, for example, when all the land is enclosed and they have no place to plant their beans. The best they can do is sell their labor to those who have land in return for subsistence, which depends no longer on their own efforts but on the wills of the rich or the impersonal market. The scarcity that Locke asserts existed at the beginning was really, Rousseau asserts, a result of the extreme extension of desire, and Locke's solution increases scarcity within wealth, a scarcity that could be corrected by moderation, a return to a simple economy directed to real needs. The expanding economy can never keep up with the expansion of desire or of longing for the means of satisfying future desire. The economy that was instituted to serve life alters the purpose of life, and the activity of society becomes subservient to it. The present is sacrificed to a prosperous future that is always just beyond the horizon. Actually

nature was not such a stepmother as the moderns thought, and it is
not so unreasonable to seek to live according to nature as they teach.

As politics turns into economics, the qualities requisite to the
latter come to define the privileged human character. Selfishness and
calculation have primacy over generosity and compassion. Dealings
among men are at best contractual, always with an eye to profit.
Differences of talent at acquisition do exist; but, Rousseau asks, does
a decent society privilege them at the expense of differences in goodness and decency? The social arrangement of property that he asserts
should follow from the study of man's natural condition is not that of
commercial societies but that of agricultural communities, where production requires only simple skills, where the division of labor is not
extreme, where exchange is direct and the virtuosos of finance play
little role, where inequalities of land and money are, if not abolished,
limited, where avarice has little opportunity for activity, and where
the motive for work is immediate necessity. The scale should not
become such that men are abstractions while money is real. A modest
sufficiency of goods and a moderate disposition, not the hope of riches
and their perpetual increase, should be the goal of political economy.
The natural equality of man can tolerate only a small amount of
inequality produced by society.

Rousseau confronts Locke's assertion that liberal economies make
all members of society richer and, therefore, palpably better off than
they were in the natural condition with the counterassertion that
freedom can never properly be put in the same balance with riches
and comfort. Perhaps the day laborer in England is better clothed,
housed, and fed than a king in America. Unimpressed by the moral
qualities Locke finds in the English day laborer, Rousseau turned back
toward the proud dignity and independence of the king. Locke took
it that his argument is sufficient to persuade the rational poor to accept
the inequalities present in society in preference to the neediness of
the state of nature. Rousseau uses the same argument to make men
rebel against the state of dependence and anxiety caused by the economies of civilized society. He goes further. In depicting the degradation
of the bourgeois, the new kind of ruler, in comparison with the greatness
of the ancient citizen, he makes the life of the advantaged in liberal
society appear to be as despicable as the life of the disadvantaged is
miserable.

The delegitimization of property's emancipation from political
control, that is, from the will of all, was one of the most effective
and revolutionary aspects of Rousseau's thought. His great rhetoric
was used to make compassion for the poor central to relations among

men and indignation at their situation central to political action. With all the freshness of original insight, before this kind of analysis became routine and tired, he outlined all that is negative about excessive concern for self-preservation and the means of ensuring it. But for all that, Locke was simply right in one decisive aspect. Everybody, not just the rich, gets richer in a system of liberal economy. Gross inequalities of wealth persist or are encouraged by it, but the absolute material well-being of each is greatly enhanced. Rousseau, followed by Marx, taught that the inner logic of acquisition would concentrate wealth in fewer and fewer hands, completely dispossessing the poor and alienating them from the means of becoming prosperous. Locke's great selling point has proved to be true. Joining civil society for the sake of protection and comfort is a good investment. This fact has been widely accepted by Americans for a long time; it is only now becoming fully recognized by Europeans. Intellectuals committed to the revolution are the last to resign themselves to the facts. The grinding sense of necessity has been alleviated and with it most of the revolutionary fervor. One may continue to believe, as somber critics still do, that the way of life of such a society is repulsive and that the motives for association are inadequate and corrupt. But that is not quite the same as the progressive impoverishment and enslavement of mankind at large. Most of all, the poor, the many, the masses— however they are now qualified—become supporters of "the system," out of crass self-interest, and that destroys the revolutionary movements. The humanness of life may be lessened, but that is not accompanied by starvation.

Locke taught that the protection and increase of property guaranteed by government based on consent are both efficient and just. The justice is harsh natural justice—the protection of unequal natural talents for acquisition from the depredations of the idle, the less competent, the envious, and the brutal. The argument for efficiency remains; but since the full effect of Rousseau penetrated the bloodstream of Western thought, hardly any of the economists who are capitalism's most convinced advocates defend the justice of the inequalities in which it results. It is at best an effective way of increasing collective and individual wealth. Rousseau's arguments for the primacy of natural equality have proved persuasive. The construction of civil society based on inequalities of property-producing gifts is seen to be a contradiction of what is most fundamental. As a matter of fact, natural inequalities of any sort—whether of strength, beauty, or intelligence—must not have any privileges in civil society because they did not in the state of nature. This is a step away from the sway of nature that Rousseau was the first to make. Nature mandates political inventiveness for the attainment of equality in civil society. Coarse pragmatism can live with a system that "works," as long as it works. But we find ourselves, at least partly because of Rousseau, in the interesting situation where we do not entirely believe in the justice of our regimes.

THE GENERAL WILL

Since man is naturally free, the only political solution in accordance with nature is for Rousseau one where man governs himself.[5] This does not mean that man consents to let others govern for him. Practically, he cannot accept the dictates of other men. He experiences them merely as wills opposing his will. Other men may force him to act against his wishes, but this is force, not right. Law is not essentially force. For law to be law, the one who obeys it must do so with the assent of his will; and in the absence of a fully wise and just ruler, other men cannot be trusted. The human law worthy of obedience is the law one has made for oneself. Only this formula combines freedom with obligation. Self-legislation is the true meaning of a decent political order.

This Rousseau contrasts with the liberal formula that one gives up a bit of freedom to enjoy the rest undisturbed. This leaves everything unresolved. Just how much is this bit? How is the ever-present possibility of opposition between what the individual wants and the demands of the collectivity to be mediated? The arrangement contains no element of morality or obligation, only contingent calculations of immediate interest. Utilitarian morality is no morality at all. Analysis reduces it at best to long-range self-interest. Real duty, the unselfregarding moral deed, becomes a will-of-the-wisp. The struggle between inclination and duty, obstinate and irreconcilable, is the psychological price paid for the liberal social contract. Only the man whose private will wills only the common good would experience no tension between his individuality and society, freedom and duty.

This analysis is the source of the general will, Rousseau's most famous innovation, his attempt to establish a moral politics that does not degrade man or rob him of his freedom.[6] The will of individuals is, by definition, individual and is therefore not concerned with the

[5]*Social Contract*, Book 1, Chapter 6.
[6]*Ibid.*, Book 1, Chapter 8.

good of others. But man is capable of generalizing. His rationality consists in it. The simple operation of replacing "I want . . ." by "we want . . ." is typical of reasoning man. The man who wills only what all could will makes a community of shared, harmonious wills possible. The society of men who will generally together dissolves the virtual war of all against all with respect to which liberal society is only a truce. General will is the common good.

Man's dividedness is not overcome by the general will, but its character is transformed. It is no longer experienced as an opposition between self and other, inside and outside. The struggle is now between one's particular desire and one's general will, a will recognized as nonarbitrary and good. Self-overcoming is the essence of the moral experience, and it is this capacity that Rousseau believed he had discovered, a discovery only dimly perceived by ancient politics and entirely lost in modern politics. Willing generally constitutes a new kind of human freedom, not the satisfaction of animal inclination but real choice. It is the privileged and profound form of rationality as opposed to the calculation of personal benefit. It is a transformation of nature that preserves what is essential about nature. Obedience to the general will is an act of freedom. This is the dignity of man, and a good society makes possible and encourages such dignity.[7]

The passage from the particularly willing savage to the generally willing citizen is the triumph of civilization, and it is man's historic activity to construct the bridge between the two. The distance is great. The soul has no such natural order, and its development is not a growth but a willful making, a putting in order of man's disordered and incoherent acquisitions during the course of time. Education is this activity of construction, which Rousseau presents in all its complexity and richness in his greatest work, Emile. The putting into political practice of this education is really the work of the legislator, who must be an artist. Beginning from the first needs and desires of a limited and selfish being, passing through all the experiences requisite to learning how to preserve itself, he ends with the man who thinks of himself as man simply, controlling his wishes by the imperative of their possibility for all men.

All this is abstract. For such a man to exist really, there must be a community into which he is woven so tightly that he cannot think of himself separately from it, his very existence formed as part of this whole. The public business is identical to his private interest, and he thinks of it when he wakes in the morning and when he goes to bed

[7]Ibid.

at night. It does not suffice that he be an unquestioning part of a traditional society governed by ancestral ways. He must understand himself as guiding his own destiny, as a lawmaker for his city and thereby for himself. Every decision, act, or decree of the city must be understood to be the result of his own will. Only in this way is he autonomous and does he maintain his natural inalienable freedom. The citizen as understood by Rousseau combines the competing charms of rootedness and independence.

It follows immediately that the citizen must choose to practice the severest virtues of self-control, for if his private bodily needs or desires are imperious, he will be too busy tending them. Moderation for the sake of freedom is his principle. This is different from the *bourgeois*'s delay of gratification, which still has as its motive the private needs of the individual and looks toward infinite increase as the end. The citizen's efforts are connected with present satisfactions that constitute their own reward. Concern with public business in the assembly of citizens is the core of his life. He works and cares for his property with a view to maintaining a modest competence, setting aside great private indulgences and personal anxieties about the future. The whole organization of community life inclines him toward generality in a substantial way. The choice of individuality would be difficult to make, whereas in a commercial society the public-spirited way of life has no support. Rousseau's city provides little opportunity for private consumer expense and imposes severe sumptuary taxes on itself.

The simplest political requisite of healthy politics is, therefore, a small territory and a small population.[8] The whole body of citizens must be able to meet regularly. Moreover, they must know one another. The extension of human sentiments is limited, and caring requires acquaintance. Love of country and one's fellows cannot be abstract; they must be continuously experienced. Perhaps the most remarkable difference between Rousseau's politics and the politics of Enlightenment concerns this question of size. The commercial republic tends to favor large territories and large populations. Large markets encourage production and exchange, hence increase of wealth. Moreover, only large countries can counterbalance large and powerful enemies. And they offer all kinds of advantages for the machinery of modern governments that rely less on the good character of men than on various counterpoising forces, on checks and balances. What is sacrificed, according to Rousseau, is autonomy and human connectedness. Concentration on local community and responsibility is part

[8]*Ibid.*, Book 2, Chapter 9; Book 3, Chapter 12.

of Rousseau's legacy, a concentration that goes against all the dominant tendencies of commercial republics in modernity. Rousseau con-
nects large size with despotism. As Montesquieu looked to great
nations like England as the models for modern regimes directed to
freedom, Rousseau looks to modern cities like Geneva as well as to
Sparta to demonstrate the possibility of what he prescribes.

Small size is also necessary to avoid the modern democratic device
of representation, which for Rousseau epitomizes the halfway modern
solution to the problem of freedom.[9] Without transforming natural
freedom into civil freedom, that is, without abandoning the habit of
living as one pleases and doing what is necessary to become a part of
a sovereign body, men hope that others will take the responsibility of
governing for them while remaining loyal to their will. The effort of
determining general wills is to be left to the representatives without
having a citizen body that wills generally. This is a prescription for
interest politics or the compromising of particular, selfish wills. The
idea of the common good disappears, and the conflict of parties takes
its place. Worst of all, representation institutionalizes divided modern
man, no longer really free, hopelessly dependent on the wills of others,
believing himself to be master but incapable of the effort of moral
autonomy.

Thus, in broad outline, Rousseau rejects most of the elements of
modern constitutionalism including those that make up the U.S. Constitution. The principles of enlightened self-interest as well as the
machinery of limited representative government only exacerbate in
his view the tension between individual and society and lead to ever
greater egotistical individualism accompanied by dangerous arbitrary
abuses of centralized governmental power. The very notion of checks
and balances encourages the selfishness of partial interests. Good institutions in this sense are predicated on the badness of men. Whether
the institutions function or not, they give way to and encourage moral
corruption.

The foundings of government Rousseau wishes to encourage are
those that make the virtue of all the citizens necessary to their func-
tioning, and they are very complicated affairs. In most modern political
philosophy after Machiavelli, there is little talk of founders or legislators. Lycurgus, Solon, Moses, Theseus, Romulus, Numa, and Cyrus
were previously the common currency in discussion of the origins of
political regimes. It was taken for granted that the union of disparate
individuals into a community of goods and purposes is the most difficult

[9]*Ibid.*, Book 3, Chapter 15.

of political deeds and requires men of surpassing greatness to achieve
it. A way of life that engages all the members had to be instituted.
But the new political discoveries seemed to indicate that the foundation of civil orders was more like the striking of a business contract,
where all that is required is individuals who are clear about their
personal interests and where they intersect with those of others. The
transition into the civil state was understood to be almost automatic,
certainly not requiring common agreement about the good life. This
hardly perceptible transition indicated the naturalness of the new
politics. All that was necessary to the founding of a political order
was enlightenment or an instruction manual. Hobbes thought that
the advantages of the civil order could be made evident to men before
its establishment. The ancients thought that the most far-seeing statesmen alone could know those advantages and that the individual citizens could know them only afterward. The foundings require
persuasion, deception, and force as well as an elaborated plan for a
way of life adapted to the particular people that is to be founded. The
ultimate goals of justice may be universal, but the ways to them are
almost infinitely diverse. The legislator must combine particular and
universal, taste and principle. Prudence rather than abstract reason is
his instrument. Such was the view of ancient politics, and Rousseau
partially returns to it, though further encumbering the legislator with
the abstract demands of modern legitimacy. All of this underlines
Rousseau's view of the great distance between the natural and the
civil states.[10]

       This treatment of legislators may be useful in thinking about the
American Framers, whose position is anomalous in modern political
thought. Their role was at least halfway between the Enlighteners and
Rousseau. Their founding activity was not based on any explicit teaching about founding in the philosophies of Locke or Montesquieu. They
were, as is Rousseau's legislator, without authority, acting as they did
before the legislation that founds all authority, and their task was
almost limitless. Surely they thought not only of the abstract contract
but of how it would fit the people they were founding. And they
reflected—individual members of the founding group more or less
coherently—on the moral character of the citizens and the national
life requisite for the success of their project. They were for a time and
in their way almost princes, legislating for egalitarian rule, preparing
their own extinction, acting out of motives of a vastness and selflessness far transcending those they expected of the citizens. All this is

[10]*Ibid.*, Book 2, Chapter 7.

discussed by Rousseau, and it provides a link between the petty egotism attributed by Rousseau to the classical liberal model of politics and the sublime morality Rousseau sought and insisted on.

CONCLUSION

Rousseau's description of what the legislator must accomplish might make the modern reader think that he is speaking of culture rather than politics. The very word "culture," first employed in the modern sense by Kant, stemmed from an interpretation of Rousseau's intention. He was looking for a harmony between nature and civilization, civilization meaning all the historically acquired needs and desires of man and the means of satisfying them discovered by him. Civilization had shattered man's unity. Although the foundation of civil societies and the discovery of the arts and sciences might appear to be simply a progress, if progress is measured by actual happiness rather than the production of the means for the pursuit of happiness, the advantages of civilization become doubtful. The restoration of the unity of man is the project of politics taken broadly. Politics in its narrow modern sense concerns the *state*, the minimal rules for human intercourse, not the happiness of man. Culture is where we think man as a whole lives; it frames and forms man's possible ways of life and his attainment of happiness. It is thought to be the deeper phenomenon. Rousseau appears to us to combine the concerns of culture and of politics. For him they are really not separable. The nineteenth-century idea of culture was completely separated from politics. It ceased to be understood as a conscious founding within the power of men to construct. It came to be understood as a growth, a result of the mysterious process of history. But however far the notion moved from its roots in Rousseau, it continued to express Rousseau's concern for the "organic" character of human association. The habitual way of using the word "culture," as something admirable, as opposed to mere cosmopolitan, superficial "civilization," reflected and still reflects Rousseau's contempt for bourgeois society and modern liberal constitutionalism as well as the critique of civilization he launched with the *Discourse on the Arts and Sciences*.

So it is perhaps helpful for us to describe Rousseau's legislator as the founder of a culture, and this makes more evident the magnitude of the task imposed on him by Rousseau. To succeed he must charm men with at least the appearance of divine authority to make up for the human authority he lacks and to give men the motives for sub-

228 GIANTS AND DWARFS

mission to the law that nature does not provide. He not only needs authority from the gods; he must establish a civil religion that can support and reward men's willing the common good. What is called the sacred today and is understood to be the summit of culture finds a place in Rousseau's project more central than the very ambiguous one it has in liberal legislation, where religion may be understood to be unnecessary or even dangerous to the civil order. As one looks at what the legislator must do, it is hard to resist the temptation to say it is impossible.[11]

This impression was confirmed for Western consciousness by one highly visible experiment, the legislative activity of Robespierre, or the Terror. The attempt to institute citizenship was a bloody business, which was sufficient to repel most observers. As Locke and Montesquieu were the presiding geniuses of Adams, Madison, Hamilton, and Jefferson in their moderate founding, Rousseau was the presiding genius of the excesses of the French Revolution. Edmund Burke's overwhelming description of the events and Rousseau's influence on them is unforgettable.[12]

In spite of Rousseau's dangerous impracticality, he could not be put aside as just another failure. His articulation of the problem of democratic politics was just too potent. His views about what effect his thought should have on practical politics are difficult to penetrate. Locke and Montesquieu would certainly in general have approved of the handiwork of their great pupils, and Rousseau would just as certainly have disapproved of Robespierre. Although his teaching is full of fervent aspiration, it is also full of bleak pronouncements about the possibility of correcting the tendencies of modernity. Whether or not he thought his kind of city could actually come into being is uncertain. But if it were possible, it would be so only in a few small places with very special circumstances, like Corsica. The universal applicability and possibility of actualization that is the hallmark of modern political science disappears in Rousseau. In this again he is more like Plato and Aristotle than a modern. But Plato and Aristotle made a distinction between the just regime and acceptable ones that permitted men to live with the less than perfect, whereas Rousseau insists that only the simply just regime is legitimate, thereby making almost all real political life unacceptable. He somehow combines the high standards of the ancients with the insistence on actualization of the good regime of

[11]*Ibid.*, Book 2, Chapter 8. Compare *Emile*, "Profession of Faith of a Savoyard Vicar," pp. 266–313.
[12]Edmund Burke, "Letter to a Member of the National Assembly," in Peter J. Stanlis, ed., *Selected Writings and Speeches* (Garden City, N.Y.: Doubleday & Co., 1963), pp. 511–13.

the moderns, thus producing the ultramodern political disposition.

The origins of this are in Machiavelli's turning away from the imaginary cities of the old philosophers toward the way men really live. He intended to reduce the disproportion between the is and the ought, in favor of the is, so as to achieve the modest goals given by men's real needs. A lowering and simplification of the understanding of man's nature would make the satisfaction of that nature possible. But somehow this moral reductionism does not work. Man's longing for justice and dignity will not accept it, and with Rousseau the old tension reasserts itself in the form of the opposition between the real and the ideal. The state-of-nature teachings, which were elaborations of Machiavelli's intention, taught that man is naturally a brute concerned exusively with his preservation. Civil society was in those teachings only a more prudent way of realizing the most primitive goals. Its establishment is a progress in that sense alone, not in the sense of a movement from brutishness to humanity. Freedom in the state of nature was only the means to preservation, and equality was only the absence of the authority of any man over any other man to prevent the exercise of his freedom. Civil society uses freedom and equality merely as means to the basic end of comfortable self-preservation. Therefore they could be greatly attenuated in the service of that end. Freedom and equality could be signed over to civil society, which adopts the responsibility for the more effective fulfillment of the goal for which they were the imperfect natural instruments. So it seems. But experience and reflection teach that, once man knows himself to be naturally free and equal, it is impossible to avoid the demand that men in society be free and equal in the most absolute sense. The freedom of man is recognized to be his essence, and civil freedom is not possible without factual equality. In practice all of society's laws remain doubtful until they can really be understood to be self-imposed, and every inequality appears intolerable. The easygoing solution of the satisfaction of the basic needs is overturned by constant demands for greater freedom and equality. They become insistent in practice as men are informed of their natural rights and act as perpetual goads to reform and revolution. What later came to be called a dialectic was set in motion, and natural freedom tends to civil freedom. Only when law is the expression of rational universality and all men are equally recognized by all as moral agents and as ends in themselves is the process complete. The chapter in the Social Contract where Rousseau describes the difference between natural animal freedom and moral freedom describes the two terms of the process.[13]

[13]Social Contract, Book 1, Chapter 8.

Whatever the consequences, once the principles appear to be self-evident, this aspiration toward ever greater freedom and equality follows, tending to challenge all prudential stopping points or efforts to counterpoise it by other principles or by traditions. The problem can be epitomized by the idea of social contract. All thinkers are in agreement that consent is requisite to the establishment of laws. But, Rousseau argued, none of them before him found any kind of rule of consent that binds the individual when the law is believed by him to be contrary to his interest, that is, in the extreme case, his life, liberty, and property. Only Rousseau found the formula for that, distinguishing self-interest from moral obligation, discerning an independent moral interest in the general will. He discovered the source of moral goodness in modern political principles and provided the flag under which democracy could march. So, at least, it was understood. Regimes dedicated to the sole preservation of man do not have the dignity to compel moral respect.

Although the attempt to incarnate the moral democratic regime in a modern nation appeared worse than quixotic to sober men after the French Revolution, they all agreed that Rousseau had to be taken account of, that his thought had to be incorporated into the theory and practice of the modern state.[14] Kant and Hegel are only the two most notable examples of this, giving an account of moral dignity in freedom based on Rousseau while using it to reinterpret and sublimate *bourgeois* society. Thus they hoped to reconcile Rousseau with the reality of modernity rather than permitting the impulse transmitted by him to lead to ever greater extremes in rebellion against triumphant modernity. Failing that reconciliation, Rousseau's persuasive depiction of humanity shattered and fragmented by the apparently irresolvable conflict between nature and society authorizes many different kinds of attempts to pick up the pieces: on the political Left, new revolutions and new Terrors to install the regime of democratic virtue; on the Right, immersion in the rootedness of local cultures without the justification of rational universality, then there are those who, like Thoreau, flee the corruptions of society in an attempt to recover natural self-sufficiency.

Taking Rousseau seriously, however, does not necessarily mean despising and rejecting the regime of the U.S. Constitution, as the

---

[14]There were strands of utopian socialism that still looked toward the establishment of small communities of the kind Rousseau prescribed. Their most notable expression is the kibbutzim in Israel, founded by Russian Jews influenced by Tolstoy, who was a most ardent admirer of Rousseau.

example of one of the most serious of those thoughtful men influenced by Rousseau proves. That is Alexis de Tocqueville, whose very obvious Rousseauism is masked to contemporary eyes by his conservative admirers, who refuse to admit that he could have any connection with Rousseau, the Leftist extremist. He turned from the spectacle of European egalitarian disorder to the United States, which he saw as the model of orderly liberty. He affirmed without hesitation the justice of equality as over against the unjust privileges of the past. He interpreted the United States as a vast educational undertaking, instructing citizens in the political exercise of their rights. He treated the Founders as men whose characters expressed a higher morality that may not have been contained in their principles. He, of course, could not believe that the United States simply solved the political problem. His view of American democracy is tinged with the melancholy Rousseau induces when one looks at real political practice. He casts respectful glances at American savages and at the great souls of some aristocratic men. He recognized the danger that the regime might tend toward materialism, to mere self-interest on the part of the citizens, and to atomizing individualism. He concentrated on the importance of local self-government, which approximated the participation of the independent city, and saw the New England town as the real foundation of American freedom, the core around which the larger government aggregated. Moreover, he introduced compassion, a sentiment alien to Locke and Montesquieu, as the corrective to the harshness of economic relations in the commercial society. Compassion he took to be the core of democratic feeling and the ground for something more than connections of interest among men. He also concentrated as liberals did not on the connectedness between man and woman and their offspring as constituting an intermediate community, a bridge between individual and society. He simply reproduces Rousseau's reflections on the family in *Emile*. And he looks to a gentle, democratic religion to mitigate the American passion for material well-being. Rousseau makes Tocqueville alert to the dangers of liberal society and allows him to reinterpret it in such a way as to encourage the citizen virtues that can emerge out of the principles of freedom and equality rightly understood.

I have adduced the example of Tocqueville to indicate the kind of meditation about politics that men of Rousseauean sensibilities might have. Rousseau's specific projects were quickly exploded. But he infected most of us with longings for freedom and virtue that are difficult to get over. He is that modern thinker of democracy who had the depth and breadth in his vision of man found in Plato and con-

Teachers

LEO STRAUSS

SEPTEMBER 20, 1899–OCTOBER 18, 1973

ON OCTOBER 18, 1973, Leo Strauss died in Annapolis, Maryland. He was one of the very small number of men whose thought has had seminal influence in political theory in our time. He published fifteen books and over eighty articles, and he left behind several generations of unusually devoted students. It is particularly difficult to speak of him, for I know I cannot do him justice. Moreover, those of us who knew him saw in him such a power of mind, such a unity and purpose of life, such a rare mixture of the human elements resulting in a harmonious expression of the virtues, moral and intellectual, that our account of him is likely to evoke disbelief or ridicule from those who have never experienced a man of this quality. Finally, Leo Strauss left his own memorial in the body of his works in which what he understood to be his essence lives on; and, above all, he was dedicated to intransigent seriousness as opposed to popularization. But an inner need to pay him tribute and a kind of filial piety urge me on in spite of the persuasiveness of the reasons that restrain me.

I

The story of a life in which the only real events were thoughts is easily told. Leo Strauss was born on September 20, 1899, in Kirchhain, Hessen, Germany. He was raised as an Orthodox Jew and had a gymnasium education. He studied at the universities of Marburg and Hamburg, and he spent a postdoctoral year at Freibourg, where Husserl was the professor of philosophy and the young Heidegger was his assistant. From there Strauss went to Berlin and held a position at the Academy of Jewish Research. In 1932, he received a Rockefeller grant and left Germany, never to return except for a few short days more than twenty years later. He lived in Paris and Cambridge until 1938, when he came to the United States. He taught at the New School for Social Research until 1949, at the University of Chicago from which he retired in 1968 as the Robert M. Hutchins Distinguished Service Professor of Political Science, at Claremont Men's College, and at St. John's College in Annapolis. He knew many interesting men and women and spent much time talking to students, but the core of his being was the solitary, continuous, meticulous study of the questions he believed most important. His conversation was the result or the continuation of this activity. His passion for his work was unremitting, austere, but full of joy; he felt that he was not alive when he was not thinking, and only the gravest mishaps could cause him to cease doing so. Although he was unfailingly polite and generous with his time, one always knew that he had something more important to do. He was active in no organization, served in no position of authority, and had no ambitions other than to understand and help others who might also be able to do so. He was neither daunted nor corroded by neglect or hostility.

There is nothing in his biography that explains his thought, but it is to be noted that he was born a Jew in that country where Jews cherished the greatest secular hopes and suffered the most terrible persecutions, and that he studied philosophy in that country the language of which had been almost identical with that of philosophy for 150 years and whose most profound philosophic figure of this century was a Nazi. Thus Strauss had before him the spectacle of the political extremes and their connection with modern philosophy. He was forced to grapple with the theological-political problem at a time when it was most fashionable to ignore it or think it solved. He certainly believed that any man who is to live a serious life has to face these questions; he devoted his own life not to preaching answers to them but to clarifying them when their outlines had become obscure. His beginning point was a peculiarly favorable one for approaching the permanent questions.

Leo Strauss was a most controversial man, and his works have not received their due measure of recognition. By calling into question the presuppositions of modern scholarship as well as much of its result, he offended many scholars committed to its method and the current interpretation of the tradition. By speaking of natural right and the community founded on the *polis*, he angered the defenders of a certain orthodoxy which insisted that liberty is threatened by the consideration of these alternatives. By his critique of the fact-value distinction and the behavioral science which emerged from it, he aroused the indignation of many social scientists because he seemed to be challenging both their scientific project and the vision of society subtly bound up with it. Philosophic doubt, the critical reflection on the horizon which seems self-evident, always evokes moral indignation, and Strauss was aware of it. But that doubt is requisite for the sake of inner freedom and for the sake of mitigating the excesses of our questionable principles. Strauss's scholarship was in the service of providing a standpoint from which sensible evaluation of our situation can be made, for alternative standards of evaluation are not easily accessible and without the search for them convention will always be criticized conventionally.

The criticisms of behavioralism that Strauss initiated became highly respectable as certain of the consequences of the new social science became evident; and some of those who had been most virulent in their criticism of his criticism shifted with the new currents, without recantation. Strauss's study of social science is an excellent example of the cast of his mind and the way in which he proceeded. His attachment to the American regime was deep. He studied its history and was charmed by its particular genius. Practically, he was grateful for the refuge it gave him, and he was aware that the liberal democracies are the surest friends of his people. From both experience and study, he knew that liberal democracy is the only decent and just alternative available to modern man. But he also knew that liberal democracy is exposed to, not to say beleaguered by, threats both practical and theoretical. Among those threats is the aspect of modern philosophy that makes it impossible to give rational credence to the principles of the American regime, thereby eroding conviction of the justice of its cause. The new social science was in Leo Strauss's early years in America the powerful form in which modern, particularly German, philosophy was expressing itself in North America. I do not believe that he took the new social science to be a very important intellectual movement. There was, and is, a tremendous disproportion between its claims and its achievements, and it is not possessed of a serious understanding of its own intellectual roots. To spend time on it took Strauss away from his central concerns. But he regarded it as his duty to have a careful look at it, because it was here and influential, and because it was always his way to ascend from popular opinion to more adequate formulations of problems, to take seriously what men say and try to see what there is in it. This was not only a form of civility, although it was that: he believed that in men's opinions is to be found the access to knowledge of the ways things really are. Only by the careful and painstaking attempt to understand our own situation can one move beyond it while avoiding doctrinairism and abstraction. Strauss's way of approaching social science was not to engage in continuing polemics or to make accusations concerning subversive motives. Nor was it to take the ordinary productions of the discipline and make the easy rhetorical refutation, although severe moral responsibility made him read almost all the literature. Rather, he looked for those thinkers who were agreed to possess the best minds and whose works inspired the movement. Moreover, as he always did, he looked to the origins, because there the arguments for a position are usually made more seriously than later when they are already victorious and have the self-evidence which attaches to success, and because there one can find the alternative perspective which has been overwhelmed by the new one. In particular, Strauss looked to Max Weber, whom he studied thoroughly and respectfully. He carried on a dialogue with him. One of the important conclusions of that dialogue was that the fact-value distinction, which although very new had come to dominate moral discourse, needed stronger philosophic grounding if it was to be taken as a fundamental category of the mind. Strauss recognized the seriousness and nobility of Max Weber's mind, but he showed that he was a derivative thinker, standing somewhere between modern science and Nietzsche, unable to resolve their tension. Thus Strauss opened up a world of reflection on the sense of the word *value* and the reasonableness of substituting it for words like good and bad, and pointed the way to profounder reflection on what is of the most immediate concern to all persons of our generation.

This was one of the sources of his great appeal to students. He began where they began and showed them that they had not reflected on the presuppositions of their science or their politics and that these presuppositions had been reflected on by great men whom we have for all practical purposes forgotten how to read. The study of those thinkers became both a necessity and a delight. This was Leo Strauss's only rhetoric. Moreover, the critique of the principles of social science was accompanied by an effort to look at political things as they first come to sight, to rediscover the phenomena which were transformed or reduced by the new methods. Strauss was dedicated to the restoration of a rich and concrete natural consciousness of the political phenomenon. His truly astonishing clarity and freshness in describing the things around us came in large measure from the way he used old books to liberate himself from the categories which bind us.

When Leo Strauss came to America, the most advanced political scientists asserted that they could dispense with political philosophy as physics had dispensed with metaphysics. Now, it can be safely said, there is more hesitation about that assertion.

II

Leo Strauss was a philosopher. He would have never said so himself, for he was too modest and he had too much reverence for the rare human type and the way of life represented by that title to arrogate it to himself, especially in an age when its use has been so cheapened. My assertion is particularly paradoxical, inasmuch as Strauss appears emphatically to be only a scholar. The titles of his books are typically *The Political Philosophy of Thomas Hobbes* or *Thoughts on Machiavelli*, and those with titles like *Natural Right and History* or *The City and Man* prove to be but reflections on more than one old philosopher. Strauss merges with the authors he discussed and can be understood to be nothing more than their interpreter. Moreover, while philosophers today speak only of being and knowledge, Strauss spoke of cities and gentlemen.

But appearances can be deceiving, particularly when our prejudices are in part responsible for them. A survey of Strauss's entire body of work will reveal that it constitutes a unified and continuous, ever deepening investigation into the meaning and possibility of philosophy. It is the product of a philosophic life devoted to an understanding of the philosophic life at a time when philosophy can no longer give an account of itself and the most modern philosophers have abandoned reason, and hence philosophy, in favor of will or commitment. It is an investigation carried on in light of the seriousness of the objections and their proponents. Strauss did not give way to the modern movement, yet neither could he devote himself to science without facing that movement. He studied the reasons for the abandonment of reason reasonably, which means that he had to test the contemporary assertions about the character of philosophy and the need for a new mode of philosophy against the old philosophy. And that old philosophy is no longer immediately accessible to us, for it is seen through a tradition which does not take its claim to truth seriously. An effort of recovery was necessary, one rendered unusually difficult by the fact that we no longer possess the equipment with which to see ourselves through the eyes of earlier philosophers rather than seeing them through ours. Our categories are inherited, questionable; they determine our horizons. Recovery means discovery, and Leo Strauss embarked on a voyage of discovery in what was thought to be familiar terrain: the tradition of philosophy. He had to throw away the maps and the compass which were made on the basis of principles alien to that tradition and which would have led him astray by causing him to pass by what was not charted. His writings were tentative but ever surer steps toward understanding writers as they understood themselves and thereby toward making the fundamental alternatives again clear to men whose choices had become impover-ished. He found a way to read so as to perceive again what philosophy originally meant. In his last writings, he finally felt free to try to grasp the way of Socrates, the archetype of the philosopher and the one whose teaching Nietzsche and Heidegger most of all tried to overthrow. Socrates came alive again in a reading of Aristophanes, Xenophon, and Plato, those writers who knew him and were captivated by him. In making the Socratic way plausible again, intransigently confronting all the objections subsequently made against it and all the ways opposed to it, Strauss believed he had accomplished the *apology* of rationalism and the life dedicated to the quest for the first causes of all things.

It is in this spirit and not as a reformer, a moralist, or a founder of a movement that Leo Strauss undertook the study of political phi-losophy. His politics were the politics of philosophy and not the politics of a particular regime. Without forgetting being, he turned away from its contemplation to the contemplation of man—who is both the being capable of longing to know being and the most inter-esting of beings, the one which any teaching about being must most of all comprehend. To begin with the human things, to save them from reduction to the nonhuman and to understand their distinctive-ness, was the Socratic way. To begin again from the natural beginning point is even more necessary today, when science more than ever is devoted to explaining man by what is not man and has thereby made it impossible to comprehend the source and instrument of that science, the soul. The world and man's mind have been transformed by science; thus, when science becomes questionable, it is peculiarly difficult to find the natural mind. Science rests on prescientific foundations which are presupposed by science but which can no longer be seen by science. All thought that proceeds without a return to the prescientific world, a world not immediately available to us, is captive to contemporary beliefs. When Leo Strauss spoke of tyranny and gentlemen and natural right and statesmen and philosophers, he was always thinking of the problem of knowledge.

To restate all this in a somewhat different form, Leo Strauss believed that the Platonic image of the cave described the essential human condition. All men begin, and most men end, as prisoners of the authoritative opinions of their time and place. Education is a liberation from those bonds, the ascent to a standpoint from which the cave can be seen for what it is. Socrates' assertion that he only knows that he is ignorant reveals that he has attained such a standpoint, one from which he can see that what others take to be knowledge is only opinion, opinion determined by the necessities of life in the cave. Philosophy, in all its various forms, always has supposed that by unaided reason man is somehow capable of getting beyond the given and finding a nonarbitrary standard against which to measure it, and that this possibility constitutes the essence of human freedom. What Leo Strauss faced as a young man was the most radical denial of this possibility that had ever been made. The objection was not that of skepticism, a view that has always been present in the philosophic tradition, but the positive or dogmatic assertion that reason is incapable of finding permanent, nonarbitrary principles. All that was most powerful either implicitly or explicitly accepted the truth of this assertion. Kantianism, in its neo-Kantian fragments, had ceased to be plausible. What remained was positivism, which understood its principles to be unprovable and dependent on their usefulness, and radical historicism, which went further by asserting that reason has its roots in unreason and is hence only a superficial phenomenon. It concluded that the positivists' principles, admittedly arbitrary, were the product of only one of an infinite number of possible perspectives, horizons, or folk minds. Heidegger, the modern thinker who most impressed Strauss, set to work to dismantle the Western tradition of rationalism in order to recover the rich sources out of which rationalism emerged but which had been covered over by it.

Now Strauss agreed that modern rationalism had indeed reached an impasse. What he was not sure of was whether the fate of reason itself was bound to that of modern philosophy. It was the elaboration of this doubt that he set as his task. The single advantage of the total crisis of philosophy was that it permitted a total doubt of received philosophic opinion that would have been considered impossible before. The belief, for example, that Kant had forever refuted the claims of ancient metaphysics became groundless. Everything was open. But such belief had fostered a forgetfulness of what ancient metaphysics was. We saw through Kant's eyes, whether we knew it or not, for even the philology which we use as a tool for the interpretation of ancient thought is based on modern philosophy. Thus, when Leo Strauss wrote a book entitled *Natural Right and History*, he was not primarily investigating the problem of justice, he was looking at the two great alternative standpoints beyond the cave—nature and history. Nature, and with it natural right, had been rejected as a standard in favor of history. Strauss dared to make that rejection, which was accepted as certain, a problem; and he did this by studying the perspective in which these standards come to light, political common sense. In short, Strauss returned to the cave. Its shadows had faded; but when one loses one's way, one must go back to the beginning, if one can.

III

But I have spoken too academically, and Leo Strauss's thought was never academic. It had its source in the real problems of a serious life. His intellectual odyssey began with his Zionism. Assimilation and Zionism were the two solutions to what was called "the Jewish problem." Zionism understood assimilation to be both impossible and demeaning. The establishment of a Jewish state was the only worthy and proud alternative. This formulation of the choice was predicated on the assumption that Orthodox Judaism—the belief in the letter of Mosaic revelation and the acceptance of the fate of Jews in the Diaspora as part of Divine Providence to be changed only by the coming of the Messiah—is no longer tenable for thoughtful men. In fact, the situation of the Jews could only be looked on as a problem, requiring and susceptible of a solution, in the light of that assumption. "The Jewish Problem" was a child of the Enlightenment, with its contempt for revelation and its assurance that political problems, once posed as such, can be solved. Strauss, while accepting the Zionist view of assimilation, wondered whether a strictly political or secular response to the Jewish situation in Europe was sufficient and whether a Jewish state that rejected the faith in the biblical revelation would have any meaning. Could the Jews become a nation like any other? And if they could, would that not be just a higher form of assimilation, of accepting the undesirability of being Jewish? Strauss saw, moreover, that pious Jews who tried to salvage Judaism and respond to the philosophical denial of the claims of the Mosaic code tacitly accepted many of the premises of their adversaries and were no longer really orthodox. Unable to accept the facile and convenient solutions available, he turned to the examination of the great thinker who suggested both the alternatives, assimilation and a Jewish state, and who initiated the higher criticism of the Bible which appeared to make life lived in adherence to the written word foolish and which prevails to this day; he turned to the renegade Jew, to Spinoza. With this, his first serious scholarly undertaking, begun in his mid-twenties, Strauss embarked on the journey from which he never returned.

As it then appeared to Strauss,[1] Spinoza directed his criticism of the Jewish tradition against two kinds of men—the Orthodox who believe in the divinely revealed character of every word of the Torah and for whom there was no need for, and a positive hostility toward, philosophy; and the philosophers, Maimonides in particular, who tried to show that reason and revelation are compatible, that Aristotelian philosophy arrived at by unaided reason is in perfect harmony with and is perfected by the Mosaic revelation. Briefly, Strauss concluded that Spinoza's method of textual criticism was persuasive only insofar as one believed that the textual difficulties cannot be explained as miracles or as the result of supernatural and suprarational causes and that Spinoza gave no adequate proof of that belief. Hence, he found, in agreement with Pascal, that the strictest orthodoxy which refused any concession to philosophy could still be maintained. And he also concluded that he must study Maimonides, for he had to see whether it was a failure of reason that made this philosopher remain loyal to the Jewish people and its sacred book. For, unlike Pascal, he was not prepared to reject philosophy.

So Strauss turned to Maimonides. His first impression was bewilderment. It was not only that he could make no sense of it; he felt utterly alien to the manner of thought and speech. But it was always his instinct to look for something important in that which seemed trivial or absurd at first impression, for it is precisely by such an impression that our limitations are protected from challenge. These writings were distant from what he understood philosophy to be, but he could not accept the ready explanations based on abstractions about the medieval mind. He kept returning to Maimonides and also to the Islamic thinkers who preceded and inspired Maimonides. And gradually Strauss became aware that these medieval thinkers practiced an art of writing forgotten by us, an art of writing with which they hid their intentions from all but a select few. He had discovered esoteric writing. By the most careful readings, the texts become intelligible and coherent to rational men. This discovery, for which Strauss is famous and for which he is derided by those who established their reputations on conventional interpretations, may appear to be at best only an interesting historical fact, akin to learning how to read hier-

---

[1]If one wishes to see the development of Strauss's thought through his studies, it would be well to compare the "Preface to the English Edition" of Spinoza's Critique of Religion (New York: Schocken, 1965) with the book itself.

oglyphics. But it is fraught with philosophic significance, for the different mode of expression reflects a different understanding of reason and its relation to civil society. When one becomes aware of this, one is enabled to learn strange and wonderful things and to recognize the questionable character of our own view, to which we see no alternative. Out of this discovery emerged the great themes that dominated the rest of Strauss's life: Ancients and Moderns, and Athens and Jerusalem. Real radicalism is never the result of passionate commitment, but of quiet and serious reflection.

Strauss found that the harmony of reason and revelation was Maimonides' and Farabi's public teaching, while the private teaching was that there is a radical and irreducible tension between them; he found that the teachings of reason are wholly different from and incompatible with those of revelation and that neither side could completely refute the claims of the other but that a choice had to be made. This is, according to these teachers, the most important issue facing man. It turned out that the opposition between reason and revelation was no less extreme in Maimonides than in Spinoza and that Maimonides was no less rational than Spinoza. Strauss also later learned that Spinoza too recognized and used the classic art of writing. Wherein, then, did the difference lie? Put enigmatically, Spinoza no longer believed in the permanent necessity of that art of writing. His use of it was in the service of overcoming it. He thought it possible to rationalize religion and, along with it, civil society. Philosophy, instead of the secret preserve of a few who accept the impossibility of the many being philosophers, or truly tolerating it, could be the instrument of transforming society and bringing enlightenment. Maimonides' loyalty to the Jewish people may have been due less to his faith in the Bible than his doubt as to the possibility or desirability of depriving them of that faith. Spinoza, on the other hand, was a member of a conspiracy the project of which was the alteration of what were previously considered to be the necessary conditions of human life. This project required a totally different view of the nature of things, and it is the essence of modernity. It began in agreeing with the ancients that the primary issue is the religious question. With its success, its origins in this question disappeared from sight. Hence, to understand ourselves, we must return to this origin and confront it with the view of things it replaced. Nietzsche, Strauss found, was wrong in his belief that there is a single line of Western rationalism originating in the ancients and culminating in contemporary science.

There was a great break somewhere in the sixteenth century. Nietzsche's critique of rationalism might well hold good for modern rationalism, but the character of ancient rationalism is unknown to us. A choice had been made by modern man, but whether that choice had led to broader horizons seen from a higher plateau is not clear.

Moreover, in his study of Maimonides and the Islamic thinkers, Strauss found that they understood themselves not as innovators, as did the moderns, but as conveyors of a tradition that went back to Plato and that they had only adapted the Platonic teaching to the Judaic and Islamic revelations. Plato, he heard, was the teacher of prophecy. What in the world that meant he could not divine. So he turned to Plato, and it was by this route that he came to the ancients. His access to their thought was by way of medieval philosophy. He had, of course, had the classical education common in Germany and was possessed of the conventional wisdom about the ancients. But that education precisely had made the classics uninteresting to him, little more than learning or general culture. No more than any of his contemporaries would he have gone to the ancient philosophers to solve the real problems of his life. Everybody was sure that the most important issues had been settled against the ancients. Now, as his thought had been drawn backward in time by the force of his vital concerns, he discovered an inlet to ancient thought through which those concerns were addressed more fully than he had imagined they could be. The unexpected perspective on the Greek philosophers which had emerged from his original needs proved to be the authentic one, for the medieval thinkers, closer in time to the Greeks and still preoccupied with the same problems as were they, had a surer knowledge of them than did the scholars who had, unawares, adopted one version or another of the modern resolution of the religious question and were most generally easygoing atheists (as opposed to atheists who faced up to the real consequences of atheism).

Strauss discovered that Plato, Xenophon, Aristophanes, and Thucydides, as well as many others, wrote like the medieval thinkers who had pointed in this direction. The execution of Socrates for impiety is the threshold to the Platonic world, and the investigation of philosophy's stance toward the gods is the beginning and end of those dialogues which are the supreme achievement of the ancient art of writing. Strauss found here the beginning point from which we would "be open to the full impact of the all important question which is coeval with philosophy although the philosophers do not frequently pronounce it—the question *quid sit deus.*"[2] The profound opposition between Jerusalem and Athens and the modern attempt to alter their

---

[2] *The City and Man* (Chicago: Rand McNally, 1964).

relation—and he now knew that this was the hidden origin of modern philosophy—became the sole theme of his continuous meditation. He was thus able to get a synopsis of the permanent human alternatives; their permanence, he argued, constituted the decisive refutation of historicism.

On the basis of these reflections, we can distinguish roughly three phases in Leo Strauss's development. It was, let me repeat, a continuous, deepening process. First, there was what might be called the pre-Straussean Strauss, represented by *Spinoza's Critique of Religion, Philosophy and Law,* and *The Political Philosophy of Thomas Hobbes.* These works treat of his immediate political-theological concerns as they first presented themselves to him. They are enormously learned and well-argued books which have a form like that of the best modern books in intellectual history. Their contents, on further consideration, strain that form and lead to his later breaking out of it. But they follow the canons of modern scholarship and their historical premises. These books put Strauss's own questions to the authors; he has not yet learned to see their questions as they themselves saw them. He finds these thinkers more caused by than causing their times. He applies a standard of reality to them rather than learning reality from them. He brings influences to them which they did not recognize, and he does not see radical breaks in the tradition which he later came to see because he accepts contemporary periodizations of thought. He knows of Epicurean religious criticism, but not of Platonic. He is seeking a standpoint outside the modern, but he has not found it. In short, he does not yet know antiquity. It is no accident that the Hobbes book, the book he liked the least, remains the one most reputed and uncontroversial in the scholarly community.

The second phase is dominated by his discovery of esoteric writing, which is, as I have said, identical with his discovery of antiquity and hence of a real alternative. He looks around the world with a fresh eye. His writing is still akin to that of other scholars, but the conclusions begin to appear outrageous; the interpretations are far from common opinion and seem based on a perverse attention to detail. Three books come from this period: *Persecution and the Art of Writing, On Tyranny,* and *Natural Right and History.* The first book elaborates the general thesis about hidden communication and gives detailed interpretations of medieval texts. The second is his first presentation of a Greek book. He chose Xenophon because Xenophon seems to us a fool but appeared wise to older thinkers. In making his wisdom palpable again, a measure of the difference between ancient and modern thought is established. Plato is always in high philosophic repute, for we can find in him themes akin to those still talked about today. But we are forced to neglect much more in him than we pay attention to. He is closer to Xenophon than he is to us, and until we understand Xenophon, we do not understand Plato. Xenophon is more alien to us, but more readily comprehensible, because he is really simpler and because we are not led astray by a misleading familiarity.

Natural Right and History provides a synthesis of Strauss's concerns and an unhistorical history of philosophy. He was beginning to see the outlines of ancient philosophy while constantly thinking of the modern alternatives and confronting them with the ancients. He could now present the classical meaning of nature and make plausible its use as a standard. Hence, he could see the intentions of the first modern philosophers who understood that view of nature and tried to provide a substitute for it. The later thinkers tried to resolve difficulties inherent in the new view or to improve on it. Those difficulties, made manifest, led not to the return to the older view but to the abandonment of nature in favor of history, which in its first stage seemed to preserve reason and provide another standard, but which culminated in the rejection of reason and the disappearance of any standard. He was always thinking of what he later called "the three waves of modernity": modern natural right, prepared by Machiavelli and developed by Bacon, Hobbes, Spinoza, Descartes, and Locke; the crisis of modern natural right and the emergence of history, begun by Rousseau and elaborated by Kant and Hegel; and radical historicism, begun by Nietzsche and culminating in Heidegger. Strauss was comprehensive yet precise, grasping each of the stages at its roots and looking to the most concrete expressions of its intention. He tried to show that all the questions are still open, but that the progressive developments, and the hopes engendered by them, had obscured the alternatives in such a way as finally to make it appear that the perspective of history or cultural relativism is simply and without question superior. Each of the great waves began with a Greek inspiration, but these returns were only partial and ended in a radicalization of modernity. Strauss took on all comers on their own terms, addressed himself to the whole tradition.

The third phase is characterized by a complete abandonment of the form as well as the content of modern scholarship. Strauss no longer felt bound to make any compromises or to see the texts through the screen of scholarly method and categories. He had liberated himself and could understand writers as they understood themselves. He talked with them as one would talk with a wise and subtle contemporary about the nature of things. The proof that he could do so is these late writings read in conjunction with those writings about which he wrote. Although their contents are extremely difficult for us to grasp, they are amazingly simple in form and expression, so much so that some might think, and some have actually thought, that he was an innocent who picked up the great books and read them as would an ordinary reader who was unaware that they are the preserve of an infinite number of scholars in a variety of disconnected disciplines who possess information without which one understands nothing of them. The distance between the naïve reader's vision and that of the scholar is as great as the distance between the commonsense perception of the world and that of modern mathematical physics; so great is the distance that there remains almost no link between them. Strauss set about restoring the naïve vision, which includes the belief that the truth is the important consideration in the study of a thinker, that the truth is always, that one can study an old writer as one would a contemporary and that the only concern is what is written, as opposed to its historical, economic, or psychological background. Strauss rather enjoyed the reputation for innocence, for it meant that he had in some measure succeeded in recovering the surface of things. He knew that innocence once lost is almost impossible to recover. The cries of indignation, insisting that what he was doing was impossible, gave him some hope. But what an effort of the mind it took to get back to the simple business of thinking about Plato and the others! He had to become aware that there was a problem; he had to spend years working through the conventional scholarly views; he had to confront the challenges posed by the great founders of the historical school and test the necessity of its emergence; he had to find a way of seeing the books under the debris and through eyes which had been rendered weak; he had somehow to have at the beginning an inkling of the ancient understanding of philosophy which he could only grasp at the end. The way to read books—so small a concern—is the point from which the problems of modern philosophy come into focus. On this question depends the freedom of the mind, both in the practical sense that he who does not know how to read can never investigate the human potential and, in the theoretical sense, that the answer to the question determines the nature and the limits of the human mind. Every sentence of these unprepossessing books is suffused with a tension deriving from the difficulty of understanding men at the level of Plato and Machiavelli, the difficulty of beginning from a cave so different from the one in which they began and trying to find the common ground of rational discourse, and the difficulty posed by the powerful argument that there is no such common ground among ages and cultures. To repeat, Strauss's refutation of historicism consisted primarily in understanding the old philosophers as they understood themselves, rather than understanding them better than they understood themselves, as did rational historicism, or in light of a privileged horizon, as did radical historicism. To be able to reproduce that older thought in full awareness of the objections to it is to philosophize.

Strauss's writings of the first period were treated respectfully, as scholarly productions of a man with somewhat eccentric interests. Those of the second were considered perverse and caused anger. Those of the third period are ignored. They seem too far away from the way we look at things and the way we speak. But these books are the authentic, the great Strauss to which all the rest is only prolegomena. The early works reveal his search and his conversion and erect the scaffold for the structure he was to build. It is only in the later works that he made the concrete analyses of phenomena, elaborated the rich detail of political life, and discovered the possible articulations of the soul. He was able to do without most abstractions and to make those readers who were willing to expend the effort look at the world around them and see things afresh. He presented things, not generalizations about things. He never repeated himself and always began anew although he was always looking at the same things. To see this, one need only read the chapter on the *Republic* in *The City and Man* and observe what he learned about *thymos* and *eros* as well as about *techne* in what must have been his fiftieth careful reading of the *Republic*. He was now truly at grips with his subject matter.

Strauss began this group of writings with *Thoughts on Machiavelli*. He found Machiavelli to be the fountainhead of modern thought and the initiator of the first truly radical break with the Platonic-Aristotelian political philosophy. From here, through the eyes of a man who really understood the ancients, he could most clearly see how they appeared to the founder of the modern project, in both its political and scientific aspects, and precisely to what Machiavelli objected in them; he could thus see what Machiavelli's innovation was. Then came *The City and Man*, which moved from Aristotle to Plato to Thucydides, from the fully developed classical teaching to its problematic formulation to the prephilosophic world out of which it emerged and which it replaced. This enabled him to see what philosophy originally meant and what the city was before it was reinterpreted for the sake of philosophy. The first of these two books was his final statement on the quarrel between the ancients and the moderns. The second was his attempt to reconstruct not precisely the quarrel between revelation and reason, but the quarrel between the divine city and the natural one, the most notable incident of which was the execution of Socrates. It is to be remarked that in *The City and Man* he, a man of over sixty who had studied Plato intensely for thirty years, permitted himself for the first time to publish an interpretation of a Platonic dialogue.

The next three books were devoted to Socrates by way of studies of Aristophanes and Xenophon, the poet who understood and accused Socrates versus the student who defended him. I need not say how fresh this approach was and what a new Socrates Strauss found for us in contemplating the old Socrates. Strauss looked, as no one else would today, for the obvious and simple way for a man of delicate perception to grasp Socrates again and see if he could ever charm us as he charmed Alcibiades and Plato. Compared with this representation, all modern studies of Socrates, including Nietzsche's, are *fables convenues*.

Finally, his last book, written in his seventies, was his first book on Plato, an interpretation of Plato's last book, the *Laws*, the dialogue which Avicenna said was the standard book on prophecy and which Strauss said was the book on the philosopher in the real city, implying that the two are really one.

Strauss told me a few weeks before he died that there were many things he still would want to do if his health were not failing. And, surely, with him went a store of the most useful knowledge. But it seems to me, now that I reflect on it, that he accomplished what he set out to do.

IV

A final word on the way Leo Strauss wrote. For those who admire gain or want to influence the world's events, his career is a disappointment. Only a tiny number of men who did not fall under the spell of his personal charm were profoundly affected by his books. He was reproached by some of his friends and admirers for not speaking in the language and the accents of current discourse; for he knew so much and had so many unusual perspectives that he could have become one of the celebrated men of the age and furthered the causes that interested him. Instead, what he wrote was at once unprepossessing and forbidding. He neither spoke to the taste of the age nor tried to create a new taste. His retreat from the stage of literary glory cannot be attributed either to scholarly dryness, to a lack of understanding of poetry, or to an incapacity to write beautifully and powerfully. His passion and his literary gifts are undeniable. Goethe was one of his masters, and it was no accident that he understood Aristophanes better than did Aristophanes' official keepers. Strauss's books contain many sentences and paragraphs of astonishing beauty and force, and in an essay such as his response to Kojève one can see a rare public indulgence of his rhetorical skills. His lack of popularity was an act of will rather than a decree of fate.

The reasons for this decision, insofar as I can penetrate them, are three. First and foremost, Leo Strauss was a philosopher, and as with every other facet of the complex impression made by this unusual being, it is to this simple fact that his choice of literary form can be traced. He often repeated Hegel's saying that philosophy must avoid trying to be edifying. He was primarily concerned with finding out for himself and only secondarily with communicating what he found out, lest the demands of communication determine the results of the quest. His apparent selfishness in this regard was his mode of benefaction, for there is no greater or rarer gift than intransigent dedication to the truth. The beauty, he was persuaded, was there for a certain kind of man capable of a certain kind of labor. The words must reflect the inner beauty of the thought and not the external tastes of the literary market, especially in an unusually untheoretical age. In converting philosophy into nonphilosophy for the sake of an audience, no matter what other benefits might be achieved, one would lose the one thing most needed. He once said of a particularly famous intellectual that he never wrote a sentence without looking over his shoulder. Of Strauss, it can be said that he never wrote one while doing so. But he is not particularly to be commended for that, for it was never a temptation for him to do so.

Second, Strauss was acutely aware of the abuses to which the public expression of philosophy is subject. Philosophy is dangerous for it must always call everything into question while in politics not everything can be called into question. The peculiar horror of modern tyranny has been its alliance with perverted philosophy. Strauss no less and perhaps more than any man was susceptible to the enchantment of the rhetoric of Rousseau and Nietzsche, but he also saw to what extent the passions they aroused and the deceptive sense of understanding they engendered could damage the cause of decency as well as that of philosophy. Aristotle or Maimonides could never provide the inspiration or the justification for a tyrant. They were no less radical, but their voices were softer and attracted less dangerous passions while abandoning excessive hopes. Rousseau was not the cause of the Terror nor Nietzsche of the Nazis, but there was something in what they said and the way they said it which made it possible for them to be misinterpreted in certain politically relevant ways. Strauss, with his respect for speech and its power, believed that men are responsible for what they say. And it was not entirely an accident of personality that Heidegger, who most of all contemporaries attracted a cult by brave talk, not only prepared the atmosphere for Hitler but eagerly enlisted his rhetoric in Hitler's cause.

This leads to the third reason, which has to do with Strauss's observations of the differences between ancient and modern philosophy. Modern philosophy hoped to ensure the union of philosophy and the city or to rationalize politics. The modern philosopher was also literally a ruler and a reformer; he therefore became much more involved in and dependent on politics. He was first the bringer of enlightenment, then the leader of revolution; finally, the whole destiny of man and even nature was his responsibility. Modern writings were public teachings, even manifestos and party programs. Ancient writings had a much more modest intention, grounded on the opinion that politics must always be less than rational, that reason must protect itself, and that there is only a tiny number of men who can potentially philosophize and hence understand the teachings of philosophy. There is an interest of philosophy, one not identical to that of any possible regime, and that is what a philosopher must defend. Ancient philosophy had a rhetoric, too, but one limited to three intentions: the preservation of what was known for those who could know it and against those who would adapt it to the needs of the time; the attracting of the few who could know it to a life of knowing and the discouraging of others; and the procuring of a good reputation for philosophy in order to ensure its toleration within the various regimes as they came and went. Strauss believed the ancient view was correct and learned to write as he read. Our special circumstances required a reminder of the severe discipline of philosophy and its distance from popular taste. Strauss had no great hopes. He left his works as resources for those who might experience the need to study the tradition, begging no one and condescending to no one. He thought it possible that philosophy might disappear utterly from the world, although he thought nature supported it. He did his best by finding out what philosophy is and by trying to tell others. At most he hoped there might someday be a third humanism, or renaissance, after those of Italy and Germany, but this time inspired neither by the visual beauty of the Greeks' statues, paintings, and buildings nor by the grandeur of their poetry, but by the truth of their philosophy. He provided the bridge from modernity to antiquity which would help this new beginning. But he never believed he could reform humankind.

Strauss's taste always led him to look at the simple, the ordinary, and the superficial. He said that only by the closest attention to the surface could one get to the core; he also said the surface is the core. It was partly a gentleman's restraint that caused him to prefer Jane Austen to Dostoyevsky, but it was more that her reserve, sensibleness, and apparent attention only to the nice things permitted the deeper and more dangerous things to emerge in their proper proportions. He detested the pose of profundity and that combination of sentimentality and brutality which constituted contemporary taste, not from any moralism but because they are philistine and boring. Most of all, he detested moral indignation, because it is a form of self-indulgence, and it distorts the mind. All of this led him to delight in Xenophon, who appeared to be the bluff retired army colonel with endless stories of the events he participated in and of the men he knew but to the level of whom he never attained, yet who really dominated with his graceful irony those who through the ages have thought they were subtle. This was the writer who presented us with the liberal Cyrus and let us figure out for ourselves what Machiavelli tells us: that there are two forms of liberality, one practiced with one's own property and one practiced with other people's property, and that Cyrus specialized exclusively in the latter form. The discovery of such an intriguing, enigmatic writer was a way of entering into an alien world of thought that Strauss preferred to the well-traveled roads which are probably of our construction. He preferred the commonplace and neglected, because that is where he could get a firm grasp on things rather than words. He learned Xenophon before he learned Plato, and when he wanted to understand Plato he studied the *Minos* or the *Apology* rather than the *Parmenides* or the *Philebus*, not because he was not interested in the *ideas* but precisely because he was.

Thus the books of his ripeness are almost as alien to us as are the books with which he dealt. I recently reread *Thoughts on Machiavelli* and realized that it is not at all a book as we ordinarily understand a book. If one sits down and reads it as one reads a treatise, its contents are guarded by seven seals; it provides us with a few arid generalizations that look like oases in a sandy desert. But the book is really a way of life, a sort of philosophy kit. First one must know Machiavelli's text very well and have it constantly in hand. And as soon as one gets acquainted with Machiavelli, one sees that he cannot be understood without knowing Livy's text very well. One must first read it on its own and try to form a Livian interpretation of Livy, and then let Machiavelli act as one's guide in order to arrive at a Machiavellian interpretation of Livy. It is in our coming to the awareness of the difference between these two interpretations that one gets one's first inkling of what Machiavelli is about. On the way one is forced to become involved in concrete details that take time and reflection. For example, Machiavelli's shockingly witty remark about Hannibal's "inhuman cruelty and other virtues" only takes on its full significance from the fact that it is based on a passage in Livy where he discusses Hannibal's strange mixture of virtues and vices; according to Livy Hannibal's major vice was his "inhuman cruelty." This is only a sample of an infinity of such charming and illuminating details which, when put in order, constitute a concrete, as opposed to an abstract, consciousness of the political phenomena. Then one realizes that Strauss's book bears the same relation to Machiavelli's book as does Machiavelli's book to Livy's book. The complexity of Strauss's undertaking is mind-boggling. It is not a complexity born of the desire to obfuscate; it is a mirror of reality. One must come to know Machiavelli's enormous cast of characters—Brutus, Fabius, David, Cesare Borgia, Ferdinand of Aragon, and so on—and be interested in their action and see the problems they represent. One must care about them as one cares about the persons in a novel. Then one can begin to generalize seriously. And Machiavelli and Livy will not do, for Machiavelli points us to Xenophon, Tacitus, Cicero, the Bible, and many other writers. One must constantly stop, consult another text, try to penetrate another character, and walk around the room and think. One must use a pencil and paper, make lists, and count. It is an unending task, one that continually evokes that wonder at what previously seemed commonplace which Aristotle says is the origin of philosophy. One learns what it means to live with books; one is forced to make them a part of one's experience and life. When one returns to Strauss's book, after having left it under his guidance, it suddenly becomes as gripping as the dénouement of a drama. As one is drawn through the matter by the passion to make sense of what has involved one for so long, suddenly there appears a magic formula which pierces the clouds like the sun to illuminate a gorgeous landscape. The distance between the appearance of this book and its reality is amazing. It is a possession for life.

What the fate of these books will be, I do not know. Those who have lived with them over a period of many years have been changed as were Glaucon and Adeimantus by the night they spent with Socrates. They learned the splendors of a kind of soul and a way of life which nothing in their experience would have revealed to them. They returned to political life, still ordinary men—for nature cannot be changed. But, since politics has as its goal the encouragement of the best possible life, they returned with a radically altered perspective, with new expectations and prayers. For the rest, I cannot help but believe that Leo Strauss's writings, even if their broader implications are not grasped, will exercise a powerful influence on the future. They are such a rich lode of interpretations of books still of concern that they will, due to the poverty of the competition, attract the young. Willy-nilly, political scientists, intellectual historians, medievalists, classicists, literary critics, and, last of all, professors of philosophy will find that they have to use his terms and his interpretations, that they will continually, with more or less goodwill, have to respond to questions outside their conventions, and that they will have to face the apostasy of their best students. Echoing the *Apology* with what will seem a threat to some, a blessing to others, I believe our generation may well be judged by the next generation according to how we judged Leo Strauss.

Raymond Aron:
The Last of the Liberals

A FEW WEEKS AGO, when I was in Paris, I went to have lunch at my friend Jean-Claude Casanova's home. As I entered the great doors of the building on the Boulevard St. Michel, I had one of those experiences which only an American amateur of things French would call Proustian. I felt a sudden shock, a powerful awareness of an absence linked to the entire substance of my adult life. I recognized that this was where Raymond Aron had lived and that I would find him there no longer.

I could not pretend to be his student or his friend, but he was the teacher and friend of all my friends, admired by everyone I admired on both sides of the Atlantic. He was the protective tent under which we lived, the urbane and always benevolent defender of reason, freedom, and decency when all these were passing through unprecedented crises. He incarnated the *bon sens* which is supposed to be the leading characteristic of liberal democracy and assumed the responsibility for presenting and representing that *political* possibility. He interpreted liberal democracy's purposes, outlined the threats to it, and continually discussed the strategies required to protect us from them. He had the broadest views and used them to guide his study of the remote details required for policy. His disappearance is equivalent to the loss of the framework in which we lived, believing it was permanent.

Aron (1905–1983) was a member in good standing of that last generation of French writers who by right of inheritance—a right extending back more than three hundred years—commanded the attention of the whole world. But he was at its edge, distancing himself from it and kept at a distance by it. He was more of an observer than a psychagogue; and he was passionately dedicated to liberal democracy, when all the charm seemed to belong to its enemies on the Right and the Left. He, too, drank at the same trough of German thought as did his contemporaries, but he reasoned about it, whereas they were more concerned with its emotive power. Thus he was more of a scholar than they, and more of a journalist, separating the two aspects of his activity rather than fusing them.

Aron began as a professor and became a political commentator during World War II when he was one of the editors of *La France Libre* in London. Afterwards his academic career led him to professorships at the Ecole Nationale des Sciences Politiques, the Sorbonne, the Ecole Pratique des Hautes Etudes, and the Collège de France. At the same time he became the regular political columnist of *le Figaro*, where he remained for more than thirty years. Of those famous Paris intellectuals, he was the only one who was really a teacher, committed to his students and accessible to them. He published countless books, twenty-six of them translated into English. Among the better known are *Peace and War; A Theory of International Relations; The Opium of the Intellectuals; Clausewitz, Philosopher of War;* and *The Imperial Republic: The United States and the World, 1945-1973.*

Because Aron was out of step with the fashions, he was more influential in foreign academic circles, as sociologist, political scientist, and philosopher, than he was in France, and his views on the political scene were more attended to by practitioners in the United States, England, and Germany than they were at home. There, his was a lonely voice until, near the end of his life, French intellectuals began to recover from their long affair with the Left and discovered that one of their great thinkers still remained and that he could give them guidance and inspiration. An extraordinary series of television interviews in 1981 (published in the United States under the title *The Committed Observer*) suddenly made him fashionable in the grand Parisian style, a position he did not seek, but one which vindicated his solitary dedication to the truth as he saw it. His teaching contributed to the formation of a generation of students dedicated to the high ideals of reason and freedom which were the essence of the old liberalism he represented.

For me, personally, he was the man who for fifty years—that is, my entire life—had been right about the political alternatives actually available to us, who had seen the real possibilities and faced them intransigently against all the prevailing temptations. This means, simply, that he was right about Hitler and right about Stalin and right that our Western regimes, with all their flaws, are the best and only hope of mankind. On the big questions he was always right and about

the daily or emergent ones as often right as anyone is likely to be.[1]
And he attempted to meet the intellectual challenges posed by the
currents of thought hostile to liberal democracy. I could go to him
for support and clarification in a world where such sureness of touch
is almost nonexistent. In all of this he resisted the fashions and did
so without doctrinairism or indignation. He was a Frenchman who
understood America, really understood America. And, although he
was temperamentally attuned to the universal, Enlightenment strand
of French thought, he knew that the intellectual world which liberal
democracy was committed to defending contained much more than
Cartesian rationalism. He was therefore a perfect link between an
American and that old culture which is essential for Americans if
their horizon is not to be utterly impoverished and which is ever harder
for them to experience.[2]

When I was a young professor at Cornell University, Aron came
to deliver an important lecture. My study, political philosophy, was
much despised as old-fashioned and unscientific by the authorities and
notables of that institution. But Aron, the famous European social
scientist, the expositor of Weber, was the object of fervid respect. A
large part of his lecture was devoted to an exhortation to American
social scientists to relax their "value-free" stance, to study ends philosophically, warning them that if they did not do so they risked losing
the one thing most needful. Aron said these things on that occasion
for my sake and because they are true. How could I help but love
him? He was good, and he was my benefactor.

All of this came back to me as I passed through the portal of that
building. Much of that great mass of good luck I call my education
could find its focus in Aron, and it then expressed itself in a mixture
of desolation and delight. It is my belief that one honors one's betters
by keeping silent about them, but memory demands a few words about
this man.

[1]The first of his dicta with which I became acquainted, one he uttered in 1949, is a
fair sample of the kind of guidance he gave us all: "War improbable; peace impossible."
[2]In America, Raymond Aron was frequently called the French Walter Lippmann.
Although the comparison is in fact ludicrous, it was meant to convey reverence for
a unique kind of man necessary to democracy but almost impossible in it; one who
both educates public opinion and is truly wise and learned. This was the ideal Aron
approached. The difference between the two men is most instructive. Lippmann was
almost always wrong on the greatest issues (i.e., Hitler and Stalin). His instinct was
unsure. He was a snob. His judgments of men were too often off the mark. (He
despised Truman.) He was ashamed of being Jewish. And his learning was superficial
and not motivated by a real love of knowledge; it was for the sake of his journalism.
He always thought power more important than knowledge. Aron had the contrary
qualities. While Lippmann merely acted out an edifying role, Aron was the real thing.
He was a trustworthy companion in judging the events of the modern world.

• •

In reflecting on Aron two salient facts insistently present them-selves. He was political, and he was really a liberal.

The extent to which Aron represented the political was impressed on me a long time ago when I was having one of my periodic visits with Kojève at the Economics Ministry. The great Hegelian, the spokesman for the end of history who had unraveled history's hiero-glyphs, was unusually agitated that day because the Fourth Republic was traversing one of its many crises. Finally he announced, "I must call Aron." It was the only time I ever heard him express the need for enlightenment from another. It occurred to me that he was ad-mitting that history is ongoing, that his *science* had to give way to *prudence*, a faculty for which there was hardly a category left in modern thought. Maybe Lenin's character was as important for the Russian Revolution as were the various determinisms of matter or spirit which fascinate the contemporary mind and drown human freedom or in-determinacy in great permanent necessities. Aron, out of his naïve and generous respect for philosophy, regarded Kojève as his superior (and Kojève was indeed an intelligence of a very high order). But Aron possessed a gift and a taste which were lacking to almost everyone else of his generation. The real activities of rulers and their decisions provided the ineluctable focus for his vision. What is in the power of men to do and what they look to in doing it were what he could not avoid being concerned with. For him the issue of our time was the opposition between Western freedom and Soviet tyranny. Anyone who tried to avoid this harsh opposition, repairing to the trans- or sub-political, was avoiding reality, which is naturally political. The political is the comprehensive order in which human aspirations for the good and the noble are actualized. It is the practical decisions of acting men which are most interesting and most revealing of human nature.

It has long been taught that politics is a superficial phenomenon and that its actors are secondary beings, with the possible exception of the extreme leaders of revolutions. Artists and intellectuals, at a remove from the position and perspective of statesmen, have been regarded as proper interpreters of politics. This is particularly true of France, and Aron's friends—for example, Sartre and Malraux—were exemplary of this viewpoint. He always sought to understand them and even to be like them. But he could not. It is not so much that ideological politics are from his point of view ideological; it is that they are not politics. They are, to employ Mann's self-description, unpolitical politics. Politics mean the governance of man, and that can only be done from positions of legitimate power. The thinker must be really an adviser of princes or an enlightener of the voting public—he must adopt their perspective—if he is to be of any use or understand the nature of the political beast. The distinction between realist and idealist is not applicable here. There is excitement and moral dignity aplenty in real political life. Aron was not a realist and never adopted abstract poses such as that of power politics. Morality is inherent in politics, but one must always begin from the real situation and goals of the political actors—how one gets from here to there. Therefore, much of his writing was devoted to describing political reasoning and what stands in the way of it in our days. He was not the man to use language like alienation, domination, self-assertion, or anything of the kind. He was constitutionally incapable of talking like that in a persuasive manner, and what he did talk about was frequently boring to people who are not truly political, who do not recognize the special character of political life, who are not enthused by "who's in and who's out," by the day-to-day observation of political detail.

I believe that it often troubled Aron that his language did not have the same resonance as did that of men like Sartre. But he was an object lesson in real responsibility to them, and he pointed toward a world deeper and more exciting than the one they inhabited. It was a rare triumph of character for Aron alone to stick by his political insight when success and esteem lay elsewhere and while others whom he knew captured the imagination of a generation. He did what he had to do, not always sure that it was the most profound thing to do, often wondering whether modern writers or philosophers were not more gifted than he. But in the long run, the one that counts, he was more useful than any of them in helping us to understand our situation.

And I do not mean that he was useful only in the sense of day-to-day guidance in the practice of domestic and international politics. It is in the realm of theory that the political has been most effectively banished. Politics as a distinctive dimension of human life, not to speak of its being the most important one, has become extremely doubtful. It has been reduced or swallowed up by other disciplines which explain it away. Economics, anthropology, sociology, and psychology, among others, claim primacy over political science. Modern abstract notions like the market, culture, society, or the unconscious take the place of the political regime as the prime cause of what counts for human beings. Older views either denied the real existence of such things as cultures or claimed that the political is their central cause rather than their effect. Aron, honest man that he was, took every academic claim seriously, but he obviously yawned when anthropologists presented their interpretations of things because those interpretations are so far removed from the common sense of life and because they ask us to concentrate on things like art styles, when freedom and peace are what we really should care about. Economists attracted his attention, but only to the extent that their theories are related to the real lives of nations and help to explain freedom or its opposite. He could never believe that the economic model of man exhausted man or that economic interest is the only kind of interest. He was in the tradition of political economy and understood Adam Smith better than did the economists who cut their science loose from its political moorings. He loved history but real history, that is political history, and he yawned, against his will, at economic, social, and intellectual history, just as he yawned at cultural anthropology. He called himself a sociologist, but it was political sociology if it was anything.

As I have said, Aron's instinct was strong, and he followed it against all that has been academically powerful, and sometimes he was not fully conscious of the unerring aim of that instinct. He visited Germany as a young man. He immediately appreciated the enormity of what was unfolding there, and at the same time he was one of the first Frenchmen to fall under the influence or recognize the stature of Edmund Husserl and Max Weber. He was always alive to what was going on. But he used his experiences to his own ends. What he saw in German politics made him aware of how high the stakes in modern politics were to be and provided the impulse for his lifelong vocation of saving reason and freedom from the wreckage provoked by the new tyrannies. And these intellectual influences freed him from French academism and certain deterministic abstractions. Phenomenology permits one to look at the world as it is without excessive reductionisms, and this gave support to Aron's natural penchant. Weber provided him with a way of looking at acting men as possibly self-determining and irreducible to the usually adduced determinants, and with arguments for the dignity and possibility of science against the background of a growing philosophically founded irrationalism. But I never saw any signs that he shared Weber's pathos, his sympathy for the irrationally committed, his anguish at the struggle of the gods. It was not that Aron was unaware of the abyss opening beneath our feet. But he really belonged to an older tradition of rationalism. He worked stolidly within the limits of the politically given and encouraged the use of statesmanlike prudence, which is neither bureaucratic rationality nor quasireligious commitment. He knew, sadly, that the good regimes could lose, but one must do one's duty, be a good citizen of the city of God, and save one's anguish for oneself.

I would call Raymond Aron a political scientist, although I believe that he never held a chair in that discipline. I mean by political science what Aristotle meant by it, the architectonic science to which the other social sciences are ancillary or ministerial. This view is founded on the premise that man is by nature a political animal, and that politics is a dimension of his being and not a derivative of subpolitical forces. According to this political science, the love of justice and glory are as primary as hunger or sexual desire, or, to refer to the latest trends, as awe before the sacred. Politics precedes ethics or psychology and can be looked at on its own grounds. The most distinctive thing about man is that he establishes regimes which claim to be just and sets down laws in accordance with them. The authoritative horizon established by these laws is derivative from nothing other than the intention or will of men. The oldest school of philosophy argued that this is *the* beginning, not only for political philosophy, but for philosophy *tout court*. This is the ground for the study and practice of politics which has collapsed. I do not argue that Aron reestablished that ground. But, somehow, he stood firmly on it, and his life was an embodiment of the political possibility. He gave encouragement to those who had instincts similar to his to come out of the closet and showed them how to cultivate and use such instincts. What unites and gives health to the extraordinarily diverse persons who clustered around his protective example is the sharing of that will-of-the-wisp, the political instinct.

Raymond Aron was a liberal, and as my title somberly suggests, I fear that he was the last great representative of the breed. I mean that he was persuaded of the truth of the theory of liberalism, that for him its practice was not only the best available alternative but the best simply, and that his personality fully accorded with his liberal beliefs. He lived—and probably would have died for—the strange spiritual asceticism, one of the most arduous of asceticisms, which consists in believing in the right of others to think as they please. It is one thing to die for one's god or one's country, another to die for the protection of the opinions of others which one does not share. The mutual respect of rights, a curious secondary kind of respect, is the essence of liberal conviction. And that respect, as the one absolute of civil society, is in reality very rare and becomes ever rarer. Aron really possessed it. He was never a conservative in any possible sense of the term, whether one looks to Burke, Hegel, de Maistre, or Milton

Friedman to define it. Whatever in him may have appeared conservative to radicals of one kind or another had to do with his defense of the essential rights, and the form of government founded on and protective of them, against previously unseen theoretical and practical threats from Left and Right.

Aron's liberalism was that of Locke, Montesquieu, John Stuart Mill, and, to some extent, Tocqueville. I make this qualification for the last named thinker, for I never saw in Aron a sense that anything truly important might have been lost with the passing of aristocracy. He, of course, knew all the arguments. After all he was an educated Frenchman. But he believed that the heights are accessible within well-constituted democratic regimes.

The creed of liberalism consists in the belief in the natural freedom and equality of all men and, following therefrom, that they have natural, inalienable rights to life, liberty, and the pursuit of property; that they possess reason to recognize those rights and to construct governments; that government is legitimated only by the consent of the governed. Bound up with this is a conviction that there can be a progress of science, that science dispels the illusions which breed fanaticism and allow for the rule of priests, and that science will "ease man's estate." In short, Enlightenment is possible and good. Aron really respected man as man. Race, nation, or religion never were decisive for human worth as far as he was concerned; the first was for him essentially irrelevant, and the other two were in principle matters of choice not fatality. He was more cosmopolitan than national, more attached to the universal principles of science than to any culture or religion. None of this was simpleminded in him. He knew the differences of nations and the importance of roots. He recognized that liberal democracy was a rare achievement, one that required severe moral prerequisites. But he never doubted that it was the achievement nor did he regard it as belonging to one particular race or tradition. In historical and cultural difference, of which he had a rich awareness, he always discerned the primacy of the unity of human nature and the common aspirations for peace, prosperity, and a just political order. All this contributed to his amazing combination of sobriety and humanity, his unfailing civility and his openness toward all opinions and the men who held them so long as they themselves were civil. The corrosive passions were almost totally absent from him although he lived in times when they were dominant all around him. He was not a hater although he was a partisan.

He knew that liberal democracy begins from selfish interests, but he also knew that those interests can be sublimated into a sense of common interest founded on our common suffering. He never gave in to the base interpretations of liberal society so popular among social scientists, not only because they were ignoble but also because they are not true. The liberal democracies are delicate mixtures of high and low, and as it is merely edifying to recognize only the high, it is a distortion to speak only of the low. He saw that men seek the common good but are often prevented from attaining it by their private interests. He was fully aware that there were moments of utter folly in democracies, but he never doubted their right to folly or contemplated favoring forms of government not based on consent.

In short, Raymond Aron was a perfect *bourgeois*. I use the term invented by liberal democracy's critics and enemies to describe the kind of man typical of it. He was reasonable, immune to the great romantic longings in the light of which the present is denigrated and sensible calculation about the future is made to appear small-minded. Such a man is a reflective rather than a passionate patriot, a good husband and father whose attachment to the smaller community attaches him more securely to the larger one, and, above all, he believes in the liberating power of education.

And this last is one of the most striking facts aboout Raymond Aron. He believed in an education that never ceases, an opportunity to look in the company of friends at life and the events around one in the light of philosophy, science, history, and literature. Democracy was for him the freedom of the mind to learn one's rights and one's duties for oneself, the overthrowing of old authority, and the discovery of the independent truth. It is amazing the extent to which he remained a Normalian all his life, with a schoolboy's enthusiasm. He was very grateful for the opportunity which the Ecole Normale Supérieure provided him. *"La carrière ouverte aux talents"* seemed just about right to him: a high-class education offered to anyone for free if he were able to profit from it, regardless of race, class, religion, or even nation. This education was, he was convinced, good for the community and good for its recipients. At the Ecole Normale he learned the best there has been, and his friends were the best there were. Throughout his life he remained fascinated by his school companions, Sartre and Nisan, and thought his confrontation with them was a privilege and a permanent inspiration. The Ecole Normale was a perfect union of the apparently conflicting demands of equality and the right to develop unequal natural gifts. Aron was quite aware that his intelligence and education were superior, but he was certain that this served the common good and that such superiority did not detract from the equal worth of all men based on their capacity for free moral choice. This set of delicately balanced convictions made possible his liberal consciousness.

Because the university was so personally dear to him, but far more because he knew that the university is the central institution in democratic society, he took a very strong stand against the wave of destruction which swept through the Western universities in the 1960s. The university is, or rather was, the substantial presence of the reason on which liberal democracy rests. If there is no reliance on, cultivation of, or respect for dispassionate reason, the rational rights which are all in all in modern democracy will wither away. The installation of the gutter in the halls of the university disgusted him. The loss of the tradition which was a source of vitality saddened him. The demagogic skewing of the only institution devoted to objectivity frightened him. If democracy cannot tolerate the presence of the highest standards of learning, then democracy itself becomes questionable. His reaction to the university crisis epitomized all that he was, and he was an ardent lover of the freedom of thought and the kind of society which encouraged it. The greatest sign of the decay of liberalism was the acquiescence of most people who called themselves liberal in the savaging of the university.

Aron was the representative of a spirit that dominated the political scene for a long time and that animated the regimes in which we live and which most of us wish to defend. They were founded and sustained at the peaks by men who believed in their principles. The politics of our time, the politics of which Aron was the committed observer, are totally dominated by the threats to liberal democracy from movements and regimes defined almost exclusively by their deadly hatred of liberal democracy. Fascism and Communism agree about their enemy, "bourgeois society." And they both agree that "rights" are "bourgeois rights." Both identify "capitalism" with "bourgeois society," and characterize the latter as the realm of selfishness, individualism, and vulgar materialism. Communism denies that reason can be free in bourgeois society; fascism insists that reason is what is wrong with bourgeois society and intends to replace it with passion. Both, therefore, take away liberal democracy's rational legitimacy. And both dismiss the homely morality claimed for mutual recognition of the rights of man, insisting that it is only enlightened self-interest.

Behind these movements is the most powerful thought of the last two centuries. Not since Kant has liberalism had the support of philosophy, whereas the enemies of liberalism can have the blessing of Marx and Nietzsche among others. All of this has rubbed off on most of us in one way or another. Hardly anyone today would be willing to defend the teachings of Locke and Montesquieu in their entirety, and hardly anyone remains emotionally unaffected by all the charms called upon by the critics of liberalism, whether they be tradition, compassion, roots, nature, religion, culture, or community. The good conscience of liberalism has been tainted, and most Westerners are only half-believers at best, if they are not utterly thoughtless or hypocrites. There now seems to be an ineradicable question mark after liberal justice, which is said to be just another form of exploitation. A debilitating relativism has grown out of liberalism's healthy skepticism.

But none of this was true of Aron. He had studied liberalism's critics better than most anyone. But finally they left him untouched. I do not assert that he had successfully refuted them, but his temperament made him immune to their appeal. He knew Sartre and Kojève and read Heidegger carefully. He spoke of them intelligently but could not be enthused by them as were so many others. He was an anachronism in the same sense Churchill was said to be an anachronism in England. They were healthy plants of an older world mysteriously flourishing in thinner soil and necessary for the protection of its offspring.

I have often suspected that liberals ultimately have to believe in progress, or something akin to it, even though intellectual modesty now forbids them to avow it. Their respect for man's freedom, and their willingness to risk so much in counting on its effectiveness, bespeaks a conviction that decency is not unsupported in this world. John Stuart Mill's certainty that the age of barbarism is past was only a particularly naïve expression of this faith. Something in Aron—and not only his good taste—forbade him the indulgence in the easy talk about nothingness so common in his time and in his milieu. For him the fundamental experience was not unsupportedness of the good. For this reason Hitler remained the obsessive puzzle of his life. How was it possible? He expressed his wonder about this to me again in our very last meeting. How could a murderous gangster who appealed to the darkest of pasts and looked forward to the cruelest of futures be the chosen leader of one of the best educated peoples the world has known? It was his great perplexity, but it never persuaded him that good is no more grounded than evil. Somehow this *fatum* in his nature sustained his sweet disposition throughout a life in which he was in daily battle with the greatest ugliness and in which all faiths were tried to the breaking point. He worked perpetually with a truly remarkable focus of energy, and his personality was a seamless unity. He must be judged not by any single part of his product but by his whole life—his scholarship, his teaching, his journalism, and his presence itself. One sees in it none of the spectacular metamorphoses so characteristic of intellectuals. He was what he was and, as such, achieved what others talked about all the time, authenticity. He was the living example of the possibility of the democratic personality. Finally all those who cared about freedom were forced to drink at this trough. He was the man who had lived liberal democracy in its best and most comprehensive sense, and to refer to him is to touch ground.

I said that I could not claim to be his student. But he was, in fact, my teacher. Not the least of what he taught me was to appreciate a man like him.

January 1990. This is Raymond Aron's historic moment. The collapse of communism and the victory of liberal democracy are what he worked for throughout his life. He was the most eloquent spokesman for the alliance which achieved this victory. He would have been the best analyst of what we can now expect and the best guide for what we should do.

The spirit of the French opposition to him is still alive. Philippe Lacoue-Labarthe, a favorite student of Jacques Derrida, in an article discussing Heidegger's affair with Hitler (the title of which summarizes its content: "Neither an Accident nor a Mistake" [Critical Inquiry, 15, Winter 1989, pp. 481–84], asserts that all great men of this century, especially Heidegger and Sartre, were swindled by either Hitler or Stalin. The capacity to be swindled was an essential aspect of their greatness, for they were awaiting the "irruption" of a new world. What about being swindled by "democracy"? "Leave that to Raymond Aron, that is, to capitalism's official thinker (a system of complete nihilism . . .)."

This statement should not be taken to be merely the rhetoric of French internecine warfare. It is now the official moral perspective of the humanities in the United States.

ALEXANDRE KOJÈVE

QUENEAU'S[1] COLLECTION of Kojève's thoughts about Hegel constitutes one of the few important philosophical books of the twentieth
century—a book whose knowledge is requisite to the full awareness
of our situation and to the grasp of the most modern perspective on
the eternal questions of philosophy. A hostile critic has given an
accurate assessment of Kojève's influence:

> Kojève is the unknown Superior whose dogma is revered,
> often unawares, by that important subdivision of the "animal
> kingdom of the spirit" in the contemporary world—the pro-
> gressivist intellectuals. In the years preceding the Second
> World War in France, the transmission was effected by
> means of oral initiation to a group of persons who in turn
> took the responsibility of instructing others, and so on. It
> was only in 1947 that, by the efforts of Raymond Queneau,
> the classes on the *Phenomenology of Mind* taught by Alex-

---

[1]Raymond Queneau, a poet and novelist, was an important figure on the French
postwar literary scene. Many of his works are illustrative of Kojève's thought, especially
the novels *Le Dimanche de la Vie* and *Zazie dans le Métro*. He, along with Raymond
Aron and Maurice Merleau-Ponty, was among those who followed Kojève's course
on the *Phenomenology of Mind* given at the Ecole Pratique des Hautes Etudes in Paris
during the years 1933–39. Queneau's notes from that course formed the core of
Introduction to Reading Hegel.
    (1990) Kojève, a Russian emigré who despised Parisian intellectuals and uni-
versities, never held an appointment in one. After the war he became a bureaucrat
in the French Economic Ministry, where he was occupied with the Common Market
and GATT, presiding as he said over the end of history. It was in his office there
that I studied with him from 1953 to his death. He was always willing to close his
door and talk philosophy. Or, as Leo Strauss put it when he sent me to see him, "He
is like Mephistopheles in *Faust,* always eager to corrupt young men." He was the
most brilliant man I ever met. Both Aron and Strauss said the same of him.

268

andre Kojève at the *Ecole des Hautes Etudes* from 1933 to 1939 were published under the title *Introduction to Reading Hegel.* This teaching was prior to the philosophico-political speculations of J. P. Sartre and M. Merleau-Ponty, to the publication of *Les Temps Modernes* and the new orientation of *Esprit,* reviews which were the most important vehicles for the dissemination of progressivist ideology in France after the liberation. From that time on we have breathed Kojève's teaching with the air of the times. It is known that intellectual progressivism itself admits of a subdivision, since one ought to consider its two species, Christian (*Esprit*) and atheist (*Les Temps Modernes*); but this distinction, for reasons that the initial doctrine enables one to clarify, does not take on the importance of a schism. . . . M. Kojève is, so far as we know, the first . . . to have attempted to constitute the intellectual and moral *ménage à trois* of Hegel, Marx, and Heidegger, which has since that time been such a great success. [Aimé Patri, "Dialectique du Maître et de l'Esclave," *Le Contrat Social,* V, No. 4 (July–August 1961), 234.]

Kojève is the most thoughtful, the most learned, the most profound of those Marxists who, dissatisfied with the thinness of Marx's account of the human and metaphysical grounds of his teaching, turned to Hegel as the truly philosophic source of that teaching. Although he made no effort at publicizing his reflections, their superior force imposed them willy-nilly on those who heard him. For this reason, anyone who wishes to understand the sense of that mixture of Marxism and Existentialism which characterizes contemporary radicalism must turn to Kojève. From him one can learn both the implications and the necessary presuppositions of historicist philosophy; he elaborates what the world must be like if terms such as freedom, work, and creativity are to have a rational content and be parts of a coherent understanding. It would, then, behoove any follower of the new version of the Left who wishes to think through the meaning of his own action to study that thinker who is at its origin.

However, Kojève is above all a philosopher—which, at the least, means that he is primarily interested in the truth, the comprehensive truth. His passion for clarity is more powerful than his passion for changing the world. The charm of political solutions does not cause him to forget the need to present an adequate account of the rational basis of those solutions, and this removes him from the always distorted atmosphere of active commitment. He despises those intellectuals who respond to the demands of the contemporary audience and give the appearance of philosophic seriousness without raising the kinds of questions which would bore that audience or be repugnant to it. A certain sense of the inevitability of this kind of abuse—of the conversion of philosophy into ideology—is, perhaps, at the root of his distaste for publication. His work has been private and has, in large measure, been communicated only to friends. And the core of that work is the careful and scholarly study of Hegel.

Because he is a serious man, Kojève has never sought to be original, and his originality has consisted in his search for the truth in the thought of wise men of the past. His interpretation has made Hegel an important alternative again, and showed how much we have to learn from him at a time when he seemed no longer of living significance. Kojève accomplished this revival of interest in Hegel not by adapting him to make him relevant, but by showing that contemporary concerns are best understood in the permanent light of Hegel's teaching. Kojève's book is a model of textual interpretation; the book is suffused with the awareness that it is of pressing concern to find out precisely what such a thinker meant, for he may well know much more than we do about the things that we need to know. Here scholarship is in the service of philosophy, and Kojève gives us a glimpse of the power of great minds and respect for the humble and unfashionable business of spending years studying an old book. His own teaching is but the distillation of more than six years devoted to nothing but reading a single book, line by line. *Introduction to the Reading of Hegel* constitutes the most authoritative interpretation of Hegel.

Such a careful and comprehensive study which makes sense of Hegel's very difficult texts will be of great value in America where, though his influence has been great and is ever greater, very few people read, let alone understand, him. He has regularly been ignored by academic positivists who are put off by his language and are unaware of the problems involved in their own understanding of science and the relation of science to the world of human concern. Hegel is now becoming popular in literary and artistic circles, but in a superficial form adapted to please dilettantes and other seekers after the sense of depth who wish to use him rather than understand him. Kojève presents Hegel's teaching with a force and rigor which should counterpoise both tendencies.

What distinguishes Kojève's treatment of Hegel is the recognition that for Hegel the primary concern is not the knowledge of anything outside himself—be it of nature or history—but knowledge of himself, that is, knowledge of what the philosopher is and how he can know what he knows. The philosopher must be able to explain his own doings; an explanation of the heavens, of animals, or of nonphilosophic men which does not leave room for, or does not talk about, the philosopher is radically incomplete because it cannot account for the possibility of its own existence as knowledge. The world known by philosophy must be such that it supports philosophy and makes the philosopher the highest or most complete kind of human being.

Kojève learned from Hegel that the philosopher seeks to know himself or to possess full self-consciousness, and that, therefore, the true philosophic endeavor is a coherent explanation of all things that culminates in the explanation of philosophy. The man who seeks any other form of knowledge, who cannot explain his own doings, cannot be called a philosopher. Discussion of the rational state is only a corollary of the proof that the world can be known or is rational. Kojève insists that Hegel is the only man who succeeded in making this proof, and his interpretation of the *Phenomenology* expands and clarifies Hegel's assertion that reality is rational and hence justifies rational discourse about it. According to Kojève, Hegel is the fulfillment of what Plato and Aristotle could only pray for; he is the modern Aristotle who responded to—or, better, incorporated—the objections made to Aristotelian philosophy by modern natural and human science. Kojève intransigently tries to make plausible Hegel's claim that he had achieved absolute wisdom. He argues that without the possibility of absolute wisdom, all knowledge, science, or philosophy is impossible.

It may indeed be doubted whether Kojève is fully persuasive to the modern consciousness, particularly since he finds himself compelled to abandon Hegel's philosophy of nature as indefensible and suggests that Heidegger's meditation on being may provide a substitute for it. The abandoned philosophy of nature may well be a necessary cosmic support for Hegel's human, historical teaching. One might ask whether Kojève is not really somewhere between Hegel and Heidegger, but it should be added that Kojève himself leads the reader to this question, which is a proper theme of philosophical reflection. Kojève describes the character of wisdom even if he does not prove it has been actualized.

The most striking feature of Kojève's thought is his insistence—fully justified—that for Hegel, and for all followers of Hegel, history is completed, that nothing really new can again happen in the world. To most of us, such a position seems utterly paradoxical and wildly implausible. But Kojève easily shows the ineluctable necessity of this consequence for anyone who understands human life to be historically

determined, for anyone who believes that thought is relative to time—
that is, for most modern men. For if thought is historical, it is only
at the end of history that this fact can be known; there can only be
knowledge if history at some point stops. Kojève elaborates the meaning of this logical necessity throughout the course of the book and
attempts to indicate how a sensible man could accept it and interpret
the world in accordance with it. It is precisely Marx's failure to think
through the meaning of his own historical thought that proves his
philosophical inadequacy and compels us to turn to the profounder
Hegel.

If concrete historical reality is all that the human mind can know,
if there is no transcendent intelligible world, then, for there to be
philosophy or science, reality must have become rational. The Hegelian solution, accepted by Kojève, is that this has indeed happened
and that the enunciation of the universal, rational principles of the
rights of man in the French Revolution marked the beginning of the
end of history. Thereafter, these are the only acceptable, viable principles of the state. The dignity of man has been recognized, and all
men are understood to participate in it; all that remains to do is, at
most, to realize the state grounded on these principles all over the
world; no antithesis can undermine this synthesis, which contains
within itself all the valid possibilities. In this perspective Kojève interprets our situation; he paints a powerful picture of our problems as
those of posthistorical man with none of the classic tasks of history
to perform, living in a universal, homogeneous state where there is
virtual agreement on all the fundamental principles of science, politics,
and religion. He characterizes the life of the man who is free, who
has no work, who has no worlds to conquer, states to found, gods to
revere, or truths to discover. In so doing, Kojève gives an example of
what it means to follow out the necessity of one's position manfully
and philosophically. If Kojève is wrong, if his world does not corre-
spond to the real one, we learn at least that either one must abandon
reason—and this includes all science—or one must abandon historicism. More commonsensical but less intransigent writers would not
teach us nearly so much. Kojève presents the essential outlines of
historical thought; and, to repeat, historical thought, in one form or
another, is at the root of almost all modern human science.

It is concerning the characterization of man at the end of history
that one of the most intriguing difficulties in Kojève's teaching arises.
As is only to be expected, his honesty and clarity lead him to pose
the difficulty himself. If Hegel is right that history fulfills the demands
of reason, the citizen of the final state should enjoy the satisfaction

of all reasonable human aspirations; he should be a free, rational being, content with his situation and exercising all of his powers, emancipated from the bonds of prejudice and oppression. But looking around us, Kojève, like every other penetrating observer, sees that the completion of the human tasks may very well coincide with the decay of humanity, the rebarbarization or even reanimalization of man. He addresses this problem particularly in the note on Japan added to the second edition (pp. 159–162). After reading it, one wonders whether the citizen of the universal homogeneous state is not identical to Nietzsche's Last Man, and whether Hegel's historicism does not by an inevitable dialectic force us to a more somber and more radical historicism which rejects reason. We are led to a confrontation between Hegel and Nietzsche and perhaps, even further, toward a reconsideration of the classical philosophy of Plato and Aristotle, who rejected historicism before the fact and whom Hegel believed he had surpassed. It is the special merit of Kojève to be one of the very few sure guides to the contemplation of the fundamental alternatives.

(Shortly after the completion of this statement I learned that Alexandre Kojève had died in Brussels in May 1968.)

The
Fate of Books
in
Our Time

COMMERCE AND "CULTURE"

WE ALL KNOW with some degree of precision what commerce is, while I, at least, have no understanding of what "culture" is, and it is a word I never use. "Culture" somehow refers to the "higher" things, to "spirituality," and shares the vagueness and contentlessness of those terms. It belongs in the family of other amorphous notions like "genius," "personality," "intellectual," and "creativity," all of which were invented with a noble, if flawed, intention and have inevitably been debased over the two centuries of their currency. This abstraction, "culture," is now used to supplant the instinctive concern with country, putting in its place a factitious loyalty and fostering a dangerous insensitivity to real politics. In the communist countries there are "culture" commissars who weave the floral overlay for the tyrannies that were supposed to produce the higher "culture." In the liberal democracies, aside from the sociologists who entertain us with descriptions of drug and rock "cultures," among others, we have a "culture" establishment which has ever less learning or inspiration and a large part of which performs the function of persuading us that the Marxist critique of crass commercialism has no relation to Stalinism, and that we can still expect dialectical materialism to eventuate in the realm of freedom and the full development of personality.

The notion of "culture" was formed in response to the rise of commercial society. So far as I know, Kant was the first to use the word in its modern sense. (Of course, every important change in language goes back to a profound change in thought.) He uses it in a context where he is discussing the contribution of J.-J. Rousseau to the articulation of *the* human problem. Rousseau's earlier works, the discourses *Arts and Sciences* and *Origins of Inequality*, had, according to Kant, revealed the true contradiction that makes man incomplete

277

and unhappy: the opposition between nature and civilization, man's animal needs and contentment, on the one hand, and his social duties and acquired arts and sciences on the other. But, according to Kant, Rousseau in his later works, *Emile, Social Contract,* and *Nouvelle Héloïse,* proposed a possible unity that harmonized the low natural demands with the high responsibilities of morality and art. This unity Kant called "culture." His three *Critiques* were an attempt to systematize "culture." The first finds limits to nature as revealed by science, a realm of moved matter where all causation is mechanical. The second establishes the possibility of a realm of freedom in which will and hence responsibility are conceivable. And the third founds an entirely new realm, the aesthetic, where imagination can have free play and man's longings for beauty and purposiveness can have substance. Taken together the *Critiques* provide the philosophic grounds of "culture," and the life informed by all three would be truly cultured. This system takes account of all the possibilities of the soul in its richness and depth. The announcement of a new clarity about the true articulation of the human potential promised fulfillments of a level previously unattained.

However, the bright promise obscures the somber background against which it emerged. Modern science had appeared to have shown that nature is soulless, that the beautiful cosmos, imitated by the fine arts, is a product of groundless imagination. Correspondingly, the modern science of man denied that man is the being naturally directed to virtue and knowledge and asserted instead that, akin to all the other beings, his sole concern is his preservation. Thus nature, the permanent ground of all things, the source of being, provides no support for man's humanity. Rousseau's powerful rhetoric was directed against the practical consequence of this theoretical understanding—commercial society and its typical atom, the *bourgeois.* Commercial society, politics stripped of imaginary goals, is dedicated to the unabashed pursuit of well-being. Its very success is vouchsafed by purifying itself of the constraints of patriotism, liberality, nobility, and other grand traits, in favor of self-interest and utility. It is in response to the economic man that the cultural movement came into being, either as a corrective to liberal society or as a radical rejection of its mercenary morals and its philistinism.

SPECTACULAR DEMANDS

This movement never seriously questioned the science of nature which underlay liberal society. There was almost no attempt to return to the older understanding of nature, a nature informed by mind. The quest was for a new dimension of reality as a supplement to nature which could account for spirituality. Dualisms like nature and freedom, nature and art, nature and history became the order of the epoch, with the latter term of each of the pairs intended to have primacy. But the weightiness or, one might say, the gravity of nature overbore or tipped the balance. No one could doubt the existence of matter or deny the power of Newtonian science; but Kant's postulates or Hegel's spirit, however impressive, do not simply compel belief. Similarly, the march of the new economy throughout the world was visible to all; the progress of the aesthetic education of mankind was, to say the least, not entirely clear. A vague sense of groundlessness pervaded those who sought for alternatives to pure naturalism. Idealism, historicism, romanticism, Marxism, and finally nihilism are the familiar names of schools which represented the new enthusiasms and corresponding disappointments in the search for the spirit. The use of the word "creativity," never before applied to anyone but God, gives some sense of the problem faced. Nature has no formal or final causes; nothing that *is* can account for the artist and his productions. He must be assimilated to God, must make something from nothing. But in the sublunar world *ex nihilo nihil fit* seems to apply, and the great structures tend to collapse back into nature. One need only look at the progress of the word "sublime" from Kant to Freud, and with it the movement from woman as the civilizer, moralizer, and object of ideal longings in Rousseau and Goethe, to woman in the science and literature of the twentieth century.

The artificial or abstract character of "culture" comes to light when one recognizes that nobody serious does anything for the sake of "culture"—or it is only recently that men do so, now that they are apparently for the first time willing to live so as to represent the conceits of intellectuals. Men and women die for their country, for their gods, and perhaps even for the truth, but not for culture. Scientists seek to comprehend nature's phenomena, statesmen to found and maintain just regimes, artists to represent beautiful bodies, and philosophers to know the first causes of all things. The motives are diverse and not necessarily conciliable. There is a commonsense reason to follow any one of these ways of life, and there are faculties appropriate to each. To establish their unity in "culture" is a task of colossal proportions, one which has not been successfully completed. Until this task is successfully completed, "culture" as a general category will have a tendency to distort its components. "Culture" somehow always means that man's higher activities have their source in human spontaneity or creativity, an interpretation which has more or less plausibility when applied to poetry or painting, but one resisted by the facts when applied to science or philosophy. The claims of science and philosophy are subverted without discussion by the "culture" interpretation. They become cultural expressions, relative to specific cultures, dependent on them and existing for them rather than for the sake of getting beyond cultures to nature. The quarrel between poetry and philosophy, which was previously thought to be the fundamental issue, is thus covered over by the triumph of the poetic perspective. Finally, God becomes man's creation rather than the reverse, a perspective fatal to religion or any kind of faith. Something like what we mean by "culture" may very well be the result of religion, but the beauty of the churches can only be understood as a denigration of human beauty and a devotion to the God who revealed himself. Only when the true ends of society have nothing to do with the sublime does "culture" become necessary as a veneer to cover over the void. Culture can at best appreciate the monuments of earlier faith; it cannot produce them.

It is most revealing that there is no Greek word that can even remotely translate "culture," and Greece is perhaps the peak example of what is said to be "culture." Pericles, in the fullest statement about Athens which we possess, attributes Athens' greatness—the peak of the peak—to the Athenian regime, to a political order to which men were committed body and soul. Alluding to the surpassing beauties which constitute Athenian "culture" for us, he says only that "we are lovers of beauty with economy, lovers of wisdom without softness." All the statues and temples and spectacles are for him merely the epiphenomena of the core, love of country. In what is perhaps the most spectacular demand on patriotism ever made, he asks the citizens to have an *eros* for the city; from this all else will flow. He is as good an authority about what is central and what peripheral as are our "culture" critics. Our regimes do not ask so much nor can we give them so much. Their sublime moments are only in their foundings and preservation. The distinction between private and public undermines the unity of spiritual strength, draining the public of the transcendent energies while trivializing them because the merely private life provides no proper stage for their action. Thucydides, who puts in the mouth of Pericles all that I have ascribed to him, ironically hides himself in the account of Athens and all of Greece while showing that the hope for perfect unity of the human powers, actually held by Pericles and parodied by Plato, is ill-founded. His book, one of the most perfect of all the beauties, is not culture-bound. He drew the lessons from Greece as a possession of use to the thoughtful for all time.

Our notions of "culture" and of the intellectuals who practice it are too grand for Periclean patriotism and refuse the lonely Thucydidean adherence to eternity. The intellectuals neither face the stern demands of the political nor the even sterner demands of the transpolitical. They advertise their superiority to political practice but are absolutely in its thrall. So many of them are Marxists because Marxism combines the charm of political action with that of philosophy. It is no accident that Marxist theory and practice use the intellectuals as tools and keep them in brutal subservience. The union of materialism and idealism in Marxism (e.g., dialectical materialism) is absolutely incoherent. The mature Marx appears to have recognized this inasmuch as he never seriously discusses the arts or education—that is, "culture." His later works show how "culture," after the supreme efforts of giants such as Kant, Hegel, and Schiller, tended to be swallowed up again by commerce. Again, nothing comes from nothing, and the higher can be reduced to the lower but cannot be derived from it. The distinction between the world of commerce and that of "culture" quickly became the distinction between infrastructure and superstructure, with the former clearly determining the latter. And this was much more sinister than the old vulgarity of commerce which made no great promises of ideal fulfillments. The intellectuals are the new class of men—neither statesmen nor philosophers—who are the purveyors of the false promise, those who most reveal the groundlessness of the spirit. This is captured marvelously well by Flaubert in M. Homais, the vulgarian who loves "culture" and finally wants to become a bohemian. The *Geisteswissenschaften* were after all just entertainment for the *bourgeoisie*. This legitimated Flaubert's incipient nihilism.

THE MOST DARING PROJECT

So the "culture" movement is something new, a response to modern society, or more correctly to liberal democracy, the commercial republic, hence a response to a novel *political* condition. This political condition was itself a product of rational choice, of a philosophic project. For the first time regimes were to be founded on reason, a new dawn for mankind, a world free of the terrible prejudices on which nations were formerly based; and at the very moment of their actualization, there was a revulsion against them on the part of much of the cultivated part of humanity.

In order to judge the legitimacy of this reaction, one must look again at the intellectual roots of modern politics (for it had intellectual roots) in order to see how the profound and comprehensive minds

who initiated it understood what they were about. It is not to be
believed that men such as Machiavelli, Bacon, Hobbes, Descartes,
Spinoza, and Locke had no sense of the fullness of the soul. It is rather
that they undertook a cost-benefit analysis with total awareness that
some losses have to be suffered in order to make some gains and were
prepared to live with the losses. We, on the other hand, have suc-
cumbed to the ever-present desire to have our cake and eat it, or to
put it baldly, have lost sight of the necessary and the possible.

I must give a superficial and popular account of the most daring
and far-reaching project ever conceived by man, of what d'Alembert
called "the conspiracy" of Enlightenment. It was an attempt to alter
completely the character of political life on the one hand, and intellectual life on the other. But above all it was an attempt to alter the
relationship between the two, and it is that relationship which is the
privileged perspective of thoughtful men. The image of the transformation is projected by Machiavelli, who appears on the scene almost
as a beggar, as a suppliant, humbly beseeching a glorious prince to
look down upon him with favor. This was the permanent relation of
wisdom and power as understood by the old philosophers. But in a
sudden shift, Machiavelli, still covertly but with expectations of perfect openness in the future, himself becomes the prince. He plots the
means for the wise to seize the levers of power and actualize the dream
of philosophers becoming kings, a dream as old as political philosophy
itself. But precisely for Plato it was only a dream, and dreams must
give way before reality. The fact that the dream is a dream meant
that philosophers in the real world have to make their plans accordingly, lower their expectations, and keep their distance from the powers. Machiavelli and his followers reversed all that, and it is in this
dispensation which we still live.

To begin from the political side, the new political science can
be understood to be a great humanitarian endeavor. For all the nobility
of ancient political science, it offered no way to realize its high goals.
Human beings still suffered from as many ills as they always had.
Practically, it offered only endurance or resignation. What men need
is peace, stability, law, order, and relief from poverty and disease. The
ancients talked only about virtue and not about well-being. That in
itself is perhaps harmless, but the moderns contended that the concentration on virtue contradicts the concern for well-being. Aristotle
admitted that "equipment" as well as virtue is necessary for happiness,
but he said nothing about how that equipment is acquired. A careful
examination of the acquisition of equipment reveals that virtue
impedes that acquisition. Liberality, for example, presupposes money

and not caring for it overmuch. But one must care for it to get it. Moreover, spending money exhausts it, so that liberality makes the need for acquisitiveness greater than it would have been without the virtue. Liberality both discourages and encourages acquisitiveness, putting man in contradiction with himself. This virtue is too weak to overcome selfishness, but is powerful enough to prevent certain positive effects which selfishness might cause. The miser is not likely to need to steal. And his quest for profit can, properly channeled, produce benefits for others. In the old system he is given a bad conscience and a bad name. But it would seem that nature is not kind to man, if the two elements of happiness—virtue and equipment—are at tension with one another. Equipment is surely necessary, so why not experiment with doing without virtue? If a substitute for virtue can be found, the inner conflict that renders man's life so hard could be resolved.

This is what Machiavelli means when he says that men ought not to do as they ought to do but ought to do as they do do. Which means that men are actually not doing as they do, but at least partly doing as they ought to do. And this they ought not to do. He puts this with outrageous clarity when he says men are never all good or all bad, implying that since they cannot be all good (for self-love is an inextinguishable part of us) they ought to be all bad. In this way alone can they overcome their dividedness. But if the distinction between good and bad in man is suppressed, then the badness, the standard for determining the bad, is also suppressed. In short, if the passions remain while the virtues which govern them disappear, the passions have unrestricted rights, by nature. They can be judged only in terms of their desirable or undesirable social effects. This is how the despised usurer is miraculously transformed into the respected banker. The new political scientists decided to abandon the pedantic and fruitless practice of inveighing against the passions and to become instead their accomplice for the sake of effectiveness. Instead of asking men to think of the common good, which they were unlikely to do, they told them to think of themselves, which they were strongly inclined to do, and to transform loyalty, patriotism, and justice into calculations of benefit. After *Prince* XVI the theoretical foundations of commercial society have been laid, just as the new argument for democracy is well begun in IX. There Machiavelli removes the moral basis of aristocratic rule by denying that aristocrats are any less concerned about money than are oligarchs. Equality begins in modern thought in the assertion that there is no politically relevant public spiritedness. Men are all equally selfish. Men's concern for their preservation and their comfort can, if the waters are not muddied by extrinsic considerations, be motors for the production of prosperity. The passions, instructed by the philosophers as to their true meaning and end, will suffice; and the collaboration of the philosophers with the passions results in the formula of commercial society, enlightened self-interest. Life, liberty, and the pursuit of property were just what Aristotle did not talk about. They are the conditions of happiness; but the essence of happiness, according to Aristotle, is virtue. So the moderns decided to deal with the conditions and to let happiness take care of itself. At most they talked about the pursuit of happiness. No longer was the concern for the rare perfection of man; the focus became our common vulnerability and suffering. Politics came to be the care of the body, and the soul slipped away.

The new vision of man and politics was never taken by its founders to be splendid. Naked man, gripped by fear or industriously laboring to provide the wherewithal for survival, is not an apt subject for poetry. They self-consciously chose low but solid ground. Civil societies dedicated to the end of self-preservation cannot be expected to provide fertile soil for the heroic or the inspired. They do not require or encourage the noble. What rules and sets the standards of respectability and emulation is not virtue or wisdom. The recognition of the humdrum and prosaic character of life was intended to play a central role in the success of real politics. And the understanding of human nature which makes this whole project feasible, if believed in, clearly forms a world in which the higher motives have no place. One who holds the "economic" view of man cannot consistently believe in the dignity of man or in the special status of art and science. The success of the enterprise depends precisely on this simplification of man. And if there is a solution to the human problems, there is no tragedy. There was no expectation that, after the bodily needs are taken care of, man would have a spiritual renaissance—and this for two reasons: (1) men will always be mortal, which means that there can be no end to the desire for immortality and to the quest for means to achieve it; and (2) the premise of the whole undertaking is that man's natural primary concern is preservation and prosperity; the regimes founded on nature take man as he is naturally and will make him ever more natural. If his motives were to change, the machinery that makes modern government work would collapse.

The historicism, romanticism, and idealism that built on the Enlightenment foundations were—from the point of view of the originators of modern political philosophy—building castles in the air, dreaming that the classical good and noble would emerge out of modern utility and selfishness, Plato's ideas out of Descartes' extension. The first discipline modernity's originators imposed upon themselves was that of self-restraint, learning to live with vulgarity. Their high expectations for effectiveness were made possible by low expectations of what was to be.

Science, then, became active; and its motto was "give us your tired, your poor. . . ." But the benefactors, too, had a motive. By their usefulness to mankind at large they expected to get gratitude and, thereby, a freedom hitherto unavailable to them. Gratitude, according to Machiavelli's analysis, is an effective motive when there is hope of future benefaction, not when there is only memory of past benefaction. Gratitude is, in other words, ultimately a function of fear. Power, present and future, and the opinion thereof, is the only guarantee of men's goodwill. Men previously did not have the opinion that science is powerful, nor was it. To have a secure position in civil society, science both had to be productive of power and to appear to be so. Innovations in politics and medicine, patently useful to men, were to be the signs of science's special status as a powerful benefactor warring against men's darkest fears of death and destitution.

ENLIGHTENMENTS

Perhaps it would be useful to describe Plato's account of the philosopher's relation to civil society, and to show how the moderns undertook to transform it. The image of that relation is projected throughout Plato's dialogues in the person of Socrates and the situations in which he finds himself, most starkly of course in the fact that the city puts him to death for being a philosopher. The discussion in the *Republic* of philosopher-kings—a passage most relevant for our considerations—culminates in the cave likeness where civil society is seen as a dark cave where men are prisoners. Escape from the cave is the central concern of the philosopher. Adeimantus, in what amounts to an accusation of Socrates, asserts that the philosophers appear to be either useless or vicious. Plato, as I have suggested, teaches that ultimately this is an appearance that cannot be reversed, and this insures the philosophers' permanent marginality. They appear useless because they are. They are neither artisans, nor statesmen, nor rhetoricians. They are idlers who contribute nothing to security or prosperity. Their peculiar contemplative pleasures are not accessible to the majority of mankind, and they do not provide for the popular pleasures as do the poets. They are relatively insensible to bodily needs and, most important, have come to terms with the fact of death which terrorizes the many. There is really no point of contact. Plato always treats the relation of *dēmos* to philosopher as that of ignorance to knowledge. He says a multitude can never philosophize and hence can never recognize the seriousness of philosophy or who really philosophizes. Attempting to influence the multitude results in forced prostitution. The natural allies of the philosophers are the gentlemen, whose bodily needs are attended to because they have money and are not compelled to make it, who have a proud disdain for death, and who display their independence by a love of beautiful and useless things, among which can be philosophy, not because they are philosophers but because they have an inkling of its nobility. The philosophers, therefore, favor the rule of gentlemen, with all their prejudices, their merely conventional superiority, their preference for the noble over the reasonable.

The modern philosophers, as I have sketched out their teaching, turned this around by making themselves useful to the many. They recognized the possible reasonableness of the people. Not that the people would ever have the desire or the capacity to pursue the truth for its own sake. But they can and usually do calculate quite well about their preservation and gain. Once one accepts their irrational premise—that death can be avoided—from there on out they make excellent use of reason in a way that gentlemen, who regard calculation about preservation and gain as base, do not. This is an observation to which Adam Smith gives the fullest testimony.

There is a kinship between the vulgar and philosophy that was recognized by the ancient philosophers as well; but, again, the overcoming of the fear of death was critical for them, and they did not envision philosophy becoming useful to that passion. But if the people learn to seek power rationally, and if scientists as a by-product of their activity provide the greatest power, then the scientists are accepted, encouraged, and deferred to by the reason of the people. There is a rational meeting ground of the people and the philosophers, and there is no further need of the aristocrats. The two great powers meet. The philosophers need money and freedom, and that is what they get. Of course, there is a certain ambiguity about what reason means, an ambiguity that must be forgotten before there can be full-blown utilitarianism. (The ironical character of the partnership is very beautifully expressed in the first sentence of Descartes' *Discourse on Method.*) Enlightenment of the cave-dwellers who had previously lived in the dark is now possible because they need only learn to follow their self-interest rather than transcend it. The communication between the people and their preceptors must always be in terms of those prosaic things about which they can calculate, mostly health and property.

As to the viciousness of the philosophers, the meaning of this complaint is succinctly expressed in the charge that the philosophers do not "hold the gods the city holds." And this accusation is most true. The quest for wisdom begins in doubt of the conventional wisdom about the highest things. The most cherished beliefs of the community, the collective hopes and fears, are centered on its gods. The unpardonable thing is to be beyond those hopes and fears, beyond the awe and shame the gods impose. Such are the philosophers who look to nature, and its unchanging uniformity, who finally deny that the gods protect the city. These men arouse horror and terror, anxiety that vengeance will be called down on the city that harbors them. From the very origins of philosophy *the* enemies of the philosophers have been the priests; the religious and wise have been at war at least since Teiresias and Oedipus fought for the trust of the Thebans. It was the charge of impiety that caused Socrates' execution. And this is where the category "culture" becomes confusing and obfuscating. The arts, particularly poetry, have very much to do with the gods, with the horizon of the cave. Whatever the poets may believe, their poetry must necessarily appeal to the needs and the tastes of the people. In the greatest cases the poets teach the people about the gods. The war between philosophy and poetry of which Socrates speaks has much to do with the religious question, especially with poetry's special kinship to the passions at the root of fanaticism. This tension in the realm of "culture" is present in all the arts.

The response of Plato and Aristotle was to attempt a reform of poetry. Contending that poetry would always be needed, they wanted it to calm and purge the passions of pity and fear. It would make men not reasonable but more open to reason, less in the grip of religious terror, more tolerant. This is the complement to their politics which relied on the gentleman. Music education was to be the formation of the gentleman's taste.

The moderns, on the other hand, regarded this solution as insufficient and declared war on the priests and along with them the arts that supported them. They undertook to cut out what they understood to be the root of religious fanaticism, imagination. From the time Machiavelli attacked the ancients for building imaginary republics, there was a sustained effort to destroy the effects of imagination in politics and science. Descartes' radical doubt is nothing but an attempt to make the world safe from imagination's productions. Hobbes tries to persuade men that the experience of the fear of violent death is the fundamental experience. It is one that dispels all the imaginary causes of fear. The moderns are much more radical than the ancients in their criticism of imagination. Plato and Aristotle are more nuanced about imagination, partly because they thought that its power in the soul is such that it must be compromised with, partly because of the purely theoretical difference with the moderns as to how seriously science must take the prescientific world. However much ancient and modern thinkers have in common, the relation between the arts, on the one hand, and science on the other, was fundamentally altered by the moderns' political project.

It is not true, as the moderns appear on the surface to say, that men in civil society are always motivated by utility, by self-interest. They could be, but actually imaginary republics affect their consciouses and consciences. They frequently do as they ought to do. This can only be corrected, as the moderns would have it, if the shadows of the "ought" are dispelled in favor of the "is." Then self-interest, informed by science, can become the enlightened self-interest on which commercial society rests. Not only must science provide the useful; it must do critical battle with the old religions on all fronts. The rooting out of the enthusiastic in man goes hand in hand with a certain anti-artistic bias in the great men who performed the operation. This does not mean that they were not men of the subtlest intellect and refined taste. But art is secondary, more adornment or entertainment than substance. Their grand styles seem to be more reminiscences of the old world than inner necessities of their thought. The response to their project by a poet who saw what was happening can be found in Swift's *Voyage to Laputa* and *Battle of the Books*.

So the answer to the question whether commercial society is hostile to "culture" must be yes. But this is in large measure because "culture" was invented to correct or oppose commercial society. It is almost a matter of definition. "Culture" implied an opposition between art and science, and a preference for the former. Science was flourishing at the moment of the cultural revolution. The profoundest element of that revolution was its criticism of the egotistic spring of action on which commercial society is founded. By its very principle such society does not find a place for the moral, political, and religious greatness on which great art is founded.

GIVING RIGHTS TO VULGARITY

The question is whether the critics of the commercial society properly assessed the greatness and subtlety of their Enlightenment predecessors. Bacon, Locke, Descartes, Hume, and all the others knew they were giving rights to vulgarity. But in so doing—in addition to caring for men's well-being—they were providing rights for themselves. The real need that commercial society has for the learned, its discouragement of fanaticism and encouragement of the tolerance necessary for trade, its effect of softening manners, all gave guarantees of an atmosphere of freedom. The production of wealth was to be beneficial to all—the refined as well as the ordinary—while breaking down the walls of prejudice which had dominated all previous societies. Thus businessmen were to be the allies of the philosophers. One need only read Adam Smith (as one fears modern economists do not) to see that there were no illusions about the characters of businessmen, and that their tastes and morals were not considered fit to dominate society. But the alliance the philosophers made with them was more surely founded on the self-interest of both parties than the unreliable alliances made in the past with priests, tyrants, or even gentlemen. For gentlemen from time to time wanted splendid things, but they were never truly attached to reason, and because they were less oppressed by the needs to which science ministered, they could never really be ruled by philosophers. Locke was surely contemptuous of manufacturers, but he hid that contempt. This was part of the arrangement. And from the heights of a Locke, or a Thucydides for that matter, the difference between what we ordinarily call "culture" and business coarseness is not all that important. The real heights never had much of a place in civil society.

In the new order a Locke was free—with almost no danger of being interfered with—to think his sublime thoughts, to seek the first causes of all things, to understand the nature of things. He could talk with his friends and teach the young. And there was money enough. The academies and universities satisfied Socrates' empty claim that he deserved to be fed in the prytaneum. The free lunch for philosophy and science was, precisely, the invention of commercial society. This marvelous situation has prevailed now for two hundred and fifty years. Of all the promises made by commercial society, the freedom of the mind is the one that has been best redeemed. This may not be the best condition for the flourishing of the mind, but that it exists is beyond reasonable doubt. Every other kind of regime that has presented itself during this long time has assaulted that freedom.

Now Bacon, Locke, and the others expected to have an effect on society—the most important effect may very well have been the respectability they gained for themselves—but they knew the effect would not be equal to the cause. The beauty of their minds could not be incarnated in the body or the deeds of the city. They were not

trying to rebuild Athens or Florence. They were not cultural deter-
minists. The potential of the human intellect can be actualized without
such a base. The highest activities are always essentially lonely and
private, and these men had a robust sense of their independence and
the ultimate self-sufficiency of the mind. In this they were just like
Socrates. The only change they operated was to bring philosophy out
of the closet into the open, instead of seeking protection behind a
little wall like men in a storm. Of course, in so doing they made
philosophy, on the one hand, more vulnerable to the public if the
hopes of controlling the public are not fulfilled, and, on the other,
put at risk that inner intransigence, that disdain for public opinion,
which is the necessary condition of the quest for truth. Not only the
rewards but the new responsibilities might provide irresistible temptations to compromise. But again, in essence they understood their
resource to be the knowledge of unchanging nature.

In the later critics there was, as I have said, perhaps not sufficient
awareness of the depth of their predecessors nor the nature of their
project. The recognition of rights which had been wrested with such
labors from a hostile mankind was taken for granted. By the nineteenth
century, the intellectuals' privileged position was an independent
given; they began openly to withdraw recognition from their partners,
the producers of wealth. The philistinism which is the condition of
the intellectuals' prosperity became intolerable to their overrefined
tastes. It is possible that commercial society is ultimately deadly to
the arts and philosophy, but then we must also abandon modern
egalitarianism and the useful science which made possible both prosperity and longer lives. Some were prepared to do this, but most
were not. Those possessed by the romantic longing for the Middle
Ages were not always fully conscious of what such a return would
entail.

Moreover, because the new movements accepted the Enlightenment's teaching about nature as well as its great social and political
activism, there was a loss of the independent footing which was the
leading quality of all the greatest minds of the past. Thought, art,
religion all became cultural phenomena, somehow in the service of a
"culture." While claiming great superiority, there was a tacit, and
sometimes explicit, awareness that the cultured belonged to this here
and now—this civilization, this culture, this cave. Their roots are in
the past, the present, or the future of this culture. Their sense of
themselves can only come from it. They need it desperately and at
the same time despise its public opinion. What was pride in earlier
thinkers becomes in them vanity. Socrates criticized the Athenians

but did not complain about them. He never expected recognition from them and above all did not need it. But this is not true of intellectuals who, in the absence of eternity, have been imprisoned by history. There was much to the criticism of commercial society, but it seems rather to have radicalized the problem. Only men of the stature of Goethe provide models of a quest to find real independence; this means, in the first place, coming to terms with what is and finding ways of greatness that do not depend on reforming the world first. As Goethe recognized, for this the old Greek philosophers are still the best guides. They knew there is always a mess.

Commercial, or liberal, society has muddled along, more or less healthy, more or less believing in itself, more or less (unfortunately nowadays rather more) intimidated by its "culture" critics. For almost two hundred years they have been of two kinds, men of the Right and men of the Left. The Left has always been more powerful and now is close to total victory. It has been more powerful because it is really just a radicalization of the materialism and the egalitarianism that proved so successful in the modern project. The Left has removed the constraints on vulgarity and selfishness that were so carefully built into the project by its originators, particularly the privacy which was essential to virtue in a regime whose public goal is not virtue. It is populism with pretensions. It points out the cultural impoverishment of the *bourgeoisie* and somehow manages to argue that the defeat of the *bourgeoisie* will restore and enhance "culture." But if, as Nietzsche and common sense argue, it is a low egotism connected with egalitarianism that threatens the higher, then the *bourgeoisie* is just a middle ground in a cultural descent from aristocracy to socialism. However that may be, there is no doubt that however foolish, merely snobbish, or even dangerous, the men of the Right (including most of the great novelists and poets) could be, some of them had a genuine concern for "culture" in whatever serious sense it might have, while the Left (particularly in its Marxist variety) is only preoccupied with economics, fobbing us off with abstractions while undermining what serious art there has been, with the possible exception of Brecht. The Right rejected the modern project in a variety of ways because its adherents had an experience of beauty for which they could not find a place in modern theory and practice. The Marxists had no such experience; their movement just wanted to include all that was said to be good, while actually they could talk seriously only about the body and its needs. Although Eliot's criticism and social theory are trivial, they certainly came out of his felt needs as a poet. There are few, if any, comparable examples to be found within Marxism.

DISTANT LIGHTS
AND APPROACHING TORCHES

But perhaps the Right/Left alternative is not necessarily exhaustive in this matter. The quiet voice of Tocqueville can teach us much. He was the last delicate bloom of that brilliant aristocracy of the *ancien régime*. His soul quivered with responsiveness to the finest and rarest things; it was surely more refined than that of most of the complainers about our vulgarity. His description of Pascal and the improbability of his like in the new order is searing. His was a rare palate. But look at the spiritual health with which he accepts modern democracy, where there is little place for his kind. He never doubted the superior justice of democracy. Against the Left, he argues that extreme equality can destroy justice and that certain good things of the past would have a difficult life in a democracy. Against the Right, he argues that there were severe intellectual failings in the order they still cherish, and he provides a model of taste in the changing world that the Right cannot match. His attempt is to preserve an awareness of the permanent and perfect in the changing and imperfect. All real regimes are changing and imperfect. It is a most serious responsibility of the thinker to glimpse the eternal while living in the ephemeral. It is a great, a fatal, error to commit that eternal to the ephemeral. Distance is what is required, but one has to begin from where one is. Tocqueville's chapters on the intellectual life of the Americans are the best thing ever written on our peculiar intellectual vices and dangers, without trying to give anyone the impression that things were ever much better in reality, without engendering sentimentality or petulance. He outlines the task that the seeker after eternity faces within the particular horizon of this regime. Each of the aspects of human spiritual endeavor is treated on its own, not lumped together as "culture." For some of them there is more hope in democracy, for others less. But there is a continuing respect for the permanence of the human longing for the true and the beautiful. Reading these chapters inevitably causes a sweet sadness. But perhaps that is just right for us. One cannot read them seriously without becoming a bit cultivated, which at least partly means to become self-aware by measuring ourselves against the permanent human alternatives. It is only when we no longer are aware of them that we will be barbarians.

And it is this loss of awareness with which we are faced, and not because of commerce or, at most, only partly so. Tocqueville prescribed for our ills a small number of universities dedicated to the study of the Greek and Latin classics, works he thought particularly suited to counterpoise our tendencies and give experience of what we are not likely to see around us. It is the universities in a commercial society that must be the repositories of the highest things because for various reasons neither the government, the workplace, nor the church can care for them. And liberal democracy lavishly supported these centers of subversion of, these standing reproaches to, its life. Practically anything could be thought or said in them.

For "culture," what are called "the humanities" is the crucial area. The humanities are now failing, not for want of support but for want of anything to say. The study of those old books, for their own sakes, for the wisdom and the taste they give us, is no longer vital, certainly not in the way the Bible was and still partly is for the religious, or Aristotle was for the philosophic. "Culture" has ended up as the collection of past illusions in a museum of which we are the curators. Truth is not to be found there. We know too much for that, and too much to start anew. Why this has happened is a complicated question. "Culture" itself is, I have tried to say, partly responsible for what has happened to culture. But I would like to end with a few words on the latest and perhaps the last threat to our sources of freedom and inspiration.

One thing the newer movements—all of which agree about the degradation of life in modernity—never doubted is that old philosophy has been refuted, that we know better, have a higher level of consciousness, if only that we know that everything is relative to "culture." Arendt may prefer Periclean Athens, but she never doubted that Heidegger was wiser than Plato. But the only way Plato, or any old author, can be taken seriously is if one believes that the decisive truth of which we are ignorant may be found in him. Otherwise study of the classics is trifling. As merely part of our heritage, or whatever, they wither on the vine. This is what made it possible to put them in the museum. But in the museum they still had an objective existence. One could go to them if one wanted to and be solicited by them.

The danger that we might be liberated by them and not play our proper role in history is now being astutely faced by what is called "deconstructionism." It is a dogmatic, academic nihilism of the Left, and proposes to do for literature what Huey Long promised in politics: "Every man a critic." There is no text, there are only interpretations. This is the final step in making modern man satisfied with himself. There is no outside, and above all there is nothing higher. This is also the final step in so-called Marxist humanism, which recognized that "vulgar" Marxism made a travesty of literary interpretation. Of course, "vulgar" Marxism is true Marxism. For the real Marx every consciousness is dependent on the objective relations of property. This new school liberates consciousness from Marx's trammels. But where does it really come from? It is just platitudinized Nietzsche and Heidegger, men of the Right whose whole struggle was against everything that Marxism represents.

Deconstructionism is a kind of circus performance in which Nietzsche is sawed into many pieces, and then the magician miraculously puts him back together and, lo and behold, Nietzsche is a Marxist, albeit not a "vulgar" Marxist. The most profound and intense effort on behalf of "culture"—Nietzsche's effort—is swallowed up by the Last Man. Nietzsche regretfully gave up objectivity in order to salvage art from Marxist objectivity. His work is used to further—however incoherently—Marxist objectivity by relativizing other kinds of objectivity. The invocation of Nietzsche on the Left is equivalent to Stalin's invocation of God—it makes no intellectual sense, but it helps with the simpletons. All the excitement of Nietzsche can then be used to disguise our alternatives, which are either Western or Soviet intellectual life. When there is no real Plato or Locke left, when the gentle light of great books is forever obscured by the burning torches of whimsical interpretation, our window to the world will have been closed.

THE STUDY OF TEXTS

I HAVE BEEN asked to address the question "How ought the next generation of political philosophers to be educated?" I suppose what is meant is really "How ought the next generation of professors of political philosophy to be educated?" We cannot prescribe to genius; and it can, for the most part, take care of itself. Philosophy is not a profession like medicine or shoemaking. Professors of political philosophy can, however, be trained, and their function is to take advantage of genius and to help to make it accessible to others. They can also help the philosophers by preserving in the form of a tradition what was taught by the philosophers—thereby both serving the public good and keeping alive the matter on which potential philosophers must feed.

But our question is a good one, for it contains an "ought": and if we succeed in answering it, we shall prove that political philosophy is possible, that it is capable of producing "valid normative statements." Our claim to recognition stands or falls with this capacity. The question is also good because it forces us to take stock of ourselves from the most advantageous standpoint: our students. We cannot, from this perspective, fail to look beyond our specialties to the whole human being we should like to see come to be: and we must look to the most general problems of our discipline. No time could be more appropriate for our questioning, for political philosophy's claim to be the queen of the social sciences or the study of man as well as the guide of statesmen is scarcely honored. Political philosophy is in crisis; its very possibility is doubted, nay denied, by the most powerful movements of contemporary thought. And that crisis is identical with the crisis of the West, because the crisis of the West is a crisis of belief— belief in the justice of our principles.

In order to educate for political philosophy, there must be some
agreement about what it is. It might be suggested that political philosophy is the quest for knowledge of the best way of life, of the most
comprehensive good, or of justice and the best regime. This implies
that there exists a good which is knowable. Both the existence of the
good and our capacity to know it by reason are denied by positivism
and historicism, and two most powerful intellectual forces of our time.
One important strand of contemporary thought denies even the desirability of such knowledge.

Of course, political philosophy is the quest for such knowledge,
not necessarily, nor even probably, its actualization. In fact, since
philosophy, by its very name, implies the pursuit of wisdom—an
unending search in which every certitude is counterpoised by a more
powerful doubt—the best political philosophy can provide is clarity
about the fundamental alternatives to the solution of the human problem. Here again there is a presupposition: there are permanent alternatives which can be identified.

Given that what is wanted is an openness to the fundamental
alternatives, what education conduces most to it? I shall note only in
passing the kind of character required for profiting from an education
in political philosophy. Its presence must be assumed; one can at best
encourage it; it cannot be made. The prime constituents are love of
justice and love of truth. These two are in some measure in contradiction, and a discrete mating of the two is rare; for love of justice
borders on and usually involves indignation, which overwhelms the
dispassionateness and lack of partisanship requisite to science, while
love of truth removes a person from that concern for the particular
demanded by justice. Aristotle says that political science lies somewhere between mathematics and rhetoric. The attempt to make it
mathematical would destroy its phenomena. Abandoning it to mere
taste would be a renunciation of reason in the most important questions. It partakes of theory and practice, reason and passion, and from
the two extreme perspectives seems either unscientific or not engaged.
It is therefore particularly vulnerable to the temptations of the extremes—to sham science or fanatic commitment. (In this light the
wildly varying dispositions toward political philosophy in the last generation can be seen as a particular expression of a perennial problem—
a problem exacerbated by a new kind of science and a new kind of
religiosity.) The man who practices political philosophy must make
that union, impossible according to Pascal, between l'esprit de géométrie
and l'esprit de finesse, and will appear open to the charges of being
unscientific and irrelevant. He must resist public opinion and his own
conscience.

Now, given this disposition, what is necessary for nourishing it properly? The answer is the careful study of texts, of the classic texts of the tradition—that and not much else. This is what is most needful—always, and particularly in our time. This assertion appeals neither to the behavioral scientists nor to those who think our purpose is not to understand reality, but to change it. It seems at best merely scholarly, denying as it does the decisive superiority of our current knowledge over that of the past and the peculiarity or essentially unique character of our problems. These objections to the study of texts are perpetually made, and political philosophy by very definition both calls them forth and rejects them. But they appear particularly strong today, when knowledge of the tradition is particularly weak. Therefore they must be addressed.

First, to speak to the reasons for the concentration on texts at all times, as opposed to our very special need, it is hard to imagine serious reflection which begins *de novo*, which is not sublimated to a higher level by a richly developed literary-philosophic tradition, transmitted in the form of writings. However radical a break from the tradition a thinker may make, the consciousness of the problems, the very awareness that there are problems as well as the knowledge of what it takes to respond to them, comes from being imbued with that tradition. This is not to deny that the problems are permanent and ubiquitous or that the human mind is at all times and places potentially capable of grasping them. It is not an assertion that the character of knowledge is essentially traditional or that the mind is essentially related to a particular culture. But there are preconditions to the mind's activity; it must above all have substance on which to work. Raw experience does not suffice. Experience comes to sight in the form of opinion, and the examination and elaboration of opinions makes experience broader and deeper. Only he who has seen through the eyes of profound and subtle observers can be aware of the complex articulation of things. Socrates without the teachings of Parmenides and Heraclitus would not have had his issues to address, nor would his superiority have been tested were his competition not of this quality. I venture to suggest that great philosophic men were almost always great scholars. They were studiers of their predecessors, not for the reasons which ordinarily motivate scholars, but because they believed, almost literally, that their salvation depended on it, that those earlier thinkers may have possessed the most important truths.

Great natural scientists have not in general needed to be great scholars. At most they have had to address themselves to the preceding generation of scientists in addition to their contemporaries. The modern natural sciences have been progressive, and their great success has made them a model for all learning. Their example would seem to prove that certain important questions can be decided forever, and that the thought of those who lived before their solution is decisively inferior to that of those who lived after.

Aristotle's knowledge of the movements of the heavens is doubt-less inferior to that of almost any college student today. The model of the natural sciences has contributed much to the contempt for tradition in philosophy. Scholarship would seem to belong to the same order of rank in relation to philosophy as does history of science in relation to science. History of science is evidently of lower rank than science and is also not necessary to it.

The issue is whether modern science is not a special offshoot of modern philosophy—which is surely questionable. Its success may very well be due to its very partialness. The doubts now current about both the goodness of natural science and its relation to the real world give some support to this view. But, without entering into these difficult and troubling questions, surely natural science is not the privileged model. From the perspective of the whole, Aristotle does not come off so badly. A scientist like Bertrand Russell may despise him, but a philosopher like Hegel can show that, in the most important re-spects, Aristotle is superior to Newton. And to do so, Hegel had to know Aristotle very well. If Hegel had stayed within the confines of the scientific opinions of his contemporaries, he would not have seen the great difficulties in them. Aristotle was the precondition of Hegel's liberation. Machiavelli, Rousseau, and Nietzsche would not have en-joyed their admirable intellectual freedom if they did not know Plato well and had accepted the prevailing notion that he had simply been refuted or outdated. Every new beginning—like that of Descartes, for example—implies a certain rejection of the past. But it takes on its significance in the light of what it rejects. The new beginning becomes a tradition in its turn, and those who follow it forget its origins in a confrontation with another kind of thought. They are tradition-bound, and when the new tradition proves to have difficulties of its own, they are no longer aware of an alternative to it. Their perspective seems natural and, although itself problematic, superior to what went before, which is only known in the light of their tradition.

If we do not have completed, final wisdom, then our most im-portant task is the articulation of the fundamental alternatives. This can be achieved only by maintaining an authentic knowledge of the best earlier thought, understood in its own terms, divested of distor-tions imparted to it by the thought which superseded it. Descartes gave a full presentation not only of the prescientific world but also of the previous philosophic interpretations of it. Those who followed him accepted his rejection of earlier thought without themselves having gone through his analysis. What was still a serious alternative for Descartes no longer was one to his followers, and knowledge of it decayed. Thus knowledge of the tradition of philosophy is necessary to philosophy and required for philosophic freedom from tradition. Philosophy has, at its peaks, largely been dialogue between the greats, no matter how far separated in time. Without the voices which come from outside the cave constituted by our narrow horizon, we are ever more bound to it. And, according to at least one version, philosophy is liberation from the bonds which attach us to the cave.

In our time the study of texts is particularly needful. Never has the challenge to political philosophy been so great. Historicism, cultural relativism, and positivism join in agreeing that the old notions about the good and the way of knowing it must be wrong, that traditional political philosophy was a dream because it did not possess the historical insight or the awareness of the arbitrariness of value judgments. Although in doubt about most things, the modern movements are sure about that. They have not succeeded in finding a substitute guide for human life, and the present situation borders on nihilism. It behooves us to reflect on that situation, and to determine whether the understanding of things which results in it is adequate. The issue is whether our thought is derivative from a particular way of posing the problems, or whether it establishes its principles independently.

For example, the fact-value distinction is taken as a given by almost everyone today, no matter whether they are behavioral scientists or committed revolutionaries. Whether it has been proven that values cannot be derived from facts, or whether that very distinction has any grounding in the phenomena—as opposed to being a mere fiction resulting from certain doubtful philosophic interpretations of phenomena—is hardly discussed. The distinction is removed from the context from which it was derived and treated as an independent truth. And the knowledge of that context and what is opposed to it has decayed.

The search for a fresh start would require a purging of acquired prejudices and of all the categories of thought and speech derived from contemporary or recent philosophy. This task requires a return to the beginning points of thought, to the prescientific or prephilosophic or natural world. Otherwise one sees the world through the screen of one articulation of the phenomena or another and is locked into the interpretation which one wishes to question. And the origins are peculiarly difficult of access for us who live in a world transformed by science and an intellectual atmosphere permeated by ideology. Ours is the age when philosophy and science—i.e., a certain kind of philosophy and science—have triumphed.

Philosophy and science have become involved in life and have changed the world. They are no longer observers or monitors. This is a unique circumstance; in the past, science did not try to replace the errors of the cave by substituting itself for them. In doing so, it risked becoming itself an error and no longer having the means to correct itself. Previously, the world had a diversity not caused by science, from which science could gather its interpretations; now the world tends to become the result of a particular interpretation, and, thus, to bear witness to it. For example, an economist's hypothesis that man's primary motive is gain can now become policy: a nation which encouraged that motive might end up producing men who prove the hypothesis. Only by looking outside that nation would one be able to regain a basis for recovering man as he is and for calling the hypothesis into question. In general, our world and our minds have much in common with my example. There is a unanimity in the world about the principles of science, while we are approaching one about the principles of politics. To see the latter uniformity, one need only compare the serious intellectual alternatives advanced in the 1930s— alternatives already relatively impoverished, compared with the past— with those available today. Now there are practically nothing but liberals and communists, who also share much with respect to ends, and there are practically no regimes with any vitality which are not supported by one of these two kinds of thought. The principle of equality, which is surely not simply self-evident, and should be the result of enlightenment and should be able to be defended against its serious opponents, has degenerated into a prejudice. Now, most serious of all, we are losing competence not only in those authors who could challenge our favorite beliefs but also in those who could best support them. The self-awareness of modern man depends on a knowledge of our intellectual roots and on a quest to rediscover the world on which the artificial world created by modernity is more or less well-grounded.

The threatened character of our self-awareness is strikingly illustrated by the most celebrated book on questions of political thought published in the Anglo-Saxon world in recent years, John Rawls's *A Theory of Justice*. It presents a new theoretical ground for liberal de-

mocracy. But it begins by dismissing discussion of its egalitarian premise. It is only an analysis of what an egalitarian society should be, if
you accept that equality is just. Rawls begins by assuming, or taking
for granted, that which political philosophy always took as its task to
prove or investigate. We can no longer take the alternatives seriously;
we intuit the justice of equality. Thus the longing to *know* the truth
about these questions is dogmatically denied its fulfillment and we are
given over to what may only be the dominant prejudice of the day.
Rawls devotes no time to proving that such knowledge is not accessible. From the outset the most important question, the one which
motivated philosophy and the possible answer to which inspired and
elevated those who think, is ruled out of bounds. But this is not what
is most striking; it is rather Rawls's easygoingness about our situation,
the absence of anguish over our impotence, the conviction that the
consequences are not dreadful.

The other salient quality of this book, related to the first one, is
the great ignorance of the tradition of political philosophy manifested
in it. Although Rawls uses ideas which come to him through the
tradition, they are accepted traditionally, used partially to support his
predetermined purposes, and very frequently distorted. There is no
indication that at any point he felt compelled to question his own
framework because of the force of what came from outside.

Rawls's book attempts to renew the contract teaching of the state
of nature theorists. But he abandons their insistence on nature and
therefore finds himself without a sanction for justice and observance
of the contract. More scholarship would have given him at least the
outline of what would have been required to construct a meaningful
contract. He would also have seen what possibilities have to be sacrificed in a contract teaching as opposed to one which, for example,
regards man as naturally a political animal; and he would have been
forced to come to grips with problems he hardly knows exist.

For example, Rawls puts forward a doctrine of "primary goods,"
ultimately derived from Hobbes. These "primary goods" are, in essence, means to any possible end, and are therefore good because
desirable to all men, no matter what their end. Rawls says that money
is one of the most important, if not the most important, of such goods.
He does not realize that the maximization of wealth can only be
considered unproblematically good if poverty is held to be a good by
no one. But Christianity praised poverty; and Hobbes, who was quite
aware of what he was doing, had to denigrate Christianity. His state-
of-nature teaching is a substitute for the biblical account of man's
original situation. One has to decide between these two positions

before an instrumental good can be considered simply good. Rawls really assumes that certain kinds of ends, for which the primary goods are evils, either do not exist or are untrue. He thus fails to present the radicalness of the political problem, which stems from the radical diversity of possible ends. He contributes to a narrowing of our horizons and an unfounded hopefulness about potential agreement among men. He accepts as a given Hobbes's transformation of religion or the world in which religion lives, and thereby reasons from a world that is unproblematic for him because, living in Hobbes's world, he no longer sees its problems. He is enabled to criticize Locke and Rousseau for intolerance when they proscribe certain religious beliefs from civil society because he sees that the religions can, contrary to Locke and Rousseau, live together in peace. What he does not see is that the religions he observes have been transformed by the Enlightenment thinkers and are only tame species of the genus religion. He utterly misses what Hobbes and Locke and Rousseau were doing. Religion is not a serious question to him. It is just another one of the many ends that can be pursued in a liberal society. He is unaware that liberal society is predicated on a certain understanding of religion, one that excludes other understandings. What is perhaps the most serious question facing a serious man—the religious question—is almost a matter of indifference to him.

I chose these two related matters of wealth and religion in Rawls because there is today a large measure of complacent agreement about them which needs most rigorous examination and doubt. The philosopher now, instead of waking us up, contributes to our sleep. Rawls is drawn completely into the circle of current opinion because he is closed to what is outside of it. He can say that universalization is not of the essence of Kant's moral teaching, showing that he has not reflected on what freedom is in Kant; he can call Nietzsche—perhaps the most extreme antiteleologist who ever lived, the man who called Darwin a teleologist—a teleologist; he can invoke Aristotle to support his view that the greatest possible complexity is desirable by referring to a passage where Aristotle says simplicity is best. If this were to be the type of nourishment provided by philosophy, our children would starve. Before we become attached to new answers, we must find out the questions.

We must turn to the greats of the tradition; but in a fresh spirit, as though they were unknown to us, almost as though they were prophets bringing news of unknown worlds and to whom we must listen with self-abandon instead of forcing them to pass before our inquisition. Above all, we must put our questions aside and try to find out what were their questions. We must avoid the example of the compilers of the renowned *Syntopicon* who indexed *justice* in all the political philosophers. One junior researcher could find no discussion of justice in Locke's *Treatises on Civil Government* and saw that he almost never uses the word. The editor said there must be such a discussion. What would a catalogue of reflections on justice which did not contain the name of Locke be? So they had to invent a thematic discussion to which the index referred. And thus they missed a great discovery.

But who are these men to whom such reverent attention should be paid? How do we establish the names on a list when I am arguing that we are in large measure ignorant about what we need to know? One can begin from the general agreement about who the great philosophers were, especially the farther away they are in time and fads have dissipated. This is not canonic! The proof of the pudding is, of course, in the eating. But it is a beginning. A second and sounder criterion is what the thinkers say about one another. Spinoza's praise of Machiavelli turns us to reflections on Machiavelli as well as teaching us something important about Spinoza. Hobbes's attack on Aristotle shows us that Aristotle is the man to attack. It is almost always the case that serious men look to serious opponents and go to the roots of that which they wish to destroy. And following this same road, one finds writers neglected by us because the limitation of our views makes them seem slight or irrelevant. Machiavelli and Rousseau had the highest opinion of Xenophon; for us he is nothing. That difference or change in taste can point the way to fundamental problems, such as the different value once set on moderation even by the apparently immoderate Machiavelli and Rousseau. This procedure results in a relatively small number of classic books, a list established not subjectively by means of current criteria, but generated immanently by the writers themselves. I argue that there is a high degree of agreement among the writers themselves as to who merits serious consideration. The writers of quality know the writers of quality. Moreover, from this internal dialogue between the books emerges a high degree of agreement about the permanent questions as opposed to the questions of the day.

The closest reading of these books is my prescription. But there is so much that stands in the way of such a close reading, at least as the core of an education. To begin with, to follow Tocqueville's analysis of American intellectual proclivities, we are not a theoretical people. The appearance of uselessness goes counter to our concentration on utility. The notion of speculation for the sake of speculation is not one that accords with any inner experience of the dominant part of the regime, and seems even to contain an element of immorality, particularly in things political which touch the passions so closely. In political science over the past thirty years, there have been two trends in regard to political philosophy, trends apparently contradictory, but issuing from the same source. Either political philosophy has been rejected as ineffective, or it has been embraced as the source of commitment to revolutionary change as opposed to the conformist tendencies of political science as a whole. Men like Pascal, who thought the only thing that counted was the unremitting quest for the knowledge of God, are not native to our soil. Nor are men like Archimedes, who destroyed all of his writings on his extraordinary inventions in engineering because they smacked of low necessity. We believe our business is too pressing for such self-indulgence. *Relevance* was just another expression of our deepest instinct. And connected with this untheoretical nature is a distrust or contempt for tradition. As Tocqueville puts it, tradition has no authoritative status for us. It is just another piece of information. Authority is no doubt contrary to the philosophic spirit, but respect for tradition helps to keep alive and give respect to what would not otherwise be taken seriously. The Scholastics took Aristotle as an authority, which was surely a mistake. But thereby he was preserved and available for those capable of understanding. We, on the other hand, free from the prejudice in favor of old authority, are likely to neglect what it can teach us. The democratic principle tends to make every man the judge of what is worthwhile, and the authority of special intelligence is not more likely to be respected than that of wealth or birth, particularly inasmuch as it is less easy to recognize. There is an ever-diminishing impact of the books which gave men a common vision and a common spiritual substance. This is merely a culmination of the penchants Tocqueville so powerfully described. And the control on these penchants exercised by our intellectual tutelage to Europe, where philosophy and the literary tradition connected with it played a greater role and were more part of the real life of nations, has almost disappeared with our emancipation from them and the assimilation of their regimes and education to ours.

Our students, in addition to not loving books, possess two contrary dispositions which combine to undermine the study of books in the quest for truth. They are persuaded that values are relative, partly on intellectual grounds, partly because such a belief seems more conducive to democracy and tolerance. Thus they know beforehand that the books are wrong in their claim to decide questions of good and bad. At the same time, they in general share an unquestioned and unquestionable—almost religious—conviction of the truth of the principle of equality. Since this is a contentious issue in the tradition, with many of the older writers against it, such writers seem to be teachers of vice rather than thoughtful men.

Once having overcome the prejudice against books, one is still only at the beginning of the task of a fresh look at them. Aside from the wide acceptance of historicism and positivism, which makes the claims of the older writers seem deluded, there are special doctrines which act as a screen between us and the books and give us the impression that we know what is most important about them before we begin reading them. The common view that economic or psychological or historical factors determine the thought of philosophers of course assumes that the philosophers are wrong, both because they all argue that thought can be free from any other determination than the truth, and because one must know that an opinion is untrue to explain its source in anything other than the truth. The sociology of knowledge is a misnomer; it can only properly be called the sociology of error. And if it is true that the philosophers are necessarily in error, then their study is the business of triflers. That it is important to know that Plato was an aristocrat or Hobbes a *bourgeois*, that Machiavelli was a man of the Renaissance and Montesquieu a man of the Enlightenment, that Rousseau and Nietzsche were mad seems so self-evident that it is almost impossible to see how one would proceed without such crutches. But as soon as one has accepted these commonplaces, one has subverted the study of the books, because such views teach us what to look for and take as facts what needs to be proved. They also presuppose that they emerge from a true framework, or one that is metaphysically neutral, that the practitioners of this scholarship cannot be subjected to a similar analysis. Almost all modern scholarship, beginning with classical philology, started from the assumption that its fundamental ideas were superior to those of the authors it studied and placed these authors in a context alien to them. Even such simple categories as idealist and realist, liberal and conservative are profoundly misleading although they seem to us as natural as night and day.

The only way to break out of this circle of subjectivism—and subjectivism it is, because, although arguing that it is objective, its adherents also admit somehow that they, too, are historically determined, and therefore tacitly accept that the next generation will interpret differently, making the philosophers nothing but the contradictory things various ages of scholars say about them—is to try to understand the philosophers as they understood themselves, to try to determine their intention, accepting the possibility that they may have fulfilled their intention and attained the truth. This is a naïve undertaking, but the recovery of innocence can be salutary. It implies a severe rupture, not only with the presuppositions of modern scholarship, but also with its results. One can be heartened by the reflection that Thomas Aquinas was a very good interpreter of Aristotle, and Rousseau of Plato, without the enormous apparatus that now stands between us and the texts.

What does it mean to understand the authors as they understood themselves? For example, Machiavelli says that he was doing something totally new. This claim is not generally accepted. More and more he is assimilated, on the one hand, to earlier thinkers, and on the other, to the more conventional thought of his own time. As I just mentioned, he is called a man of the Renaissance. But if Renaissance means anything, it means the rebirth of classical Greek and Roman antiquity. Machiavelli, however, rejected both the thought and the practice of classical antiquity. He believed he had found a new and superior ground on which to erect the structure of politics. In adopting the myth of the man of the Renaissance, one assumes what one cannot know—what the Renaissance was really like, and whether there was a typical man and thinker—and distorts with this imaginary standard what we can know—Machiavelli's text. We note the similarities between Machiavelli and his contemporaries, and become blind to the differences separating them. This provides a second general maxim: in what appears similar, one should look for the differences; and in the different, the similar. But it is especially the differences on which one must concentrate. It is taken for granted that when Machiavelli adopts the language or the tone of his contemporaries that he does so fully and sincerely, but that when he argues for his peculiarity he is mistaken and vain. It is true that *The Prince* resembles the traditional mirrors of princes in some respects. But nothing in them resembles the teachings of e.g., *Prince* XV and XXV. Thrasymachus, to take another familiar comparison, surely agrees with Machiavelli that men pursue their private interest exclusively; he is "hardheaded," but he never suggests that this self-interest can be the basis of a policy conducive to the public interest.

All of these appealing generalizations are nothing but impediments. One should pick up *The Prince* and read it as though it were written by a contemporary, as though it were a personal communication to one about something of common concern. In this way we abandon the categories which we allow to become habitual due to a lack of a sense of urgency. A line-by-line, word-by-word analysis must be undertaken, for Machiavelli is a difficult writer and we do not have the habit of reading carefully. The hardest thing of all is the simplest to formulate: every word must be understood. It is hard because the eye tends to skip over just those things which are most shocking or most call into question our way of looking at things. One simple definition of the philosopher is that he is the man who thinks concretely without the aid of abstractions which order things but at the same time really hide them. The study of great philosophers is an education in concrete consciousness, but it can easily degenerate into a support for abstractions. This is the reason the novelist and the poet are great helps to the philosophic intellect. They, at their best, stay close to particulars; and their rich consciousness of particularity, combined with judicious generalization, is a way toward the formulation of philosophic principle. This is why Plato and many others wrote in a form resembling poetry in which all explicit generalizations are false and the real generalizations are left to the reader to make for himself on the basis of the experience provided by the book. Thus the books are not only educations in concreteness but provide powerful lessons in the deceptiveness of easy generalizations and, properly studied, liberate us from them. In this way they make that union of *l'esprit de finesse* and *l'esprit de géométrie* of which I spoke earlier. He who reads books which do not display inquiry itself but its results, like those of Aristotle and Hegel, risks misunderstanding the depth and breadth of common sense experience presupposed by their general formulations. They write for those who are already philosophers. This is why, for us, the study of thinkers like Plato, Machiavelli, and Rousseau is most appropriate. They show the way as well as they present the end. Relying again on Tocqueville, there is a peculiar democratic addiction to general ideas. The tendencies which our regimes foster most need counterbalancing. The study of texts, however distant it may seem from the phenomenological movement, has a similar motive and is a reaction to the impoverishment of the world of experience as a result of general ideas and is an attempt to recover that world in order, ultimately, that one have better general ideas. I have implied earlier that the study of texts is superior as a means to this end, inasmuch as the new beginning requires a new self-awareness which is not likely to be obtained by unaided self-examination.

However that may be, in reading Machiavelli we tend to miss the obvious. The argument or example that seems irrelevant, trivial, or boring is precisely the one most likely to be the sign of what is outside of one's framework and which calls it into question. One passes over such things unless one takes pencil and paper, outlines, counts, stops at everything, and tries to wonder. Our failure to see is a result not only of laziness or lack of intelligence but of our unwillingness to believe that Machiavelli could have thought or taught this or that thing. This unwillingness is a result either of our moralism or of certain notions about what men in the Renaissance thought. How often I have heard men of high intelligence, goodwill, and learning reject an obvious point, clearly stated in the text, with the remark, "No man in the sixteenth century could have thought such a thing!" To take another example, in the study of Plato, it is practically taken for granted that Socrates' trial was politically motivated and that the charge of impiety was only a pretext. This interpretation goes counter to everything the texts of the *Apology* and other dialogues say. Why is the text taken so lightly? Because from modern scholarship we learn that the Athenians were not serious about such things. The real source of that modern scholarly opinion is an argument made in the seventeenth and eighteenth centuries by men like Bayle, Gibbon, and Montesquieu that Christianity was the source of intolerance. They consciously rationalized Greek and Roman politics in order to present it as a favorable contrast in matters of religion to modern nations so much affected by the religions founded on biblical revelation. Thus the real charge against Socrates is ignored because we are influenced by earlier thinkers who knew what they were about. But we think we have founded our knowledge of the Greeks on scientific philology. The blindness to our own thought and to the text of Plato is fraught with consequences. The importance of religion and the critique of it in Plato is missed. This only supports the current easygoingness concerning the religious question about which I have spoken. The value of Plato as an articulator of problems we forget is thus lost. A curious contradiction in contemporary thought leads to the view that, on the one hand, the Athenians did not take the gods to be the most important beings and, on the other hand, that Socrates was conventionally pious. The text of the *Apology* teaches that Socrates was guilty as charged: that he did not believe in the gods of the city. And this is not a merely scholarly point, because the case of Athens and Socrates is typical, according to Plato. All cities must have gods, and all philosophers must doubt their existence. If this is the case, the rationalization of politics is impossible. The possibility of that rationalization is taken for granted in most of modern political thought. (Only Rousseau—the greatest modern reader of Plato—makes the rejection of that possibility an important part of his teaching. For this stand Rousseau is taken to be a crank.) And this belief is one of the most important and pervasive influences in contemporary politics. The alternative to it is obscured by apparent science. Just looking at Plato open-mindedly would free us from our prejudice.

Openness is the general principle in the study of texts. But it is a different kind of openness from that which is most praised today. Contemporary openness is based on closedness to the possibility of the truth of the thought of the past, whereas the openness required is one that can call into question our openness and the specific modern thought on which it is based. To achieve such an openness nothing more is required than deideologization and the love of truth. There are no universally applicable rules of interpretation, for each author has different intentions and a different rhetoric. Each must be understood from within. He must be worn like a pair of glasses through which we see the world. It is unlikely that we shall be able to read many books in such a way, but the experience of one book profoundly read will teach more than many read lightly, because the most important experience is not the dazzling succession of ill-conceived ideas, but the recognition of seriousness. He who has read one book well is in a position to read any book, while he for whom books are easy currency is rendered incapable of living fully with one.

In all this what may seem most perverse is my apparent denigration of scholarship, particularly historical scholarship. Books have something to do with the time and the language in which they were written, and they are full of references which only the learned can understand. It is almost inconceivable that it should be argued that we are not greatly aided by all the research of the last ages. And I would agree that learning is a good thing, if it is not learning for its own sake and if that learning serves the understanding of the books instead of encouraging the use of the books as raw material for the scholar's system. Another maxim is that our learning should be guided strictly by the author's understanding. We should learn about history from Machiavelli; look to those authors to whom Machiavelli refers us; take seriously the teachings he takes seriously. He should be our preceptor, and we should follow his curriculum.

The first thing a student will observe is that Machiavelli is written in Italian. If he does not know Italian, he must learn it. There are translations, but one cannot trust them. But if he learns Italian as the translators learned Italian, he might as well not learn Italian. For example, none of the translators translates *virtù* as *virtue*, at least not uniformly.[1] They say that it does not mean *virtue* in Machiavelli or in the Renaissance. When *virtù* seems to designate what the translator

---

[1] Now there is finally a very good translation, by Harvey C. Mansfield, Jr. (University of Chicago Press, 1985). Even he would agree, however, that this does not do away with the need to learn Italian.

thinks virtue is, he renders it virtue. When it does not, he will use *ability, ingenuity,* or whatever. But Machiavelli uses the same word and actually plays on the traditional use to indicate his transvaluation of values. In one place he uses it three times in two sentences, designating radically different things and thus says something very shocking. But the translators use three or at least two different words, thereby destroying the teaching. The problem is not one of philology, but of the conventionalism of mind of the translators. They think Machiavelli could not mean what he says. Inaccurate translation reflects inaccuracy of understanding, the tyranny of the scholar's prejudice over the matter to which he should be subservient. To learn Italian for the sake of understanding Machiavelli as the translators understand him is a waste of time. Most of the important words Machiavelli uses can be understood by following his use of them, and to do that requires no sophisticated science, just a lot of work. Anyone who takes the trouble to study Rousseau's use of the expression *le peuple* will find that this great friend of the people means pretty much the same thing as does Plato when he uses *dēmos:* the hopelessly prejudiced many. Someone might retort that one has to know Plato to recognize that. But Rousseau himself refers the reader to Plato in the clearest way. And this is only another proof that it is not Rousseau's own time that is most helpful in understanding him. Plato is much more important for interpreting Rousseau than is Voltaire. The education required for studying Rousseau can be learned from Rousseau. And incidentally, one gets a better understanding of Plato from a man of Rousseau's caliber than one would from the most learned philologist. This is only indicative of how the study of one author can lead to a grasp of the tradition as a whole and entirely from within.

Our students must, then, learn languages, and that is not to their taste. But they must be guided by their philosophic concern in the study of languages and not be carried away into the infinite labyrinths of philology. Far more important is that they keep thinking of the book of the world and comparing the words in the philosopher's book to the things in the world.

Similarly, Machiavelli talks about historical events and persons. Must we not know what happened in its fullness to see whether Machiavelli is right and how he interprets? But this presupposes that we have a true account against which to measure Machiavelli's account. In reality it comes down to accepting some modern historian's view as opposed to Machiavelli's. Moreover this supposes that Machiavelli's intention is to give an accurate historical account rather than to make a specific point for which he is willing to distort the facts. In *Prince* II Machiavelli speaks of two dukes of Ferrara as though they were the same. But a moment's reflection will prove that this is intentional, that he wishes to indicate that in solid, traditional states it makes little difference who rules. In III he speaks of Louis XII's invasions of Italy. In VII and XI he gives very different accounts of those invasions. Putting the three accounts together, one can see that Machiavelli wishes to show that Italian politics are controlled and corrupted by the Roman Catholic Church. He first presents Louis as an independent actor, and gradually reveals, to those who pay attention, that Louis was the dupe of Alexander VI. This history can be constructed internally, and most scholarly history would stand in the way of recognizing it.

Finally, in *The Prince*, Machiavelli refers to other books, most especially the Bible and Xenophon. One is expected to know their significance. It goes without saying that Machiavelli counted on more cultivated readers than can today be expected, and we must make every effort to be what he wanted us to be in order to teach us. But, again, to understand the Bible or Xenophon, we must begin by recovering what Machiavelli thought the traditional understanding and use of these books was. He refers not to the Bible of the higher criticism, but to the Bible of the believers and the Church. To know the Bible one must be familiar with its text as it is written and at least have some sense of what it means to believe. Then Machiavelli takes over from there. All the contemporary erudition about the Bible does not help us see Machiavelli's interesting use of it—for example, how he rewrites the story of David and Goliath, or his blasphemies about Moses founding a people. Likewise, classical studies have reassured us that Xenophon is simple and a bore, so Machiavelli's learning from him the two forms of liberality—the legitimate, using other people's property, the illegitimate, using one's own—loses its sense. This passage in Machiavelli is essential for understanding his agreement and disagreement with Greek political philosophy. Machiavelli should teach us the wonders of Xenophon, whereas some classical scholarship has given Machiavelli a lesson as to Xenophon's defects.

Study of the texts in this way is an endless task; but so is the study of nature, and the two studies go hand in hand and are almost the same. This is the truly liberal study. One would, of course, ultimately become very learned by means of it. But the learning would have a coherent and authentic character, one related to the highest purposes of life. Great books are full of hidden references and quotes which reveal themselves only to initiates. But there is no shortcut to the initiation: the route goes only by way of the ever-deepening reflection on the books as they relate to the problems of the world.

• • •

An example of the kind of awareness which is not immediately accessible on the surface of the books, which is dependent on a history that emerges immanently from the books, can be drawn from Tocqueville. Tocqueville often is called a conservative and is almost always contrasted with Rousseau, the radical and revolutionary. These are categories—simple ones, ones that seem almost to be of perennial common sense—used in academic and popular discourse. History comes to the aid of these categories to explain Tocqueville's position as a result of reaction to the French Revolution, his aristocratic origins, etc., as opposed to that of Rousseau, the optimist of the Enlightenment, the resentful poor boy. All of this is very plausible and such explanations have a particularly exhilarating effect on the modern mind. But the more one really knows, the less one finds them helpful. I had always accepted this interpretation of Tocqueville, and only recently, forced by facts, my reflections have begun to take a different turn. Tocqueville rarely mentions Rousseau and speaks denigratingly of the *philosophes*. But, while studying *Emile*, I had to teach *Democracy in America*. On coming to the passage on the role of compassion in democracies I was compelled to recognize that it was based on the discussion of compassion in the *Emile*. Not only is the argument the same, but Tocqueville makes the same literary reference, to La Fontaine, as does Rousseau. The latter cannot be an accidental connection, for it is so idiosyncratically Rousseauean. Now this is not a minor question. Compassion is Rousseau's supplement to self-interest as the social bond. This is his correction of the natural right teaching of Hobbes and Locke. Tocqueville agrees with Rousseau that egalitarian society brings forth this disposition and that it is what tempers the selfishness of democratic principles of right. Beginning from there, I looked back over the whole scheme which Tocqueville used to analyze American democracy and realized how great a debt he owes Rousseau. The alternative facing modern man, according to Tocqueville, is egalitarian democracy or egalitarian tyranny. And this is precisely Rousseau's teaching. Aristocracies for both are dead; they were unjust but contained a certain real nobility which is likely to disappear in democracies. Thus the political project for Tocqueville is to preserve freedom in equality and a tincture of nobility in democracy. Such is also Rousseau's intention. What is the way of achieving freedom in equality? Small communities with religious foundations. That is straight Rousseau. The concentration on the size of community was Rousseau's restoration of a classical theme within the context of modern political thought which denied its significance. And the civil religion described in the *Social Contract* closely parallels Tocqueville's descriptions of and prescriptions for religion in democracy. Tocqueville on the family, the role of women, the arts, the habits of mind, and even rhetoric is derivative from Rousseau. In his description of an Indian he once saw Tocqueville even echoes Rousseau's ultimate doubt about the superiority of civilized life for happiness, this again as over against Hobbes and Locke. Tocqueville looked at the king in America, whom Locke said was worse clothed, housed, and fed than the day laborer in England, and asked, as did Rousseau, whether the critical question was put by modern thought: is that king less happy?

One could say much more about this intimate relation between Rousseau and Tocqueville. But I limit myself to indicating the harmony of their views. Why then does Tocqueville not acknowledge his great teacher and why does he appear so moderate? One must look to his addressees and his explicit intention. He writes to reconcile the well-born and the well-educated to democratic principles and life, in order that democracy will not be torn apart by the opposition of its most talented elements and will be tempered by their leadership and participation. Rousseau was a red flag waved before such men. It was not vanity but prudence that caused Tocqueville to hide his debt to Rousseau. The more moderate tone is partly illusory, for Rousseau was much more moderate in expectation than is often thought. Moreover, the principles of the rights of man, revolutionary in the *ancien régime*, were no longer so after the revolution. That debate was over. Tocqueville's business was to make them work politically. I do not argue that Tocqueville is simply the same as Rousseau; but the more I think about it, the difficulty is more on the side of differentiating them than of assimilating them.

To conclude, I should like to say a word about Rousseau himself and the way he should be read. It is often noted that Rousseau is the philosopher who attacked philosophy. This is a blatant contradiction and would seem to stem from the vain love of paradox. But on living with Rousseau, one becomes aware that he attacks philosophy but praises Socrates. That would seem to be a continuation of the same paradox, for Socrates, the founder of political philosophy, did nothing but defend philosophy and try to make it appear divine. However, Rousseau makes it clear that Socrates lived in a world in which philosophy was new, where it was thought to be dangerous and it played no role in public life. Philosophy needed a defense in order to be preserved; it had to be made to appear to be good for political life. But the situation had changed in Rousseau's time. Philosophy was the rage; it had become the adviser to enlightened despots and the comforter and helper of the peoples. Philosophy was becoming a tool of the prejudices and a servant of the selfish passions. For the sake of political virtue and the preservation of true philosophy, the public philosophy had to be attacked. The very opposition in speech between Socrates and Rousseau is indicative of the profoundest agreement in thought. Rousseau's critique of modernity—which means us—comes to light only by way of such reflections.

It is obvious that much stands in the way of the education I propose. Its actualization seems almost impossible—except that it is so simple, so available, and so charming. I have found that young Americans are seduced by the discovery of books—in a book-drenched society—books unadorned with alien paraphernalia. They are thirsty for clarity and inspiration, and they can find both so readily at hand. This is my hope, for almost all that is institutional stands in the way of the study of books. Such an education, whatever its other results, gives the students an experience of the possibilities of human greatness and of community based on shared thought that cannot fail to alter their expectations from politics.

JUSTICE:
JOHN RAWLS VERSUS THE TRADITION
OF POLITICAL PHILOSOPHY

THE PROMISE AND THE PROBLEM

JOHN RAWLS's A *Theory of Justice* has attracted more attention in the Anglo-Saxon world than any work of its kind in a generation. Its vogue results from two facts: it is the most ambitious political project undertaken by a member of the school currently dominant in academic philosophy; and it offers not only a defense of, but also a new foundation for, a radical egalitarian interpretation of liberal democracy. In method and substance it fits the tastes of the times. Professor Rawls believes that he can provide persuasive principles of justice that possess the simplicity and force of older contract teachings, that satisfy utilitarianism's concern for the greatest number without neglecting the individual, that contain all the moral nobility of Kant's principles, that will result in a richness of life akin to that proposed by Aristotle, and that can accomplish all this without falling into the quagmires of traditional philosophy. This is a big book not only in the number of its pages, but in the magnitude of its claims, and it deserves to be measured by standards of a severity commensurate with its proportions.

Liberal democracy is in need of a defense or a rebirth if it is to survive. The practical challenges to it over the last forty years have been extreme, while the thought that underlies it has become incredible to most men living in liberal democracies. Historicism, cultural relativism, and the fact-value distinction have eroded the bases of conviction that this regime is good or just, that reason can support its claims to our allegiance. Hardly anyone would be willing to defend as truth the natural-right teachings of the founders of liberal democracy or of their philosophic masters, as many, for example, defend Marx. The state of nature and the natural rights deriving from it have taken their place beside the divine right of kings in the graveyard of history. They are understood to be myths or ideologies of ruling classes. One need only recall the vitality of the thought of liberal democracy's great opponents, Marx and Nietzsche, and reflect on the absence of comparable proponents to recognize the magnitude of the crisis. A renewal in the light of these challenges, theoretical and practical, is clearly of the first importance.

But, disappointingly, A *Theory of Justice* does not even manifest an awareness of this need, let alone respond to it. In spite of its radical egalitarianism, it is not a radical book. Its horizon does not seem to extend to the abysses which we have experienced in our own lifetimes; the horrors of Hitler and Stalin do not present a special or new problem for Rawls. Rather, his book is a correction of utilitarianism; his consciousness is American, or at most, Anglo-Saxon. The problems he addresses are those of civil liberties in nations that are already free and of the distribution of wealth in those that are already prosperous. The discussion is redolent of that hope and expectation for the future of democracy that characterized the late nineteenth and early twentieth centuries, forgetful of the harsh deeds that preceded it and made it possible, without anticipation of the barbarism that was to succeed it.

Just as the political concern which appears to motivate Rawls is narrow and thin, so is his view of the theoretical problems facing anyone who wishes to accomplish what he proposes to accomplish. Simply, historicism, whether that of Marx or that of Nietzsche and the Existentialists, has made it questionable whether an undertaking such as Rawls's is possible at all; yet he does not address himself to these thinkers. He takes it for granted that they are wrong, that they must pass before his tribunal, not he before theirs. Marx is not treated, and Nietzsche is quickly dispatched, improbably, as a teleologist. I am aware that it is not Rawls's intention to write a history of political philosophy, and it is not incumbent on him to present a critique of Marx and Nietzsche. But the issues raised by Marx and Nietzsche must be dealt with if Rawls is to be persuasive at all. If liberal democracy is just a stage on the way to another kind of society, then Rawls is merely an ephemeral ideologist. And if rational determination of values is in the decisive sense impossible, then Rawls is only a deluded myth-maker. He supposes that his method makes a detour around these roadblocks, that there is no need to discuss nature and history. Throughout this book one wonders about the status of Rawls's teaching. Is it meant to be a permanent statement about the nature of political things, or just a collection of opinions that he finds satisfying and hopes will be satisfying to others? One finds no reflection on how Rawls is able to break out of the bonds of the historical or cultural determinism he appears to accept, and no reflection on how philosophy is possible within such limits or what it means to be a philosopher. Is he a seeker after the truth or only the spokesman for a certain historical consciousness?

What Rawls explicitly undertakes to do is to provide principles for our preexisting moral sense, to elaborate the implications of our institutions or convictions, to tell us what we mean when we speak of justice, to find a basis of agreement among our contemporaries. He believes that there is a *via media* between subjectivity pure and simple and telling us what the world is really like. But, again, the question always present is whether that moral sense is anything other than a mere preference, one conditioned by our time and place. Rawls takes it for granted that we are all egalitarians. Aristocratic teachings are inadmissible, but it is not clear whether this is because they are based on an untrue understanding or because we do not like them any longer. Conversely, it is unclear whether our egalitarianism is a result of the revelation of the fact of men's equality or whether it is just what we happen to like today.

Rawls thinks that his procedure is Socratic. Socrates, however, did not begin from sentiments or intuitions but from opinions; all opinions are understood by Socrates to be inadequate perceptions of being; the examination of opinions proves them to be self-contradictory and points toward a noncontradictory view which is adequate to being and can be called knowledge. If opinion cannot be converted into knowledge, then the rational examination of opinions about justice, let alone of senses about justice, is of no avail in establishing principles according to which we should live. It is even questionable whether such examination is of any use at all. Rawls begins with our moral sense, develops the principles which accord with it, and then sees whether we are satisfied with the results; the principles depend on our moral sense and that moral sense on the principles. We are not forced to leave our conventional lives nor compelled, by the very power of being, to move toward a true and natural life. We start from what we are now and end there, since there is nothing beyond us. At best Rawls will help us to be more consistent, if that is an advantage. The distinctions between opinion and knowledge, and between appearance and reality, which made philosophy possible and needful, disappear. Rawls speaks to an audience of the persuaded, excluding not only those who have different sentiments but those who cannot be satisfied by sentiment alone.

Thus those who turn to Rawls hoping to find a reasoned statement of the superiority of liberal democracy to the other possibilities or a defense of the rationalist tradition of political philosophy will not find what they are looking for. They will find reassurance that their sentiments are sufficient, that they need not enter the disputes of the philosophers; they will be made to feel at home rather than made to long for distant worlds; they will be nudged in the direction of more reform and tolerance in accordance with the prevailing tendency of our regime; and they will be given a platform that would appeal to the typical liberal in Anglo-Saxon countries: democracy plus the welfare state—leaving open whether capitalism or socialism is the most efficient economic form (so that one need not be a cold warrior); maximum individual freedom combined with community (just what is wanted by the New Left); defenses of civil disobedience and conscientious objection (the civil rights and antiwar movements find their satisfaction under Rawls's tent); and even a codicil that liberty may be abrogated in those places where the economic conditions do not permit of liberal democracy (thus saving the Third World nations from being called unjust). This correspondence, unique in the history of political philosophy, between what is wanted by many for current political practice and the conclusions of abstract, rigorous political philosophy would be most remarkable if one did not suspect that Rawls began from what is wanted here and now and then looked for the principles that would rationalize it.

JUSTICE AND THE ORIGINAL POSITION

A theory of justice must show what a decent regime is and what duties citizens owe to it. Rawls's problem is the classic one: what kind of a civil society would a reasonable man choose to live in and why should he obey its commands when they go against his grain? Rawls assumes that there is a form of civil society that can reconcile public and private interest and hence that a true political philosophy is possible. He argues that the principle of utilitarianism—the greatest good of the greatest number—is the one generally accepted today and that it does not suffice. Out of the many possible criticisms of that principle he selects the one that it does not satisfy the demands of the few, in particular of the economically disadvantaged few. He accepts the utilitarian position that each individual's view of his good is his good and that it is the business of society to attempt to satisfy the individual to the extent the fulfillment of his wishes does not do harm to others and not to propose or impose a view of the good on the individual or to have a collective end. The objection to utilitarianism is that it does not insure consideration of each individual and that, in spite of its individualist basis, the disadvantaged are sacrificed on the altar of the collective. Rawls proposes a contract according to which every man gives his adherence to civil society only on condition that he be guaranteed certain minima which one might call rights. Such a contract serves to set the goals and limits of civil society, to prescribe duties to rulers and to motivate the citizens' adherence as well as to define their legitimate claims.

Although Rawls goes back in time to seek a model for his theory of justice, he brings a fresh set of concerns to the contract doctrine. It must somehow be transformed to accommodate sensibilities that have emerged historically out of utilitarianism and popular dissatisfaction with it. Men must have equal rights not only to "life, liberty, and the pursuit of happiness," but to the achievement of happiness. Inequalities, whether they stem from birth, fortune or nature, should be offensive to us. Thus to the familiar principle of liberal democracy that each person is to have an equal right to the most extensive basic liberty compatible with a similar liberty for others, Rawls adds a second principle that all goods are to be equally distributed or, if unequally distributed, this unequal distribution must be agreed to be the advantage of all as measured by the desires of the least advantaged member of society. Rawls seeks a new morality which will constrain the advantaged to admit that the possession or use of their advantages depends upon the permission of an egalitarian society, one which will persuade the disadvantaged that whatever inequalities exist are to their advantage. Rawls's innovation is to incorporate the maxims of contemporary social welfare into the fundamental principles of political justice. Not only must material goods be provided to each citizen, but also an equal sense of his own worth, recognized by others; for, after all, man does not live on bread alone.

The disadvantaged or, to say what Rawls really means, the poor, must be listened to, not condescended to or told how they should live; and the attention paid them must be grounded on the most fundamental right which precedes institutions and in accordance with which institutions are formed. A man does not, as Plato said, have a right to what he can use well; or, as Locke said, to that with which he has mixed his labor; or even, as Marx said, to what he needs; he has a right to what he thinks he needs in order to fulfill his "life plan," whatever it may be. With respect to ends, government for Rawls must *laisser faire*; with respect to the means to the ends, it must *beaucoup faire*.

Once Rawls has determined what is wanted, he seeks for a way of deriving or demonstrating his two principles of justice that will be persuasive and that will exclude conflicting principles. A contract made by all the future members of the new society to abide by these principles would fill the bill. But why would superior men agree to a contract that requires them to make sacrifices for the benefit of the disadvantaged? A common ground of advantage, more fundamental than any particular advantage, must be found in order to gain unanimous consent. This need for a common ground is the source of the elaborate construction of "the original position" which is *the* feature of this exceptionally complex book.

Every understanding of man must have some vision of the fundamental situation, free from the accidents and trivia which distract us from the one thing most needful, a situation in which a man can discern what really counts and on the basis of which serious men guide their lives. The Best Regime of Plato and Aristotle, the City of God of Augustine and the State of Nature of Hobbes, Locke, and Rousseau come immediately to mind as powerful alternatives according to which we are asked to take our bearings. Now comes Rawls's "original position" which, if we are willing to assume it, will compel us to accept his two principles of justice and his version of society.

The "original position" amounts to something like this: Ask a man, any man, what kind of a society he would like to live in, assuming that he wants to live in a society. He would describe one that fulfilled his idea of the good, one that would make him happy. But he knows that the other men have different ideas of the good that conflict with his, so that it is unlikely that his idea will prevail; and even if it were to do so, those other men would be deprived of their happiness. If he were to imagine that he did not know what view of happiness, what "life plan," he were going to have, but did know that he would have a "life plan," what kind of society would he choose? In this case he would be choosing under what Rawls calls "the veil of ignorance." Since there are many possible "life plans," none belong to man as such; therefore, it is not unreasonable to assume that men in the original position do not know their goal but know only that they must have one. The different final goods cannot be reconciled, and it is undesirable that they be so. Inevitably, according to Rawls, a man in this situation would choose a liberal society, for at least he would be permitted to pursue his goal, if it did not do harm to others, whereas he would otherwise risk losing his happiness altogether. Better a little than nothing—so cautious calculation would seem to indicate. This provides a ground for agreement among men who are similarly situated. They would accept Rawls's first principle of justice.

Further, although this man does not know the good, the final end, he knows that there are certain things that will contribute to the fulfillment of his life plan, no matter what its content. These things one can call primary goods, good because they serve whatever good is final. They are things like rights, liberties, birth, talent, position, wealth, a sense of one's own worth. Our typical man would want to have as much of these primary goods as possible. Some are natural and others are effects of social arrangements; but possessing them depends on chance. He would want a society which encourages the use of what nature gives and assures that he gets the most of what society can give. But, if the veil of ignorance descends again, he would opt for equality, since, given the fact of the relative scarcity of primary goods, he would be likely to have less rather than more of an unequal distribution. The natural primary goods he would choose to use and develop only insofar as they contribute to the happiness of all and they are harnessed by the institutions to that end. The social primary goods, like wealth, he would allow to be unequally distributed only to the extent that the least advantaged member of society, which he might be, would gain from that unequal distribution and could hope to improve his own situation thereby.

In this condition of ignorance, calculating men will agree to Rawls's second principle. A contract is made for mutual advantage on a basis of equality. This contract sets down the rules of the game; justice in a man is abiding by his agreements, keeping his word. Justice is fairness in the sense that it is only fair to abide by the results of a game the rules of which are seen to be reasonable and just, even though one might have wished for another result and would like to alter the rules for one's personal advantage. Rawls's recipe contains equal measures of selfish calculation in the original position and public spiritedness—in the form of fair play—after real social life has begun. A man cannot be expected to join a group in which his happiness is not promoted equally with that of others. A society which gives him that equality of treatment deserves his adherence. Once men are aware of the original position they will abandon their overreaching: they will recognize that there are no legitimate claims to special privilege and will be dissuaded from using the power deriving from any unequal possession of primary goods to command such privileges.

The "original position" is an imaginary foundation which Rawls wishes to insert beneath the real edifice of liberal society in order to justify that society. It is invented rather than discovered, and one may well doubt whether it is substantial enough to support such a structure.

THE "ORIGINAL POSITION"
VERSUS THE STATE OF NATURE

In order to see the difficulties inherent in the "original position," it must be compared to the "state of nature" in the contract teachings of Hobbes, Locke, and Rousseau, for Rawls intends his invention to play the same role in his presentation of justice as did the state of nature in theirs. And the change of name is indicative of the decisive difference in substance. Rawls banishes nature from human and political things. The state of nature was the result of a comprehensive reflection about the way all things really are. Hobbes, Locke, and Rousseau could not be content with a figment of the imagination as the basis for moral judgments. Nature is *the* permanent standard; what the good man and the good society are depends on human nature. The state of nature is the result of a specific understanding of nature founded on a criticism and a rejection of an older understanding of nature and its moral and political consequences. The state-of-nature theorists, therefore, agreed with Plato and Aristotle that the decisive issue is nature; they disagreed about what is natural. Metaphysics cannot be avoided. If there is to be political philosophy, they believed, man must have a nature, and it must be knowable. Rawls does not wish to enter into such disputes, the validity of which has once and for all been refuted by his school. And his political goals are furthered by the imperatives of his method, for he does not wish to accept the iron limits set by nature on the possibilities of transforming the human condition. Although he sometimes rests an argument on what he calls human nature, his thought is directed not only at overcoming those injustices which are against nature but at overcoming nature itself. He wants the advantages of the state-of-nature teaching without its (to him) unpleasant theoretical and practical consequences.

The state of nature presented a picture of man as he really is, divested of convention, accident, and illusion, a picture grounded on and consistent with the new science of nature. Man, according to the real contract theorists, is a being whose primary natural concern is to preserve himself, who enters into the contract of society because his life is threatened and he fears losing it. That fear is not an abstraction, a hypothesis, an imagination, but an experience, a powerful passion which accompanies men throughout their lives. This passion is sufficient to provide a selfish reason, a reason that men can be counted on having, for adherence to a civil society which is dedicated to preserving them. The conflict between particular interest and public good disappears. The reason why this passion is not ordinarily effective enough to guarantee lawful behavior is that men in civil societies which protect them forget how essential that protection is. They get notions of self-sufficiency; they pursue glory; they break the law for their pleasures. And, above all, their religions persuade them that there are things more important than life or that there is another life, thus calming the fear of losing this one and encouraging disobedience to civil authority. The state of nature is intended to reveal the nullity or secondary character of these other passions and these hopes of avoiding the essential and permanent vulnerability of man. Death is the natural sanction for breaking the contract, and the state of nature shows both that this is so and that the goods which might conflict with desire for life are insubstantial. The positive law is merely derivative from this sanction and gets its force from nature. The state of nature demonstrates that the positive goals of men which vary are not to be taken seriously in comparison with the negative fact on which all sensible men must agree, that death is terrible and must be avoided. They join civil society for protection from one another, and government's sole purpose is the establishment and maintenance of peace. This origin and end of civil society is common to the contract theories of Hobbes, Locke, and Rousseau in spite of their differences. And whether they believed the state of nature ever existed or not, it was meant to describe the reality underlying civil society. Man's unsocial nature and the selfish character of the passion that motivates men's adherence to civil society limit the possible and legitimate functions of that society.

Now, Rawls's "original position" fails to achieve what the state of nature teaching achieved. Apart from the fact that there is nothing in the original position that corresponds to any man's real experience, the fear of death disappears as the motive for joining civil society and accepting its rules. Rawls is very vague about the reasons for joining civil society and, because he does not want to commit himself to any view of man's nature, it cannot be determined whether the attachment to society—attachment in the sense of obeying its laws—is really so important for a man in fulfilling himself. With the disappearance of the fear of death as the primary motive, the sanction for breaking the contract also disappears. In civil society contracts are protected by the positive law and the punishment it can inflict. Prior to civil society, there must be a natural punishment or none at all. A man whose desires or view of happiness urge him to break a contract that has no sanctions, no authority, would be foolish not to do so. After all, life is not a game. He exists naturally, while civil society is merely conventional. Either there is some essential harmony between private and public good or there is none. If there is none, on what basis can one arbitrate between the two? Rawls does not provide a basis for the reconciliation or anything more than a sermonizing argument for the nobility of sacrifice to the public good.

What Rawls gives us in the place of fear is fairness. But that is merely the invention of a principle to supply a missing link. Why should fairness have primacy over the desire for self-fulfillment? Once we leave the "original position" and the "veil of ignorance" drops, the motive for compliance falls away with it. When we leave the state of nature, the passions found there remain with us and provide powerful reminders of that earlier state and our reasons for preferring the civil one. But the original position is a bloodless abstraction which gives us no such permanent motive. Fairness is a reasonable choice of enlightened self-interest only in the original position. Fairness as something more, as choiceworthy for its own sake, cannot be derived from the original position. It is a tattered fragment of an earlier tradition which argued that man is naturally political and that the practice of justice will make a man happy. The state of nature begins from the natural isolation of man and teaches that society and its justice are good only as means to an end. The natural sociality of man is inconsistent with individualism or anything like the freedom of choice among ends which Rawls wishes to preserve, or the notion that man's relation to society is in any way contractual. It requires a rigorous subordination of particularity to the community and all the harder virtues of self-restraint about which Rawls never speaks. He is an individualist, but he does not wish to accept the harsh practical and theoretical consequences of that individualism. In order to pose the issue clearly he would have to confront the views of human nature underlying the contract teaching with those that assert that man is by nature a political animal. Fairness simply does not cohere with his shrewd, calculating individual in the original position.

Rawls's egalitarianism is similarly without foundation, for he does not want to accept the low common denominator of the true state of nature theory. He wants an equality which extends beyond mere life to all the things social men care about. All men, no matter what their qualities of mind or body, no matter what their virtues or their contributions, must have a legitimate claim to all goods natural and social, and society's *primary* concern must be to honor that claim. He must therefore abstract from all the evident inequalities in men's gifts and achievements, but he can find no firmer ground for this abstraction than that it is what he wants, that it is required for his "original position" to work. But it is a long way from the rights of nature to the rights of the original position. The latter rights are hardly likely to inspire awe in anyone who believes himself to be superior. The contract theorists consciously lowered man's sights and his view of himself in order to make equality plausible and found a common interest. It is not in a situation of neutral "reflective equilibrium" that man chooses civil society, but in the grip of powerful natural passions which control and direct his reason and reduce him, willy-nilly, to the level of all other men. Rawls does not want to follow these theorists in this respect, although he wants to have all the advantages he sees in their teachings. The state-of-nature teachings are connected with a denial of the nobility of man and thereby of the nobility, if not the utility, of morality, and their authors were aware of this. Rawls does not wish t stoop low enough to benefit from their solidity, but what he adopts from them prevents him from soaring to the moral heights to which he aspires.

As opposed to the contract theorists who taught that the strongest thing in man is his desire to avoid death and who took their bearings by that negative pole, Rawls insists on the positive goal of happiness. The contract theorists took the tack they did because they denied that there was a highest good and hence that there could be knowledge of happiness; there are only apparent goods, and what happiness is shifts with desire. Men have always disagreed about the good; indeed, this has been a source of their quarrels, particularly in matters of religion. The contract theorists tried to show that this factual disagreement reflects a theoretical impossibility of agreement. Out of this bleak situation which seems to make political philosophy impossible, they drew their hope. If the importance of all particular visions of the good can be depreciated, while all men can agree on the bad and their inclinations support its avoidance, then solid foundations can be achieved. But it has to be emphasized that a precondition of this result is the diminishing of men's attachment to their vision of happiness in favor of mere life and the pursuit of the means of maintaining life. Rawls, while joining the modern natural-right thinkers in abandoning the attempt to establish a single, objective standard of the good valid for all men, and in admitting a countless variety of equally worthy and potentially conflicting life plans or visions of happiness, still contends, as did the premodern natural-right thinkers, that the goal of society is to promote happiness. Thus he is unable to found consensus on knowledge of the good, as did the ancients, or on agreement about the bad, as did the moderns. He is able to tell us only that society cannot exist without a consensus, but he does not give any motive for abiding by that consensus to the man who is willing to risk the breakdown of actual society in order to achieve his ideal society—which is what any man who loves the good must do. Only the "veil of ignorance" in the "original position" makes consensus possible; but once the scales fall from a man's eyes, he may very well find that his life plan does not accord with liberal democracy. Rawls asks that only those life plans that can coexist be accepted, but he is not sufficiently aware of how far this demand goes and how many life plans must be rejected on this ground—and all for the sake of a peace the value of which is unproved.

THE GOODNESS OF THE "PRIMARY GOODS"

Because Rawls does not take seriously the possible conflict of important values, because he really presupposes the existence of the consensus he believes he is setting out to establish, because he would prefer to simplify the human problem and narrow our alternatives rather than face fundamental conflicts requiring philosophic reflection, Rawls does not see that the contract theorists could not be satisfied with rejecting some views of the good as merely incompatible with the contract but had to find grounds for showing that they are untrue. Their understanding of nature was requisite to their political teaching, for opposing doctrines to which men were passionately committed denied the authoritative status of the civil law and the contract from which it stems, as well as the value of the life the contract is intended to protect. Rawls speaks condescendingly of Rousseau's assertion that men who think their neighbors are damned cannot live in peace with them. We know better than Rousseau; our experience shows that pluralism of religious belief works just fine. We need not worry, for only a few fanatics who constitute a clear and present danger need be restrained. But Rawls does not know what faith is. He looks at the believers around us, not knowing that religion has been utterly transformed, partly as a direct result of the criticism of the contract theorists, partly as a result of the liberal society of which they were the inspirers. The kind of men who fought the wars of religion could not be asked to give up their quest for salvation for a peace they despised; they had to be made to disappear. Either they were wrong in their beliefs, or their actions were justified.

The state of nature was intended as a substitute for the biblical account of the origin of man and society, a rational account in place of the one provided by revelation. Its theorists had no objection to a tepid faith, one that would not lead men to challenge civil authority.

But in order to achieve this result the meaning of faith had to be drastically revised. Rawls, looking at the believers of our day in America, whose religious views are the fruit of Enlightenment thought, assures us that faith is no threat to the social contract and that Locke and Rousseau were needlessly intolerant. Thus he profits from their labors without having to take on their disagreeable responsibilities. Hobbes, Locke, Rousseau knew that their teaching could not be maintained if biblical revelation were true and that there was no way to avoid confronting it directly. Rawls, counting on men's having weak beliefs, simply ignores the challenge to his teaching posed by the claims of religion.

This becomes clear in Rawls's discussion of what he calls the primary goods. The notion "primary good" plays the same role in Rawls's teaching as does "power" in Hobbes's, and Rawls's list of primary goods is similar to Hobbes's list of powers. But for Hobbes powers are not simply neutral. They depend on ends, and there are some ends or life plans for which all the listed primary goods would be evils. What is wealth for him who believes that it is easier for a camel to go through the eye of a needle than for a rich man to enter into the kingdom of heaven? What is health for him who believes with Pascal that sickness is the true state of the Christian? And how does the sense of one's own worth, rather than humility, accord with the man who believes he is a sinner? To treat these things as goods is equivalent to denying that view of things in which they are the opposite.

And Hobbes does deny the validity of the opinions which are incompatible with the powers on his list. Rawls avoids denying such opinions by not paying attention to them. He only takes seriously opinions which fit the society he proposes. For example, the possibility of revelation was a question which occupied much of the best energies of Hobbes, Locke, Rousseau, and Kant. It is quite evidently not a question that bothers Rawls very much. At the very least, Hobbes must argue for the preeminence of this life and deny that happiness in this life can be achieved or maintained without these powers. A comprehensive reflection about the nature of things is implied in this list of powers. Hobbes argued that we cannot know what will make us happy (although we must know what will not and cannot make us happy) but that we can know the means to the satisfaction of desire. It follows, therefore, that we should pursue those means, we should seek power. And thus it also follows that, consequent to the depreciation of the ends, power in a way itself becomes the end. The low tone, the philistinism, the concentration on preservation and wealth in Hobbes is a result of the primacy of power in his teaching. The popular criticism of the *bourgeois* is really the criticism of Hobbes's man. But that tone follows inevitably if the great and noble ends are merely insubstantial opinions whereas health and wealth are the stuff of being. Moreover, in the establishment of public policy, one inevitably concentrates on what is real and what the citizens have in common. It is by way of Hobbes and of Locke—who follows Hobbes in this respect—that economics comes to the center of politics, where it remains for Rawls.

Rawls's acquiescence in the emancipation of the means from the ends makes him an unwilling collaborator in Hobbes's moral revolution. He would undoubtedly protest that his interest is men's happiness, but he has little to tell us about it. When it comes to the primary goods, however, he has much to say. His political proposals are nothing but a means for their distribution. This means that his society promotes the kinds of happiness dependent on his primary goods. Or, put another way, the purposes of his government are alien to those emphasized in classical political philosophy or biblical revelation. Government, instead of making men good and doers of noble deeds, as Aristotle would have it, has as its goal providing what Aristotle would call equipment or external goods. And the ends of government almost inevitably determine the characters of men. The beginning point of Rawls or rather Hobbes-Locke fixes the outcome. His democratic man hardly resembles the classical object of admiration: Socrates, who was born in poverty and lived in poverty but was the happiest man of his time. Even the way Rawls treats his own addition to Hobbes's scheme, the sense of one's own worth, partakes of this mode. The sense of one's own worth, he reiterates time and again, depends very much on the esteem of others. Socrates required only his own testimony, but Rawls's man cannot withstand unfavorable public opinion. Rawls tries to provide him with esteem no matter what his life plan may be; Rawls's man is in every way dependent, "other-directed." Hobbes determined the worth of a man on the basis of others' consideration of him; as he put it, in his direct and vigorous way, a man's worth is his price. Rawls differs from him only by engaging in price fixing.

QUALITY VERSUS EQUALITY

Rawls, because he substitutes the equal right to happiness for the equal right to life, must equalize not only the conventional primary goods like money but also the natural ones. This latter is harder to envisage (apart from the salutary work of geneticists who, Rawls believes, might one day improve all our progeny). One thinks of Herodotus' account of the Babylonian law by which all the marriageable girls were auctioned off; the beautiful ones brought high prices from the rich and voluptuous men; the city used the money so derived to provide dowries for the ugly girls, thus making the naturally unattractive attractive. Nature's injustice to the unendowed is what the thoroughgoing egalitarian must rectify. The redistribution of wealth is hardly sufficient, for, as we all know, the most important things are those "that money can't buy." The ugly girls will surely be grateful. And the beautiful ones, who are forced to sacrifice the satisfaction for which they are equipped to the greater number whom nature has endowed less generously but whose dreams are of similar stuff, will not be discontented, for when the veil of ignorance still covered their nakedness in the original position, they had no idea that they would be beautiful. Rawls is not in agreement with Aristophanes who, in the *Assembly of Women*, indicates that, when the law compels the beautiful to be at the command of the majority, not only does tyranny result but *eros* rebels. The original position works miracles, in the precise sense of the word, for it stops the course of nature.

This leads to the further questions of the relation of quality to equality, a question which Rawls treats only obliquely. Although the desire of the least advantaged persons remains decisive, Rawls assures us that the less fortunate have no interest in policies which would reduce the talents of the more fortunate. Not only does he fail to offer us proof of this assertion, he does not seem to be aware of the possibility that the majority, with all the goodwill in the world, might not appreciate what the higher talents or activities are and hence might not be willing to allocate scarce resources to them or set up the "structures" necessary to encourage them. Leveling does not seem to be a serious danger to him. One might suspect that he does not address himself to the problem of the great man for fear that it would undermine the persuasiveness of his argument that his version of civil society can reconcile all legitimate interests. Aristotle, for example, did address this problem and concluded that republican cities would either have to ostracize the great man or renounce their nonmonarchic regimes and make him their ruler. Both alternatives are unsatisfactory, but Aristotle presents them because the nature of political things forces him to it. Rawls suppresses the conflict. But the suspicion that he avoids it in order to make his case stronger is probably unfair to him. It is rather that he does not see it. If "life plans" are merely a matter of preference and are in principle equal, then the distinction between the great man and the common one disappears. If everyone is to have an equal sense of his own worth, superiority must not exist. The habit of such beliefs has, I fear, the effect of making a man incapable of distinguishing the great from the mediocre. The very distinction is seen as the result of injustice and snobbishness.

In Rawls one finds none of the concerns which preoccupy Tocqueville, who, although a democrat convinced of the justice of the principle of equality, argued that intellectual and moral superiority would not find fertile soil in modern society. Hard choices had to be made, according to Tocqueville; it was essential for democrats to be aware of the fact so that they might attempt to mitigate the loss. Similarly, although Rawls admires John Stuart Mill, one would never know from Rawls's account of him that the primary intention of On Liberty was to protect the minority of superior men from the tyranny of the majority, that Mill believed mankind was threatened by universal mediocrity. For Rawls, as for most Americans who speak of it, the tyranny of the majority is a threat only to the disadvantaged. One can only hope that the problem posed by Tocqueville and Mill has not been solved by the loss of the capacity to recognize the great and the beautiful—or by the very disappearance of the great and beautiful themselves.

But Rawls's treatment of Nietzsche does not provide much foundation for this hope. He takes it that Nietzsche has a subjective "value" preference for men like Goethe and Socrates and wishes to impose it on the majority who are not like Goethe and Socrates. Rawls's reading appears to be slight and uninformed. He does not see that Nietzsche really addresses the questions which Rawls from his own point of view has to address: how one creates a "life plan" or horizon when there is no objective good, or, what is the same thing, how values are created (Nietzsche was the first to use "value" in the modern sense; Rawls unawares adopts Nietzsche's invention); what the self is, if one believes as does Rawls, that there is a "self" and that it is productive of values rather than determined by them; how philosophy is possible, if human thought is historical. Rawls discusses only the preconditions for making life plans and value creation, not the ways in which they are actually made. Nietzsche teaches that only a certain kind of man is capable of creativity, by which he does not primarily mean the writing of poems or the painting of pictures, but the production of values by which man can live. He wants the very thing Rawls claims to want— a variety of rich and satisfying "life plans"—but he has thought through how one gets them and has some inner experience of what they are.

Let us, however, assume that Rawls is right and that Nietzsche has a mere preference for "culture" in the current watered-down sense of the word. Surely it would nonetheless be distressing if there were to be no more Goethes or Socrateses. One would have to reflect on the conditions for their existence and try to determine whether they coincide at all with the conditions for Rawls's society. But, although Rawls seems to take it for granted that such men will be present, his teaching holds that it makes no difference whether they are or not, for pushpin is as good as poetry—unless one or the other appeals more to the least advantaged. All talents are but resources for the greatest happiness of all and get their price in today's happiness market. Anyhow, Rawls has a solution, for he has established an exchange branch of government which distributes resources for the public benefit. Nietzsche can go to it and make an application for a study grant. To characterize this solution to the problem of greatness in democratic society one would need the talents of a great satirist.

THE MISUSE OF KANT

To complete his reincarnation of contract teachings, Rawls attempts to lend his "original position" the glow of Kantian moral nobility. As always, he reads older philosophies only for support for his own much narrower thought. He picks and chooses, never really caught up in the necessity of their arguments, sure that he looks down on them from a higher plateau. Rawls not only does not accept the truth of the *Critique of Pure Reason* and the *Critique of Practical Reason*, which is the precondition of establishing the possibility of a realm of freedom, and which is presupposed in Kant's moral writings. More important, he does not understand what Kant means by morality. Morality must be chosen for its own sake; it must be a good, or rather the highest good; the goodwill is the only unconditional good. There must be an interest in morality just as there is an interest in money or in food and one which has primacy over all other interests. Rawls has done nothing to establish such an interest. Surely it is not interest in morality that motivates men in the original position, whose goal is to enjoy as much happiness as possible. If happiness, however conceived, is the end, then morality is a means to that end, good instrumentally rather than in itself. Happiness, to use Kant's language, is a heteronomous rather than an autonomous motive for obedience to the moral law.

Kant's morality is not that of the social contract, for the social contract teachings are all heteronomous. Morality in them is only a

GIANTS AND DWARFS

tool constructed by men for the fulfillment of prior, nonmoral, natural ends. Part of Kant's political teaching is indeed hypothetically contractarian, but there is a problematic relation between his political and moral teachings. Morality and civil society are linked by a philosophy of history which is itself problematic for Kant. The three moral postulates—God, freedom, and immortality—are necessary supplements to morality, without which it would be overwhelmed by politics and history. Morality does not look to consequences, for that would make it contingent. Social benefit is Rawls's goal, whereas morality in Kant's view need not be helpful in the establishment of a just society or in making a man happy. Kant says, consistently with his principles, that a moral man must never break a law. Rawls preaches the legitimacy of civil disobedience and conscientious objection. The preservation of his life must not, for Kant, be any consideration for a moral man, nor should his conduct be affected by the actual state of affairs. Rawls makes it clear that heroic sacrifices are not a necessary component of his social man and that prudential modifications of principle are legitimate and desirable.

Rawls's fuzziness about morality is summed up in his denigration of the primary importance of generality or universality in Kant's thought. For him the essential element of Kant's moral teaching is autonomy, i.e., the combination of freedom and rationality. But Rawls fails to see that what Kant means by freedom and rationality is universality. A man *is* autonomous if he is able to act according to laws derived by universalizing the maxims of his action; one is both free and rational when one so universalizes. In order to act freely a man must obey the law he has made for himself, without being compelled by other men or by particular circumstances or by nature. Acting according to his own desires is not freedom, for he does not make those desires; they are given. A man may desire to tell a lie, but he can immediately see that lying cannot be accepted as a rule of conduct for all men. If he is able to obey the rule possible for all men in opposition to his particular desire, and if he is not motivated by future gain or by fear of punishment, ridicule, bad reputation, or anything other than a respect for the universal principle, then he can be said to act freely, independent of the contingent and conditioned; otherwise he is the slave of man, institutions, or nature. He is free because the principle is arrived at by the examination of the meaning of his own desire. And he is free in a higher sense by virtue of his capacity to overcome his own desire for the sake of the universalized principle based on it. This proves his capacity to act for the sake of morality alone.

Rawls's men in the original position act in terms of individual desire; they are deprived only of the knowledge of their particular circumstances, so that they will choose those rules which will be most useful for satisfying whatever desires they may turn out to have. For Kant, the moral man acts with full awareness of his particular circumstances and chooses to obey the universal rule in spite of them. Particular desire and universal law are only coincidentally harmonious, so that the man who always acts according to the law shows that he is free. And in acting freely, a man is also acting rationally, for universalization is the activity of unconditioned reason, and universality is the form of reason and of any rational law, political, moral, or natural. The calculation of a man seeking to satisfy his passions (or to set up principles in the "original position") is only an instrumental use of reason to attain ends which reason played no role in establishing. But if his end is not the substantive intention of his action but the universalizability of the maxim governing his action, he is dedicated to reason simply, to noncontradiction. Kant's categorical imperative is the imperative of universality, and it comprises both freedom and rationality. Therefore, a true Kantian interpretation of Rawls's man in the original position is that he is neither free nor rational.

Rawls's denial of the crucial significance of generalization is most revealing about the character of his enterprise. Rousseau, while accepting the view of nature contained in the state-of-nature teachings, insisted that the natural inclinations cannot provide a basis for a decent community or for anything but mercenary morals. Nature provides preservation, low selfishness, as a common ground. Natural freedom is to act according to one's inclinations without concern for others. If there is to be concern for others, another and higher common ground must be found. Rousseau found that ground in the will to generalize one's desires, to think of oneself as a citizen and not as a man (although the motivation for doing so remains the natural desire for preservation). When men think generally, they are at one. Hobbes and Locke brought men together as passengers on a ship whose interests are private but who all equally have the desire to keep the ship afloat. Rousseau, and Kant following him, bring them together by giving them the same interests. This is obviously a profounder and more certain harmony, but it goes against nature; this moral freedom requires what Rousseau calls the denaturing of man. This denaturing is effected by a severe morality, which is established in the name of freedom but requires the overcoming of natural inclination. The natural man and the citizen are at opposite poles. Generalizing is itself easy; the will to generalize is difficult to attain, because it requires indifference to one's own happpiness.

Rawls to the contrary, Kant is an austere moralist, because he recognizes the demands of morality. A choice must be made between natural satisfaction and moral action, between the private and the public, between the particular and the universal. These tensions make it impossible for man ever to be simply whole. Sentiments of justice are as much inclinations as are sentiments of selfishness and have no higher status. Rawls does not like such choices; he does not like restricting inclination. The struggle of self-overcoming is not at home in his relaxed society. In sum, his thought has nothing to do with that of Kant, for whom, at most, the moral man can hope for happiness and the coming to be of a just society, but cannot alter his conduct to realize these ends. To repeat, Rawls's teaching is only utilitarianism made contemporary, and utilitarianism is in its turn a modification and simplification of the teachings of Hobbes and Locke. That tradition was not influenced by the moral criticism of Rousseau and Kant. Its concentration was and is on the satisfaction of particular desire. Rawls's teaching is almost entirely of that tradition. The goal of his society cannot by any stretch of the imagination be taken to be Rousseau's citizen or Kant's moral man. His refusal to think about nature makes it easy for him to confound natural and moral freedom, as well as the two alternative and opposed grounds of community in modern thought. There is no halfway house between Hobbes and Kant; and Rawls's Kantian interpretation of the "original position" does nothing but lend it a spurious moral dignity.

REASON AND THE GOOD

Limitation of space makes it impossible to discuss the institutional castles Rawls builds on the sands of his original position. These amount to a restatement of American constitutional arrangements, reinterpreted to include the imperatives of the welfare state. Whether the more detailed practical consequences he arrives at actually follow from his premises is more than questionable. He constantly returns to our common wishes and familiar experiences to make his undemonstrated conclusions appear convincing. He is persuasive because he supports familiar contemporary beliefs, not because he provides rational grounds for them.

We must, however, turn to the last and most intriguing part of the book. It is here that Rawls promises to show that there is a rational way of determining what is good for us and that the practice of justice will make us happy. For all its apparatus, the first part of A *Theory of Justice* really only tells us the obvious: society needs rules, and it will only survive if most men in a society obey those rules. Rawls has not, up to this point, succeeded in showing in any convincing way that the individual interest and the public interest are identical. Consequently, he feels constrained to go back to the oldest question in political philosophy, the one posed to Socrates by Glaucon and Adeimantus in the *Republic*: "Is the just man the happy man?" The answer must be yes if the law is to be compelling for a man who seeks happiness. Only by abandoning happiness as the goal could Kant avoid answering this question. Rawls, despite his Kantian pretensions, is, in Kantian language, a eudaimonist and tries to approach the old theme in the new mode. The difficulty is great, for his liberalism keeps him from excluding any preferences; his egalitarianism keeps him from saying that some goods are more reasonable or of a higher order than others; and his method keeps him from talking about the true nature of things. But he must make the attempt if he is to avoid relativism and nihilism.

If there is to be political philosophy, reason must be capable of guiding our fundamental political actions. Now Hobbes, Locke, and Rousseau argued that the fundamental human fact is the desire for self-preservation. Reason cannot establish the reasonableness of that passion or talk men out of it. Reason does not establish the end. But it can find the means to the end. Reason is crucial but only instrumental. Community is established by the fact that for all men this passion supplies the most important motive. Reason cannot establish its reasonableness, but it can establish the unreasonableness of views of the good which contradict it. This is sufficient for the possibility of a political philosophy. But the society founded on that philosophy is limited to the ends which passion provides to it. Rawls, who wants society to do much more than is legitimated by the contract teachings, wants reason to give what the passions refuse. In this section he engages in an endeavor more characteristic of ancient philosophy which taught that reason can establish the ends as well as the means. It is, therefore, not surprising that here he invokes the name not of Kant but of Aristotle.

The last part is entitled *Ends*, and it contains three subsections: *Goodness as Rationality*, *The Sense of Justice*, and *The Good of Justice*. Rawls's strategy is first to show that reason is sufficient to determine ends, then to describe the sense of justice in us, and finally to show that the society which embodies the principles implicit in the sense of justice and allows that sense its activity would be chosen by reason as good, as *the* end. His stated purpose is to show that collective activity is good; actually he wishes to show that collective activity is the highest, the unconditional good.

Rawls's discussion of goodness as rationality immediately disappoints the expectations aroused by his title. He does not even show that it is good to be rational. That is finally left up to the decision of each individual. What he thinks he shows is that reason can be of use in establishing a "life plan"—if one wants to have a rational life plan. Furthermore, a rational life plan is not rational in the sense that the ultimate goals are established by reason, but only in the sense that reason has played some role in the formulation of the plan. Desires, tastes, preferences, values, what have you, are the ultimate determining factors in a life plan, and Rawls does not tell us where they come from. He apparently believes that, without determining the desires by reason, he can develop rules which will limit or constrain the indeterminacy of desire sufficiently to make a community possible. The bait which will draw men to the acceptance of these rules is the promise that they will be happier if they follow them.

Happiness, according to Rawls, is the purely subjective contentment accompanying success in the fulfilling of one's plans and the expectation that the success will continue. Instrumental reason can, of course, help to insure the means of fulfillment, but the only way reason, in Rawls's presentation, could call into question a life plan is by showing that it cannot succeed. Success becomes the real criterion. If you have safe life plans, you are likely to be happy, if happiness is only contentment.

Rawls tells us that "For Royce an individual says who he is by describing his purposes and causes, what he intends to do in his life. If this plan is rational, then I shall say that the person's conception of his good is likewise rational" (p.408). He then proceeds, through tortuous argumentation, to set down the rules for determining the rationality of a plan. The means for it must be available. Its success must be likely. It must be compared with other possible life plans. The intensity of desires must also be considered. It must include as many desirable ends as possible. Its compatibility with the plans of others must be considered. The probability of its continuity must be evaluated. And then . . . we have to decide. That decision is a leap, and there is no reason to believe that the abyss that must be leapt over has been narrowed by this machinery of "deliberative rationality" that Rawls provides. He talks about the rationality in life's decisions, but his discussion underscores their essential irrationality. A rational man would be reduced to nihilistic despair or irrational commitment. Only a man irrationally attached to safety and contentment could remain satisfied with such a solution, for safety and contentment are merely "values" like any others. It is a laudable thing to wish to advance the cause of reason, but to do so one must have an under-standing of the world such that reason can play an important role in it. Rawls devotes no discussion to what emerges, albeit unconsciously, as the most important component of happiness—the irrational for-mation of ends or values.

But let us listen to Rawls in his final statement on the matter: "But how in general is it possible to choose among plans rationally? What procedure can an individual follow when faced with this sort of decision? I now want to return to this question. Previously I said that a rational plan is one that would be chosen with deliberative rationality from among the class of plans all of which satisfy the principles of rational choice and stand up to certain forms of critical reflection. We eventually reach a point, though, where we just have to decide which plan we most prefer without further guidance from principle (p. 64). There is, however, one device of deliberation that I have not yet mentioned, and this is to analyze our aims. That is, we can try to find a more detailed or more illuminating description of the object of our desires hoping that a fuller or deeper characteri-zation of what we want discloses that an inclusive plan exists after all." The only rational way out is to combine all competing charms. One can frequently have one's cake and eat it.

Rawls continues, "Let us consider again the example of planning a holiday (p. 63). . . . Often, however, a finer description fails to be decisive. If we want to see both the most famous church in Christen-dom [in Rome] and the most famous museum [in Paris] we may be stuck. . . ." (p.551). And so we are. This eloquent summation of the human condition also summarizes Rawls's thought. Its ridiculousness quenches indignation. How could a man who is telling us how to live turn to the example of a holiday when discussing the most important question of all? Why not reason versus revelation, love versus duty to one's country, life versus dedication to the truth? Can one wonder that a generation has turned away from reason when this is the level of its most eminent representatives, when this is the sort of guidance it can get from them? Rawls speaks to men with the souls of tourists.

The reason for Rawls's behavior is that this irrationality of ends is not a problem for him. He is convinced, as the weight of his book proves, that we know what is most important—society, i.e., preser-vation. He is not tormented by these questions; they are matters of indifference. One can believe what one wants and do what one wants, so long as it does not get in the way of liberal democracy. His rational rules, such as possibility and inclusiveness, are fit only for that cramped little risk-fearing man in the original position. They determine the kinds of ends possible before those ends are even considered. Single-mindedness, dedication to the one most important thing, facing impossible odds, are now irrational. Rawls counts on an audience of men whose horizons have been so confined that the great dangers in the great decisions are no longer visible to them. He devotes no attention to those varied and rich expressions of individual nature which he promises will flourish in his society. In order to do so he would have to water the irrational roots out of which values grow in his system. By being fed on reason they grow frail and colorless, for it is only the reason of utility. The kind of diversity he thinks of is that found in obscure but harmless religious sects or in obscure but harmless sexual practices. The kind of diversity which produces great actions, great art, or great new civilizations is out of his reach. He provides a soil which is not salubrious for the growth of a diversity that is worthy of the name. The solid thing is survival; in a world where the great value decisions are akin to the choice between vacationing in Paris or Rome, where they cannot change the fundamental character of civil society, there is no reason for difference. Man will be alike or will differ by their insignificant differences of preference or their insignificant perversities.

Rawls counterattacks. "Human good is heterogenous. Although to subordinate all our aims to one end does not strictly speaking violate the principles of rational choice . . . it still strikes us as irrational, or more likely as mad. The self is disfigured and put in the service of one of its ends for the sake of system" (p. 554). If we pursue contradictory ends, no matter. That is but the proof of our freedom. The principle of contradiction, the foundation of reason, strikes our philosopher as irrational, nay, mad. Such formulas provide us with a fine-sounding excuse for not thinking about the important questions. This rationalist makes a virtue out of unreason when it suits his purpose. The ship he has so painstakingly constructed sinks to the sound of his applause as it slides down the runway. He thinks it is afloat.

He adds that "the self is prior to the ends which are affirmed by it" (p.560), which means that the self creates the ends instead of being determined by them. It knows no masters, including reason, and it cannot be comprehended by reason. Professor Rawls owes us and himself a fuller account of the "self." A little study would teach him that this notion had its origin in thinkers who were friends of neither reason nor liberal democracy, and that it is manifestly inconsistent with his project.

THE MISUSE OF ARISTOTLE

Once having established the goodness of rationality, after his fashion, Rawls gives reason a new tool, for the judgment of the rationality of life plans—the "Aristotelian principle." This principle is invented to show that men want to use the capacities required and encouraged by Rawls's society, and that therefore we should rationally choose that society and its form of justice.

Kant was brought in to pronounce the benediction over a society grounded on selfishness. Now Aristotle, the central contention of whose moral and political teaching is that there is a highest good and who is according to Rawls therefore mad, is constrained to give his blessing to a notion of happiness founded on whatever a man believes to be the expression of his value. The Aristotelian principle, which Rawls admits was not enunciated by Aristotle, but alleges to be in accord with Aristotle's intentions, holds that "other things equal, human beings enjoy the exercise of their realized capacities (their innate or trained abilities), and this enjoyment increases the more the capacity is realized or the greater its complexity" (p. 426). Rawls cites Nicomachean Ethics, VII, 11–14, and X, 1–5, apparently unaware that Aristotle in these passages is showing that there is one highest activity which accords with human nature and which is productive of happiness. Far from praising inclusiveness and complexity, Aristotle attributes whatever need we have of them to the weakness of our nature, which we should try to overcome. He concludes in VII 14 that "God always enjoys a single and simple pleasure." Far from praising the interdependency of social life, Aristotle teaches that the only real pleasures are those that are self-sufficient, that are connected with eternal things, and that can in principle be enjoyed in solitude. In short, Aristotle teaches that philosophy is the only way of life that can properly be called happy. He arrives at this conclusion after examining all the claims to happiness and showing that all the others besides philosophy are without foundation and self-contradictory. The philosopher is not as such a social man; Aristotle never even says that the moral virtues, including justice, are necessary to the philosopher in order to philosophize.

It is true that Aristotle teaches that the activity of our faculties is what makes us happy. But he does not mean by faculties what Rawls

means by capacities—"innate or trained abilities." Aristotle's faculties
are natural components of our constitution like sight or intellect. They
have a proper development and are exercised on appropriate objects.
Men may possess and exercise these faculties in greater or lesser degree,
but they are accordingly more or less men. There is a structure and a
hierarchy of the faculties based on their contribution to happiness.
Aristotle can tell us in quite detailed and concrete terms precisely in
what happiness consists. But Rawls, for all that he may use the word
"nature," means nothing by it. Whatever a man does express his
capacities; whatever he believes himself to be, he is. Rawls believes
that man has a self; Aristotle believes he has a soul. These terms are
mutually exclusive. The self is self-determining; at best it is a mysterious and elusive source, infinite in its expressions. The soul has a
nature, for it has an end which determines it and of which it is not
the cause; but the self has no nature, it is protean. Rawls, in order to
avoid being incapable of saying anything about ends emanating from
the self, insists that a man must first deliberate and suggests that the
more complex activity in any genre should be preferred (for example,
chess over checkers). Rawls draws the inspiration for this suggestion,
God knows how, from Aristotle. Rawls's criteria for the actualization
of capacities are purely formal and external, not helping us to determine whether they are true or counterfeit expressions of a man's nature
or to distinguish skillful safecracking from the making of beautiful
statues. And, after all, Rawls tell us, the man who enjoys counting
blades of grass may be fulfilling his nature, too. Aristotle might very
well agree, but he would insist that such a person, other things being
equal, was an inferior man. This Rawls will never do. He will simply
try to find a group of men who will support this man's sense of his
own worth.

THE SENSE OF JUSTICE: NATURE OR INDOCTRINATION?

The Aristotelian principle enables us to reach the penultimate
stage on our journey to the promised society. This is the elaboration
of the sense of justice. It is one of those "capacities (innate or trained
abilities)" the exercise of which human beings enjoy. The sense of
justice is the condition of our being members of and maintaining a
good society, and the good society will make us happy because it
satisfies our sense of justice. The sense of justice is a psychological
principle, and Rawls presents a three-stage history of its development.
Once the sense of justice is developed, we have an unbreakable psy-

chological need for and attachment to society. It becomes as much a part of our psychological constitution as any other sentiments. We are social because we possess the sense of justice. The ambiguity of Rawls's "innate or trained abilities" leaves us with an exquisite doubt as to whether the sense of justice is natural or only the result of habituation. However that may be, Rawls tells us that if this sense exists, and society meets its demands, the society will be stable. This leaves the further doubt whether the society is truly just or merely satisfies the sense of justice.

The three stages are, roughly, as follows: When we are children we obey out of love, trust, and respect for our parents. This is the morality of authority. It is childlike but is preserved in men like Thomas Aquinas or believers of any kind. The second stage is that of our youth. When we are attached to our group we see our good in it, and we are motivated by praise and blame. This, too, though useful, has its evident limitations. It is the morality of George Washington and patriots. Finally there is the morality based on rational adherence to principles, on the recognition that one's society is reasonable and fair, that it follows the imperatives of the "original position." It is the morality of adulthood and is practiced by Rawls and philosophers like him, as well as all members of the promised society. Rawls does not show us that these three moralities are harmonious or that the third achieves the synthesis of the first two. To do this, one would have to study regimes founded on reverence or piety and on loyalty, honor, or patriotism, compare them with those founded on reason, and determine the various advantages of each. It would require an achievement comparable to that of Hegel to show that the society founded on reason contains the political and moral advantages to be found in holy awe of the sacred or in selfless loyalty to friends and undying hatred of enemies. There is no reflection here on what really constitutes rootedness. Only after the completion of such an undertaking could one look down on these older principles as an adult looks down on a child. On the surface, it would appear that reason substitutes selfish, low, and sure motivations for noble ones. Does this reason really perceive great goals beyond calculation of advantage? Rawls, as always, has no taste for examining alternatives.

But more important, Rawls has not proved either that adherence to the principles developed in the original position is rational or that reason can demonstrate the goodness of strict obedience to the laws of a society founded in accordance with these principles. In the absence of such proofs one can say only that the morality of principles does not rest on impulses, feelings, or instincts as do the other two kinds

of morality and that it involves the use of reasoning—though it may
culminate in rationalizations or ideologies rather than reasons. This
three-stage doctrine of moral development looks suspiciously like what
is today called political socialization, that is to say, a way of making
men part of the group whether it is natural or good for them to be so
or not. Rawls must prove that these stages are part of men's development in the same sense as is the formation of their organs, or risk
acquiescing in a process of indoctrination for the sake of social goals.
His abandonment of nature does not open new domains of human
freedom so much as make way for the unlimited manipulation of man.

THE OMNIPOTENCE OF SOCIETY

And, now, at last, we are at the goal, "the idea of social union,"
the community that reason chooses and that makes us happy while
unifying private and public interest. Not only is society necessary, not
only does it give us satisfactions we would not have without it; it
incorporates us so that we are parts of it. From the atoms of the state
of nature Rawls has constructed a social organism in which we feel
with the whole and are pleased or pained along with it. Socrates'
extreme and ironic paradox is here presented deadpan. Nothing good
is outside of society; nothing transcends it. We are wholly of it, but
we do not even know what that society is like. It is very "Aristotelian"—i.e., very complex—so that everything that can be contained
in man finds its expression, and we all enjoy it. It is based on a moral
and intellectual division of labor which increases the quantity and the
kinds of production for the enjoyment of all, without risk of the
deformation wrought by narrow specialization or alienation of our
labor. We get everything from society, and we owe it our total allegiance. If man had a nature, it would be social. We are always partial;
only society can have all the perfections, but we possess them through
it. We should not try to be self-sufficient, but should accept our
weakness, join the team and play fairly, recognizing that everyone
makes an equal contribution to the collective result. The man who
is not sociable is radically imperfect and has a deficient life. He is the
only man Rawls is not willing to treat as an equal. For Aristotle the
man who does not belong to civil society is either a beast or a god.
For Rawls he is only a beast. For Rousseau, the solitary is the only
good man. For Rawls he is the only bad one. All the ambiguity of
social life disappears.

Rawls has accomplished the complete socialization of man by

beginning from the weakest and most vulnerable individual and en-visaging a social arrangement which will protect him in his weakness, guarantee his subsistence, allow him to pursue and fulfill his wishes and plans, and give him the same sense of his worth that the rich, successful, and honored individual has. Going far beyond the more modest goals and hopes of earlier thought, Rawls proposes to make it the purpose of society to fulfill men, to make men happy, accepting as happiness what each believes happiness to be and providing each with what Rawls takes to be the universal elements of happiness no matter what its form. Since neither God nor nature fulfills any such plan and might even be viewed as opposing it, society must take on the whole burden of providing and distributing the elements of hap-piness; and the disadvantaged person recognizes that it is only society that considers his interests and battles a hostile nature and chance for his sake. Society exists for him, but he, in the most decisive sense, is its creature.

It is easy to win the allegiance of the disadvantaged to this scheme, just as it is not difficult to obtain the participation of the poor in a plan for sharing the wealth. The real problem is the stronger or the more advantaged, for they might be willing to take their risk in a less equal arrangement or even try to be substantially self-suffi-cient. Thus Rawls's book is in large measure a polemic against them. He socializes them by persuading them that they too are weak; by confounding natural with social inequality; by denying that there can be self-sufficiency; by habituation and the inculcation of shame and guilt; by obliterating alternatives; and above all by endless sermonizing. The harmony between the advantaged and the disadvantaged is not natural and is brought into being by a suppression of nature. The rough edges, the fundamental conflicts, always present in earlier practice and theory, can, therefore, be understood by Rawls to be the results of mere perversity. Since man has no fixed nature, social planning, even the use of genetics, can ultimately smooth all of this away. Rawls's original perspective from the point of view of the disadvantaged makes other considerations vanish. The consequence is a closing of the exit from the cave. There is no way out and no hiding place. "In justice as fairness men agree to share one another's fate" (p. 102).

What Rawls creates is an enormously active government whose goal is to provide the primary goods, including the sense of one's own worth, and therefore to encourage the attitudes that support the pro-duction and equal distribution of those goods. What can the future of liberty be in such a scheme? Liberty is, to be sure, Rawls's first principle of justice, but it is qualified by having to be "compatible with a similar liberty for others." Rawls does not elaborate the extent of that qualification. There is, to repeat, no natural-right teaching in Rawls, no absolute limit of any kind. All freely chosen life plans must be restricted by the fundamental demands of social union. Conflict will be resolved practically and theoretically in favor of society. We have only Rawls's assurance that nothing important can fail to find acceptance within the terms set by the original position. Man's plasticity, made even greater by the absence of nature and its limits, permits all those little adjustments in men which will make the idea of social union possible. Society is the one absolute in Rawls's thought, although it is without foundation.

And what is the purpose of all of this? An artificial happiness of an artificial man. Rawls's promised society is a desert. It feeds on false tales—stories about its being the final product of evolution and history, stories that make unequal things appear to be equal. Democracy, which was to free us from the myths which perverted nature, becomes the platform for a strident propaganda that denies nature for the sake of equality, as the myths of conventional aristocracies denied nature for the sake of inequality. The community desired is one without tension, without guilt (except for those who do not go along), without longing, without great sacrifices or great risks, one made for men's idle wishes and for the sake of which man has been remade. The language of maximum liberty, diversity, and realization of capacities is so much empty talk, the only function of which is to support our easygoing self-satisfaction.

CONCLUSION

The greatest weakness of A *Theory of Justice* is not to be found in the principles it proposes, or in the kind of society it envisages, or in the political tendencies it encourages, but in the lack of education it reveals. Rawls's "original position" is based on a misunderstanding of the state-of-nature teachings of Hobbes, Locke, and Rousseau. His "Kantian interpretation" is based on a misunderstanding of Kant's moral teaching. His "Aristotelian principle" is based on a misunderstanding of Aristotle's teaching about happiness. And these three misunderstandings constitute the core of the book. An authentic understanding of these thinkers would have given him an awareness of the problems he faced and of the nature of philosophic greatness. We are in no position to push ahead with new solutions of problems; for as this book demonstrates, we have forgotten what the problems are.

The most essential of our freedoms, as men and as liberal democrats, the freedom of our minds, consists in the consciousness of the fundamental alternatives. The preservation of that consciousness is as important as any new scheme for society. The alternatives are contained in the writings of the greatest men in the philosophic tradition. This is not to assert that the last word has been said, but that any serious new word must be based on a profound confrontation with the old ones. That confrontation has the added salutary effect of destroying our sense of our own worth and giving us higher aspirations. Rawls is the product of a school which thinks that it invented philosophy. Its adherents never approach an Aristotle or a Kant in search of the truth or open to the possibility that these old thinkers might have known more than they do; and since they have a virtual monopoly on the teaching of philosophy, there has been a disastrous, perhaps irreparable, loss of learning and extinguishing of the light which has flickered but endured across so many centuries. His book is a result of that loss of learning and contributes to it in turn. His method and the man he wishes to produce impel me to think that Nietzsche—abused by Rawls, although not culpably because ignorantly—might provide a more appropriate title for this book: *A First Philosophy for the Last Man.*

The following two essays on the universities in the 1960s were written with a three-year interval between them—the first in 1966 and the second in 1969. Although they deal with permanent questions, they comment on changing events. I present them as they were written, to reflect my thinking as it emerged and to show how the events appeared to me then. The first reveals me to have been innocent and good when I was young, full of that passion which most feeds on illusions, hope. By the time of the second, I had abandoned hope and replaced it with clarity, the child of distance and detachment, the beginning of my mature age. My concern with the fate of reading good books in America has been a constant. The reform I actually proposed in the earlier one is about the same as the modest reform I would still propose—the union of a small group of like-minded professors against the tide. The Greek Civilization Program mentioned in it became a reality—for one year, after which its animators left Cornell. But of those dozen or so freshmen, at least six became scholars with whom I am still in contact after more than twenty years.

In the second essay I did not forecast that the scene of extremist reform would move from the social sciences to the humanities and that the students of the sixties would be the professors of the eighties. Henry Louis Gates, Jr., suggests that his generation progressed from taking over buildings to taking over curricula. Now the professors are way out in front of the students. In the great Stanford reform it was the professors who used the students to further their "post-modernist agenda" in the battle against Euro-centrism.

THE CRISIS OF LIBERAL EDUCATION

Two events appear to have had the greatest impact on American academic life in the postwar period: the launching of Sputnik and the recent campus revolts and threats of revolt. In them can be seen the character of the crisis of liberal education in this country.

The Russian success in space resulted in a general belief, probably unjustified, that the United States had fallen behind the Soviet Union in scientific capability. The myth that modern science could flourish only in a democracy was shattered. It was recognized that there must be concerted support of the sciences and that certain educational programs must be encouraged; the free operation of the marketplace does not by itself produce the kinds of men with the kinds of training necessary.

The alarm experienced set in motion a transformation of our educational institutions. The easygoing era dominated by the notions of individual "self-fulfillment" and academic egalitarianism was past. Standards had to be set and the raw talent mined from the earliest high school years. The result was the establishment of great rewards, moral and material, for excellence, particularly in the sciences, although this concentration was also gradually transmitted to all the disciplines. Terrific competition became the order of the day. The Scholastic Aptitude Tests grew ever more important in ranking students, and apparently objective measures of talent are ever more in vogue. Some twenty or thirty colleges and universities have become elite institutions, constituting a sort of caste structure. The system begins to resemble that of France, with its monolithic national standard and the careers which are fixed from the age of twelve. The old American academic world and the opportunities it afforded for beginning anything at any time, in which there were few encouragements but also few obstacles, is disappearing. Within the universities the prestige of intelligence and achievement has gone up correspondingly. Now the most respected students are not the socially prominent nor the athletic but those who succeed at what the university is primarily intended to promote.

No one could doubt that some of the effects of this pressure have been salutary. We are using our resources better, and the general respect for intelligence has increased. The university has come to the forefront of American life, and more and more of the best of the young intend to spend their lives in it. All the professions require university-trained men, and they look for their new directions in the results of research undertaken by the university. The university has become omnicompetent and sensitive to the needs of the community. As such, however, it is less a preserve for the quiet contemplation of the permanent questions which are often forgotten in the bustle of ordinary business and the pursuit of those disciplines whose only purpose is intellectual clarity about the most important things, and more a center for the training of highly qualified specialists. This change has been consecrated by a transformation of name: what was once the university has become the multiversity.

It is here that the difficulty arises. The multiversity does not appeal to the students' longings for an understanding of the most serious problems, in particular, their doubts about the route to follow in order to live a good life and their questions about the nature of justice. These are not technical problems, and technical education assumes that these problems are solved, generally, by an acceptance of the status quo. This is not a particularly disturbing situation for the great majority of young people who are content to make careers and do not feel called upon to reflect generally about themselves or the whole of society. But for that most interesting few who can become leaders, pathfinders, and revolutionaries this is a great source of dissatisfaction. They can find no place for training in what most concerns them. The various specialties do not add up to a general overview, and the best students must turn elsewhere to educate themselves and satisfy their cravings.

I venture to suggest that the campus riots of 1965 were largely a result of the failure of our schools to educate the tastes, sentiments, and minds of the best endowed young people. Their sense of what is significant—and it can only be a *sense*, for they have not cultivated themselves sufficiently to have any *knowledge* of what is significant—could find satisfaction only in unpolitical politics. On the one hand they protested against *bourgeois* society on the basis of a crude existentialism, an unstudied worldview which they have picked up on the winds of the time. On the other hand, they protested against the indifference of the university. The complaints were untutored, but they reflected the awareness of an absence or a lack. They wanted more attention and thought smaller classes, more freedom, and no moral responsibilities would change things.

This is not correct, but it is the best they could do in finding means to a goal they had no experience of. I am convinced that such unrest will not occur in institutions where the students do not sense a great disproportion between what they study and the lives they wish to lead, where the ancient questions of philosophy and theology are honestly and seriously treated and occupy a central place in the curriculum. Students will not rush to action when they believe they are preparing themselves for the problems they know they must face. The situation of our educational institutions is defined by the high level of proficiency they demand and by the fact that that demand emerged in response to certain specialized, technical challenges which run somewhat contrary to the demands of liberal education. The righting of the balance is the great responsibility and opportunity of liberal education in the coming years.

The current generation of students is unique and very different in outlook from its teachers. I am referring to the good students in the better colleges and universities, those to whom a liberal education is primarily directed and who are the objects of a training which presupposes the best possible material. These young people have never experienced the anxieties about simple physical well-being that their parents experienced during the Depression. They have been raised in comfort and with the expectation of ever-increasing comfort. Hence they are largely indifferent to it; they are not proud of having acquired it and have not occupied themselves with the petty and sometimes deforming concerns necessary to its acquisition. And, because they do not particularly care about it, they are more willing to give it up in the name of grand ideals; as a matter of fact, they are eager to do so in the hope of proving that they are not attached to it and are open to higher callings. In short, these students are a kind of democratic version of an aristocracy. The unbroken prosperity of the last twenty years gives them the confidence that they can always make a living. So they are ready to undertake any career or adventure if it can be made to appear serious. The ties of tradition, family, and financial responsibility are weak. And along with all this goes an open, generous character. They tend to be excellent students and extremely grateful for anything they learn. A look at this special group tends to favor a hopeful prognosis for the country's moral and intellectual health. However, it would be hard to imagine a generation with so little in the way of roots or real education. Their tastes have been given no formation at all, and the learning that has been poured into them gives them competences but fails to move them. The student's interpretations of the world come from the newspapers and from what is in the air, and neither church, home, nor school add much to that. They know mathematics, for example, but it is taken as a skill and does not inspire them to the theoretical life; nor do they conceive of it as a tool with which to understand nature and hence themselves.

An older form of primary education, not entirely intellectual, devoted itself to giving the young standards and depth of conviction. If further study changed the content of the beliefs, it was done from this starting point, which provided a model for comprehensiveness and seriousness. Today religion, philosophy, and politics play little role in the formative years. There is openness, but that very openness prepares the way for a later indifference, for the young have little experience of profound attachments to profound things; the soil is unprepared. In short, much of the heritage of the West, which had been passed from generation to generation in living institutions and in the books which supported them, is unknown or meaningless to our young. Most come to college ready to follow one specialty or another and let the rest of life take care of itself. They do not expect to change their tastes, amusements, or ways of life. The only way they plan to become different is that they will acquire a profession which will give them a place in the world and permit them to enjoy its advantages. Others come nurturing a vague longing for "meaning."

What they find in the university is a dazzling array of courses in a bewildering variety of fields which compete for their allegiance. Their professors are typically members of professions who are engaged in research in particular areas considered important by those professions. There is almost no reflection about the relations of those fields to each other, and their various premises may well be in contradiction with each other.

The undergraduate education reflects the situation in the graduate schools which are now the most respectable part of the university and are presumed to be at the frontiers of knowledge. The young people are prizes to be captured by the special disciplines. They have no real guidance as to what is truly important and what one must know in order to be a human being and a citizen. In most schools the students are forced to take a few courses in several disciplines during their first two years. But this only introduces them to each of the disciplines as a specialty, helps them to decide in what they would like to specialize, and adds a few quickly forgotten facts to their already bulging storehouses. They also have elective courses, but these are usually chosen helter-skelter and just add a patina of general cultivation; a science major may study some medieval poetry or a philologist some atomic physics, but this only gives a momentary thrill and in no way contributes to the understanding of the major subject.

The problem of liberal education is a result of the fantastic growth of specialization. This is trite. It is so well-known that some of the sophisticated are beginning to deny it. It is, however, true, because of the demands made on a student's time. But, more important, it is true because, in order to admit all these specialties into the curriculum and give them equal status as they demand, all sense of unity and hierarchy has had to be abandoned. The only principle visible in this system is that of tolerance, each field respecting the rights and dignity of the other. The only criterion for what should be admitted to or excluded from the university is tradition, and the pressures of public demand and foundation support can easily overcome that.

It is no accident that a university administrator, one who has to preside impartially over the mob of disciplines, coined the term "multiversity." The very word solves the problem by denying its existence. An institution of higher learning is a series of parts which constitute no whole, or the whole of which is beyond the survey of any single man and is determined by a series of accidents. Philosophy and theology, ancient pretenders to the throne of the sciences, have been banished, or they have become democratized and have accepted their positions on a level with their former subjects. It is not that the university represents many competing ways of life, but that it offers none. Everyone is the same, pursuing some goal set by the system, and each differs only in that he represents a different cog in the machine.

Universities once presented a view of the ends of life, and the studies pursued were directed to those ends. They were preserves for the encouragement of the higher human alternatives. To become pious, wise, or prudent were the goals. At different times one or the other dominated, or they were competing with each other. The merely technical things were not a part of the university. Now all agreement about the goals has disappeared. But that is not what is serious. The university could, after all, still be the place where they are debated, where one learned what is necessary to participate in that debate in an informed way.

The serious problem is that our studies do not even raise these questions any longer. To be sure, many professors speak out on the great issues, but very few as a result of their learning. They speak as private persons; their sciences teach them little about those issues which are admittedly so important. The trivial is well-known; the great is left to passion and personal taste. The university is in better possession of the means to ends than ever before; but never has it been able to shed so little light on these ends.

At the root of the problem is modern natural science. Superficially, it has this effect because it needs so many highly trained practitioners to fulfill important social and political needs which are subtheoretical. The science explosion has bloated the universities with persons and disciplines which are clearly ancillary to theoretical studies, although vital to practical projects. Very few men and women have the true temper of science, and the majority of the recruits to natural science must hence be only technicians. But, as a majority, they help to set the tone. And much of the research done is of little theoretical significance. All this has had its effect, and if it were not for the huge government efforts in this field and the university's willingness to take over almost the entire burden, there can be little doubt that the strains on the university's unity would be much diminished.

But, more deeply, the changes in natural science itself, not its use, have resulted in an almost unbridgeable gulf in the university. The crude formula, the two cultures, expresses the difficulty. The distinction between the scientists and the humanists, in the current senses of the words, is a phenomenon of relatively late origin. To be sure, there were always men who were more interested in politics and poetry than in astronomy, and vice versa. But is was also always understood that such men were incomplete, not just in the sense that they did not know everything that can be known by a man, but in the sense that one cannot know man if he is not seen in the context of the nature of which he is a part, nor can the heavens be known by one who does not have a grasp of the observer of the heavens. There were not two worlds, starting from different premises, employing different methods and arriving at different kinds of "truths." The disciplines were divided according to subject matters which were integral parts of a whole which could be grasped as a whole.

But in the last century or so, somehow the natural sciences have become metaphysically neutral and emancipated themselves from the unifying grip of philosophy. And their conclusions are so far from the common sense of everyday life that the two seem hopelessly disparate. Science apparently tells us little about the world which is of concern to us, although it is crucial to our mastery of it. And the human sciences cannot attain the rigor demanded by the natural sciences without deforming themselves. Thus they lose the confidence and the authority lent by science. The very distinction between sciences and humanities is a rear-guard action of the humanists attempting to protect themselves from the destructive onslaughts of science by setting a limit to scientific reasoning. This Maginot Line succeeds only in cutting the humanities off from their only source of salvation—a support in nature.

The study of the sciences, formerly the surest road to the rational discussion of the most comprehensive principles, hardly leads in that direction any longer, and a doctor in physics as such hardly qualifies as a wise man. The humanities still try to make such claims, but they are hardly justifiable without a rational foundation in nature; any humanistic interpretation of man is always threatened by a counter-explanation emanating from a psychology which has its roots in modern theoretical science; the human has no separate status. There is a cleft in our understanding of the world, and this is necessarily expressed in the university and its members. The two worlds go on independently. The situation is not remedied by the suggestions that scientists should read poetry and humanists learn the second law of thermodynamics. The two sides do not appear to need each other for the pursuit of their disciplines as they are currently conceived; a man will not be any less a scientist for want of a humanistic training, nor will a humanist be any less a humanist for want of scientific training. This is particularly true of the sciences, which in their splendid isolation continue progressing according to their own standards. The two kinds of learning and men live together in the university, but they have no vital connection, and their relationship is a rather tense administrative one.

The split in the world of learning is the most decisive intellectual phenomenon of our time, and there is no easy healing of the breach. It is the real source of the crisis of liberal education, and the serious study of that crisis would be a liberal education in itself. Here, I can only discuss its effect on the university as it is faced by the undergraduate. In general his professors do not feel that the university's lack of unity is a problem because they have made their life decisions and are convinced of the importance of their fields. They wish to get ahead with them, and the nature of their studies—particularly in the sciences, but also in some aspects of the humanities that slavishly and unnecessarily imitate the natural sciences—leads them to smaller and smaller topics of research, ever further from the orientation and questions of the students. The student is really asked to perform an act of faith in his choice of field and learn its tools in the promise of future fulfillments which he knows from the outset can only be partial. And a large proportion of his teachers are primarily researchers for whom teaching is secondary and whose researches, built on the researches of still others, are such that they have never, or not for a long time, raised the first questions.

But still, against the tide, some educators and citizens insist that there is an education of a human being as a human being and that a person cannot be minted into a small coin and still remain human. They are aware that the only living knowledge is that united in the head of a single individual, and thirty individuals, each with a part of the knowledge of Newton or Rousseau, do not equal a Newton or a Rousseau. Such educators have been given encouragement by the student unrests; attention has again been turned to the problems of the undergraduate which seemed to have been forgotten in the period of the apparently triumphant professionalism.

Money and the time of university administrators are now being devoted to the improvement of the undergraduate education. This is in itself promising, for, willy-nilly, the attention paid to the problem of the undergraduate requires some consideration of the total formation of a human being and a standpoint beyond the specialties. Of course, much of the proposed reform evades the issue and merely gives way to unreasonable and inappropriate student demands, such as removal of all university control over student conduct, or admission of students into the decision of questions which are properly the responsibility of the faculty. In some cases one suspects that there is a tacit complicity of faculty and administration in irresponsible political and moral behavior of the students just so long as it does not affect the campus life too seriously; this provides the supplement to the students' lives which is necessary due to the spiritual impoverishment of their education. This aspect of a young person's training is thus no longer a duty of the university. There are, also, the usual efforts to provide for more classrooms, smaller classes, and more faculty-student contact, all of which are desirable but also peripheral.

But when it comes to actual discussion of what a liberal curriculum should be, there is an extraordinary poverty of ideas. It seems that the substance of general studies has been exhausted, parceled out among the specialties. There is a great deal of talk about the vanished universal man, and it is argued that we must at least try to simulate his comprehensiveness, but what such a man was is widely misunderstood. It is assumed he was a polymath, a man who had the curiosity to learn each of the fields at a time when none was so vast that it required the entire life of an exceptionally able man. Now the fields have become much more complex and filled with detail so we are faced with the choice between a careful knowledge of one or a superficial acquaintance with many. If this were the case, what must be done would be clear, and liberal education would be a thing of the past.

But the so-called universal man was not an idle browser in the plurality of sciences. Men like Aristotle, Descartes, and Leibniz began and ended with unique interests in certain fundamental questions that do not belong to any single domain and are presupposed by each, questions like what is *knowledge*, what is *good*, etc. They did not have to be practitioners of all the arts any more than an architect has to be a carpenter and a bricklayer in order to build a house. The architect must know what each of the subordinate arts can accomplish and how they fit into the whole plan, but the special arts are rather more dependent on the architect's knowledge of the whole plan than the architect is dependent on their skills. The architect, without being a specialist, contributes vitally to the specialties.

Similarly, the interesting cases of the universal man were occupied with the special sciences insofar as they shed light on the universal problems, and their contributions to those special sciences were a consequence of their larger view. This possibility exists today as much as it ever did, and its actualization is even more necessary inasmuch as many new fields of endeavor are developing aimlessly. That actualization is admittedly more difficult today, but it can be attained by a careful study of one or two fields with respect to the general questions and a constant canvass of the others, ruthlessly cutting away the irrelevant, with a view to the effect their conclusions have on our understanding of the whole and the legitimacy of those conclusions in the light of the whole.

What I argue is that the questions which relate to the first principles of all things and the nature of the good life are as real as they ever were and that they constitute a study which is not contained in the special disciplines although those disciplines presuppose such reflection. The universal man is adept at this architectonic science, and his contributions to the various fields are a result of his larger knowledge. He is the only one who is open to the whole by the very nature of his studies, and he is a model of the proper intellectual concerns of a man who wishes to be complete. However difficult our particular problems may have made his quest, the issues remain, and we become self-conscious only by getting a glimpse of them.

This is what our rebellious students sense when they try to get a grasp of the whole by the easy route of mere feeling. And this is what is lost when professionalism dominates; each profession prefers to get ahead with the business at hand and avoid the sticky questions at the beginning. They like to give the appearance of self-sufficiency and to treat the philosophic interest as dilettantism. The world is divided up among the disciplines, and there is nothing left. What is forgotten is that the division is itself a question, and that each discipline must have something more than the right of the first occupier to justify the possession of its terrain. If we have lost touch with the way in which one approaches such a question, there are models of it in the literature of the tradition, and our first step would be to study that literature to see whether the earlier attempts were adequate and, if not, to determine why not. If this is not done, one remains a prisoner of the tradition which established our division of the disciplines represented in the university. There is indeed a subject matter for liberal education; it is only obscured by our particular situation.

It is usually agreed today that time should be left in the curriculum for general studies, but when it comes to filling that time not much is said. The disappearance of the general under the cloud of the particular has left the impression that beyond the specialties there is a vacuum. There are suggestions for the inclusion of exotic specialties which are nevertheless still specialties. The most characteristic solution is to give up and, under the guise of freedom, let the students do anything they please, construct any kind of program they like. In the last two or three years the most prominent reforms in the Ivy League institutions have all had to do with providing more freedom. Distribution requirements are being relaxed or abandoned altogether; one school lets some of its best students spend their last year doing whatever interests them, another suggests they go away for a year, and still another is going to permit good students to graduate as quickly as they want.

All of these plans are declarations of bankruptcy on the part of the universities, a renunciation of their function of teaching the students, and an avoidance of the difficulties involved in making the decisions as to what a student ought to know. Of course, none of the specialties have any such problems, and so *that* fixed pole remains and dominates the student's course of studies. The argument that this freedom makes the student more autonomous remains to be proven, and there are other ways to make him responsible.

No one can be against freedom, but one wonders whether this truly provides it. Students can take whatever they want, but if there exist only the alternatives which naturally proliferate in our day, then they are cut off from the rarer alternatives. How can the student be expected to know of important fields of study which he hardly sees represented around him? Only if the university encourages and makes respectable what is important and neglected can it be preserved and the students made to pay attention to it. The university is responsible for the atmosphere which forms the student, and to make no decision about what should and should not be a part of that atmosphere is to make the decision that what is generally acceptable in the society at large will dominate. The university should not impose a single course of study or way of life on its students, but it must see to it that the various serious alternatives find a place within it. Almost all of the proposals that are now being made by those who have power to institute them are totally devoid of any substance and are mere techniques of organization.

Another characteristic recent approach to liberal education, that represented by Daniel Bell, attempts to cut the Gordian knot created by the tension between general concerns and specialization by finding the common element in all the disciplines. This is found to be method, and the proper training then becomes the technique of inquiry. The problem with this is that it is at too great a remove from the first natural questions of students, or for that matter of anyone. Method is secondary, a tool for the study of the problems which interest one; and the kind of method adopted depends on the nature of the subject matter. The beautiful quote from Hegel at the end of Mr. Bell's article[1] seems to argue against the burden of his thesis. Hegel thinks the greatest danger is what we call conceptualization, for the abstract concepts characteristic of modern thought impoverish and deform the phenomena. The Greeks, notoriously unmethodological, are his model. They possessed a rich natural consciousness of nature in its immediate concreteness. This is the proper beginning point. The theories and concepts can then be tested against such a consciousness.

Before one starts studying the methods of scientific psychology one should have a solid experience of the varieties of men and women; otherwise one is likely to see in man only what our psychology permits us to see. Ordinarily the concentration on method means an acceptance of the techniques of modern natural science and their applications in social science, for the centrality of method is a modern fact connected with the growth of the new mathematical physics. That method itself actually was a result of the new articulation of the various subject matters which preceded it. Whether that centrality of method is appropriate to the study of man is a question, and that question should precede any methodological study. What sciences have in common methodologically reduces to rather thin stuff. And by the concentration on method one ends up pretty much accepting what each of the disciplines is doing and studying how they do it.

[1]In *Higher Education and Modern Democracy*, ed. Robert A. Goldwin (Chicago: Rand McNally, 1967), pp. 121–39.

Far more important are such questions as whether the presuppositions and conclusions of psychology are compatible with those of physics or the law and what to do about it if they are not. And surely the question of what a state is, what an individual's duties to it are, and what constitutes a good one have primacy over the way social scientists are studying developing states. And such questions cannot be handled quickly, but require time, concern, and continuing study. They are the questions answers to which are always presupposed but rarely thought out.

It would be easy to demonstrate that the questions are the same today as they were for Socrates. It is these questions which are permanent and the consideration of which forms a serious man. It is the role of the university to keep these questions before its students. Its curriculum should not be grounded on implied answers to them which exclude other possible alternatives. It may be true that "method" or "conceptual innovation" is at the core of the learned disciplines, or that "values infuse all inquiry," but a curriculum should not assume the truth of these assertions, as does Mr. Bell's. They are products of a particular view, which should be considered along with other views. For in these various perspectives, the fields of knowledge look very different. Plato may reflect and express the "values" of ancient Greece; but it is also *possible* that he saw permanent truths and that our interest in "method" and our notion of "value judgments" are only a reflection of certain transient needs of our time.

There is no reason why one should work within Mr. Bell's framework any more than that of someone else. That framework gives an appearance of openness but is actually grounded on very narrow and dogmatic premises. The only real openness is to see the world as it was seen in the most thoughtful perspectives, attempting to understand them as they were understood by their authors, not fitting them into a preexisting framework, not forcing them to respond to our perhaps misguided concerns. The proper curriculum must begin behind such assumptions as Mr. Bell's. There is nothing spectacular or new in what must be done. The old questions must be learned and their relevance to our particular situation seen. This can be accomplished most adequately by making the center of the curriculum consist in the best things that have been said about them and in the studies that prepare the character, imagination, and intellect of the student to receive those teachings.

For this reason those universities which used some version of what are called the great books—institutions like the Experimental College at Wisconsin, St. John's College, and the College of the

University of Chicago—have succeeded in creating the greatest enthusiasm among their students. Those books contain much of the
profoundest reflection about the nature of man, and the contact with
them is an inspiring intellectual and moral experience, one which has
a great liberating effect on those who are brought to it.

Much has been said about the inadequacy of the great-books
approach. The chief criticisms are that it is too bookish, meaning that
it begins from books, not things, and seems to put all that is great
into a single inappropriate category. It unavoidably rushes students
through much too much. Better a smaller number of books well understood than one hundred lightly read, for the kaleidoscopic effect can
well result in an indifference to all its elements. But for all that, those
who proposed this curriculum were almost alone among American
educators in pointing in the right direction. Their polar star was the
formation of thoughtful men and women, for the moment forgetting
all pressing concerns of the day. They saw that this education was to
be found in the posing of the fundamental alternatives and that the
awareness of these alternatives is what is most threatened in modern
democratic society.

The great-books approach has disappeared almost everywhere
now, except at St. John's College. Whatever the intrinsic defects of
its curriculum, they do not prevent it from being the best curriculum
available to American undergraduate students in recent years. It is
not so much a criticism of St. John's College as of American higher
education to say that it is too far away from the specialized interests
of professors and the trend in the universities to gain solid support.
The picture would be bleak indeed if it were not for the insistence of
the students. It is perfectly clear that the idea of a liberal education
still persists and that all of the changes in our world have not made
such an education impossible.

What our students most want and need is training in a few books
in the great tradition which give them models for the serious, rather
than the sham, universality, books which integrate the various studies
and present their relevance to life as a whole. Such books provide not
only an intellectual education but also a moral education insofar as
they involve the reader's concern with living the good life. They refine
the taste and present alternative explanations of experience. And they
are a theme for association among students who today have little to
talk about because their studies give them nothing in common. These
books must not be studied as parts of literature, politics, or history,
but as contributing to them all.

The only way a program of liberal education devoted to the careful study of the classic literature can gain acceptance with some assurance of permanence and the participation of the modern faculty is to construct it in such a way that it draws on the specialties as specialties while maintaining the general focus by its very structure. The professors must not be asked to devote their time to courses which have nothing to do with their specific interests or do not meet their standards of professional competence. They must rather be teaching their discipline and competing for adherents to it, but in a context where they are forced to relate it to certain general issues and to persuade students who are not already convinced of its importance that it contributes to their understanding. (This will have the added advantage that professors will undergo the perhaps salutary experience of relating their work to unprofessional common sense; this is done less and less today as professors live more and more among their specialized colleagues who do not raise these first questions any longer.)

One program which attempts to utilize the resources of the contemporary university to overcome the obstacles to a liberal education today is being planned by Cornell University. It is a course of study in classical Greece intended to take three-fifths of the freshman and sophomore years of a select group of students. The first two years of a student's college career are chosen because he or she is most open at that time and is likely to choose his later course of specialized study on the basis of these earlier experiences. Later he or she judges everything in terms of his major subject. Moreover, these two years do not conflict with the major, and hence the ire of the established interests is not aroused. This program will take the place of the universally criticized "distribution requirements" and will give the students a substantial and useful content to fill up the time which so many feel is being wasted and the emptiness of which has led to proposals to shorten the college years. And the students will have free courses with which they can fulfill the technical requirements for an intended major or follow up any other interests they may have.

The content of the program is simple; there are no great didactic innovations. The students will follow a series of seminars in Greek philosophy, political thought, literature, history, mathematics, and science, and there will be a special summer session on Greek art. Throughout the two years they will be studying the Greek language intensively. It is hoped that there will be a high standard of precision and concentration, narrowing the study to a few capital texts and a short historical period. The expectation is that the students will: (1) learn about Greece; (2) see the relationship between the learned disciplines while gaining some experience with them; and (3) become intimately acquainted with the permanent questions revealed in the tradition of Western thought at its very origins. It is hoped that the students' sensitivity to greatness in general will be increased by this grasp of one of its forms. There will be nothing artificial about their experience—they will be studying a reality, not an academic construct, in all of its aspects.

It is remarkable to what extent senior professors can become enthused by such a project. A number of distinguished scholars are anxious to participate in it because it allows them to satisfy their scholarly consciences while doing what they know undergraduates want and need. And, although the program is not intended to lead anywhere beyond itself, they cannot help hoping that some good students will be attracted to their discipline who would not otherwise have been. It would appear that the best strategy for the development of liberal arts programs is that of involving small groups of professors who already have some interest in common rather than by trying to establish university-wide programs which will necessarily aggravate vested interests and have little hope of survival. Other programs could be constructed on similar lines, hence presenting students with a variety of choices for a training which combines professional solidity with philosophic openness and avoids the lack of direction or unity connected with the elective system.

This is not a humanities program. The sciences are an integral part of it. The student could not possibly approach this subject matter "humanistically" or "scientifically." Each is part of the whole of Greek thought. What man can be is determined by what science knows of that nature of which man is a part, and science is directed by what is known of man and the recognition that any understanding of nature which cannot comprehend man is incomplete. The students will not study the history of science or the "Greek view of nature" but will learn to solve Euclid's and Ptolemy's problems as they did. Although this will not familiarize them with the operations of contemporary science, it will enable them to see the kinds of questions science always poses and to judge the relation of what science does to the rest of what men believe and know. And, perhaps, some students might even find in the somewhat different ancient science questions to be asked of modern science.

This is no substitute for learning the results of modern science, but it will give those who are not going into the sciences a more meaningful experience of scientific reasoning, and more real reflection on the purposes of science than they could possibly get from an introductory physics course. And for those who do have the intention of becoming scientists, this additional study may prove itself most worthwhile, for the whole scientific enterprise is discussed at length and with great clarity in classical thought, and they can consider the ends of science, its proper applications, its limits, and its relation to the other important activities of life. This program is beyond the split between the "two cultures."

In popular discussion today, the goal of almost everything, including the university, is said to be diversity. To the extent that this is not merely a means to avoid discussing what is good, we mean that in a free society many high or noble ways of life must exist for men and women to choose among. But the concentration on diversity as such is self-defeating. For in order for a new and serious way of life to emerge and maintain itself, its founders must believe in its truth and its superiority to other alternatives; hence they cannot hold that diversity is simply desirable. The quest can never be for diversity but must be for the truth—the truth about the highest good and the end of life. Diversity will take care of itself, given the various talents and characters of human beings. Never has there been so much talk about diversity and so little true difference among persons. To be sure, there is the diversity of specialization, but this presents a most monotonous aspect, for the practitioners do not differ in life principle. Although the workers in a factory are divided among many tasks, they can be, and usually are, men and women of similar tastes and beliefs. Does it constitute pluralism in religion to have many sects if the teaching presented in all the houses of worship is fundamentally the same? We are diverse in this almost quantitative sense, but intelligent observers can call us conformists, for a certain way of life derived from our political and economic system settles itself on most of us. It does so, *faute de mieux*, because we are ignorant of alternatives or because we are told that all alternatives are equally true or untrue.

To supplement the diversity of specialization, there has arisen what might be called the diversity of perversity. Writers, in their escape from the desert in search of interest and variety, have taken to celebrating the obscure peculiarities which can afflict some of us. But this too becomes boring, for there is no depth in mere deviation; once our clinical curiosity is exhausted we discover that it is less interesting than the merely "normal."

To repeat, the only true diversity comes from difference of principle about the final ends—serious thought and conviction about whether, for example, salvation, wisdom, or glory is best. This we lack, and it is the function of the university to maintain the awareness of these alternatives in their highest forms. We have all the negative conditions of freedom. Our young can think or do almost anything they please. But in order to act differently one must have ideas, and this is what they lack. They have access to all the thought of the past and all of its glorious examples. But they are not taught to take them seriously as living possibilities for themselves. This is the problem of our educational institutions.

THE DEMOCRATIZATION

OF THE UNIVERSITY

"Do you too believe, as do the many, that certain
young men are corrupted by sophists, and that there are
certain sophists who in a private capacity corrupt to an
extent worth mentioning? Isn't it rather the very men who
say this who are the biggest sophists, who educate most
perfectly, and who turn out young and old, men and women,
just the way they want them to be?"

"But when do they do that?" he said.

"When many gathered together to sit down in assemblies, courts, theaters, army camps, or any other common
meeting of a multitude, and, with a great deal of uproar,
blame some of the things said or done, and praise others,
both in excess, shouting and clapping; and, besides, the
rocks and the very place surrounding them echo and redouble
the uproar of blame and praise. Now in such circumstances,
as the saying goes, what do you suppose is the state of the
young man's heart? Or what kind of private education will
hold out for him and not be swept away by such blame and
praise and go, borne by the flood, wherever it tends so that
he'll say the same things are noble and base as they do,
practice what they practice, and be such as they are?"

"The necessity is great, Socrates," he said.

"And yet," I said, "we still haven't mentioned the greatest necessity."

"What?" he said.

"What these educators and sophists inflict in deed when
they fail to persuade in speech. Or don't you know that they
punish the man who's not persuaded with dishonor, fines,
and death? . . . So what other sophist or what sort of private

365

speeches do you suppose will go counter to these and pre-vail? . . . Even the attempt is a great folly. . . ."[1]

The modern university was that great folly of an attempt to establish a center for reflection and education independent of the regime and the pervasive influence of its principles, free of the overwhelming effect of public opinion in its crude and subtle forms, devoted to the dispassionate quest for the important and comprehensive truths. It was to be an independent island within civil society, the sovereign Republic of Letters. It tried to disprove the Socratic contention that he who shares bed and board with the rulers, be they kings or peoples, would soon have to share their tastes and way of life, and that thus the thinker must separate himself in heart and mind from the currents of party passion in order to liberate himself from prejudice. The modern university has as its premises that free thought can exist in full view of the community unthreatened by the public passions and that it can be of service while preserving its integrity. Academic freedom was to protect scholars from the most obtrusive violations of their independence and was designed to draw them from private isolation into the public institutions; tenure is the most visible expression of that principle in the modern university.

Previously, it had been understood that democracies were in particular need of the enlightening function of the university, both because democracies necessarily have a large proportion of uneducated rulers and because public opinion reigns supreme in them without the counterpoising effect exercised by an aristocratic class which incorporates different principles and to the protection of which dissenters can repair. The presence of the university was the means of combining excellence with equality, reason with the consent of the governed. But precisely because it is so necessary to democracies, it is particularly threatened in nations where equality takes on the character of a religion and can call forth all the elements of fanaticism. In the first place this is so because democracy's fundamental beliefs are difficult to question; flattery of the regime and of the people at large is hard to avoid. Democratic sycophancy becomes a great temptation, one not resisted without difficulty and risk. And, in the second place, the university is, willy-nilly, in some sense aristocratic in both the conventional and natural senses of the term. It cannot, within broad limits, avoid being somewhat more accessible to the children of parents of means than to the children of the poor, and it forms men and women of different tastes from those of the people at large who are,

[1]Plato, Republic, VI, 492a–e.

it is not to be forgotten, the real rulers. And the university is supposed to educate those who are more intelligent and to set up standards for their achievement which cannot be met by most men and women. This cannot but be irritating to democratic sensibilities.

The most obvious, the most comprehensive, the truest explanation of what is going on in our universities today is the triumph of a radical egalitarian view of democracy over the last remnants of the liberal university. This kind of egalitarianism insists that the goal of a democratic society is not equality of opportunity but factual equality; it comes equipped with all the doctrines which are necessary to persuade its adherents that such an equality is possible and that its not being actual is a result of vicious special interests; it will brook no vestige of differentiation in qualities of men and women. It would more willingly accept a totalitarian regime than a free one in which the advantages of money, position, education, and even talent are unevenly distributed. The liberal university with its concentration on a humane education and high standards had already been almost engulfed by the multiversity, which is directed to the service of the community and responsive to the wishes of its constituency.

Now the universities have become the battleground of a struggle between liberal democracy and radical, or, one might say, totalitarian, egalitarianism. Therefore, it is not only the fact that universities are so much in the news that makes them central to any discussion of how democratic America is; it is also because they educate the best of our young, now more than half of them; because what they teach will ultimately determine the thought of the nation; and because the struggle going on in them concerns the interpretation of the meaning of our institutions and their goodness or badness. All this discussion takes place within the context of democracy, for both the defenders and critics of our regime accept the premise that democracy is the one legitimate regime, the only issue being whether the United States is sufficiently or truly a democracy.

The gradual politicization of the university can be seen partially by the extent of the concern expressed about it in society at large. Political men are constantly talking about universities and what they should or should not do. The universities have lost their neutrality as well as control of their destinies. Previously matters of curricula and student conduct were thought to be properly matters of internal university policy. Now the sense of the university's mission has been lost, and, at the same time, what has been going on within it has succeeded in frightening and arousing the political community. The former Secretary of Health, Education and Welfare, Robert Finch, has even gone so far as to make an attack on the tenure system, the vital heart of academic freedom. Following professional and student radicals, he accurately assessed the fact that it is the faculties which are most likely to be recalcitrant in an attempt to make the universities responsive to immediate concerns and that tenure protects them. He characterized faculties in much the same way as Marxists do the *bourgeoisie* in a capitalist system. They are, according to him, a privileged class protecting special and private interests. He sees no principle embodied in their unusual status; the issues are so clear, as he sees them, that only private vice could be the source of their unwillingness to change with the times. We are overburdened by the pontifications of journalists as well as politicians, and professors, administrators, and students look to the newspapers and television for publicity and support. All of this indicates the extent to which universities have become a part of the system of public opinion.

But these are only symptoms. One must look within the universities themselves to see the magnitude of what has happened. The primary fact is the advent of student power, which, if it means anything, means an extreme democratization of the university. It is a democratization in several senses: it extends the range of power to everyone present (things have gone so far that maintenance personnel are to sit in some university legislative bodies); even the usually accepted notions of age and stake in the community as standards for participation are considered discriminatory; and, most important of all, the special claim of competence is ignored or rejected. Professors, as well as students, frequently deny that their learning gives them title to govern the university or to determine what is important for it to represent. Everyone is listening to young people these days, and they are talking.

The most stunning example of this about which I know is what happened at Cornell. When black students carrying guns and thousands of white students supporting them insisted that the faculty abandon the university's judicial system, the minimal condition of civil community within the university, and backed up that insistence with threats, the faculty capitulated. Most of the faculty members who voted for capitulation argued that this was the will of the community, what the students wanted. They had talked to many students, and the students strongly desired that the faculty reverse itself. These professors could satisfy their consciences by turning to public opinion. So democratic had they become that they accepted a mob gathered in an atmosphere of violence as a true public. So weak were their convictions about what a university is that they could find legitimacy only in public approval by their student constituency; their scholarly competence provided no source for independent judgment. Their souls had become democratic and egalitarian to a degree far greater than that demanded by the principles of the regime; the regime requires that every citizen abide by the duly expressed will of the majority, not that the mind of man be determined by the taste of the community at large. In this instance there was a realization of Socrates' comic comparison of a democracy to the solemn deliberations of a group of children who are empowered to choose between the dietary prescriptions of a doctor and those of a pastry chef. Here, though, the doctors accepted the legitimacy of the tribunal.

In order to see the full dimensions of the situation and to recognize that the only real element in the changes occurring and the reforms demanded is radical egalitarianism, one must listen carefully to what is said. The key word is *relevance*. The whole of education must be guided by the standard of relevance. Now, of course, no curriculum was ever intended to be irrelevant; and even if scholars have lost the habit of justifying the importance of their disciplines, there is embedded in each a serious argument for its study. Relevance is obviously a relative term, implying a standard by which relevant and irrelevant things are judged. Classical liberal education set as its standard the formation of a human being possessing intellectual and moral virtue; relevant studies were those that tended to the perfection of the natural faculties, independent of the particular demands of time or place.

This is not the criterion of relevance referred to by today's students. Those students who are doing most of the talking and popularizing the notion of a relevance—that is, the Leftist students—mean that education must be directed to the problems of war, poverty, and, particularly, racism as they now present themselves, in other words, to the problems of contemporary democratic society. They not only argue that these are the fundamental issues to which the universities should address themselves, they also insist that certain kinds of solutions are self-evident. When they talk about justice they do not regard knowledge of justice as a problem; it is almost inconceivable to them that there can be a theoretical questioning of the principle of equality, let alone a practical doubt about it. The universities, as they are seen by these students, are meant to preach certain principles and to study their implementation. The movement is antiintellectual and has the character of a democratic crusade. The theoretical person who stands outside of the movement, who urges that the university's primary function is the pursuit of clarity about such questions, is easily accused of complacency. Such idle lack of commitment can only be tolerated when we have brought peace, prosperity, and equality to the earth. Not even the richest country ever known can afford to devote any of its resources to the useless cultivation of the mind.

The relevant curriculum is to be promoted, watched over, and used by students. Student participation is the catchword in all talk of university reform. The goals to be achieved by student participation are never explicitly defined. It is enough to refer to the democratic view: everyone has the right to vote. Faculties and administrations everywhere are bustling to "restructure" the universities with a view to greater student participation in everything; it has become an end in itself. To point out that students do not participate in disciplinary procedures, choice of faculty, establishment of curricula, and so forth is sufficient to demonstrate that decisions are illegitimate. There is almost no concern to show that such participation improves the quality of those decisions or contributes in any way to serious educational goals or even that it satisfies the students' wishes, let alone their real needs. I would venture to suggest that none of the moves toward student participation made in the last four or five years have done anything but generate new demands on their part and cause a deterioration of academic standards, an increase of demagogic teaching, and a loss of the sense of a university's purpose. There is a craze for change, but educators have no vision of the purposes of this change; they have nothing to offer but change itself. The direction is given to the drift by the prevailing winds of democratic extremism. Whether an educational institution can be treated as a political community or whether democracy needs any restraints seems never to be a question.

This is a democratic age, and democracy is the special place of the young. According to Plato's analysis, the young in their turn exacerbate the weaknesses of democracy and impel it toward anarchy and ultimately tyranny. He describes our situation before the fact: "As the teacher in such a situation is frightened of the pupils and fawns on them, so the students make light of their teachers, as well as their attendants. And, generally, the young copy their elders and compete with them in speeches and deeds while the old come down to the level of the young; imitating the young, they are overflowing with facility and charm, and that's so that they won't seem to be unpleasant or despotic."[2]

The young are powerful in democracies for many reasons. Estates are not easily transferable within them, so the authority of fathers is diminished. The hierarchies from which the young are excluded and which characterize other regimes are absent in a democracy. The older people lose their special privileges; and, in the atmosphere of liberty, the bodily pleasures, of which the young are more capable, are emancipated and have a higher status. Equality renders illegitimate most

[2]*Ibid.*, VIII, 563a–b.

claims to rule over the young: age, wisdom, wealth, moral virtue, good family are all banished, leaving only number, or consent, and force; and it is more difficult to exclude the young from ruling on the basis of these titles. All of this gives ground for believing that when the young become more demanding and the old more compliant, a new stage of democracy has been reached. The young are taking full advantage of their condition, making use of both their special claims to rule, consent and violence, however contradictory the two may appear to be.

In our democracy there is a further reason, of which Plato did not speak, for the dominance of the young. The radical political movements attempt to establish new kinds of societies, to find solutions to what older wisdom said was insoluble, to overcome necessity and master chance or, as Machiavelli put it, fortune: "I judge that it is better to be impetuous than circumspect, because fortune is a woman; to keep her down it is necessary to beat her and thrash her. One sees that she lets herself be conquered by the impetuous rather than by those who proceed coldly. And, of course, as a woman she is always a friend to the young, because they are less circumspect, more brutal, and command her with greater audacity."[3]

Those who wish to ride the wave of the future know that the young are most skilled at it and do deference to them as such. Only those who have some conviction of the rightness of their principles can stand against the sea of change, and, as we shall see, this con- viction is what seems no longer to be generally possessed.

The democratic ruling body constituted by the students estab- lishes, as do all ruling bodies, policies which further its interests. The substantive reforms, as I have said, have no basis other than that they conduce to the equality of all. Open admissions is the new cry. All citizens must go to college; everyone must be allowed into the halls of learning. And this means, in effect, that everyone must graduate from college, for it will soon be found that it is impossible to fail great masses of students in the age of student power. It immediately follows that standards must be lowered or, rather, utterly abandoned, no matter under what shining banner this change is presented. One of the first points of attack is grading; grades are said to degrade, to make students "grinds" rather than independently thoughtful, to make stu- dents part of the system, to encourage bad motivations for study. Although these allegations are not without merit, the real reason for the criticism is that grades make distinctions and indicate that some are better, at least as students, than others. Similarly, required courses

[3]Machiavelli, The Prince, Chapter XXV.

and traditional majors begin to be abandoned. It would be hard to argue that these courses and programs of study were very well conceived, but they represented the tattered remnants of some thought about the natural articulation of the kinds of knowledge and what a person must know in order to be called minimally educated. A vacuum called freedom takes their place.

Each student is to be permitted to construct his own curriculum and discover his special genius or realize his unique self. The university can no longer provide guidance as to what is important and set standards based on a view of human perfection. It is blithely assumed that the student is capable of doing so for himself and that he has no need of sublimating discipline. In technical studies, of course, fixed courses of study will remain, because, for example, professors of engineering know what they must teach and what a student must know. But the best students in the better universities are no longer interested in a technical education; they are strongly inclined to what are very loosely called the humanities and the social sciences, and here the universities have abandoned their pedagogic function. It is a perfect solution for educators: in the hallowed name of freedom they are relieved of the responsibility of elaborating a curriculum. The true result of all of this is that the most vulgar and philistine things which proliferate in society at large will dominate the university, for the university cannot, as it should, counterpoise them. If the university does not provide alternatives to the prevalent, where else could the student find them?

One thing is certain: the serious study of classic literature will be sacrificed to the reforming spirit. It does not seem relevant to our students, and it is not to be expected that it would. The importance of classic literature, particularly the philosophic literature, could be recognized by young people only after long and exacting discipline. This is particularly true in America, where nothing in the students' past or the world outside the university attests to the significance, or even the existence, of these rare and fine things. It was because the university insisted on them that they were preserved and that a university education could be understood to be a transforming experience rather than an exercise in self-expression or "doing one's own thing," no matter what it may happen to be.

The fate of classical languages is the model for what is happening in general. They are less and less studied, for they require an effort which seems pedantic and constraining, and they do not simply relate to the students' untutored, unguided experience. In the absence of knowledge of the languages, there can be no serious study of the texts written in them. In our current atmosphere everything has its place, and no one need feel uncomfortable or left out. At the end, whole new kinds of ephemeral study programs emerge, brought into being by the most popular issues of the day or the inclinations of groups of students.

Finally, the criticism is turned on the professors who not only are the protectors of the old ways but also are charged with being negligent of their students. The professors are understood to be primarily teachers who have lost their taste for teaching. The notion that a professor in a university is, in the first place, a scholar and that this must take most of his time is gradually becoming unintelligible. It used to be considered something of a vice for a man to be too much of a teacher because that would lead him into the temptation of adapting his thought to the demands of the market. He should not have to attract students but should provide a model for them of integrity and independence, of a higher motivation, whether they like it or not. The opportunity to be with a learned person should be considered a privilege and not a right, a privilege reserved for the competent and respectful. This was believed to be for the good not only of science but also of the student. But now it is everywhere deemed appropriate that the professor should teach more, be in closer contact with students, and accept their judgments as to his competence. It is not to be denied that a professor sometimes learns from students, that many professors are bad teachers and also bad scholars, and that often criticism can help them to right their ways in both respects. But to assert that students, as a matter of principle, have a right to judge the value of a professor or what he teaches is to convert the university into a market in which the sellers must please the buyers and the standard of value is determined by demand.

It was precisely to provide a shelter from the suffrages of the economic system and the popular will they represent that universities were founded. Now that the student right to judge has become dogma, the universities have become democracies in which the students are the constituencies to which the professors are responsible. A whole new race of charlatans or pastry chefs has come into being who act as the tribunes of the people. One can expect a wholesale departure from the universities of professors of real independence.

Thus we have gone very far down the road toward equality. It is somehow now held morally reprehensible to believe that equality is limited by natural differences in men's and women's gifts and that a reasonable understanding of democracy is as a regime which allows them to develop those gifts without conventional or arbitrary hindrances. It is now doctrine that all men are factually equal, and if they do not meet high standards it is due to deprivation or the falseness of the standards. In the theory and practice of our universities we have come to that stage of democratic sentiment at which Tocqueville warned that men prefer equality to freedom, where they are willing to overturn the institutions and laws necessary to freedom in order to gain the sense of equality, where they level rather than raise, indifferent to the deprivations they impose on the superior and on the community at large.

I

What, then, is the future of liberal education in the face of these powerful tides? By *liberal* education I mean education for freedom, particularly the freedom of the mind, which consists primarily in the awareness of the most important human alternatives. Such an education is largely dedicated to the study of the deepest thinkers of the past, because their works constitute the body of learning which we must preserve in order to remain civilized and because anything new that is serious must be based on, and take account of, them. Without such a study a man's mind is almost necessarily a prisoner of the horizon of his particular time and place, and in a democracy that means of the most fundamental premises or prejudices of public opinion. This study has long had only frail support in the United States, and it is what is most threatened at this moment. It is the sole reason for the being of the university as anything more than an advanced high school for the training and detention of the young.

Addressing myself to this question, I wrote an article in 1966 assessing the condition of universities with respect to liberal education.[4] At that time the picture was bleak, but there was some basis for hope that in the interstices of the universities with all their bigness this small vital center might be maintained, not because it had any place guaranteed in the principle of the university but simply out of habit supported by the great wealth and diversity of the American university. That hope has all but disappeared. I saw then that the multiversity had no principle of organization, that it was directed to public usefulness rather than knowledge for its own sake, that the university had lost any sense of the unity of knowledge. It had become a place for specialists without any view of, or longing for, wholeness. The students were beginning to be aroused, and their stirrings seemed to express that longing for wholeness which was absent in the rest of the university. However, they, too, shared the belief of the specialists that the end of the university is public service, practice not theory.

[4]See "The Crisis of Liberal Education," pp. 348–64.

And the intensity of their demands, in sharp contrast to the easygoing, live-and-let-live disposition of the specialists, could easily result in a deterioration of the university's intellectual atmosphere. The liberal arts were likely to be crushed between the aimless diversity of the specialists and the spirit of political reform of the students.

I also saw that administrators were likely to become accomplices of the students, for they have almost no education other than that in efficiency; without a clear view of the goals of a university they would, I knew, give in to the greatest pressures. But I based what hopes I had on my belief that the undergraduates did have a *feeling* of what was lacking in the specialist's education; and that their concern for living their lives well might be a wedge for the development of some liberal curricula which would respond to that concern and help to restore some limited sense of the unity of education in a rational and scholarly way. What I did not foresee was, on the one hand, the speed of the collapse of the administrators, and, on the other, the lack of conviction of the professors about the importance of what they were doing. The pieties of the professors about academic freedom and civility have turned out to be largely empty. They are ready to transform the university totally in terms of the untutored wishes of the students. The professors have proved to be so accommodating because they lack clarity, or because they too wish to share the students' idealism, or because they make the interested calculation that their specialties will be spared.

As for the students, I saw in them a potential for good or evil. They were freer in some senses than their parents. Necessities of life were better provided to them, and they lived in a world in which most principles of morals, religion, and politics were without great persuasiveness or binding force. This gave them the equipment for a reconsideration of such questions without external constraint. But they were lacking in rootedness, and their almost total lack of education in the tradition gave them no experience of greatness in thought or deed; no books meant much to them. There was that longing for wholeness, partly genuine, partly spurious (in order to have the exhilaration of the sense of depth). Properly controlled and guided, I believed, this longing could be the motor which would drive them to the effort requisite to learn.

But somewhere along the line this dangerous mixture has begun to fall out of balance; perhaps it is, and was always, inevitable, for there is not enough intellectual and moral substance available to discipline the students' aimless freedom. It was only a small minority of well-endowed students who could have been touched and finally trained, but they required protection and, at the least, an atmosphere of calm in which there is some respect for liberal studies. I suppose that this minority still remains, but all the honors go to a loud group of protesters furnished with easy and appealing ideologies as a substitute for thought; they either attract the really able students, because they appear to represent the only thing that has real force, or they reduce them to a confused silence. At first they seemed to be questing for guidance and leadership of a sort to respond to their sentiments. But, of course, they are easily dupes of movements, political and intellectual, which play to their tastes and are largely sham.

How can they judge, having neither experience nor knowledge? Every year their souls are thinner from want of spiritual nourishment; their openness becomes emptiness, the soil within incapable of sustaining any deep-rooted plant. They test the possible authorities to which they turn and find that none has the power to inspire them or resist them. The adult world makes itself contemptible, seeming to represent nothing itself, and, in what can only appear to the young to be cowardly flattery, praises the idealism and morality of those who have never had the chance to practice either. The great change comes when students no longer quest but teach, confident that they know the answers and are sufficient unto themselves. One of the ugliest spectacles is that of a young person who has no awe, who is shameless, who does not sense his imperfection, for it is the charm of youth to be potentiality striving to perfect itself, to be an essential incompleteness which may one day be truly complete. Adults are almost always imperfect; a youth is surely imperfect, but he at least offers the hope of development. But self-contempt is the basis of self-improvement, and this generation has nothing left in god or man against which to measure itself. Plato's description of the democratic man now seems most appropriate:

> ". . . he doesn't admit it if someone says that there are some pleasures belonging to fine and good desires and some belonging to bad desires. . . . He shakes his head at all this and says that all are alike and must be honored on an equal basis. . . . He lives along day by day, gratifying the desire that occurs to him, at one time drinking and listening to the flute, at another downing water and reducing; now practicing gymnastics, and again idling and neglecting everything; and sometimes spending his time as though he were occupied with philosophy. Often he engages in politics and jumping up, says and does whatever chances to come to him. . . ."[5]

[5]Plato, *Republic*, VIII, 561c–d.

To Plato's account must be added a somewhat more sinister element: a rage at the emptiness of this life, and a desire to commit oneself to acts of revolutionary violence. Nonviolence has more or less silently been dropped from the creed of the New Left. College now means to more and more students a place where the young educate the nation and practice self-expression. It should not be surprising that the aristocratic aspiration which democracy frustrates should find its outlet on the Radical Left. Under the banner of equality these privileged students can lead and, with impunity, express their contempt for the people.

The universities were a fertile field for this development. A survey of the so-called liberal arts segments of the universities reveals that they are unarticulated heaps of departments, each teaching specialized disciplines which have presuppositions that are hardly discussed and are frequently incompatible with those of other disciplines. These disciplines have aggregated to the university at various times over the last thousand years. There is little coherence to them, nor does a view of life and the world evidently emerge from any separately or all together. The most important question has been forgotten, and even the means for a rational discussion of the unity of the university or the unity of life seem to have been lost. We seem to have to make do with tradition or whatever the winds of the day bring along. The state of academic philosophy, which should be the unifying discipline, indicates the severity of the problem. Today it is largely dominated by linguistic analysis, which is merely a method for studying discourse rather than itself a source of discourse; it is a universal rulebook for playing the game, but it does not tell us what the game is or play it itself. The natural sciences are a world unto themselves, dealing with what are presumably important problems, but they are unable to do anything about conveying their meaning within the total picture. The humanities have also become specialties, and it is rare to find a convincing explanation of their importance; the literatures studied are very rarely understood to be of vital significance for life today, and certainly they are undermined by the notion that science is the domain of reason and cannot understand the world of poetry. And the social sciences are slavishly imitating the natural sciences and are further hampered by their own principle, the fact-value distinction, from speaking about the moral and political good, which is what agitates the students.

Thus when students ask about the good life and the nature of our world, they are met by a deafening silence, for there are no persons in the university whose competence enables them to respond to such questions. Many professors are answering the students but not on the

basis of their competence; they are biologists or psychologists, or whatever else, speaking about what they have never studied, never adequately reflected on, and what is in no way connected with the things
they can claim to know. The questions and pressures of students during
these past six years have created a stir among academic men, but it
has not caused them to undertake a serious reconsideration of the
state of our learning or to look toward a philosophic and scholarly
treatment of the issues raised. That just seems impossible; the whole
is approached by way of feeling, by identification with popular movements, by "commitment" or "concern." The professors do not try to
educate these longings; they try to share them without transforming
them. What some social scientists proudly name "postbehavioralism"
consists in nothing more than an attempt to keep the "value"-hungry
wolves from the door.

The university has proved itself incapable of teaching students
about the good life because that is not a subject that any part of our
universities even knows how to discuss; it belongs to no department
or any group of them added together. The education of our professors
has been a specialized, technical one, with more or less old-style
humanities mixed in but not really taken seriously or penetrating the
special discipline. We have hardly a reminiscence of what was once
the central business of universities. During and just after World War
II, America was the beneficiary of many generally and humanely educated European scholars. Whatever the difficulties of the teachings
many brought with them, these men and women had roots deep in
the best thinkers and had the habit of justifying what they taught by
them. One might have thought that the example of their learning
and persons would fundamentally affect our universities. But the enormous expansion of higher education and the growth of the multiversity
simply drowned their influence. Now, even in the unlikely event that
it were to be thought that the philosophic, unifying, synoptic education needed to be reestablished, we would not be in a position to
do so, for we no longer have the teachers who sufficiently know or
care for the great tradition or are capable of working through the
prejudices which seem to have rendered it meaningless and irrelevant.

Until the students became vocal, the university was characterized
by easygoing indifference to larger purposes; each discipline followed
its own internal development and the administration held the whole
together. In the new era, scientists and humanists have come out to
meet the students, praise them, agree to reorder "the priorities," and
announce that the real purposes of the universities are those proposed
by the political movements of the Left. Thus a direction and purpose

is again given to the university, and a community is established around this purpose. The only problem is whether that purpose is in any way consistent with the premises of science and scholarship.

Some professors become disturbed when they recognize that they must change their teaching in order to fit the movement and that the integrity of their discipline is threatened, that the passionate desires of the indignant are not consonant with the results of dispassionate rational inquiry. But such worried professors are more than counter-balanced by those professors who, excited by their new roles and liberated from what they now recognize to be the fragmented character of their existence, are willing to make their disciplines "relevant." The strength of this group is reinforced by the more or less active support of another group of professors, composed most particularly of natural scientists, who see no threat of a new Lysenkoism in their disciplines and who therefore are of the opinion they can have their cake and eat it. The fact that the interests of the professors can differ so much indicates how little of a real *intellectual* community there was and hence how partial the lives of the professors had become. In these circumstances, the university was an easy conquest for the first move-ment which exposed its lack of purpose or conviction and which proposed to restore the wholeness of life, the absence of which was even beginning to trouble the complacent professors. This movement usurped the position in the university which by right belonged to liberal education and in the process abolished the throne—occupied by weak and illegitimate pretenders—of the only legitimate ruler, philosophy.

II

Although the universities have had little to offer in the way of reflection or leadership in recent years, there are those who have jumped into the void created by the absence of philosophy and spoken to the general issues. There is not much thought reflected in what they say but there is the decay of a certain kind of thought here and its language is the only language which appeals to students. Although there have been few political movements which make such modest demands on the minds of their adherents or which have been so profoundly anti-intellectual, this one, too, is, of course, founded on a comprehensive view of things and is guided by that view. That view was not a product of the founders of the movement, and, because its followers are so unselfconscious, they are unaware of its sources and its implications. They are prisoners of certain European, particularly German, teachings which migrated to the United States and have been so successfully assimilated that they now seem native and part of common sense. We have adopted the language and the consequences of these teachings from the European professors who helped to bring them but have absorbed almost none of the learning which should accompany them. At all events, when thought out, these teachings lead to views and ways of life which are antithetical to this regime, and their dominance would surely undermine it. The German thought reflected in the current language of politics is the thought which is at the roots of both communism and fascism. Although the present political movements are democratic in that they propose to speak for all men, and they are egalitarian, they are based on a critique of liberal democracy and a hostility to it. The egalitarian movement has gathered into its bosom the teachings of men who were, to say the least, not friends of democracy and has used them to the furtherance of equality. The only sacrifice is free society as we know it. Prudent observers who knew something of modern philosophy were not surprised to find that kind of irrationalism which is open to violence, tyranny, and racism emerging in the New Left. This was a necessity of its principles, as I shall try to show.

In the events that have occurred within the universities these past few years, the most sobering fact which has emerged is that neither in the things that are taught in them nor in the actions or reactions of those who are supposed to be responsible for their preservation is there much evidence of a conviction of the truth of the principles on which liberal democracy and the liberal university are founded. When such conviction is lacking, institutions and laws have lost their vitality and maintain themselves only by inertia; their replacement by new modes and orders is only a matter of time. This is not to suggest that by preaching the principles one can give them life; it is only meant as an observation. Somehow our principles are no longer persuasive. Our condition is beautifully characterized by a passage in Dostoyevsky's *Possessed:*

> Do you know that we are tremendously powerful already? Our party does not consist only of those who commit murder and arson, fire off pistols in the traditional way, or bite colonels. . . . Listen. I've reckoned them all up: a teacher who laughs with children at their God and at their cradle is on our side. The lawyer who defends an educated murderer because he is more cultured than his victims and could not help murdering them to get money is one of us. The school-

boys who murder a peasant for the sake of sensation are ours. The juries who acquit every criminal are ours. The prosecutor who trembles at a trial for fear he should not seem advanced enough is ours, ours. Among officials and literary men we have lots, lots, and they don't know it themselves. . . . Do you know how many we shall catch by little, ready-made ideas? When I left Russia, Littré's dictim that crime is insanity was all the rage; I came back and find that crime is no longer insanity, but simply common sense, almost a duty; anyway, a gallant protest.[6]

That is a nihilist speaking, looking at the dissolution of the horizon within which his people had lived. The similarity of this situation to our own is no accident. The speaker is not referring essentially to the decay of the Czarist regime but of Western justice and morality, and that is what we are experiencing in all liberal society today. Dostoyevsky was one of a small group of clairvoyant men in the last half of the nineteenth century who saw that somehow the old world was sick and dying, not meaning by the "old world" states or regimes, but the biblical and classical morality which stood behind and made possible all states and regimes as we have known them or can imagine them. Nihilism was a response to the incipient death of all that had gone before, an expression of the meaninglessness of life without a compelling horizon of values, an attempt to destroy the lifeless body which remained after the vital center had died, and, perhaps, a hope of a new world, the outlines of which we cannot yet perceive but to which we must be dedicated for the sake of life. Civil societies are constituted by what they respect, by what men bow their heads before in reverence. When they no longer have anything before which they can bow, their world is near its end, and all the suppressed and lawless monsters within man reemerge. One might suggest that our New Left is a strange mixture of nihilism with respect to past and present and a naïve faith in a future of democratic progress.

To put this more compellingly for Americans, the old liberalism is no longer of real concern to today's students. By the old liberalism I mean either the thought of the Founding Fathers who believed in the natural rights of man, established by reason and applicable to all men, and who constructed a nation dedicated to life, liberty, and the pursuit of happiness, or that of men like John Stuart Mill who believed in the open society dedicated to free speech and the

[6]Constance Garnett trans., The Possessed (New York: Modern Library, 1936), p. 427.

self-determined private life. To the extent that Locke, the Declaration of Independence, the *Federalist*, or Mill are taught in the universities, they are historical matter and hardly anyone supposes that they can be believed or taken as guides for our lives. Without entering into the merits of that older liberal thought, it somehow no longer satisfies the soul of this generation of mankind and seems to be taking its place alongside the teachings which legitimized monarchy and aristocracy in the graveyard of history. Adults still refer to its principles, but when protests against war, poverty, or racism contradict them, those protests carry the day. It is not believed that liberal society insures substantive justice. And anyone whose "life-style" is hostile to that of liberal society is considered justified or even heroic in "opting out" of it. What appeals to students now is the language of Marxism and Existentialism; it seems to them to describe their situation.

It is a most striking fact that since Mill there has not been a single really influential book supporting liberal democratic society, and Mill cannot be compared in power or depth to men like Marx or Nietzsche who were his critics. Liberal democracy has come to seem to be negative; it wishes to provide the conditions for freedom or the good life, but it does not give prescriptions for the use of freedom or define the good life. Its neutrality permits the dominance of any one of very many possible ways of life, some of them unattractive. Marx could plausibly assert that it was merely the condition for the existence of *bourgeois* capitalism, and that freedom meant primarily freedom to be a worker or an owner in this kind of system. And Nietzsche argued that liberal democracy was the home of "the Last Man," a being without heart or conviction, a shriveled manikin dedicated only to preservation and comfort. All of this criticism has become commonplace in the unremitting attack on white, complacent, middle-class America; it was vulgarized in America by men like Fromm and Marcuse. The models for admiration are no longer statesmen but bohemians or revolutionaries.

But in the improbable wedding of Marx and Nietzsche which has recently been arranged, it is clear that Nietzsche is the dominant partner in spite of his Rightist inclinations. Marx's egalitarianism, concentration on the poor, hatred of imperialism, and so forth have been maintained, and Leftists would still like to style themselves Marxists. But they no longer read the serious Marx; *Capital* seems both boring and irrelevant; the only Marx which is attractive is found in the early, so-called humanistic, writings, the study of which is of very recent origin. And the attack on reason, the use of terms like self, authenticity, and commitment, which are on everybody's lips, show plainly enough to what extent the Marxist teaching has been adulterated by a newer and more compelling kind of thought and a different understanding of the goals of politics. The New Left is not the Old Left, but is rather a result of the assimilation of the thought of Nietzsche and Heidegger to that of the Old Left. However this may be, the prevalent discussion in the highest seats of learning is, to a greater or lesser degree, in the terms of postliberal thought, and this means that soon everyone will think in this way.

But it would perhaps be best to see the changes in our thought by looking to the recent history of the social sciences in America. The social sciences are the discipline in which one would most expect the political and moral life of man to be discussed and are the sources of our understanding of them. For more than thirty years the social sciences have been dominated by the fact-value distinction. This distinction was made by German sociologists in the 1890s and most influentially propounded by Max Weber. It was imported to this country by sociologists and political scientists in the 1920s. This distinction was based on the assertion that no judgments of good and bad, no moral distinctions, could be grounded on reason, that they were subjective acts of the mind, preferences. The goals by which we guide our lives constitute a horizon by which we orient ourselves, but that horizon is an act of human creativity, not one of reason; no horizon can claim to be authoritative or demonstrable. Weber was persuaded of the truth of this analysis and attempted to salvage some possibility for the existence of science, of the reasonable quest for objective truth. Science was to be the noble endeavor of overcoming one's own values in the name of truth. The consequences of all this for our lives are, as Weber knew, quite far-reaching. Little attention was, however, given by American social scientists to assessing the effect of the distinction or, for that matter, to proving its validity. They accepted it and devoted themselves to the elaboration of an objective social science based on it; they were enchanted by the vision of a value-free social science which would be comparable to the natural sciences.

Although the science itself has not been very impressive, the success of the viewpoint has been breathtaking. Today even schoolchildren use the word *value* where another generation would have spoken of good and evil. The new social science had the effect of banishing good and bad, the discussion of the ends, from the domain of the sciences or reason. That was no longer a scholarly theme. The social scientists still had to live as men and women as well as scholars; but they were almost to a man liberal democrats; they accepted that as their value. And, unlike Weber, they used the fact-value distinction as a means of sparing themselves the necessity of being concerned about the status of their value. This was just fine until that value was challenged. It had lost its dignity; liberal democracy was just one value among many, and it had eroded from long neglect.

When the students wanted to implement certain policies and found apathy and indifference among adults, they, and their professorial camp followers, launched an attack on value-free social science, insisting that the social sciences should be primarily concerned with values. They accused the social scientists of being easygoing accomplices of the established order. The social scientists were indeed supporters of this order and were also unable to give an account of their reasons for being so. They simply believed that no sane man would question the superiority of liberal democracy to all available alternatives. Indeed, the fact-value distinction had become the last intellectual bastion of liberal democracy: in the absence of any demonstrable superiority of one value over another, that regime which tolerated all values might be understood to be preferable to one which did not. Moreover, since values are equal, they seem to be democratic. Every man has a right to his own values; no one need feel inferior. But the social scientists were utterly unprepared to resist a large group who insisted that its values had to be accepted no matter what others wanted. After all, why not?

It is to be noted that the students, as was to be expected, themselves adopted the fact-value distinction. They made no attempt to return to Marx, who thought that the true goals of human life could be determined by reason. They merely looked at the fact-value distinction and recognized that there was no intrinsic reason why we should concentrate on facts, that that choice in itself is a value judgment. Science seems to have demonstrated that the most important thing—the right way of life is the most important thing—is not amenable to scientific, that is rational, treatment. This means men must abandon reason and turn to the establishment of values. This is precisely the analysis made by the profoundest European thinkers in the last century who took the value question seriously. The positing of values is, in this perspective, the most important human activity, and all the specialized activities are guided by the values posited. Thus the social scientists, men so dedicated to reason, were astonished to see their students, even their own children, denying reason, turning to Eastern religions, addicted to drugs, toying with violence, becoming a new breed or species unintelligible to rationalists. But in a sense they were going to the end of roads which their teachers and parents had opened but had themselves not traveled. Phenomena such as the use of drugs cannot be understood on mere sociological and psycho-logical grounds. They are the consequences of the problems in our thought. If reason is superficial, then the irrational must be cultivated for the enrichment of life.

Much of what we recognize to be the most advanced contemporary opinion follows as a consequence from the fact-value distinction. Man is the value-producing being; that is the great discovery implicit in the distinction. If it is values which guide reason, then one must look beneath rational consciousness, the *ego*, to an unconscious, an *id*, a self, in order to find out what man is and discover a source for a meaningful life. This self cannot be understood by reason; it must be creative and hence beyond prediction; it must be listened to as an oracle. One cannot know what it will produce or whether what it produces is good or bad. It is the absolute beginning. With this we see the origin of our concentration on the self and its fulfillment. It is the modern substitute for the soul, which is a rationally ordered structure and is dependent on and subordinate to the order of the *cosmos*. The self has no order and it is dependent on nothing; it makes a *cosmos* out of the chaos that is really outside by imposing an order of values upon it.

In most discussion today one finds little elaboration of what the self is; rather the self is defined by what it is opposed to. The great illness of modern man, according to our critics, is alienation or other-directedness. This means to live according to other people's values, whether they are expressed in laws, schools, work, or whatever. A man who lives in that way is divorced from his self and is hollow. Education must not impose values on the student but let his own values develop and grow. In the absence of any objective standard for judging a man's words or deeds, the only test can be whether they are his own or another's, whether he is a true self or alienated, inner-directed or other-directed, authentic or hypocritical. Authentic is really the word, the replacement for good. Many different ways of life can be authentic; the standard is only in the honesty or sincerity of the expression of that way of life. No matter how criminal or foul you may be, you are cleansed if you are sincere about it; hypocritical obedience to law is the human crime; Jean Genet is superior by far to the *bourgeois* father and citizen.

How can one then be sure that one is sincere, that one's values are authentic? Such assurance cannot be achieved by comparison of one man's values with those of another. The only proof is in the intensity of one's *commitment*, in the ultimate case by being willing to die for one's value, in the assertion of one's value against the chaotic outside, bravely facing all risks. It is the strong-willed versus the weak-willed instead of the good versus the bad. We praise men now, not for the rightness of their cause, but because they care; the primary thing is not truth but concern. This, of course, puts a premium on fanaticism, not to speak of fakery.

At all events, man as the value-needing and value-producing animal leads directly to the view that the good society is one which allows selves to commit themselves to authentic values and to grow in terms of them. This is exactly the prescription of the New Left. It is, of course, in the absence of elaboration, empty. One has no idea what such a society would be like; it is utterly unprogrammatic. But it is just such a vision which allows for the most complete rejection and destruction of the present regime and the greatest self-indulgence without guilt; and to be committed to this vision gratifies moralistic vanity at the same time. It is the best of many possible worlds.

Nietzsche, who was the first to present a profound teaching of the self, understood it to be an aristocratic teaching, for true selves are rare. The kind of man who can create a horizon for a whole people and make his values theirs and thus ennoble their lives is extremely rare. This is a natural distinction among men, and democratic society, according to him, effaces this distinction. But, as is easy to see, this teaching, or a corruption of it, easily becomes grist for the mill of radical egalitarianism. Objective standards encourage distinctions of rank among men; each self is a standard unto itself, and there is no rational basis for comparison of one self with another. The self justifies the most extreme freedom, for there is nothing in nature to which the self is subservient; the self is the creator, the biblical God possessed uniquely by everyone.

In politics, teachings tend to be transformed by what is most powerful in the regime and in turn transform the regime in the direction of its most dangerous tendencies. The corruption of a teaching which was intended to be noble is peculiarly revolting. Not content with understanding democratic citizens as self-regarding but decent men who try to live by laws they themselves set down for the good of the community, we have had to make them into gods to whom nothing can be compared. Every man must be understood to be creative, no matter how much the standards of art and taste have to be debauched in order to do so. Political restraint and moderation must give way to ugly fanaticism in order to give everyone the chance to be committed. The grossest indecencies are permitted in the name of sincerity. And the wisdom of the ages must be forgotten in order to avoid alienating a growing self.

All of this tends to intensify the conformism—the increasingly monolithic quality of life—which it is supposed to overcome; for in the absence of real goals to strive for, human beings are most likely to fall back into their animal sameness, into the common instincts in the satisfaction of which all men and women are alike. Real diversity is never the result of the concentration on diversity. And at the same time as we are likely to produce greater conformity, we do not stop to consider whether the *laissez aller* we encourage is consonant with civility or political justice. No one asks whether we have any right to be so hopeful that every healthy self will posit nice civil values for itself which are consonant with everyone else's self-realization. Is there any built-in assurance that the unrestrained growth of each individual will not encroach on the vital space of other individuals? Yet this is all that seems to be talked about; the situation is parallel to that in which Rousseau's rhetoric of compassion was used by every dry, self-serving French bureaucrat in the nineteenth century. One thing at least is certain: in all of this there is no concern for justifying or preserving those restraints which have been necessary to the life of every community ever known to man. If neither reason nor tradition can bring about consensus, then the force of the first man resourceful and committed enough must needs do so.

It cannot be doubted that the status of values is a most perplexed and difficult question. Great men have contributed to the present view of things. They must be studied carefully, and the alternatives to them must be equally considered. Reason can only be abandoned reasonably; without this serious examination the modern view becomes empty and dangerous nonsense. It is precisely in this context that the value of liberal democracy becomes manifest: it is the only regime which permits and encourages such a quest. It should be the university's vocation to carry out this quest. In order for it to restore itself today, its faculties would have to make common cause in defense of free inquiry and at the same time protect and encourage those students who wish to learn. It is highly questionable whether it would any longer be capable of such an effort, for it lacks the awareness, the desire, and the personnel. Instead, radical egalitarianism is a dogma within it. Given the increasing and menacing pressures for conformity growing up within the university, it seems reasonable to ask whether it will not be necessary for thinking men and women to return to the isolation of private life in order to be able to think freely. This is not a happy thought for our universities. However, there is also a larger question: is liberal democracy conceivable in the absence of the liberal university? The liberal university appears to be both the highest expression of liberal democracy and a condition of its perpetuation.

ACKNOWLEDGMENTS

"Giants and Dwarfs" is reprinted from *Ancients and Moderns: Essays on the Tradition of Political Philosophy in Honor of Leo Strauss*, ed. Joseph Cropsey, pp. 32–52, © Basic Books, New York, 1964. By permission of the publisher.

"Political Philosophy and Poetry" is reprinted from *Shakespeare's Politics* by Allan Bloom (with Harry V. Jaffa), pp. 1–12, © Basic Books, New York, 1964. By permission of the publisher.

"Richard II" is reprinted from *Shakespeare as Political Thinker*, eds. John Alvis and Thomas G. West, pp. 51–61, © Carolina Academic Press, Durham, 1981. By permission of the publisher.

"The Political Philosopher in Democratic Society: The Socratic View," copyright © 1971 by Allan Bloom. Originally published in *Mélanges en l'honneur de Raymond Aron*, pp. 147–66, ed. Jean-Claude Casanova, Editions Calmann-Lévy, Paris, 1971.

"Hipparchus or the Profiteer," translated by Steven Forde, is reprinted from *The Roots of Political Philosophy: Ten Forgotten Socratic Dialogues*, ed. Thomas L. Pangle, pp. 21–35, © Cornell University Press, Ithaca, 1987. By permission of the publisher.

"An Interpretation of Plato's *Ion*" is reprinted from *Interpretation*, Vol. 1, No. 1, Summer, © 1970. By permission of *Interpretation*.

"Aristophanes and Socrates: A Response to Hall" is reprinted from © *Political Theory*, Vol. 5, No. 3, pp. 315–30, August 1977. By permission of Sage Publications, Inc.

"Emile" is reprinted from Rousseau, *Emile or On Education*, tr. Allan Bloom, pp. 3–27, © Basic Books, New York, 1979. By permission of the publisher.

"Rousseau: The Turning Point" is reprinted from *Confronting the Constitution*, ed. Allan Bloom, pp. 211–34, © American Enterprise Institute, Washington, D.C., 1990. By permission of the American Enterprise Institute.

"Leo Strauss" is reprinted from © *Political Theory* 2(4), November 1974, pp. 372–92. By permission of Sage Publications, Inc.

388

"Raymond Aron: The Last of the Liberals" in *Commentaire*, March 1985.

"Alexandre Kojève" is reprinted from Alexandre Kojève, *Introduction to Reading Hegel*, pp. vii–xii, © Basic Books, New York, 1969. By permission of the publisher.

"Commerce and 'Culture' " is reprinted from *This World* 3, pp. 5–20, Fall 1982. By permission of the Institute for Educational Affairs.

"The Study of Texts," Richter, M., ed. *Political Theory and Political Education*, pp. 113–38, © 1980 Princeton University Press. Reprinted with permission of Princeton University Press.

"Justice: John Rawls versus the Tradition of Political Philosophy" is reprinted from © *American Political Science Review*, 69(2), pp. 648–62, June 1975. By permission of the APSR.

"The Crisis of Liberal Education" is reprinted from *Higher Education and Modern Democracy*, ed. Robert A. Goldwin, pp. 121–39, Rand McNally, Chicago, 1967. By permission of Kenyon College.

"The Democratization of the University" is reprinted from *How Democratic Is America?*, ed. Robert A. Goldwin, pp. 109–36, Rand McNally, Chicago, 1967. By permission of Kenyon College.

INDEX

Achilles, 130, 149, 188, 204, 205
Adam, 52, 89, 93, 189, 204, 205
Adams, John, 228
Adeimantus, 62, 197, 254, 285, 335
Agamemnon, 204, 205
Aglaophon, 128
Alcibiades, 116, 117, 119, 250
Alembert, Jean Le Rond d', 282
Alexander VI, Pope, 311
Alexander the Great, 57
Al-Farabi, 244
Anacreon of Teos, 98
Anaxagoras, 125n
Andersen, Hans Christian, 35
Andromache, 130
Andros, 137n
Anne, Queen of Great Britain and Ireland, 45
Antilochus, 132
Antiphon, 9–10, 74
Antisthenes, 138
Antoninus, Marcus Aurelius, 25
Antonio, 67–81
Anytus, 119
Apollodorus of Cyzicus, 137
Aquinas, Thomas, 27–28, 38, 306, 341
Aragon, 76
Archilochus, 125, 127, 140, 141, 145
Archimedes, 304

Aristogeiton, 100, 116–20
Aristophanes, 37, 45, 108, 170–175, 240, 245, 250, 251, 329
Aristotle, 16, 25, 27–28, 40, 47, 49, 111, 163, 164n, 170, 198, 228, 249, 251, 255, 262, 271, 273, 284, 287, 288, 293, 296, 298, 302–4, 306, 307, 315, 320, 322, 328, 329, 335, 339–340, 342, 344, 345, 356
Aron, Raymond, 256–67, 268n
Asclepius, 124n
Athena, 98n, 124n
Augustine, Saint, 52, 320
Aumerle, 91, 92
Austen, Jane, 253
Averroës, 27–28
Avicenna, 250

Bacchus (Dionysus), 129n
Bacon, Francis, 247, 282, 289
Balthasar, 80
Balzac, Honoré de, 25
Bassanio, 71, 72n, 75–78, 80
Bayle, Pierre, 308
Bell, Daniel, 358, 359
Bennett, William, 24
Bernstein, Richard, 16–17, 24
Boccaccio, Giovanni, 35
Bok, Derek, 14–15
Bolingbroke, Henry, 83, 84, 86–88, 90–93

ABOUT THE AUTHOR

ALLAN BLOOM is the author of several books, including *The Closing of the American Mind,* a national best-seller. He is codirector of the John M. Olin Center for Inquiry into the Theory and Practice of Democracy at the University of Chicago, where he is also a professor on the Committee on Social Thought. He has taught at Yale, Cornell, the University of Toronto, Tel Aviv University, and the University of Paris.